LANDMOOR

JEFF WHEELER

AMBERLIN BOOKS

LANDMOOR

Published by Amberlin Books

PUBLISHING HISTORY
Trade paperback edition published May 2003

ISBN 1-58649-001-X

*Published simultaneously in the United States
and the United Kingdom*

12 11 10 09 08 07 06 05 04 03   1 2 3 4 5

Visit our website at
www.amberlin.com
www.deep-magic.net

Amberlin Books
791 Fir
Pocatello, ID 83201

To Brendon and Jeremy who suffered the first drafts

To Rodney, Peter, Ays, and Ally who suffered the last

And to all the readers of Deep Magic

I

He had been confined to a silent world of sleep. An engulfing blue light surrounded him that maintained the awful prison. He wanted to be rid of it, to sit and stretch and walk about. But the bond was powerful, and he couldn't rouse himself from it. There was no hunger, no sense of thirst. No weariness either. No, that had abandoned him a long time ago. If he ever did awaken, he knew he would never need to sleep again. He would never dare sleep again. Or was this blue existence really his own death – this gradual feeling of loss and timelessness? Thoughts formed and then scattered. The only real thing was the blue light – the source of the prison he had chosen for himself. What a foolish choice.

And in an instant, it changed. The blue light winked out.

He blinked. Wincing at the colors and shades streaking across his eyes, he realized he could see again. Greens and browns and grays – rich earthy colors. The blue light had vanished. His insides thrilled with the freedom. For a moment, the barrage of sounds disoriented him. He was in the woods surrounding the watchpost. Wasn't he? The shrill chatter of a jackdaw echoed, winging its way through the grove. Fat bumblebees spun in wide circles nearby. And a small waterfall! A melodious churning waterfall. It took a moment for him to realize that marsh water had seeped into his boots, making his feet cold. The discomfort of it was new, invigorating. The Everoot surrounded him, growing across the rocks and trees, wet and glistening like damp moss. Memories flooded him as well, thoughts sticking together and holding. Excitement surged through his stomach. He was alive again! And then he felt the presence of Forbidden magic coming nearer.

As he turned around, he discovered the woman moving through the woods. She was blurred, distorted by the crackling sheets of blue lightning flashing off the canopy of wetland trees – a wall of magic separating them. The roar of the magic swept through the marshy grass as it fought to keep her out. A feeling of darkness and fear settled into his bones at seeing her. A smell also – a stinging smell that reminded him of cinders and dead flesh. He knew in an instant she was an intruder to the warding. Tingles of fire gathered through his fingers as he summoned Earth magic from the spongy mat of grass and moss, breathing it from the mud and stones. He inhaled its cloying smell. Again the thought came to him. He was here for a reason. She was an intruder. He – the guardian. He remembered nothing else. Summoning the rush of the magic to aid him, he raised his arms to unleash it on her.

In the blink of a moment, the magic abandoned him, leaving only the scent of smoke. It was like a silver candle-snuffer quenching a taper. He tried to summon the Earth magic again, but it slipped from his fingers like water. The warding was also gone. Panic seized him as he realized that no barrier separated them. The blur of the warding was gone and he could see her clearly now – dark sleek hair and an ageless face. Her eyes were depthless and as dark as her hair and robes. She was his height and moved with a suppleness that defied the tangle of the woods. She reeked of Forbidden magic.

"Who are you?" He gagged on the terror rising in his chest. He had been bound for this moment – for this moment only. To defend the warding – to stop anyone from seizing the Everoot.

No answer.

"Who are you?" He squinted against the thickening shadows, watching as the afternoon sunlight faded and blackness gathered in its wake. The marsh water had soaked through his boots, but he was cold with fear. She opened her hand. A ball of reddish light glimmered against the curtain of long black robes she wore. His eyes widened, recognizing the shade of the flame. Terror writhed up his throat. He couldn't breathe. He couldn't think. He knew exactly what had come to kill him.

"Yes, you do know what I am," came her whisper, answering his thoughts.

He took a tentative step backwards, waiting with dread for the rush of magic that would destroy him. "How did you find...?"

"I am the one who called you. I am the one who has tamed you. Serve me."

The ground lurched as he fell to his elbows and knees, weeping in shame and loathing. He shook with cold as the marsh water soaked into the rest of his clothes.

* * *

The city of Landmoor hunkered on a wide flat hill overlooking the Shoreland moors. It was an odd-looking hill, a little lopsided on the eastern slant, with teeth-like rows of stone jutting between splotches of green sedge. The fortress-city occupied the summit from end to end, its tall, ridged walls interspersed with dominating watch towers, bastions, and two gatehouses. From the center of town rose the sprawling governor's palace, square and proud, higher than any of the uneven walls. Yet, despite the slouching look which he inwardly admired, Allavin Devers knew that Landmoor was a defensible and well-built keep, one of the strongest in the Kingdom of Dos-Aralon and one of the most remote. He stood just within the fringes of the Shadows Wood, staring across the low hills towards the heights where the city perched. A placid river snaked around the western bounds of the hill, wandering this way and that. A few narrow stone bridges spanned it, joining with the single road leading north to the woods. The lazy road came up the side of the hill before straightening out and reaching the gatehouse. It looked the same on the other side too; he had seen it a hundred times. Yet it was the first time Allavin had ever known of an enemy army being so close to it unaware. The watchmen patrolling the heights couldn't see the gathering masses of soldiers and horsemen within the depths of the Shadows Wood. Allavin shook his head in disgust and scratched his beard. The army had been roaming the woods for days now, mashing their tracks and clearing out any witnesses with their dangerous cavalry. It did well to hide their numbers as they converged on the king's road. The city could withstand a formidable siege. But would the king of Dos-Aralon be able to send an army down soon enough to lift it? Fuming, he shook his head again. He doubted it. Not unless they learned about it first. He'd been tracking the army for several days now, and he knew his trade better than the Bandit Rebellion scouts. But how quickly could he get the news to the king?

Waiting within the protective screen of trees, Allavin sensed the movement more than heard it. Looking over his shoulder, he saw the Shae approaching him. They would have been able to sneak up on any man on either side of the war, but Allavin knew the Shae. He envied how well they blended in with the marsh surrounding Landmoor. The browns and greens of their field garb fit the shadows and scrub of the woods. Their features were hardly remarkable, if you knew them as well as he did. Most of his kind thought of the Shae as a freakish, cunning race. Most were disturbed by the fact that they all had pale skin that burned easily in the sun and light-colored hair. Their eyes were beautiful, but only certain colors – green, blue, and gray. He'd seen a few with lavender eyes over the years, but those were rare. They spoke a different language among themselves, an ancient language, with words hauntingly familiar and twisted with multiple meanings. It took a while to pick up all the nuances. Maybe that was another reason why humans distrusted the Shae so much.

But Allavin Devers preferred their company. He smiled in greeting as the four Shae scouts gathered around him.

"It's only a matter of days now before they are in posi-

4

tion to strike," Allavin said in the tongue of the Shae. *"The Rebellion's army is big enough to take the city and control the moors. It'll be a nasty fight rooting them out of here."*
"How many soldiers do they have?" Tiryn asked. He was the leader of this group of Shae scouts and had stunning blue eyes. Allavin had known him for years. *"From what I've seen, it's the entire Shoreland army. Several thousand foot soldiers at least. And they have the Kiran Thall with their horses waylaying wagons and teams from both sides of the king's road. And not simple hit and run raids like they normally do, they're spreading out far, watching for trouble from the north. I'm sure the garrison at the castle is wondering why the traffic from Castun has all but halted. What have you seen?"*
"The same as you. The Bandits have gathered an army here. Another one is starting to gather itself in the west. The Kiran Thall are ruthless, my friend. They have no regard for Life magic. They offend us."
Allavin nodded. *"They do indeed. I need to get north to warn my king. Where are your alerion tethered?"*
"Nearby. They hate the moors. We can't stay long."
"Well, our dukes prefer it when the Bandits gather together in one place. Makes them easier to come down and squash." He clucked his tongue. *"Not this time though. It will be an agony to re-capture Landmoor. Keep watch for me, Tiryn. I'll need you and your scouts watching from the skies until I make it back."*
"There is something else," Tiryn said with concern. *"We came across it on our journey over here. I think you should see it. The Bandits have soldiers clearing out part of the forest."*
Allavin was puzzled. *"For a camp?"*
Another Shae from the group shook his head. He had gray eyes with green edges. *"No, it's in the middle of a marsh. I've never understood humans anyway. We wanted you to look at it. It's peculiar...even for your race."*
"Show me what you found then."
Tiryn nodded and beckoned with a hand signal. Allavin slipped next to him, watching the quick play of their fingers as the orders were passed out. The quiet way they could talk

with their hands had always impressed him. This particular group of Shae were among the best trackers in the western rim of the valley. Tiryn motioned for one of his scouts to take the lead.

A single scout darted into the trees ahead, his longbow held low and level with a steel-tipped arrow already nocked. Tiryn motioned again and the other two took to the flanks. It was a masterful tactic, Allavin thought with a smile. The leader couldn't see the first man, but he could see the other two who both relayed information back to him in surreptitious hand gestures – a silent language for a clever people. Allavin was taller and broader across the shoulders than the average Shae, but he moved with a practiced step, mimicking their own and set an arrow in his longbow as well. His worn leather shooting-glove felt comfortable and snug on his hand and wrist and he curled his main fingers around the string, letting his knuckles wedge the arrow into the groove.

They crossed the woods at a swift pace and came upon the swamp Tiryn had mentioned. It was a wet tangle of scarred cedars, uncontrolled vine maple, and matted nets of marsh grass. Wilt and moss grew over drooping branches and tinted the huge boulders with flecks of green and black. The air was heavy and wet and smelled like a sodden cloak that hadn't been laundered in a month. Allavin cleared away a silky net of spider webs, feeling its unseen strands across his beard. A thick canopy of entwining cedar limbs blocked the sinking sun, veiling the swamp with patches of gray. Sweat beaded up on his forehead and his armpits were soon soaked. The moors were always humid.

Tiryn held up his hand, and Allavin stopped. It meant that the Shae scouts had also stopped. He listened, straining to hear past the whir of roach moths. The leader nodded, gesturing. He turned to Allavin.

"Jerrinwey crossed a warding."

Allavin squinted, confused. *"A warding is... magic, isn't it? I've never understood all the meanings of that word."*

Tiryn furrowed his brow, thinking. "In your language then. A warding is magic. Crossing one, for us, is a little like passing beneath a waterfall without getting wet. We can feel

even a broken warding. They leave a smell...or a taste."
Allavin looked at Tiryn. "Is the warding Forbidden magic?"
"The warding isn't. But Jerrinwey smells Forbidden magic ahead. The Bandits are using it."
Allavin nodded. He had expected that. "I'll go closer. Don't risk your patrol, Tiryn."
The Shae smiled. "You are our brother, Allavin. The paper kings will listen to you."
Allavin returned the smile. The Shae called the Kingdom of Dos-Aralon the paper kingdom because of the treaties they liked to sign. It was a good joke, because the Shae sold them the ink. He nodded to Tiryn to move on and the Shae motioned the others to go deeper. Through the mesh of leaves, their boots sank into a small rivulet of murky water cutting in front of them. Tiryn froze after stepping past it, hand on his heart. He swallowed and composed himself, looking back at Allavin in assurance, before continuing after the others. He'd obviously felt the warding too.
Allavin felt nothing save the damp heat. But the Shae were different in that respect too. They could taste and smell magic in all its colors and shades. Aside from the whickering noises of insects, he heard the quiet rush of a small waterfall and stream.
Tiryn held up his hand and made a gesture of alarm. *Jerrinwey hears them,* he said with his hands. *We are close.*
Crossing another dozen paces, Allavin heard it too – the chugging sound of shovels through mud, sinking and slopping. As one, they moved towards the noise. Soon the sound was joined by heavy grunts, and Allavin saw the dim fringes of lantern light ahead through the swamp choked with thimbleberry bushes and witch-thorn. Allavin wiped the sweat from his mouth with the back of his hand and stared ahead. He saw the other two Shae in position, watching the workmen in the middle of the swamp.
Tiryn beckoned Allavin closer.
Ahead in the gloom, he saw the glimmer of water cascading down a huge rock outcropping, washing off the rock steps in thin white rivulets. It collected at the base of the beautiful

falls in an overgrown pond, thick and teeming with moss. The moss was everywhere – blanketing the rocks and fallen branches. Even the outcropping and the falls were green with it. In the dim glare of the lanterns, he could see the moss cover the forested glen for thirty paces at least.

Half-clothed men with heaving muscles tore at the swamp with root furrows and shovels, hurrying to finish a network of wooden gutters to drain the pond. Lanterns hung from sagging lengths of twine, offering pale rings of light to the soiled crew. Sluggish gray water coursed through the tilting conduits, dumping into a flat gully forty paces away. Allavin and the small band of Shae skirted the workmen to the left, moving closer to the falls. The sucking sound of the shovels was replaced by the crack of scrapers and pickaxes. Standing in the pond water, the workers scraped the moss from the rocks and tossed the clumps into hand-barrows. Allavin stared at the scene, wondering what was happening. The Bandit Rebellion was collecting…moss? He studied the scene as other workmen approached and poured fresh water from jugs over the soiled moss. It turned a rich shade of green and even in the poor light it sparkled with buds of blue and violet.

Allavin motioned to the plant and made the sign of Forbidden magic. Tiryn shook his head, scrutinizing the workmen. He looked angry at the devastation of the grove. The falls would have been beautiful and quiet, but the workmen were destroying the peacefulness. Tiryn motioned again and Allavin watched the two scouts he could see raise their longbows and choose their targets. The Shae never allowed the earth to be desecrated like this.

Allavin put his hand on Tiryn's arm, stopping him. He motioned to the moss and pointed to his own palm with the flat of his finger. He wanted some of it to bring back with him. Tiryn nodded begrudgingly and made a quick series of hand signals. There was plenty of moss in the area, and it wouldn't be difficult for one of the scouts to creep in and snatch some. Allavin crouched, wiping the streaks of sweat from his face. He had to find out what the Bandit Rebellion was stealing from the swamp. Was it a poison? A cure? He knew a Zerite healer in Iniva who might know. Tiryn raised his hand again and pointed. The bows quietly bent.

From the shadows of the swamp on the east side, a knight approached the workmen. The glint of field armor became visible in the pallid light. The workmen slowed and regarded the new arrival. The dark armor was sculpted with a metal trim of ivy and leaves. It was the design of a particular regiment of knights in Owen Draw – a regiment that was now another word for treason. Allavin tried to swallow and found he could not. *Sweet Achrolese,* he thought in shock. *It's Balinaire.* He knew the man before him better than most in the valley. He had tracked this man's army throughout the vales and hills of the entire realm. It was Lord Ballinaire himself, the leader of the Bandit Rebellion and its three armies. Allavin had last heard he was entrenched in the Kingshadow Mountains, building a fortress. But here he was... in the Shoreland itself preparing the siege on Landmoor.

Ballinaire spoke in hushed tones to the men in the grove. His black eyebrows were stark against the creased folds of wrinkled skin. His thin hair and short beard were white, like shaded snow. The workers rested, their muscles quivering and dripping sweat. The quiet rush and patter of the falls muffled his words, but Allavin watched him with growing anger and determination. King don-Rion would pay a hundred Aralonian pieces to know that Ballinaire was hiding down here. He'd pay more and he'd rouse every knight and soldier under the Crown. But it wasn't the golden mint from the king's coffers that Allavin craved. No, he wanted peace. *Maybe the Rebellion will end at last,* he prayed. Dos-Aralon had been sundered by the Rebellion and would continue to be riddled with disaster until Ballinaire hung stiff from a gibbet. Ballinaire had enough men in the Shoreland to take Landmoor. But not enough to hold her against the brunt of Dos-Aralon's armies.

Tiryn clutched his arm. *"Jerrinwey is gone."*

Allavin looked at him and felt his heart lurch. The point scout was never supposed to leave the sight of the flank scouts. Never. He was about to tell him to send another in when Tiryn jerked at his cloak.

"Run!"

Allavin didn't argue. In a start, he plunged back into the moors, no longer cautious of the sound they made. Cries of alarm came from the watch, but Allavin knew how to elude the Bandit army. Tiryn's lithe body sprinted next to him, his longbow ready with an arrow. Shouts rose up in pursuit, but the Shae and the tracker had a tremendous lead.

A flash of blue lightning lit the murk of the swamp. A rushed cry of fear and pain followed instead of thunder and then silence. Allavin looked back and saw an inky black shape silhouetted against the trees as the light of the blue fire died. It wasn't Ballinaire.

"Quickly!" Tiryn said.

Allavin nearly stumbled through a juniper shrub and managed to keep his footing in the slick mud on the other side. With Tiryn next to him, he plunged into a narrow gully and started up the opposite slope, clutching the cedar roots as handholds and tearing his fingertips on witch-thorn. His hands stung and burned. Allavin hoisted himself and risked another look backwards. One of the Shae scouts was twenty paces back, bounding over rocks and shrubs. Then blue light exploded, blinding Allavin with its startling heat and fire. When the spots cleared from his eyes, the Shae was dead, smoldering with a charred scorchburn through him.

"Shenalle protect us from the Firekin," Tiryn prayed in a frantic voice, scrambling up the slopes with naked fear blazing in his eyes. *"Shenalle protect us and keep us. Shenalle bring peace to the troubled..."*

Allavin Devers grabbed Tiryn's arm and pulled him up the slope. He started for the ring of trees, but he was alone. Tiryn had spun around and raised the trembling bow. *"Keasorn guide my arrow. Keasorn give me courage to strike my enemy."*

"Tiryn, run!"

"Vannier grant me luck. Vannier give me cunning."

"Run!"

Allavin saw the black shadow across the gully. With a look of determination on his face, Tiryn let the steel-tipped shafts loose, one after the other, a trained and deliberate motion from quiver to string. Allavin watched the arrows warp left and right of the shadow and clatter against the wet bark of the twisting vine maple. The shadow raised its arms. Allavin dove clear as the blue light lit the sky like a thousand searing candles. Before he could loose another arrow, Tiryn screamed as the bolt of blue light struck his chest, lifting him with its blazing fury and tossed him against a stand of prickle-vine. The magic seared through his chest, leaving a smoking gap and his face transfixed with terror.

Allavin Devers scrambled through the brush, keeping low to the ground. He dodged around trees and stands of juniper, trying to get clear of the forest. He heard nothing, but he knew he was being followed. The black shadow was hunting him. Wrenching his sword from its sheath, he thrashed at the low-hanging boughs and cut away the vines that tried to snare him. The entire scouting party was dead. A Shae scouting party!

The mud tugged at his ankles, clumping on his boots and slowing his escape. It was lighter ahead, meaning he was close to the edge of the woods. He stumbled through the maze of cedar and sedge. Something black pricked his side vision and he changed directions, trying to outdistance it. Huffing with exhaustion, he risked a look behind. The light gave the shadow a form – the form of a man draped in midnight colors. A Sleepwalker. It must be a Sleepwalker! Allavin's heart thundered in his chest. He turned back again, too late. A tree sent sparks of light and pain into his eyes. Blood gushed from his broken nose, and the pain rocked his body. Pushing away, he staggered for the sound of a stream somewhere in the thick folds of the Wood. His broken nose throbbed in agony, sickening him.

Crushing a stand of reeds, Allavin stumbled down a deep inlet and splashed into a pond of quicksand hidden there. The gritty waters immersed him, a smothering bath of sand and shallows. He tried to swim free of it, but the sinking pull dragged him slowly down into the sinkhole. Allavin thrashed upwards, trying to get a last mouthful of air, but he swallowed blood and sand. No! his mind shrieked. He could feel his lungs screaming for air. He was going to die. The thought

11

haunted him in a rush.

The black shadow watched him struggle in vain from the lip of the rise. Just beyond the rows of gnarled cedar, the fortress of Landmoor began flickering awake with torchlight as night and mist descended over the moors.

II

It was just before dusk when the Council sentries came to arrest Thealos Quickfellow. Both sentries wore the sharp, green and gold colored uniform of the Council Elder of Vannier. They had swords belted to their waists, but the weapons looked more ceremonial and polished than the clean, practical kind that Shae soldiers carried. They arrived at the Quickfellow manor and sternly demanded that Thealos accompany them to meet with Council Elder Nordain. Sorrel treated the sentries with cool disdain, as was her inclination, but Thealos had been expecting this. Leaving his room, he looked at Sorrel calmly, seeing the disquiet in his mother's face.

"You've done enough to shame us already, Thealos," she said in a low voice. "You know what you must do now."

He stared at her and then followed the sentries without a word to her.

The streets of Avisahn were empty for the most part. The heavily wooded grounds of the Quickfellow manor fell behind them and the horses' hooves clacked against the smooth paving stones of the main city road. From his vantage near the window of the carriage, Thealos could see the tall spire of the Temple of Keasorn rising in the center of the beautiful city like a mountain amidst of sea of slate-shingled manors and gilded churchyards. The carriage picked up speed as they started down the slope of the wooded foothills towards

13

the center of Avisahn. But that majestic temple was not his destination. The Shae had three gods: Keasorn, Shenalle, and Vannier. Thealos' family worshipped the third, as was customary among trading families. These deities had their own High Council with a stern Council Elder to rebuke the wayward young. An ironic smile twisted Thealos' mouth. He knew what he was doing went well beyond wayward young.

It was dark by the time the sentries escorted Thealos into the keeping chamber of the High Council of Vannier. Though its dome couldn't rival the spire of Keasorn's temple, Vannier's temple was just as opulent and situated closer to the docks near Barters Row. It had always reminded Thealos of a giant eggshell. He watched the two sentries take taciturn positions by the entry door after shutting and locking it. Turning, he stared blankly at the double doors leading into the High Council chamber. He'd been here four times in the last year. Each time, the Council Elder had tried coaxing him into obeying his parents' wishes or repenting some foolish childhood thought. Thealos wasn't expecting any coaxing this time. He'd get a stern warning and a few threats to unman him. Thealos swallowed, preparing himself for it. His eyes bored into the double doors, wondering who had been gathered to witness this meeting. Would Correl be there? He'd been gone all afternoon, and Thealos wondered where his father was. Trying a last-minute bribe probably. The fluted scrollwork of the door shone with a heavy waxed polish. It was an immaculate design and finish, stained a rich auburn, and revealed the symbol of the god Vannier – entwining crescents facing opposite ways. Looking closely at the trim edges, he saw little gouges in the wood. He wanted to click his tongue, but he'd run out of spit along the way. Instead, he sighed nervously. No, this wasn't the first time he had been summoned to speak to Nordain. But it was the first time he'd been summoned anywhere under guard.

"Sit down, Quickfellow," one of the sentries said, a disdainful clip to his voice. They both regarded Thealos with open animosity. They should, after all. According to the customs of his people, he was practically anathema just being there. Was it only a formality now? A foregone conclusion in everyone's mind?

Thealos regarded them coolly and then began to pace the keeping chamber. He was never one for sitting quietly for long bouts of time, and he walked in a short circle, thinking about what he would tell the Council Elder when he was brought in to speak to him. He was expecting another censure, that unless he followed the Shae customs as he ought, he would be banished from Avisahn and attainted from his family name. From that moment on, he would be Thealos Kil-Quickfellow. Being a Kilshae was enough of a threat to bully most from abandoning the Shae homeland. But Thealos thought that if he could show Nordain that he wasn't frightened of it, perhaps he could convince him to change his mind or at least open it a little. Was that asking too much?

Knowing Nordain as he did, it probably was.

"You might as well sit down," the taller sentry said. They were both shorter than Thealos, though wider around the chest. The sentry who addressed him had crisp blue eyes and a narrow face. "Elder Nordain will call for you soon enough."

"Am I breaking a rule of Forbiddance by standing?" The last thing he needed was advice from the very men who would be called to escort him out of the city into exile. It would be done hours before dawn, before the city had awakened to witness the shame of it. Avisahn didn't want its dirty linens wagging in the streets for all to see.

"Don't mind him," the other sentry said. "We'll see how proud he stands when the Elder finishes with him. I've seen lads two Silvan years older than him weeping like babies when it's over." He gave Thealos a challenging glare.

He's mocking my youth, Thealos thought and tried not to smile. *What an idiot.* Thealos then ignored them, focusing his thoughts on what would happen beyond the sculpted doorway. The gnawing considerations infuriated him. Correl didn't understand. Neither did Sorrel. How could they? They had both followed the proper paths of the Shae all their lives. They were content to spin out their days in Avisahn even though the Shae had once controlled the entire valley. Did they even know what he was going through? Could they know? Thealos clenched his fists, pacing swiftly. It was time to leave Avisahn. Not for the rest of his life. Not until the gods returned with Safehome and made the world new again. Only for a season or two. Why? How could he explain it? A feeling – a prompting. A whisper from the gods? Or maybe from his own mind, desperately hungering for what lay beyond the borders of the Shae kingdom. For knowledge, not just history lessons. For a chance to wear a sword and not only as a decoration like the two sentries did. But if Nordain banished Thealos from Avisahn, he would never be able to return. Was a little freedom truly worth risking that?

The council door opened.

"Thealos of the house of Quickfellow," the robed attendant said. He stared at the young Shae with emotionless eyes. As if the young Shae were a rock or a pond – some unliving thing.

"I am Thealos."

"The Council Elders will now see you."

Elders? Thealos thought in confusion. He was expecting to see Nordain and his priests, certainly not the Council Elders of Shenalle or Keasorn too. Thealos nodded and followed the attendant into the chamber. He was greeted with the flavored scent of spice candles, a musky smell that always made him think of Nordain. He saw the fat Elder sitting in the cushioned armchair behind a wide desk. Two thick candles illuminated the polished desk inset with streaks of blue marble. A sheaf of papers sat arranged before him along with a tall chalice of spiced wine, the Elder's favorite drink. He was a big man, for a Shae, with curling ash-blond hair that was cut above the frill of his shirt. He was already balding, but his face was smooth except for a single pockmark on his right cheek. His eyes were gray and fierce. A platter sat just within arm's reach, and his belly showed his weakness for the delights of the baking guilds assembled there.

Entering the council chamber, Thealos saw the witnesses assembled in the stuffed chairs around the room. He recognized the Council Elder of Shenalle, Trinton by name, and two captains from the Legion Army of Avisahn were obviously representing Keasorn. There were other witnesses too.

His eyes quickly scanned those assembled, one from each section of society. There were more than enough already to banish him tonight. His blood went cold. Nordain obviously wanted an audience.

"Greet the Council Elder, Thealos," Correl whispered from behind him. Thealos felt his father's tight grip on his arm. He twisted free of his father's grasp and gave him a challenging look. "I've been here before, Correl," he said, seething, uncomfortable with the stares pricking him.

"Be seated, Thestyr," Nordain said, casually waving Correl away. "You're his Correl, but I'd like to speak to your son for a moment. Yes, your seat...over there. Very good. Come in, Thealos."

Thealos took a deep breath and approached the table. He dropped to one knee, bowed his head and then rose. "I come as summoned, Council Elder."

"Oh, I do appreciate your obedience," Nordain said with a mocking smile. He sipped from the silver chalice and regarded Thealos coolly. "Do I understand correctly that you have not chosen your calling yet?"

Thealos was forced to stand in the center of the hall, all eyes upon him. That was intimidating enough. He could feel the intensity of their eyes, so he stared down at the floor to steel his courage. Nordain would not make him cry. No matter what happened. He quelled the trembling in his stomach so his voice wouldn't falter. Nordain would try and trick him with his words if he could. He always did. "No, I don't think you do, Elder Nordain."

"Then you have decided?" He sounded amused. "Which of our three gods will you serve then?"

"That's not what I meant. I don't think you really understand what my calling is."

"Ahh, your 'true' calling. This...calling of yours is the one we've spoken of before?" Thealos nodded. "And you feel – what, inspired that you should leave the home of the Shae to wander about aimlessly with the humans in the valley?"

Thealos' stomach twisted with frustration. Nordain was trying to belittle his feelings again. He gave the Council Elder an arch look. "Didn't this entire valley once belong to the Shae, Elder Nordain? From the Ravenstone to the Kingshadow and down to the sea. Am I wrong? Then how can you say I'm leaving my homeland?"

Nordain's gray eyes crackled with fury. His voice was controlled. "How old are you, Thealos?"

"You know very well how old I am. That's what this is all about, isn't it?"

"This isn't a debate. I expect you to answer the questions I pose you. Obedience is the First Order, not a Rule of Forbiddance. Now, do I ask too much to have you give me your age?"

"Tomorrow, I earn the age of seven Silvan years." Oh, the debate was only beginning!

"And what do Shae youths do at such a distinguished age?" Nordain prodded. "What is the tradition of our people?"

"We are told by the Council Elders that we must tithe one Silvan year to the service of the gods. To whichever god we choose."

Nordain took a sip from the wine chalice. He rubbed the lip of the cup with his thumb as he contemplated. "That is correct. And after that you have your entire life to waste or flitter away as you choose, Thealos. You know we live much longer than our human neighbors in Dos-Aralon. And if you so desire, you could waste thirty of their lifetimes pursuing your own selfish ends." Each word stung as he spoke. "Can you please explain to me why you cannot fulfill such a token responsibility then? To give back one-seventh of what you've already been given, not to mention the dozens more you have ahead of you. I tell you, young man, that if you despise our ways this much, that you cannot bring yourself to make even a paltry offering...you do not deserve to associate with those who have and those who do." The gray eyes flashed menacingly. "Please, do share with us what gives a lad of your limited age and experience the wisdom to know what it best for you, when hundreds, even thousands of your forebears have done what is expected with willing and grateful hearts." He shrugged with the incomprehensibility of it. "Do you feel the length of service is too long? One Silvan year. That is all, and then you have your entire life to yourself. Or are you afraid you may learn something? That you might learn to forget your own selfishness and be of service or betterment to the Shae? Is that what you fear, Thealos?"

"May I answer yet?" Thealos asked, wrestling with his anger.

"Yes, you may. I expect to hear an answer from you. I want to know what gives you the right to abandon our traditions."

Thealos swallowed. "Council Elder, my deepest fear is that our traditions are destroying us as a people. In Vannier's name, let me finish!" he said when he saw Nordain open his mouth. "For once, listen to me. Truly listen. Our people once controlled this valley. But we have given it over to Dos-Aralon. They have taken it away from us, piece by piece. We may control the trade along the Trident River. We may barter with the humans and reap their riches. But there will come a time when they will cross the river. We must start preparing for it, Elder. My calling is to go among them, to understand their ways, to try and teach them ours like was done when the Shae first came to this world. I love our people." He felt tears start to choke him and quickly cleared his throat to stifle them. "More than you will ever know. I love my family and I know my choice is hurting them deeply. But I'm convinced of this, Elder Nordain. If we do not take sides this time, the Shae will lose to whoever wins. Dos-Aralon used to be our ally. Now we only sell them weapons and food. But the Bandit Rebellion is getting stronger. It's worn on long enough – and you can't deny that it's affected us. It's barely safe to trade in Sol any more. This is our chance to change what will become of our people in the future! And I tell you, Elder Nordain, that I am also convinced the reckoning will happen before one Silvan year is through. I'm hearing talk of war in the Shoreland by summer. We cannot stand by while it happens without us – again."

Nordain smoldered. Thealos saw it in his eyes that he didn't believe him. Nordain set the goblet down and folded his arms imperiously. "Are you privy to the secret council of King Silverborne? Do you discuss war tactics with the Legion Army commanders? If it is war you crave so much, choose Keasorn as your calling and join the Shae army. We know what's going on in the valley better than you think. If we got involved in every little..."

"But we won't fight in this conflict either," Thealos tried to say, clenching his teeth. "We haven't since the Purge Wars, and the humans mock us for our weakness."

"And how do you know so much about the Bandit Rebellion? We have watchposts along the Kingshadow still. If there was anything to concern us in the Shoreland, our scouts will tell us. What is the source of your knowledge? Isn't this just gossip you've heard in alley taverns across the river? Ah, you didn't know that I knew about that?" he said triumphantly, seeing Thealos flinch. "Your speech was noble and brave. But the truth, Thealos? The truth is that you tire of the Rules of Forbiddance. You feel tethered by our customs and you seek to spoil yourself with the gratification's of Dos-Aralon. As a barter's son, you've been exposed to their life. It's tainting you."

"That is not true."

"You are deceiving yourself! I have seen young Shae itching to sip from the forbidden cups. I tell you from my experience, I have seen these Kilshae when they try to return, to gain admittance back into the protection of our society. To the very shelter they once took for granted. They are heartbroken when they come to learn that they cannot! Anathema is forever." He leaned forward, giving Thealos a hard stare. "Will you risk that? Are the pleasures of Dos-Aralon truly worth that?"

Mutters of assent rumbled through the chamber. Thealos didn't dare look behind him.

"You're twisting my words!" Thealos said, stepping forward. "I've never had a sip of ale or eaten their burned meat. I've never done anything to bring dishonor on my name or my family. What sin have I committed to earn this? Our culture is in danger, Nordain. What will you do when the humans come here? Do you think they will grant you one morsel of honor because you're a Council Elder? They will take your chalice and dash your head against the paving stones."

"Are you threatening..?" Nordain roared.

"No! Sons of Fire, I am trying to get you to see what will happen if we continue to sit and do nothing! If I forsake the Rules of Forbiddance out there, I have no right to return. I know that. You do not believe me strong enough to resist their ways. I tell you that I am. As the son of a barter, I must be! Let me see the world as it is. Let me see it for myself, Elder. Without all our shade and illusions. That is all that I ask. If I am wrong, I will humbly submit to any penance you have for me, and I covenant to dedicate two Silvan years to a calling. I ask for a brief while to see if I am right. To follow where my heart leads me, just as our forbears did following Silvermere to this valley all those years ago. Was he a Kilshae to do so? Then I am in good company."

"And what gives you this right? You think that the gods of the Shae cannot protect us?"

"Not from our own foolishness. They never have."

"And by what authority do you make this claim? Our ruler is the only one who can interpret the gods' will for the Shae. That is the direction we must all follow. You must follow it, Thealos!"

The young Shae stared at him passionately. "I cannot."

"You deny the authority of the King of Avisahn?"

"No, I deny the wisdom of the Shae hierarchy."

"They are the same. If you accept our values, you must accept their decisions. By your soul, Thealos – you must accept it!"

"I will not accept what is wrong – what has been wrong since we've let a stupid bureaucracy overwhelm our freedoms. Look where following frightened hearts has brought us? We've lost the whole valley to the humans. King Silverborne is a coward for letting it happen during his reign. And so are you for not seeing it. May our gods have mercy on us for the way you're destroying this people." And Thealos knew before the last words were out of his mouth that he should have kept that last thought to himself.

III

The Council Elder's private chambers were lavish with gifts from the guilds he represented in Vannier's name. Tall flawless vases, crystal dishes with sweet smelling confections, bedecked curtains bearing the lily-and-rose of the clothweavers guild. Each more dazzling than the last. Expensive trinkets from as far away as Sheven-Ingen littered an onyx table top nestled against the wall near the door. These rattled as the door slammed shut.

"I told you to frighten him, Nordain," Correl said. "Not send him to the block for sedition! In Vannier's name, what do you think you are doing!" Thealos had never heard Correl angry enough to actually shout at the Council Elder.

"What should have been done earlier, Thestyr," Nordain replied, giving Thealos a sharp look. Thealos jerked free again of his father's grasp and started pacing. "He's a headstrong lad. Too headstrong. But he's also a victim of high station. You've spoiled him horribly, Thestyr."

Thealos saw the venomous look that Correl gave the Council Elder. "I think I've spoiled you too much, Nordain. You never would have become Council Elder without me. And you're not going to get away with this. Do you know how many votes in the Sunedrion you'll need to condemn him? I'll have Corbund and Val-Mestro make sure it never reaches the general audience..."

"You're getting old to be playing favors with the council..."

22

Nordain said with a chuckle. "There is nothing you can do. He condemned himself in a hall full of witnesses! Trinton is hardly as pious as a gosling, but he heard heresy tonight. I assure you, your son will be under arrest before the night is over." He gave Thealos an arch look. "You do well to look so fearful, Thealos. You should be afraid. I doubt the Sunedrion will cry for your blood, but you won't be a free man when you come of age tomorrow morning."

"It's not fear," Thealos said through clenched teeth. He was furious.

"You're in enough trouble as it is, Thealos!" Correl snapped. "For once, be silent!" He fixed the Council Elder with his finger. "I know what you're doing, Nordain. I may be old, but I am not blind. How much do you want?"

"What?" Nordain laughed.

"You caused this dilemma. What will it cost me to repair it?"

"Save your purse for the morrow, Thestyr. I'm doing this for the sake of the people. We don't need the Kinslayer Wars to start again. Thealos will stand trial for speaking sedition. It's the only way to save your family's honor. Wouldn't you rather he die as a traitor than knifed in some back-street alley in Dos-Aralon?"

"You did this on purpose," Thealos said. "The summons... the witnesses..."

"I did it for your soul, lad," Nordain replied smugly, his eyes shining. "I gave you ample opportunity to cease this foolishness. You refused. Did you think we would let you walk away in shame? What, a Kilshae? The son of Thestyr Quickfellow? You've always been a very passionate lad. But it is only a matter of time before someone tries to use that."

"You son of Pitan," Correl swore, shaking his head.

"Be careful," Nordain said. "There will be many who will say he learned this sedition from you."

When he saw Correl flinch at the accusation, Thealos longed to strangle the Council Elder.

"You know I didn't..." Correl stammered.

"Ahh, that is the true issue, Thestyr. What do I know? And how much, exactly, is my good opinion worth to you?

As I said, we'll discuss those terms on the morrow." Nordain stepped around to a soft-stuffed couch and seated himself. He gave Correl a hard look. "You may go. I must take the boy's confession tonight so we can proceed with the formal charges tomorrow. And I'm sure the palace will be interested in hearing this right away."

Thealos looked pleadingly at Correl. "Don't let him take me."

The Council Elder raised his eyebrows insistently.

"Let me bring my son home with me," Thestyr asked after swallowing.

"Impossible. I said you may go."

"He hasn't been put under arrest yet! For the love of Shenalle, give him one last night at home with his family!" Nordain scowled at the suggestion. "Whatever it costs me," Correl sighed at last. "Whatever the cost to us, I don't care. Let us make our peace with him before he goes to the Sunedrion."

Thealos was galled with Nordain, at the power he wielded over the Quickfellow family. At last the Council Elder sighed, bored. "He's under your wardship then, Thestyr. But I tell you, if he's not here tomorrow at dawn, I'll have the Council Elder of Keasorn send the Crimson Wolfsmen to find him. Do you understand what that means? If I must send them, he's as good as guilty."

"Upon my word," Thestyr Quickfellow said, nodding vigorously.

"Very well." He gave Thealos a measured stare. "If I have my way, lad, you'll spend your calling in prison instead of roaming the valley like a drunkard. It could have been different, but remember your obstinacy prevailed in the end. Hopefully, you will become a good lesson to others."

I hope so, Thealos was about to retort, but Thestyr grabbed his arm and directed him to the door.

"Use my private retreat," Nordain insisted, motioning to a fluted screenwork across the chamber. "My last piece of generosity for the evening. And Thestyr – the cost." He tapped his mouth thoughtfully. "I could use twelve reams of satin-cloth and damask. I particularly like the pattern with the yellow primroses." He took a deep sip of spiced wine. "Have it delivered to my attendant in the morning."

"Very well, Council Elder," Thestyr Quickfellow replied tonelessly, hauling Thealos out of the Shae High Council and into the gardens beyond.

* * *

The pale blue moonlight glimmered on the silver window panes. Thealos could hear the sharp voices of Correl and Sorrel arguing in the keeping chamber across the main hall. In between the hard-edged voice of Correl he heard angry words that spoke of his mother's pain. He listened, pausing in the darkness to savor the sounds. He rarely heard her curse.

"I told you that we couldn't trust Nordain," Sorrel said. "He is a greedy, conniving thief. He'll ruin us – ruin you! I'd sooner trust little Arielle to the Dos-Aralon army than that back-stabbing..."

"I did what I could!" Correl thundered. "He's our son. They were planning to hold him tonight."

"No!"

"I know, I know! This will cost us dearly enough. But what else would they get him to confess? That I'd prompted him to shout off to the Council Elder of Vannier? Sons of Fire, he did it in front of everyone!"

"What are we going to do?"

"I'm dispatching a messenger to the palace – to the Princess. Maybe she'll speak for him."

"Against her father?" Sorrel was incredulous.

"What other choice do we have? I'll send messages to the members of the Sunedrion who owe us favors, but I don't have many friends from Keasorn or Shenalle. Normally, this would never go so far so quickly. Nordain planned it from the start."

Thealos bowed his head and tried to bury the rage in his heart. He knew what he was doing would cost his family. He only hoped they would come to forgive him. Opening his eyes, he stared out at the moonswept gardens, filling his eyes with its sights. He'd miss all the comforts of the manor house, but it was the family gardens that would tug at his soul. He'd miss his parents and brothers, but it was his little sister that he would regret leaving behind. He closed his eyes for a moment, trying to trap the good memories inside. Pushing away from the window, he went to the door and opened it.

"I hear him," Sorrel said. As he crossed the hall, he saw Correl and Sorrel face him from the doors of the keeping chamber.

"I am sorry," Thealos said as meekly as he could pretend. He looked at Correl. "I've failed you yet again."

Correl's eyes narrowed. "You've always had your own will, Thealos. Ever since you were a boy. Why couldn't you, for once in your life, have sought the family good instead of your own?" He shook his head, too choked with anger to speak.

"How could I expect you understand me now?" he replied softly. "You've never tried to before."

"You've been doing things your way for so long," Sorrel said with great bitterness. "But you are still our son."

"I always will be." He sighed, hating that it had to be this way. "I'm going to talk to Arielle for a little while. Maybe we can talk later? I thought the worst that could happen would be an exile. I never thought Nordain..." He sighed again and shook his head.

Sorrel nodded, folding her arms and pacing the tiles. Thealos smiled inwardly. He'd gotten his pacing habit from her. But she didn't try and comfort him. No, she was still too angry. Their eldest son was abandoning the Shae tradition of manhood. Not only that, he had committed a serious crime. This would humiliate them. Giving Correl a final look that tried to be conciliatory, Thealos went up the long flight of steps and down the wide hall, running his palm over the flat banister. He stopped at the hall cross-way where a huge silver-gilt mirror faced him and swallowed the image of the room behind. He resembled Sorrel more than Correl, with her wide forehead and narrow face. But he had Correl's green eyes, a startling color that matched his temper. The face staring back at him was a handsome one – Thealos knew that. He was an incorrigible flirt, especially at parties. But he stared at the image and wondered why the glass didn't show his heart, his thoughts – all the ideas twisting and struggling to come to life inside his mind. It was only an image, and it revealed nothing of the person within. Much like the Shae. What they were on the surface, the polish, glitter and flash, was nothing what they had become deep within themselves. Frightened, reclusive, stubborn. Nordain was hiding from it. So many did.

After closing the distance, he rapped on his little sister's bedroom door. He waited a moment and then entered. Arielle was flinging the sheets away like a thrush caught in a thicket.

"Thealos!" she gasped, running up to him and squeezing him so tightly around the middle it hurt. "I was scared that you weren't coming back. They were yelling so loudly. I couldn't tell what was happening."

"Shhh," Thealos said soothingly, leaning down and kissing her hair. He cupped her chin and looked into her eyes. She was a beauty, the darling youngest of the Quickfellow family. "I'll be all right, Arielle. I don't want you to worry."

"Worry! I'm scared and excited for you at the same time." She sighed. "You're my favorite brother."

"You say that to Jaye and Jedian too," he reminded her.

"You're all my favorites," she replied with an impish grin. "But you are my special brother, Thealos. Are you really going to become a Kilshae?"

He gave her an understanding grin. "That depends on whether you can keep a secret."

Her eyes widened with delight. "I can!"

"I came to say goodbye, Arielle. Because you're my favorite sister."

"I'm your only sister."

He kissed her cheek. "Tell them you were asleep. Tell them the only thing you remember is that I kissed you and promised that I would come home someday. Will you tell them that?"

"You're leaving? Right now?"

He nodded. "I'm not going to get another chance."

"Can I come with you?" Her eyes were so serious it hurt

him to look at her.

He shook his head. "And add kidnapping to the charges? I'd better not, Arielle. Pretend to sleep." She slipped beneath the thick wool and linen covers and shivered. Her eyes were misty with tears, and she squeezed him tightly.

"I'll miss you, Thealos." She tugged on his shirt to bring him down and kissed his cheek. Then she remembered something and dug beneath the covers. "Take this with you," she said, giving him a leather bundle. "I want you to keep it. For when you get lonely."

He stared at the bundle she'd pressed in his hand and swallowed. He knew it contained her wooden hoppit doll. "Thank you," he whispered, giving her one last hug. "I am going to travel the whole valley, Arielle. I'll camp under the pines of the Vale, watch the tide off the Cliffs of Demos, and drink from the Dayspring Rush. And I will bring you a gift when I come home." He rose and approached the bedroom window.

"A White Rose of Tharkin?" she asked, excited. "If you find one...?"

"If I find one." He gave her one last smile and disappeared through the window before she could see him cry. He shut the glass and felt the cool wind touch his face high up on the balcony. He breathed slowly, shuddering. Leaving her was harder than he expected. Climbing over the rail, he lowered himself down the black-iron slats and then dropped into the bushes of heather below. Keeping low, he waited and watched. Nothing.

With the practiced Shae step-walking pattern, Thealos went around the side of the Quicksilver manor, staying on the dark rich soil and behind the rows of hedges and feather-fern. He reached his bedroom and found the stash he had left out the window earlier that day. A wool tunic and a long-sleeved linen shirt were folded in a stack and he put them on before wrapping himself in a thick green cloak. Thealos secured his favorite hunting bow to his travel sack with leather ties and slung the burden around his shoulders. He shoved a long dagger into his belt. He listened at the silver windowpanes but he could not hear anything.

Thealos wondered how long he would have before Correl went to Arielle's room looking for him? An hour or two? Not much time.

Parting the branches of a fragrant azalea bush, he looked up at the glittering ocean of stars. The blue light of the moon Eroth bathed his face. He stared at the road, letting his vision adapt to the night colors. He waited patiently, knowing Nordain. Sure enough, he saw the two sentries who had kept him at the Shae High Council. They were watching the moonlit face of the manor with a good view of Thealos' room. Arielle's room was on the other side of the manor. Without a sound, he crossed behind the manor and disappeared into the dark gardens, following the side of the paving stones to keep hidden in the trees. Thealos crossed a small brookstone bridge, feeling the darkness of the wooded grounds absorb him into its bosom, and he savored the smells in the air. He knew the back woods better than anyone else in the neighborhood.

If Nordain had made sure that Keasorn's Crimson Wolfsmen had been watching for him, Thealos knew he would never have made it sixty paces from the manor house that night. Inwardly, he was pleased his family worshipped Vannier instead. Their god may have made men good at trade. But they were terrible watchmen.

IV

The harsh yellow glare of torch fire washed over Thealos' face as he climbed the shoal docks from the barge and entered the city of Dos-Aralon. He dropped a few Aralonian pieces into the grubby hand of the ferry-keeper and joined the ranks milling about the crowded pier. He had chosen the southern trading docks deliberately, knowing well in advance that they would be crowded for hours yet to come. Darkness had already fallen over the jammed city, but with torches and lanterns to play the sun's part, there would still be many willing to deal. Even with a Shae.

Thealos passed beneath the high bastions and ramparts facing the river. He knew the trading streets better than most in Avisahn and quickly marked the barters his father traded with – the clothweaver and draper guilds. Avoiding those, he ducked down side alleys where he could avoid curious stares. The night was warm, but he wore the green cowl up over his head to hide the tell-tale features that branded him a Shae – the straw-blond hair, light eyes, and pale skin. There were other traits that distinguished him from the humans of the valley. He could feel the tremor of the Earth magic and discern whether it was Light or Forbidden. He could smell color, and he could see in the dark like a cat born to walk the rails at night. He knew the humans were afraid to see the eyes of a Shae glowing in the dark. He smirked. Let them fear.

30

Thealos walked quickly and confidently, one hand on the sharp dagger in his belt. He used the Shae step-walking pattern of the woods to keep his soft boots from clipping loudly on the stone. More than anything else, he wanted to get out of Dos-Aralon and into the open plains before the gates were shut. Nordain would send sentries for him in the morning. Once Nordain was certain Thealos had abandoned Avisahn, he would ask the Council Elder of Keasorn to summon the Crimson Wolfsmen. They were the defenders of the Shae kingdom, more highly trained than the regimental knights of Owen Draw, but Thealos doubted they knew Dos-Aralon as well as he did.

Out of the corner of his eye, he thought he caught a subtle movement behind him. Whirling, Thealos drew his dagger and stared down the empty alley. He gripped the hilt, ready in a defensive crouch for a thief or robber. He could see the light from the street at the other side of the alley. There was nothing, not even the scuttling of a rat on the cobblestones. He stared for several long moments, letting his breath out evenly. He usually trusted his instincts and his reflexes. Lowering the cowl, he listened, trying to catch any clues from the wind. Laughter glided past him from one of the many taverns on Highwater Street. He smelled the raw rich flavor of ale and honeyed mead – both Forbidden to the Shae. He tried to sense the Earth magic, but it was crowded down and stamped beneath the layers of street and filth. The sense of the magic was almost inaudible in Dos-Aralon. It had been so since the humans had settled there, or that was what he remembered from his studies.

Keeping his guard up, Thealos raised his hood and continued south, frequently checking the mouth of the alley behind him for any sign of pursuit. As he entered the next street, he kept with the flow of wagons and guild carts. Along the city wall, the stalls and booths were corded down with tarps. Paid sentries walked down the ways, protecting the wares during the night. Theft was common, Thealos knew, but only on the human side of the river. Painted signs and crooked flat boards spoke of the linens and trinkets for sale. He'd seen them so many times. He hoped he would never have to

31

cheat a man for another bolt of cloth again.

The south ports of Dos-Aralon wedged down against the furthest walls and gates. The walls were easy enough to follow, but sometimes the gatehouses were nearly indistinguishable from the high watch towers and cobbled steps rising to the bastions. He'd never negotiated through Dos-Aralon at night, but he found his instincts were still true and quickly approached the South-Bannik porter door leading out to the valley plains. Something tickled the back of his neck again, an awareness, a whisper of doubt. He paused at the street edge and turned around, looking back once more. He didn't know what he was expecting to see, for there were plenty of shopkeepers and journeymen about him, even a cluster of hired guards. It was a nagging feeling, like an itch between his shoulder-blades he just couldn't quench.

Something was following him.

Dos-Aralon was a dangerous city. He knew that well enough, and recognized that safety would only be found out in the hills and hollows of the valley. His instincts were better attuned than those of the human neighbors. He sheathed the dagger in his belt and hurried to the porter door. There were five sentries posted at South-Bannik wearing the army uniform of Dos-Aralon. This was typical.

"The moon greet you," Thealos said in the common language of the high kingdom. "I need passage tonight."

"Leaving?" the porter captain asked. "What for?"

"I have business elsewhere," Thealos replied. He looked over his shoulder, but saw nothing to mark his premonition. He still felt it.

"The gates are closed for the night. Come back in the morning."

Thealos tensed. "I can see the gates are closed, captain. But this is the quickest way. By the time I reached Kimberton Gate, it would be curfew. I need to..."

"Not tonight, lad. They're going to ring the bells soon, anyway. Pack up for the night. You can leave in the morning." He folded his arms, immune to Thealos' pleas.

Thealos scrutinized the porter guards. "This is a delicate matter," he said, unslinging the travel pack from across his shoulders. It was obvious they were expecting a bribe. In quick motions, he untied the mouth and reached inside. "My father is expecting a wagon shipment from the Radstill vineyards. If it arrives early," he continued, withdrawing a sealed bottle of Silvan wine, "we stand to make quite a profit from the sale."

"Sweet Achrolese," one of the guards gasped, staring at the bottle. "Is that...?"

"Yes, it is," Thealos answered with a greedy smile. "See these symbols? It's a dark red from the Silverborne kegs. As I said, gentlemen, this is an important meeting I must attend to. If you let me out tonight, I'll let you share this one. Even though it will cost me," he said with an exaggerated sigh. "Do we have a deal?"

The porter captain stared hungrily at the bottle and nodded. Fetching the gate keys from an iron ring around his belt, he unlocked the doors. Thealos nodded approvingly to the captain and handed him the bottle. He listened with smug confidence as the porter doors were closed and sealed behind him. He wondered whether any of them knew the bottle cost barely thirty silver pence in Avisahn. It was a modest table wine that even Arielle drank mixed with water – though still good by human standards. It did come from the Silverborne kegs. Of course, that's what the label declared on nearly every bottle of wine from Thealos' home.

* * *

When dawn broke like a foamy wave over the woodlands, Thealos shook his head wearily. It didn't feel like that much time had passed. The purple sky brightened until it shone a lustrous blue, hiding the stars in the light. Woven blankets of gray clouds floated along the channels of wind, bringing the smells of wildberries and decaying bark. The city of Dos-Aralon was well behind him, and he walked at an even pace, keeping away from the river. His plan was simple, and still a little unformed. Thealos wanted to walk the whole valley, to get a feeling and friendship with the people of the land. He wanted to meet farmers and soldiers and spinners

– even members of the Bandit Rebellion – and learn from them. He knew he should be cautious. There were stories of what men did to the Shae away from the homeland. Of course, the stories were meant to discourage exactly what Thealos intended to do. But if he could find a small group to travel with – a group of humans he could trust – it would increase his chances of surviving. With that in mind, he continued south, following the Trident River because he thought Nordain would look to the western lands for him first and Correl would search the city. Besides, Thealos knew the eastern ridge of the valley from the trading routes that Correl used, and he thought it wise to stay near familiar ground until he reached the Shoreland. Once he was down there, he could catch a ship to anywhere in the world and his trail would be impossible to pick up. Bluejays squawked from the branches of tall poplars, fluttering from tree to tree, chasing flying beetles. By midday, a rim of sweat had formed on Thealos' brow. Lowering the hood so he could feel the wind on his neck, he swept his long blond hair back and kept it loose. He was tall for a Shae, but still recognizably one even at a distance.

By mid-afternoon, Thealos could see the inland valley for miles. He stopped to eat on a low rangy hill crowned with trees. It overlooked a rich land with pastures dotted with stands of oak, ash, and maple trees. A hawk circled in the sky before dipping down to snatch a jackrabbit. He saw a few riders in the valley coming up from one of the many farms and towns scattered throughout the Inland. He knew his green cloak would conceal him in the tree line. Biting into a ripe wrepfruit, he felt its juice trickle down his chin and mopped it with his sleeve. The strangest part of being in the valley was the nakedness he felt without the thick woods around him. Avisahn was an intricate forest-kingdom that stretched nearly the entire western slope of the Ravenstone Mountains. But its borders ended abruptly at the Trident River. He was used to spending the day in shade, not under the hungry burn of the sun. Growing up, he had stared down at Dos-Aralon's valleys as if they were the low countries, not a land that had once been a mighty forest. He wanted to laugh. A mighty forest. That was long before the Purge Wars. It was during the time of King Silvermere, the first Shae king to settle the valley.

When nightfall finally came, Thealos hid himself in a small grove of birch and nestled with his cloak in a patch of broad-leaf brush. He dared not build a fire, even though the air was cool. His vision was sharper in the darkness without a fire glaring in his eyes, and he had no intention of being caught off-guard. Cradling his short bow in his arms, he set out three arrows where he could easily reach them and fell into a light sleep. He awakened with a start each time an owl hooted. It was an exposed, unprotected feeling, not as comfortable as hunting in the woodlands of Avisahn.

When Thealos awoke the next morning, he was covered with chilly dew. A heavy white mist hung all around him, so thick he couldn't see farther than he could toss a stone. The trees looked skeletal outside the grove. Thealos had seen the fog from a distance before – the docks at Avisahn and Dos-Aralon were always thick with it in the morning – but it had never claimed the highlands of the forest. Not being able to see was frightening, but exciting as well. Walking in the soft wet kisses of mist, Thealos discovered it had a taste – a little like tart apples dabbled with salt. Without the help of the sun, it was difficult to determine which way to go. He tried to keep heading south, but he caught himself straying further inland.

About midmorning, the fog dissipated and he could see the valley again. Long diagonal rows of wheat and corn grew in farms surrounded by stone fences. Fruit orchards running for miles deeper inland flaunted a rich harvest, and Thealos stopped at midday to have a snack of plums at the southern edge of a farm. He left a few Aralonian pieces at the foot of the tree to pay the farmer for the fruit he took. The farther south he went, the more the land became rugged with hills and riverbeds. Just before nightfall, he saw an old man sitting on the porch of a small home smoking a long-stemmed pipe. He lit a lamp and sat back on the crafted porch and watched, scanning the horizon. Thealos saw the old man raise his hand and wave, and he felt awkward that he had been seen. He waved back, but chose not to stop his journey. He wanted to be at least three days out of Dos-Aralon before making contacts with the humans. That would make him even harder to find. Cutting east, he went to find the river and shelter for the night.

The prairie grass whisked at his boots, and he kept his stride long. As he came down the slope leading towards the majestic Trident, he spotted a campfire in a tight cluster of vine maple near the riverbank. It was a large fire, and he could smell smoke and stew as the wind shifted towards him. The stew smelled like wild onions and rabbit meat, but it was laced thickly with bay leaves. The campfire flickered as something passed in front of it. It was nearer the Trident than he expected for a human camp. But the stew smelled good, not scorched. Curiosity leading, he stepped carefully down the slope and dodged between trees as he approached. About forty paces or so from the fire, he could hear them.

"Fetch the lantern," a gruff voice said. "Can't you get that fire any hotter, Tomn? It might frost tonight."

"Any hotter, and you'll be cutting your stew with a dagger. It's bubbling like Pitan – you want me to burn it?"

"Aaahh, quit moaning. Jurrow, get over here with that thing. You two, don't stand there..."

"Eat trope," another voice snapped. "I'm almost through."

There was a jangle of pots and metal spoons and then a hiss and a curse. "Sweet hate, this is hot! Get me that glove so I don't burn my hand."

"Get it yourself. Here's the lantern, Tannon."

Thealos saw a wink of flint and steel and then a steady glow appeared. It lit the eastern side of the camp, and he could see the man holding it. He had a stubby beard and a shock of gray-streaked hair. He wore the leather tunic and buckles of a field soldier, but he didn't wear any livery. A wide brown belt wrapped around his thick waist with short flat daggers shoved in the band. Wrinkling his eyebrows at the glare of the lantern, the man stood and held it away from him.

"You're crazy holding that thing. Now every Wolfsman on

the other shore can aim for your throat." They all had similar armor, each missing a badge or rank.

Tannon held up one of his hands. "I'm not asking you to do this. I'm not asking none of you. You do what I say, the quicker we make some pieces and get back north."

There was a chuckle from one of the other men. "You just want to get back to Holly's. Admit it. If you're so banned impatient, why didn't you just bring her along..."

The man stuttered when a knife landed between his legs. Thealos blinked, having barely seen Tannon's reflexes. He was a heavy man, but he threw a knife like a whip-snap. Tannon frowned and planted his fist on his hip. "That's enough, Beck." They were quiet for a few moments. "You know why we're out here. We looked through that banned snag of maple for a week. Now, let's see what we've got to show for it. Open up the sack again. Show us the sash."

Thealos craned his neck, staring closer. He saw one of the muddied soldiers withdraw a Crimson Wolfsmen sash. Thealos started, blinking with surprise. Surely these men couldn't have taken down one of the Shae defenders. It was impossible! Slipping from behind the tree, he started creeping closer. He could see the others around the crackling fire, each offering something to the stash, something they had found during their search. Thealos wanted to get closer to get a feel for what they had found. Whose side were these men on? He'd heard the Bandit Rebellion wore black and gold — well, at least the officers did. Were these men from Dos-Aralon? He didn't know, but he wanted to find out, especially if they were baiting Shae and killing them. Drawing closer, Thealos crouched and waited, studying each individually. One held up a smooth battle dagger, the hilt tarnished, but Thealos recognized the slant of the blade. It belonged to a Crimson Wolfsman. He scowled at the humans for the irreverent way they touched such an elegant weapon.

The one tending the fire had reddish brown hair and a long nose. He bent over a small cauldron of stew and he tasted it eagerly and then fanned his mouth. Slipping a bodkin arrow out of his quiver, Thealos fit it to the tight bowstring. He wanted to be ready just in case...

"In the trees!" someone shouted from his right side. "Over there! He's got a bow!"

Ban! Thealos cursed silently. He needed a diversion now. Dropping to one knee, he raised the bow and firmly pulled the arrow back to his ear. Thealos let it fly. The arrow hissed into the mass of burning logs. Sparks and cinders exploded in a spray, knocking the cook back with a howl of fright. He brushed the glowing embers off his leather tunic and stumbled back from the flames.

"There!" Hoth pointed, drawing his weapon – a notched polearm with a jagged cleaver. The soldiers spread out, rushing from the fire's perimeter as if live ants were biting their ankles. Before Thealos could rise and back away, he heard a shutter click and then a beacon of light fell on his face and chest. Tannon held up the lantern and scanned Thealos warily. It was time to run. These weren't just soldiers, they were thieves.

"The eyes!"

Behind him, Thealos heard the quiet crunch of leaves before a knobbed mace struck the back of his head.

V

Pain and nausea soaked through Thealos in waves. He struggled to open his eyes. How long he'd been unconscious, he didn't know. As his sight came into focus, it took a moment to realize that he was laying on his side, looking at the blazing white tongues of the campfire. He tried to sit up, but found he had nothing to prop himself up with. His arms were bound behind him, the ropes digging into his wrists. Dirt and bark shavings painfully cushioned the side of his face. Blinking, he struggled to move and found himself helpless. His ankles were also tied.

"He's awake."

A fit of panic nearly overwhelmed him, but he forced it down. He had never been in bonds before. Rolling onto his back, he tried to sit up. His head swam with dizziness and he thought he might throw up.

"You hit him pretty hard, Cropper," the one they called Tannon said with a half-smile. "Thought we'd have another dead Shaden on our hands."

"He wasn't very good," came the reply. Cropper was a thin, spidery man with sack-wheat colored hair and livid eyes. "No Wolfsman anyway."

"Could have been," Tannon said. "Could have been a Sleepwalker too. Good work."

The others were asleep around the fire, their faces filthy and haggard. They smelled like Silvan wine. His mouth went dry. Thealos' clothes were rumpled, his pockets empty. His travel sack lay in a heap, the supplies he had thoughtfully packed were already spilled out and shared. A cold, growing fury started to ball up in his chest.

Tannon studied him. "You didn't know what you were doin', did you, boy?"

Thealos fought to sit up and nearly sank back down with the effort. "That depends," he answered.

"Hmmm?"

Thealos knew he'd have to be careful with what he said. But he was the son of a barter, and he knew how to twist things to his advantage with words. "I saw your camp, Tannon." He gave the thickset man a cunning look. "At first I wanted to share your fire. But when I saw your little collection, I thought I'd help you."

"That's horse trope," Cropper said. "I saw you. You drew your bow first, Shaden. You were gonna shoot us down and steal it."

Thealos ignored the comment. He focused on Tannon. "Either I'm a poor aim, or I didn't mean to kill anyone here tonight." He knew what the humans thought of the Shae. He had to talk quickly to dispel Cropper's first impression. "I did get an arrow off," he continued, nodding towards the fire. "It's pretty obvious you're the leader, Tannon. If I'd wanted to harm your group, I wouldn't have missed you."

Tannon rubbed his mouth. "He's got a point."

"We should just kill him and dump him in the river," Cropper said offhandedly. It was said in such dispassionate tones that Thealos' skin crawled.

"Do you want to know why I came so close?" Thealos challenged.

"Because you're a half-wit?" Tannon replied.

The young Shae shook his head slowly, ignoring the throbbing in the back of his head. *Please Vannier, let them believe me.* "Because I wanted to read what's on the Wolfsman sash. That fabric I saw one of your men hold up. You can't read it, can you?"

The wizened soldier frowned.

Thealos swallowed. "Where did you get it?"

"Don't trust him," Cropper warned, shuffling his legs. "He'll trick you, Tannon. They all do."

"He can try," the soldier replied.

"You have the advantage here," Thealos pleaded. "I'm trying to save my neck. So would you in my place. I'm just trying to show you that keeping me alive will be to your advantage. Can any of you read Silvan?" He looked at Cropper then. "Can't you?"

Tannon picked up the Wolfsman's dagger and studied it in the firelight. "How much would this fetch me in Dos-Aralon, boy?"

He grinned. "The dagger of a Crimson Wolfsman? You can't buy one from the weaponsmith's guild. I can't even buy a blade like that in Avisahn. It can be worth a lot to a collector."

The soldier captain nodded, testing the tip of the dagger with his finger.

"Dump him in the river," Cropper said. "I hear it in his voice. This one's a barter."

Tannon shrugged. "I'll decide in the morning after we've all talked about it. Get some sleep, boy. This might be your last chance."

Thealos nodded. He didn't think he would sleep at all.

* * *

"What's your vote, Beck, Hoth?" Tannon asked, hooking his thumbs in the wide brown belt. The Wolfsman dagger had joined the others in the brace he wore. Thealos remembered how quickly he used them. Swallowing, he glanced at the last two in Tannon's Band who hadn't voted yet.

Beck was the one with the sash. He fingered the fabric, gazing at the strange markings scrawled in a language he didn't know. "I want to hear what he has to say."

"Banned fools," Cropper muttered, chewing on the stem of a pipe. He blew a haze of clove smoke from his lips. The smell was stale – pungent yet sugary. Smoking cloves was also Forbidden to the Shae. Thealos wanted to chuckle with the irony. His life came down to two more votes and all he could think about were the Rules of Forbiddance.

The one called Hoth sniffed and shrugged. "Kill him or don't. It doesn't matter to me."

"I've heard that the Wolfsmen...that they can hear Shaden blood singing," Tomn said. He was the cook, the one Thealos had startled the most with his arrow. Of all the men in their gang, he was slow, but he was grateful Thealos' arrow had missed, and he spoke strongly to save Thealos from Cropper. He had dull green eyes. His face was grimy, but earnest. "Is that true, Shaden?"

"My name is Thealos."

"It's a silly myth," Cropper snapped. He gave Thealos an angry stare. "Just another one of their lies."

Thealos gave Tomn a deep look. "It doesn't sing," he answered in a steady voice, hoping their ignorance would help. "But we do know when the earth drinks our blood. Even some humans say the Earth magic sings to them."

"So...so you could tell if a Shaden were murdered?" Tomn pressed.

Thealos nodded. "Is that what happened to the Wolfsman you...found?"

"We didn't kill him," Tomn insisted. "He'd been dead a long while. Isn't that right, Tannon? Just a skull, some bones... plus the clothes. Can't sell a stitch of it, except maybe the sash and the dagger." He gave Tannon a furtive look. "If we kill him, the Wolfsmen will come after us, won't they?"

"If they were coming, Tomn, they would have by now," Tannon replied with a smirk. He gave Thealos a cunning smile. "Well, it looks like the band will let you live today, boy. If Hoth changes his mind, well...you just keep praying to Shedang, Achrolese, and Vinderhopper that he doesn't." The group cackled at his mocking rendition of the Shae deities.

"Fools," Cropper spat. He tapped the burning cloves out of his pipe and crushed them with the heel of his boot. He left the group, sulking. Thealos stared at the tiny wisps coming from the scorch marks where he had stood. It was another act of defilement, something deliberate to tarnish the land. It made the ball of rage in his heart grow.

Beck came over and dropped down next to him, showing

him the mottled sash. His fingers were dirty and strong.
"You said you could read this, Shaden."

"Untie me first," Thealos said.

"What?" Tannon chortled.

"What can I do, Tannon?" Thealos snapped, his temper
flaring. "Escape? You've taken my bow and quiver. You have
my knife and my provisions and all the Aralonian pieces
I own. I am a good woodsman, but not without supplies.
If I ran away, I'd be in worse shape than I'm in now." He
shrugged, his wrists cramped and numb from the tether. "To
be honest, I doubt I could walk on my own right now without
falling down. Please – untie me."

Tannon nodded to Beck. The soldier grunted and slipped a
dagger from the cuff of his boot. Thealos felt the ropes stretch
and snap as the blade sliced through the bonds. Blood rushed
into his hands, stinging his fingertips with pricks of life. He
chafed his wrists, trying to keep from wincing at the bloody
sores. Gingerly, he touched the back of his head where the
mace had struck him and felt the matted blood. Beck untied
the bonds around his ankles.

"How's that, boy?" Beck asked.

Thealos nodded appreciatively. "Thank you. May I see it?"
He gestured for the sash. Taking the cloth, he brushed his
hand along the length, finding where the stitching held the
drape together. He examined the workmanship closely. It had
obviously been steeped in mud or earth, but the fabric was
of the highest quality, a rugged blend of wool and linen that
kept well even outdoors. It was treated to protect it from the
elements. Flipping it over, he examined the edging again.

"What does it say?" Beck asked excitedly.

"I haven't started reading it yet," Thealos replied. "My
father is in the cloth business. It's definitely Silvan-made.
See how the stitching is so tight and close?" He ran his
forefinger over the tight weave. "No loose threads. Not
one. A few good washings and you could sell this for a high
price." Beck's eyes gleamed. "Now for the markings. Let me
see." He started to read it in his mind, struggling with the
cryptic notes of the ancient Shae language. He learned the
Wolfsman's name and rank. "His name was Jade Shayler,

and he bore the rank of a Lor. Impressive."

"What does his name mean?" Tomn asked, edging closer. He looked fascinated. "Don't Shaden names mean something?"

"You know a little about us, don't you?" Thealos said approvingly to the simple man.

Tomn grinned, embarrassed. "A little. But not much. So what does it mean?"

"Literally, Jade Shayler means 'green eyes.' There are some nuances too, but I doubt any of you would understand them." He gave Tannon a wry look. "The writing here and here describes his life, who trained him, what action he has seen." He rolled the fabric down, showing them the Silvan script. "But as you can see on this half, the fabric is empty down to there. He was young, for a Shae. But I think I know how he died."

"And how could you know that?" Tannon asked.

"You're full of trope," Hoth said.

Thealos shook his head. "I'm only guessing. But the last thing written here is an encounter with a Sinew dragon. One that apparently menaced the Shae side of the river. Jade Shayler went after it." He looked from face to face. "I didn't think your band could have killed a Crimson Wolfsman. But a Sinew dragon could."

"A Sinew dragon," Tannon said sternly, folding his arms.

"A Sinew dragon," Beck agreed, his eyes lighting with mischief.

"You obviously know about them," Thealos continued.

"You'd find nary a man in Dos-Aralon who would," Hoth said with a grin. "But those in the army, especially the scouts...we know what's out in the valley. Sinew dragons lurk in a clutch in the swamps and woods, things you don't find anywhere near the city."

"Then you know that Sinew dragons like shiny things," Thealos said conspiratorially. "Greedy beasts, they kill to steal. Do you know why they're called...?"

"Because they're land dragons," another soldier butted in. Thealos didn't remember his name, though he recognized his voice from the night before. "They don't fly."

"They jump," Hoth added.

"I'm impressed with your band, Tannon," Thealos said with a charming grin. "You know a lot about this valley."

"More than you probably do, boy," the leader replied smugly. "What was your name again? Thallis?"

"Thealos," he replied. "Thealos Quickfellow."

He didn't dare ask if they were part of the Bandit Rebellion. Not yet.

* * *

Thealos squirmed uncomfortably and tried to pull the blanket over his legs, but his fingers were numb from the ropes and it took him a minute. The campfire crackled nearby and Cropper's shadow fell across him as he walked around it, near Thealos.

"Get out of my way," Cropper growled.

Thealos tried to scoot over, but he wasn't quick enough and Cropper kicked him hard in the chest. It hurt like fury, but he managed to bite back all but a grunt of pain. Thealos massaged his ribs, letting the air out of his chest slowly. He watched the ornery soldier stalk away from the night fire. Thealos swore under his breath, one of his favorite of Correl's curses that he reserved for doing business with humans. His wrists were bound in front of him this night, offering a little more comfort than he'd had the last two nights. His ankles were hitched together and snagged to a tree. They trusted him with information, but not freedom. As confidently as they talked of their skill as a band and in fighting, there was an unspoken fear of the Shae in their eyes. That somehow, if he were left without bonds, he would manage to steal a knife and cut their throats as they slept. Thealos didn't condone murder – it was certainly Forbidden. But he might have kicked Cropper in the ribs on the way out.

"He shouldn't have done that to you," Tomn said in a low voice across from the fire. He looked angry as he scrubbed the cauldron he used for cooking. Flakes of ash and hunks of soot were caked into the sides, making Thealos wince every time he ate the stew or broth that came out of it. The stew wasn't burned, which would have been Forbidden, but the pot itself was disgusting.

"He must have hated pups as a child," Thealos joked, earning a smile from the timid cook. "I've really tried not to yelp too often." He gave Tomn a sad smile and rolled up against one of the thick maples in the grove. "You clean while the others sleep?" Tannon snored off to the left, his huge chest rising and falling with the ragged breathing.

Tomn shrugged, then scrubbed the inside of the small cauldron furiously. Dropping the blackened rag, he brushed his hands on his pants and went around the fire, closer to Thealos. "How do your eyes glow like that?" he asked, staring at Thealos' face. For an instant, the cook looked as if he were tempted to put his finger in Thealos' eye.

"It's just the light from the fire. Have you ever seen a cat in the dark?"

"A mountain cat? Out here in the valley?" Tomn laughed. "Oh, there's the little ones in the city. They're expensive. Even in Dos-Aralon, and you can rarely find a good seller. So the firelight makes them glow like that? Do mine glow?"

Thealos nearly rolled his eyes. "Of course yours don't, Tomn."

"Why do yours then? Does it hurt?"

"No. What do the Druid-priests tell you?"

"It depends which Druids you ask," Tomn replied, sitting comfortably. "The Council Druids say your eyes glow because you have knowledge and truth. But the Valley Druids, the ones down here, say you glow because you stare at the moon too long. I've been watching you the last few nights, Thealos, but I haven't seen you stare at the moon more than once or twice. Just glances, really."

Thealos laughed. "Do you know why they say we stare at the moon, Tomn?" The grubby cook shook his head no. "In our tradition, that's where our people came from. There are other worlds out there, Tomn. Not just this one. We came from that world on a floating city," he said, nodding towards the northern sky where the luminous blue crescent of Eroth could be seen through the gaps in the trees. Tomn smelled like cinders. "One day we'll return home when the city comes

46

back for us. But not for a while, I think."

"You really believe that?" Tomn asked, his eyes betraying doubt.

Thealos nodded simply.

"The Valley Druids would say you're mad then. They don't believe in all those myths and things."

"Why would they? They just forget that what they know about the world, they learned from us. We came to this world to teach your kind, Tomn."

"Teach us what?" he laughed, amused.

"I'll save that for another night," Thealos replied. "If there's going to be another night."

Tomn's forehead wrinkled. He started scrubbing on the pot again. "I won't...I won't let them kill you, Thealos." He leaned forward, his face intense. "If you help us find that Sinew dragon treasure, I'll talk Tannon into letting you go. We don't want trouble with the Wolfsmen. We just need your help a little while."

"I don't think Tannon will listen to you," Thealos said with a wary smile. "Cropper hates me. And Tannon listens to him." He nodded towards the woods where the angry soldier stood watch.

"Tannon listens to me too," Tomn replied, dejected.

"I hope so," Thealos said, letting doubt syrup his voice.

Tomn flushed and leaned forward with a light whisper. "I could cut you loose and no one would know how or why. Don't think I couldn't. You could have stole a knife or something and waited until we were asleep. Right?"

Thealos felt a smile twitch at the corner of his mouth. "I'm glad I have you looking out for me, Tomn. But I want to help you find that treasure. It could be worth a lot if the Sinew dragon is dead."

"I thought you said the dragon killed that Wolfsman?"

"I'm pretty sure he did," Thealos answered enigmatically. "But not many things can get the best of a Crimson Wolfsman. And a Lor is about as dangerous as they come."

Tomn nodded. "Yeah, I heard they're as good as the Sleepwalkers."

"The what?"

"That's right, you don't let Sleepwalkers into Avisahn, do you?" He must have seen the confusion in Thealos' eyes. "You've never heard of one? They dress in black and can walk in and out of a castle at midday without anyone even seeing their shadow on the ground. Trackers can't find them. Kings hire them to find things that are stolen or to kill someone who is high up and protected."

"Assassins?" Thealos probed.

"They do that too," Tomn agreed. "Except I hear they use magic. That or they're made out of magic. When they don't want you to, you can't see them." He shook his head in wonder. "Not even a Knight of Owen Draw can take one down."

"Is that so?" Thealos replied with a nod. "Tell me more, Tomn," he probed, seeing the excitement in the cook's eyes.

* * *

After midnight, Thealos lay quietly in the camp watching the dying embers of the fire wink out one by one. He had already worked out how he was going to escape.

VI

Dujahn shifted in his saddle, squinting against the night sky at the black tangles of the Shadows Wood. The air was warm and muggy, but cool breaths of wind teased his neck only to vanish beneath the hot dampness of the moors. He sat on a stolid bay mare out in the middle of the grasslands, silently, feeling sweat trickle down the sides of his face. He mopped it up on the back of his glove. "Where are you, Folkes?" he muttered, scanning the trees.

Twisting in the saddle, Dujahn turned around and stared up at Landmoor. It rose high on a lopsided hill, surrounded by misty ponds and protected on the west by a bend in the river. The moon bathed the marsh grass in blue and caused winks of light to dance on the pools. From high in the watchtowers, torches burned brightly, making the fortress shimmer with patches of yellow and orange. It was dark and he was too far away to see any of the sentries patrolling the outer walls, and he knew they couldn't see him either. Even if they could – what was a lone horseman compared with an army poised within the forest? A mosquito buzzed near his ear, and he swatted it sharply. He wore a plain brown tunic over a shirt of embroidered leather, tight at the sleeves. His hair was also brown and his face had an ordinary shape. To some he looked lazy – to others he looked bored. It made him perfect as a spy.

Dujahn wiped his mouth, trying to count the number of

months he had been on this assignment. His true employer, the Gray Legion, was a ring of mercenary spies that snooped into just about every kingdom's affairs east and west of Dos-Aralon. They had a few well-placed spies in the court of Dos-Aralon, mostly women, and so far King don Rion had refused to hire any or even try and purge them from the realm. Dujahn didn't exactly enjoy working for the Bandit Rebellion, but at least a Bandit commander was better than counting gnats for some regiment weasel. He smirked. The Bandit Rebellion needed spies and the Gray Legion needed a foot in the politics from these lands. He hoped that Lord Ballinaire would eventually ask for his services. *Now that would be an interesting assignment!* he thought.

In the distance, Dujahn heard the trample of hooves coming down the Iron Point Road. It was the only road through the Shadows Wood and so overgrown in places that wagons had to waddle just to get through. Plunging from the thick cedar trees came a huge roan, its hooves clomping against the paving stones marking the old Shae highway. Dujahn shook his head, wondering if Folkes was a fool or if he just didn't care how much noise he made. Gripping the handle of the hooded lantern he had secured around the saddle horn, Dujahn lifted it and pointed it towards the inbound horseman. He raised the shutter quickly and then closed it. A single wink of light went out.

The noise of the hooves slowed and hissed into the grass. Commander Folkes eased his horse up to where Dujahn waited for him. He was big – nearly as tall as General Dairron, the commander of the Kingshadow regiment who had arrived earlier that day. Dujahn was always comparing people, sizing them up and matching them against others he knew. It was how he kept things straight in his mind. As a Gray Legion spy, he needed that. Always look for the unusual. With Folkes, that wasn't hard to do. The Bandit commander's mismatched suit of armor showed an almost absent-minded laziness instead of tokens of his battles and opponents. A breastplate taken from a vanquished Knight of the Blade. His sword from a Vale Shae. The greaves and gauntlets were of different design, all scratched and marred beyond polishing. Unique – Folkes liked it that way. Dujahn suppressed a smile. The Provost Marshals of the East Kingdoms would have laughed at the Bandit commander with scorn. But then again, they were more known for fastidiousness, not their battle sense.

"How long...you've been waiting?" Folkes asked, trying to catch his breath. He lifted a leather flask to his lips and took a long drink. It smelled like ale.

"Sunset," Dujahn answered simply. "How was the ride from Anikesh, Commander?"

"Long and thorny," Folkes answered, wiping his mouth. "I saw a few patrols of knights, but none of them saw me."

"Well...they would have been banned surprised to catch you out all alone." Dujahn sat back and smirked. "Now, do you think they would have hung you right there – or bothered dragging you all the way to Owen Draw for a trial first?"

Folkes frowned and corked the flask. "I don't pay you for jokes, Dujahn. I pay you for information. Why were there so many patrols?"

Dujahn shrugged noncommittally. "The Kiran Thall have been busy down here, Commander. Whenever they raze a village, don Rion sends down the knights to chase them away. It's that simple. Word in don Rion's court these days is that he wants to send the dukes of Amberdian and Cypher on a march down here to hang some Bandits."

Folkes nodded and let out a big breath and snorted with contempt. "That rumor again? It costs too much and it takes too long. Amberdian is spineless and Cypher won't go it alone. Nothing before year-end at least. Let's go in," he said, nodding towards the fortress of Landmoor.

Dujahn turned his horse around and spurred it forward lightly. He led them off the main road, about a mile or so from the fortress, veering off into the grasslands just before the hill jutted out of the valley. Steering around a pond, they pressed towards the bottom of the hill that Landmoor crowned.

It was certainly a privilege to be invited into the Rebellion's council. The other two commanders had special advisors who joined them when answering Ballinaire's summons. Folkes had decided it was time that he had an advisor as well, so he insisted that Dujahn be allowed to represent him. Ballinaire was distrustful, of course, but even he recognized the value of having one from the Gray Legion handy. He needed every ally he could muster.

"What did you learn about this meeting?" Folkes asked, his voice low and his eyes riveted on the torch fire high on the walls. "Do you know what Ballinaire wants?"

"He's managed to keep that secret," Dujahn muttered in response. "But I have managed to find out what he's done down here so far. As you saw coming down the road, the Shoreland Regiment is bunched up together in the Shadows Wood – less than a day's march away. Looks to me like Ballinaire is preparing to lay siege." He nodded to the keep as they started up the rugged slopes. "He has some troops in one part of the wood, but I couldn't get close enough to see what they were doing. I'm a spy, not a Sleepwalker – sounded like they were digging. Making trenches, maybe. I don't know."

"Trenches? Ballinaire won't sit still long enough for trenches. Not if don Rion sends more than a single duke's army."

"I agree with you. So, in addition to the regiment, we have the Kiran Thall roving the woods and blocking the road."

"Hmm," Folkes murmured. "Who else is here?"

"Dairron, of course. The General came in on his Dragonshrike before the sun had even set. I asked a contact in Dos-Aralon about him. He told me that Dairron flies over Avisahn regularly – trying to catch a peek at Silverborne's daughter, no doubt. Wants to abduct her, I've heard. Who knows for sure. Now, what about that advisor he's always with? I couldn't get much on her."

"Miestri," Folkes said with the look on his face as if he'd eaten a bad onion. "She's a Sorian, Hate thank him. How he got her to support him, I would pay in Aralonian pieces to find out." He gave Dujahn a sidelong look. "You still haven't been very useful there yet. Maybe I should hire someone else."

Dujahn chuckled. "Inlanders," he laughed, rolling his

eyes. "King don Rion could pay me three times what you do. We could have your rebellion crushed before the first winter snow. But," he added comfortingly, "The Gray Legion wants Ballinaire to win. He's getting old, though. I've heard General Dairron will take over then. Is that true?"

Folkes shrugged. "That has not been decided yet. Maybe I will take over, Dujahn. It's true that Lord Ballinaire depends on Dairron the most. Without the soldiers he's recruited and his defensive tactics, the Bandit Rebellion would be half its size right now."

"Or dead," Dujahn pointed out. "Wasn't Dairron's father a regimental knight also? Like Ballinaire?"

"He was," Folkes replied, annoyed. "Served him during the Purge Wars, then rebelled with him too. Stanjel Dairron is a first generation Bandit, Dujahn. It's in his blood to hate don Rion. But that doesn't mean he could take over the Rebellion," he said in a warning voice. "Not without a fight."

They approached the outer wall of Landmoor and stopped talking. It was too dangerous now. Their horses grunted as they followed the base of the steep hill. Near a bend in the river, Dujahn stopped. There was a blackened inlet in the face of the hill, darker than the night. There was some old shrine buried under the hill that led to the catacombs beneath the city. Nudging his mount forward, he reached the edge of the entryway and swung his leg over the saddle. The smell of thistle and moss was thick in the air. In moments, several Bandit soldiers emerged from the shadows and took their steeds. There was a gap within the tiny entryway leading to a small ingress with a stone stairwell at the far end. Some old Shae markings were chiseled in the stone on the inside, but they had faded and crumbled to the point that Dujahn couldn't read them. His grasp of Silvan writing was still mediocre. The horses were left below as they started up the stairwell.

"The garrison commander would have a seizure if he knew about this," Folkes muttered. "Does the Governor know?"

"Haven't met the man," Dujahn replied with a shrug. "Would you like me to?"

Folkes gave Dujahn an angry look and ignored the question.

He doesn't know when I'm being serious, Dujahn thought blackly. *What an oaf.*

Within the shadowed alcove of the inner bailey, a detachment of Bandit officers met them. The officers had neatly trimmed beards and short hair, common for the humid Shoreland region. They wore the black plate mail and gold trim of Bandit Rebellion officers. Dujahn noticed how none of the common Bandit soldiers were armored the same way – only the officers. It was a remnant, he knew, of Ballinaire's own days leading don Rion's army. Long, long ago. Dujahn already kept a mental note of the twists and turns of the tunnel. He knew where to go. Torches glared from racks mounted on the walls, offering smoky light to the dark, broken corridors. After walking some distance, they arrived at a huge cellar that had been fortified with beams and stone – a fortress beneath a fortress. It was cool in the tunnels, and Dujahn sighed with relief. If Ballinaire didn't want him as an advisor, Dujahn hoped his next assignment took him to the milder northlands. Or maybe the Bronnfisher Islands. That would be interesting too. He remembered something about a plague jewel there...

The Bandit officers opened the door and allowed them both to enter. Dujahn inhaled the smell of burning cloves and peered around Folkes. He saw General Dairron leaning against the far wall, but the smoke came from an older man in dark robes. He stopped short, trying to remember who the old man was. That's right. The other Sorian.

Between the Ravenstone and the Kingshadow there lived two of the Sorian order. He knew that Miestri – Dairron's supporter – lived with some renegade Shae in a valley cut into the Kingshadow Mountains. He had never met her, but had heard she was very beautiful. Some said she looked like a Shae, except she had ebony hair and dark eyes. The other Sorian in the valley sat right in front of him, smoking a pipe. He had been told the man called himself Mage. He wore simple black robes with a patterned green hem. He was of medium height and, by the wrinkles around his eyes and cheekbones, between fifty and sixty. But it was whispered in the Gray Legion that he was older than the world – that all the Sorian were. The Gray Legion had sent plenty of spies to learn more about them, but none had ever returned...not even the Sleepwalkers. Dujahn didn't think he was in any danger as long as he stayed near Folkes.

The one called Mage sat in a high-backed oak chair, his green eyes studying the spy and the Bandit Commander.

Folkes took one of the high thick-stuffed chairs around the table. Dujahn stepped casually into a far corner and watched. He had a good view of the room. Folkes grabbed a goblet and filled it with ale. He took a deep swallow and set the cup down with a thump. Looking up, Folkes seemed to notice Dairron for the first time, leaning against the far wall, his arms folded across his chest.

"When is Ballinaire going to get here?" Folkes muttered at last, wiping a trail of ale from the day's growth on his chin.

"When he pleases," Dairron replied. "You know that."

"Do you know why we're here?" Folkes demanded, and Dairron shrugged and stood still, looking unconcerned and composed.

"I thought it was obvious. He wants to start the war."

"And that doesn't worry you?" Folkes challenged. "I'm surprised you're not pacing and muttering about supply trains, sieges and sappers."

Dairron smiled. "I've rather been looking forward to it, Folkes. We've been baiting the bear too long. It's time to call down the wolves."

"Oh cut your tongue for once, Stanjel. You know what we're up against – what don Rion can put in the field. We're in Landmoor for Hate's sake! This is still one of don Rion's cities. If he knew we were here, he'd have the knights swoop down so fast our heads would be spinning on a pike."

Dujahn studied the Bandit General for a reaction. General Dairron shook his head, chuckling, and unfolded his huge arms. His hair was the color of dark soil with a few wisps of gray. He wore the armor of the Bandit Rebellion with pride, the mail shirt encased in black plate. Four gold general bars, pinned to his thin traveling cloak, glinted in the lamplight.

Dujahn remembered hearing how Dairron had earned them. Even in the Gray Legion, he was a legend for what he had done. Nearly every kingdom outside the valley had offered him a military command. He continued to refuse them all. Dairron wanted Dos-Aralon. He wouldn't leave.

"If is the keystone," the General reminded Folkes, snapping Dujahn out of his reverie. "If he knew. I think the King of Dos-Aralon should spend less on his velvet court and polished knights, and more on intelligence." He gave Dujahn a sidelong look iced with enmity. "Besides, Phollen's Regiment is close enough. Quit fussing."

"Be assured, Commander Folkes," Mage said softly. "We would not be meeting in Landmoor if it were not secure." His voice was like worn leather gloves that fit perfectly. Dujahn saw his eyes pierce right through Folkes.

"Where are the others?" Folkes asked the Sorian, trying to ignore Dairron's mocking eyes.

"If I've heard correctly," Dairron interrupted with an etched smile, "the Commander of the Shoreland Regiment is heading to Sol." He chuckled again. "Probably chasing a serving girl."

"Your ears listen that far east, General Dairron?" Mage said in his whisper-like voice. "That surprises me." Dujahn caught the subtlety, but he saw that Folkes didn't. No, Folkes never paid attention to the details. Dujahn understood that Miestri claimed the western half of the valley as her land. And Mage claimed the east. Dujahn thought a moment, trying to put it together. Dairron was a general and commanded a brigade – the largest force the Bandits controlled and he occupied the heights of the Kingshadow with it. Then there was Mage and Tsyrke Phollen, the Shoreland commander, who had a regiment of soldiers and the Kiran Thall. Folkes had the third regiment, the smallest, stationed in the Shadin Mountains. And all three of these men would start hacking each other to pieces if Ballinaire lost control of them. Dujahn had to cover a grin at their idiocy.

"You know plenty about chasing tykes, Dairron," Folkes blurted out. He planted his elbows on the table with a rattle. Dujahn closed his eyes, knowing what was about to come out of his mouth. *Ban it,* Dujahn swore to himself. *I shouldn't have mentioned the Princess of Avisahn.*

"At least Phollen can get the women he dotes after, Dairron," Folkes blundered on. "What about the bleeding Princess of Avisahn? You fly over Silverborne's castle on your pet Dragonshrike just to peek at her. Have you even seen her yet, or only in your dreams? Silk socks ready for the dance? You dote after the Shae like..."

General Dairron took several slow steps forward, his blue eyes cold and menacing. His shadow fell on the table. "Rather than using your tongue to spite me," he whispered acidly, "You might learn better ways to use your brain instead. If you mock the Princess of Avisahn or the Shae again, I'll cut out your tongue."

"You may frighten my spy, but not me," Folkes warned. "Don't cross me Dairron. Or you'll be facing the end of my sword."

Dujahn saw granite resolve in General Dairron's blue eyes, and he silently fumed. He wouldn't get a higher position in the Rebellion if Folkes got himself killed so quickly. Folkes was a seasoned battle commander, but Dairron was stronger in every way that counted. *That man fears nothing.* Not the Shae, not Dos-Aralon, not a Sorian. Dujahn knew it was the ruthlessness of Dairron that Folkes coveted – which he found lacking in himself. It was jealousy, and it was poison to Folkes.

"Face the end of your sword? Trust me, Commander, it would take a bigger sword than yours," Dairron answered. "You've had your warning. Another taunt, and you're a dead man."

The cellar door creaked open and a woman wearing velvety black robes entered. Her eyes were black and sparkling and a sly grin spread across her mouth. Dujahn stared – she was the most beautiful woman he had ever seen. Not one in a thousand harlots in Zhoff could have matched her flawless face. And Dujahn had seen the harlots of Zhoff. The feeling in the room cooled with her presence. She smelled like cinnamon and bitter herbs. Midnight hair, inky and smooth, spilled down from the cowl as she pulled it down. She was a

Sorian. Dujahn could feel it as she passed by him. Her voice was soft.

"I hope I have not missed any bloodshed." She smiled playfully, but her eyes betrayed her contempt for Folkes. Folkes stared at her, and Dujahn could see the passion rise up in his eyes. He was half-drunk anyway, but not even he would dare to touch a Sorian. Not if he wanted to live.

"Choose your enemies wisely, Folkes," Dairron warned, backing away. "We are equals only so long as Lord Ballinaire stands over us. When he falls, you will answer to me. I do hope you remember that." Turning to Miestri, he added respectfully, "Welcome, Lady of Vale."

The Sorian gave Dairron a sultry smile. Her face was beautifully cold and compelling. Dujahn thought it strange – ageless but young. She wasn't the blossom of youth – not really. But was she just as ancient as Mage? Were all the Sorian alike in power, or were some greater than others? These were questions the Gray Legion would pay handsomely to have answered. It was one of the main reasons he was there on assignment. The Sorian were not found in every kingdom, yet this land had two. So strange...Dujahn wondered where her Shae escorts were. She supposedly never went anywhere without them. Or was that another false rumor?

"Welcome to Landmoor, Lord General," she answered Dairron with a smile. Her eyes passed quickly over those in the room. "Lord Ballinaire will see us now. And I think he's angry enough to kill one of you."

Dujahn swallowed.

VII

The well-oiled shudder of armor sounded in the stillness of the underground tunnels along with the thud of marching boots. There were easily twenty men coming, Dujahn reasoned, cocking his head and listening. He had started to sweat again. The cellar door opened and the leader of the Bandit Rebellion entered – Lord Stroth Ballinaire. His white-plumed helmet was cradled in the crook of his arm, showing his long snowy hair down to his shoulders in the Inland fashion. His face was hard aged skin, split by wrinkled crags. He was easily seventy years old, but he wore his Bandit armor well. Five gold general bars and a golden star were pinned to his cape along the shoulder. The star, Dujahn remembered, signified the rank of Champion of Owen Draw. A title no knight had held since Ballinaire rebelled against King don Rion. Bloodshot blue eyes stared at them from beneath bushy black eyebrows flecked with gray. A thin white beard garnished his lower jaw. His voice was strong.

"Why are we missing one of my commanders?" Ballinaire said. His voice was strong and angry. Twenty warriors fanned out around him, filling the cellar. They were his personal guard, and he had seen to their training. The sculpted black ivy and leaves of their armor matched his. Had General Dairron ever been one of them? Dujahn didn't know that. There was still so much to learn. He kept perfectly still, inconspicuous.

"Commander Phollen is near Sol, my Lord," Mage answered, bowing his head slightly. "I will speak on his behalf."

"Were my instructions not clear?" Ballinaire snapped. "I wanted all my commanders here tonight. Has he rebelled against me? Why isn't he here?"

"Certainly not, Lord Ballinaire," Mage answered with patience and calm. "He sends his regrets, but it was not possible to make it here in time. He has to provision the regiment overseas, and he struck a deal on some stout Sheven-Ingen blades. But you may expect his arrival within the week." The green eyes narrowed triumphantly. "The summons is finished, his regiment has gathered. He will come to take Landmoor as you ordered. When all is ready."

Dujahn inhaled slowly, grateful that Folkes had hurried to the meeting. He would not have wanted to answer to Ballinaire for any reason. *My apologies, Lord Ballinaire, but Commander Folkes was just too drunk to obey the summons. I'm assuming he'll arrive after he's cleared all that Spider Ale out of his bowels.*

The leader of the Bandit Rebellion relented and nodded his head curtly. "I trust for good reason, Sorian. I trust he made every attempt to be here. In addition to the Shoreland Regiment, you speak for the Drugaen Nation as well?"

Mage nodded. "Naturally."

The Drugaen were somewhat of a mystery to Dujahn. He knew little of their race other than that they were sturdy, blocky fellows who had been enslaved by Sorian to work the mines of the Ravenstone. He knew there were two factions within the Drugaen Nation – the Faradin and the Krag. The Faradin had revolted and proclaimed their freedom and still fought to uphold it. The Krag were still loyal to some Sorian who had enslaved them a thousand years ago. The Krag were superstitious and followed anyone who could muster some spark of magic. And it didn't surprise him that another Sorian, like Mage, had met their need.

Ballinaire bowed his head. His gnarled, gloved hand trembled with age as it stroked his short white beard.

Dujahn did not take it as a sign of weakness. No, Ballinaire was still strong enough to keep General Dairron from usurping his place, two Bandit Commanders from killing each other, and a pair of Sorian at his disposal. Dujahn wanted to chuckle. The King of Dos-Aralon didn't know what he was up against.

"The time for war has arrived," Ballinaire said suddenly. His eyes went across every face in the room. "No more waiting or plotting. No more attempts at insurrection. We have come far and fought boldly. The swords of both armies have been sheathed in blood again and again. But this time, it will be different. By year's end, we will sup in don Rion's palace. The valley will be ours at last." Dairron glanced at Miestri, surprised. Folkes took a long swallow from his goblet and wiped his mouth. "Our efforts have stirred rebellion, to take what was wrongfully denied me after the Purge Wars. That insufferable king owes me a debt in blood, and I will take payment in blood. I promise you," he added with an excited edge in his voice, "That our ranks will swell as the flood engulfs the valley and those who support Dos-Aralon. King Birtoss don Rion will lose his crown, and those who defy us will be no more. No more knights of Owen Draw. No more dukes of Amberdian and Cypher. Even Iniva and the Yukilep will come in line or crumble." His eyes glittered with hatred. It was an emotion so intense in feeling and conviction that Dujahn felt it coiled deep within the old general's bones. "When I march to war this time, they will all fall. Every one."

"When?" General Dairron interrupted, his eyes gleaming and wary.

"Tonight," Ballinaire answered. "It begins this instant."

General Dairron stepped forward, his eyes exultant. "You've considered my plan then? Shall we seek a union with Avisahn, combine with them to destroy Dos-Aralon?"

"The Shae?" Ballinaire coughed, amused. "What have the Shae ever done for us? When have they ever sought an alliance with me? I tell you, General, the Bandit Rebellion will spread like fire through dried weeds this time, until this entire valley is ablaze. I will not bargain – I will not cajole with those fools across the river. I will march on this valley until the governors and princes and kings cry to me for peace, until they submit to the rule they denied me so long ago." Lord Ballinaire shook his head slowly. "My plans have nothing to do with the Shae. We will conquer don Rion, the Yukilep, and even the Shae. We will do it alone."

Dairron shook his head. "My Lord, we number no more than a tenth of what don Rion can put in the field. The lowlands are vast, we cannot attack with total surprise. And yet you suggest we can siege and break the city of Dos-Aralon before the winter snows? With all the other Dukes collapsing on our flanks like lions? And we can do this...by ourselves?"

"Listen to him," Miestri said assuringly. Her black eyes glittered with mirth. She spoke to Dairron but her eyes were on Mage. The two Sorian glared at each other, almost defiantly. Folkes watched Ballinaire and Dairron. He missed out on the interplay.

"You are wrong, General," Ballinaire replied. "We already know that don Rion can put more in the field than we can." He shook his head, his fist tightening. "But now numbers are of no consequence. A smaller force can withstand a mightier one through many advantages."

Dairron's eyebrows raised. "What? You will taunt him into attacking the mountains? You know he won't. Or do you think this fortress is enough to stand against him?" His laugh was cold. "I could take this castle in a fortnight. It certainly won't stop don Rion. Prince of Fire," Dairron swore, "I enjoy your rhetoric, Lord Ballinaire, but you must convert my sword too. Our men won't fight fed on stuffed morale or promises. We cannot match don Rion's ability to wage war without an alliance. And the Shae are the only way. Their chief city is across the river from our enemies, vulnerable..."

"You are the one mistaken, General. I say that our forces not only can match don Rion's, but can defeat them with minimal casualties. Listen to me, my friend, my cautious commander. Not even the Shae will be able to stand against us with their timid sparks of Silvan magic. I tell you that don Rion's head will hang rotting on a spike in the entrance gate of Dos-Aralon!" Ballinaire reached into the pouch he wore at his belt and produced a handful of green moss with flecks of blue and violet. It dripped moisture on the floor. Dujahn stared at it. He remembered the digging crews in the forest. He hadn't been able to get close enough to see what they were digging up.

"What is that?" Folkes said, his face pinching with curiosity. "It looks like...moss."

"Where did you find that?" Mage demanded, leaning forward. To Dujahn, it looked like the Sorian was about to come out of his robes. "It doesn't exist any more. It was all destroyed..."

"No, wise one," Miestri countered with a trace of mock in her voice. "There is more of it...here."

* * *

The sun sneaked through the gray folds of the cloudy sky, swelling the haze with golden hues. The morning fog lingered over the damp marsh grass, swirling thick enough in some pockets to gutter out a weak candle. The field beyond the northern walls of Landmoor was quiet, save for the lilting warble of swallows and the occasional shriek of a jackdaw. Dujahn crept up and nestled behind a droopy bush. He waited.

The Sorian Miestri stepped through the shrouded pasture, her black robes hissing against the thick stalks of marsh grass. Two figures flanked her, gripping ash longbows fitted with bodkin arrows. Each wore drab green cloaks that hid their faces and concealed the glint of fine mail. She walked straight through the field, not deviating at all as the fog roamed about her. A shadow loomed ahead, but she walked steadily toward it until the form coalesced. It was huge, hulking. Dujahn kept his distance, but stayed close enough to see them both. He could not stop looking at Miestri. He hadn't been able to since the night before. This was his chance...what he had been preparing for. To get into a circle of Sorian and learn about them. The knowledge would be worth enough to buy a village...maybe even a castle.

The general's Dragonshrike hunched forward, its glossy

black scales shifting as its serpentine-scaled wings shrugged and its eagle-like head swung around toward her. It's thick beak opened, hissing. Glassy black eyes blinked once. The leather shoulder harness creaked and General Dairron eased from the stirrup straps and landed on the grass with a soft sound. His glinting plate mail was gone, replaced by a black riding uniform made from thick sections of leather stitched tightly together at the elbows, shoulders, and knees. He tugged his gloves on securely. Dujahn squinted and cocked his head. He advanced to a closer shrub, careful of every step. Not too close...just enough to listen in...carefully...

"That was a brilliant performance last night, General," Miestri said, stepping up to the tall Bandit. "You actually seemed surprised and angry. Did you see the look on Mage's face?"

"I think he nearly choked," Dairron replied smoothly. "You've done well down here, Miestri. Does the old fool have any other orders for me this morning?"

"Which old fool?" she replied with a silvery laugh. "Yours? Lord Ballinaire is growing impatient for you to leave. He had hoped you would be gone before dawn."

Dairron shrugged. "Patience has never been his foremost quality." He sighed. "I'm furious he ordered you to stay in Landmoor. I need you in the Kingshadow, not frittering your talents down here."

Miestri's voice was light, almost musical. "It is a pity – but necessary. It is still too early to let the top spin out by itself without any coaxing. And I discovered the hall below the tunnels where the Silvan Records were kept. They date back half a millenium, so we may find what you've been searching for. The information about the Crystal will certainly be very useful now."

"But it is information that Lord Ballinaire could also use," he warned. "The fool is going to get himself killed this time. No more border raids, no more splintered agreements. He's digging a hole deep enough to bury us all." He shook his head angrily. "We've come too far for him to ruin everything."

"He just may live, Stanjel. What if he discovers the secret of the Everoot?"

"Isn't that why you are staying then?" Dairron reminded her. "Make sure that he doesn't. And make sure the other Sorian doesn't convince him to abandon the idea. Not only did Mage look shocked, but greensick as well. He knows everything about that plant. Who is to say he doesn't know about the Crystal as well?"

"Don't fear the old man," Miestri replied. "He is waning. And when he falls, I will take his dominion. He never knew about the Crystal. He never knew what the Shae did to protect it. That is our advantage. Just be sure your army never leaves the mountains, General. I will meet you in Vale when it is time to take command of the Bandit Rebellion."

Dairron shook his head and chuckled. "You saw Ballinaire last night – he doesn't consider the Shae a threat! When they find out, every Crimson Wolfsman in the whole banned eastern forest will be down here with the Silvan high army behind. If my plan is going to work, I don't want them finding out too soon. Nor do I want any needlessly killed. Laisha Silverborne won't support me if she thinks the Bandit Rebellion are nothing but Shae-killers." He paused. "Unless we can get her to believe that Dos-Aralon is."

"I've already begun the arrangements," Miestri said. She cocked her head. "Your care for Silverborne's daughter is quite beyond me. You know it is Forbidden to the Shae to cavort with you." Her voice was low, seductive. "Is Laisha truly worth all that trouble?"

"She is worth any trouble. Prince of Fire, not only is she fair, but cunning, too! She rules that kingdom, not her father. We have always fought against the Shae, Miestri. If we manage it right, they will fight for us." He nodded to her escort. "And not just the Shae from the Wilderness of Vale, but all of Avisahn."

Dujahn stopped breathing. This was worth even more than he thought. Folkes was an idiot – he would never rule the Rebellion. It would be Dairron and Miestri – he knew it instinctively. This was the kind of plotting that the East Kingdoms did, not some out-of-the-way protected vassalage. The scheming was cold and utterly ruthless. Dujahn loved it.

65

Miestri bowed her head. "As I have said, I am already engaged in that effort."

"Good." He rubbed his lip. "The meeting with Lord Ballinaire changed our previous plan, but it can also help us." He folded his gloved hands together over his mouth. "Ballinaire is leaning over the edge of the pit he's dug. I want to do what I can to push him in."

"Indeed," Miestri agreed. "What else would you have me do, General?"

Dairron pointed north, away from the city. "One small favor. The Shoreland regiment is camped in the Shadows Wood. While Mage hurries to Sol, do what you can to stir dissension in the regiment. See how many officers and Kiran Thall will follow you. Cause some havoc," he added with a grin. "You're so good at that."

She laughed. "That would prove entertaining. Ballinaire is preoccupied with hoarding his find in the swamp. He won't know what I'm doing."

The Bandit General smiled. "Then I will prepare in the Kingshadow. You are my eyes and ears in Landmoor. I especially want to know how he reacts to what we do."

"What about Folkes?" she asked with a little yawn. "He knows something is happening."

"Leave Folkes to me. Either he joins us or the Duke of Owen Draw and the Governor of Iniva hangs him on a rope. I'll give him a chance to decide."

"Be sure you teach him the consequences." She smiled, and touched Dairron's arm affectionately. "Safe journey, General," she said with a nod and stepped back a few paces. "These beasts hate the moors. You had better go. But if you fly near Avisahn again, be sure to stay out of bow range. They may be waiting for you with their own alerion this time."

The Dragonshrike twisted its shoulder to the grass and Dairron gripped the leather harness and pulled himself onto the saddle as it straightened itself. Cinching the leather straps around his legs, he looked down at the black-robed woman with midnight dark hair and gave her an etched smile.

"If there are, I will deal with them. Remember why we are

here," he said from above, offering her a simple nod.

Miestri smiled and flashed him a sultry grin. "Oh, my memory is very good, General. I will join you in the Kingshadow as soon as I am able. It has been very dull in the Vale recently. Wars can be amusing."

Dairron nodded and slid his arms into the harness fittings. He touched a glass orb at the saddle's pommel and the Dragonshrike rose on its legs, its huge razor-like wings unfolding as it flexed its shoulder muscles. The plumage was dark on the back, like a crow's.

Dujahn squinted, staring up at the looming silhouette. He was perfectly still.

"Do you think the spy has heard enough?" Dairron stated. "The one over by that bush."

"I've let him listen in on us," the Sorian replied. "*Venay shaye nu!*" Miestri ordered crisply in Silvan. Her two escorts whirled around, their longbows pulled tightly and arrows aiming straight for Dujahn.

He cringed in the mud, not daring to move. From the mist came a whisper of cloth and Miestri appeared in her flowing black robes. He stared at her midnight eyes. She was going to kill him. She was going to rip out his entrails.

"An early morning stroll for the Gray Legion spy...Dujahn, isn't it?" Dairron asked, folding his arms casually and leaning forward in the saddle harness. "Or can you think up another inane excuse that's more convincing?"

"I came...I came to seek you out, General," Dujahn spluttered. "The Gray Legion can help you. We want you to rule Dos-Aralon. The other nations fear it more than anything."

Miestri reached into her robes and withdrew a sphere of red glass. Something twitched inside of it, an orange smoky light that hungered to reach out and snap at him. Dujahn watched it, mesmerized – terrified.

"I came to help you!" he insisted. "By Achrolese, I swear it! I have information about Folkes. About don Rion and the Shae!"

"I know," Miestri replied. "And you will."

VIII

D awn broke into the little camp by the river over a haze of fog. Thealos had noticed it getting thicker each morning the further south they went. The day began as it typically did, with Tomn trying to coax the ashes back to life with fresh wood and a snapping flint-stone. Tannon was always one of the first up, sharpening the brace of knives he wore with a slow methodical ring from a whetstone. Not that the knives needed it, but the sound was nearly impossible to sleep through. Beck and Hoth came awake more slowly, each stumbling a few paces into the surrounding glen to relieve themselves against a tree. Thealos writhed in disgust.

"You look tired," Tannon mumbled to the cook between the ringing strokes on the whetstone.

"Didn't sleep well," Tomn replied with a shrug, casting a surreptitious glance at Thealos.

Sitting in the grass, Thealos rubbed his ankles. "How far are we from the woods where you found the Wolfsman?" he asked Tannon.

"Another day's walk at least. About half-way to the Shoreland."

Thealos had already guessed that. He knew the Trident River followed the western borders of the Shae kingdom until it split into three tributaries and dumped into the sea. There was a human city down at the base of the nearest one, a trading port called Sol. To the east, further away, was Jan-

Lee, a Shae watchpost.

"I've been thinking, Tannon," Thealos continued with a purposeful voice. "If the Sinew dragon did kill the Wolfsman, it might still be guarding its clutch. You never found the dragon's body, so it could be waiting for us. Have you thought about that?"

Tannon nodded and sheathed another dagger into his belt. "We can handle a Sinew dragon, boy. It's the clutch we were looking for and couldn't find."

"I don't doubt it. But at what cost?"

"You scared of it?"

"A wise man would be," Thealos replied with an even tone. "Is anyone in your band an archer?" The way he had seen pock-faced Jurrow handle the short bow he had stolen, he didn't think so.

"A Flaming Arrow?" Tannon groaned. He chuckled. "We don't need any of those."

Flaming Arrow? Thealos had no idea what that meant, but he shrugged. "Just a suggestion. I'm a pretty good aim, despite what you may think. Maybe I'd be useful in a fight, that's all." He let it go, let the idea seed and sprout in Tannon's mind. He continued to massage his ankles.

Tannon gave him a wary look and then glanced over at the bow next to Jurrow. "Let him loose," Tannon ordered. "His bowels are probably near ready to burst."

The rest of the morning went by quickly. Gulping down some heavy porridge spiced with sugar and cloves, Thealos observed Tannon's Band break camp. It disgusted him in every aspect. To the Shae, fire was more than burning sticks. It was a power only carefully handled. It seemed to Thealos that half the Rules of Forbiddance related to it in some way. Putting out a campfire or a hearthfire was done methodically, to make sure every ember died out. Ashes were buried and covered with stones. It was even Forbidden to char meat, so the Shae dinner platters were served a little rare. But Tannon's Band burned even their stews, they kicked out a fire and left it smoldering, abandoning their responsibility for taming it. Their arrogance for the land galled him.

They continued the long march alongside the river.

Thealos watched the interplay between the members of the band. At first, they had all looked alike to him, but now he saw the subtle shades between them. Beck and Hoth were inseparable, keeping to themselves and joking about women and gambling. Both were considered handsome for humans and their thoughts were never far from the taverns they had left behind. Cropper was a skulk and always took the rear, his eyes never leaving Thealos' back. Jurrow was pock-marked so badly that he had grown a reddish beard that covered most of his face. Tomn had Shae-green eyes and appeared to be the closest to Tannon emotionally. Twice during the trip, Thealos overheard Tomn say they should give Thealos' things back to him. Tannon rebuffed him.

After stopping to rest at midday, Tannon loosed Thealos' wrists and had Jurrow give him the short bow and a brace of steel-tipped bodkins. Thealos fondled the wood and then re-strung it, feeling more confident with it in his hand. They gave him the bow just in case the Sinew dragon left its clutch and came after them. The bow came with a warning.

"You use one of those against us again, boy," Tannon said, "And not even the Crimson Wolfsmen will be able to tell you were a Shaden."

Thealos nodded that he understood. It took every bartering instinct inside him to keep his face straight, to hide the fear writhing in his stomach. But he had his bow back.

* * *

Before dusk, they reached the borders of a decaying forest of maple trees, nearly five miles wide. There was no road or trail through it, and the river cut directly into it, creating gulches and a network of gullies around the waterfront. As they set up camp again for the night, Thealos cautiously approached the wood and stared at the dark strips of bark splintering from the trunks. The trees were growing too close together, their branches interlocked, causing a web of leaves to blot out the sun. Huge bullfrogs croaked by the river, and the wind hissed as it shook the limbs. A fetid smell greeted him, something sick. Thealos walked around the edge of the forest and examined the trees. He touched the bark and sifted through dead leaves with his fingers. Craning his neck, he looked up to the top and listened for the familiar bugs and beetles. There were only a few but that gave him a little hope. No birds nested in the limbs, no animals scuttled away. It was practically empty of wood life – at least for now. Kneeling in the grass, he pulled up a clump of grass by the roots. He smelled the mud and then frowned and blinked his eyes shut.

"What is it?" Tomn asked, crouching by him.

"Forbidden magic," Thealos said in a low voice. The others from Tannon's Band crowded around. "This forest didn't grow like this, it was twisted this way."

"It smells like trope," Hoth muttered, stamping the swampy grass to dislodge cakes of mud from his boot.

"But you smell magic?" Jurrow questioned skeptically.

Thealos nodded. "Not just smell it, Jurrow -- I can feel it. My people are very sensitive to Earth magic, and we can tell when its been poisoned. It has its own smell." He replanted the clump of grass and stood, brushing his hands. "I don't know whether the Sinew dragon is in there or not." Hoth laughed, but Thealos ignored him. "It takes a long time for the Earth magic to restore ground after it has been infected. If my people lived on this side of the river, we would help clean it up and it would recover sooner."

Beck and Hoth rolled their eyes. Tomn nodded with interest.

"We're running out of daylight," Tannon said. "And I don't want to go after it in the dark. Jurrow, fetch some wood for the fire. Hoth and Beck – see if you can find a rabbit or something. I'm tired of eating wild onions. If we find that clutch, I promised you thirty days leave in Dos-Aralon."

Hoth and Beck grinned at each other and started out in search of food. Cropper glowered at Thealos with dark eyes, but he met the stare with one of his own. While Tomn brought out the dirty cauldron, Tannon sat down against a jagged tree stump and started oiling his knives with a dirty rag. As Thealos stood there, he felt them all around, like ashy smoke that stuck to his clothes. There was a mocking look in their eyes as they glanced at him, except for Tomn. It was some grand joke that he was a part of but didn't understand. Thealos knew they did not understand the Shae. They didn't even care to understand.

But the joke would be against them. Somewhere, in the thick tangled maple, he had felt something else. Something he had learned from the Wolfsman's shawl and hadn't shared with them. There was another magic in the wood, and he could sense it – like a pure chord of music none of them could hear. It whispered through the branches and hummed against his skin.

Silvan magic.

* * *

Tannon smirked, the firelight painting his face in reds and oranges. "So did we all, boy. And granted, we did a banned decent job of it. But the truth is, you just can't make someone obey who's determined not to. Sure, King don Rion rules this valley in name, but the regional governors and the dukes actually rule. He has a strutting court in the city, full of his dukes and knights and princes. But down here, down near the Shoreland, it's ruled by whoever has enough strength. There's a saying that goes with it..."

"What a man can take with his sword is his own," Thealos answered. "I've heard about it. We don't believe in it, though."

"Sure, Shaden," Cropper said. "You believe what a man can steal with his mouth is his own. You could barter a man's arm off his shoulder and he'd think he was getting a bargain. Banned liars, all of you.

Tannon scowled at Cropper for interrupting.

"How did the Bandit Rebellion begin?" Thealos probed, dipping the rabbit meat into the stew. Tomn had been careful and given him a cut before he charred the rest.

"You've got to look at it two ways, with two different leaders, Shaden. Back during the Purge Wars," Tannon explained, "The Rebellion was by the League of Ilvaren – led by that pirate, Kiran Phollen. It was Shorelanders versus

Inlanders back then. Phollen refused to obey the king's summons and to pay the king's taxes. It started a war that lasted for years. Sure, they killed him and all, but his sons lived. One became the new pirate leader, and the other formed a cavalry group of Bandit horsemen called the Kiran Thall."

Beck and Hoth whistled. "I hate the Kiran Thall," Beck said with a shudder.

"I see," Thealos said with a nod. "Then what about Ballinaire? How does he fit into this?"

Jurrow grinned, his red beard widening. "Inlanders versus Inlanders now. He joined the Rebellion, Shaden. And now he leads it."

"But why? What made him turn from don Rion?"

Tannon took a long drink from his flask of ale and wiped his mouth on his sleeve. "Who cares," he replied, stifling a burp. "Why does anyone?"

Thealos was appalled. "You're part of Dos-Aralon's army and you don't even know why you're fighting?"

"Why should I care about anything except getting paid? Does it even matter whose grudge is more important? It's nobles squabbling. They've always done that. Except this time Ballinaire turned the Rebellion into a banned regimental army, and he does a banned good job keeping don Rion from sleeping nights. The dukes try and box him in, but Ballinaire wiggles out and stabs at the flanks. We're always sent here and there, chase him to that ravine, follow him in that hole." He scowled. "All we get is ten pieces a month. It isn't worth enough to care about any of it."

Thealos looked at Tannon curiously. "Have you thought about joining the Rebellion then?"

"They get paid even less. Remember those Kiran Thall that tried to woo us, Cropper? Showed them where they could put their seven pieces. But you know, Shaden, in our own way, we are a little rebellion," Tannon answered smugly. "Here, you look thirsty, boy. Have a drink." He offered the flask.

Thealos shook his head. "It's Forbidden."

"If you're going to sleep with us, you might as well drink with us," Tannon pressed. He offered the flask again.

"It's against my customs," Thealos replied. "I would have shared the Silvan wine with you, but it's already gone."

"What's the banned difference?" Hoth snorted, gulping down his own. "Both make you drunk."

"One is Forbidden," Thealos replied. "The other isn't."

"Leave him alone," Tomn said from the fire, scraping the sides of the scorched cauldron to fill another bowl.

"What's the matter with you, Tomn?" Beck jeered. "You wish you were a Shaden too?" He gave Thealos a cutting look. "Here's a question for you, boy. You've asked us about the valley, but I want to know about your people." His voice was slightly slurred, and his breath stank of ale.

"I'm sure you do," Thealos said under his breath.

"Tell me about your land. Is it true that you pray to the trees? Oh, and what about that lovely lass Laisha Silverborne! Does she really dress in silk socks and dance around the Palace grounds? I've heard that. Haven't you? She's so high and snooty, some royal wench. Or do you dance just praying for a peek at her or does she come out wearing..."

"You mock what you don't understand," Thealos said tightly.

"Then I'm right, am I?" Beck hooted.

"No – you're just displaying your ignorance. Is it true that humans grunt like rabbits when they breed?"

"What did you...?" Beck challenged, rising quickly.

"Sit down, Beck," Tannon stamped.

"But you heard what he..."

A dagger flashed in Tannon's hand and the soldier stared back at it warily. "We need him alive. He's been a good help to us."

"He hasn't done a banned thing," Cropper fumed.

"I think I want to change my vote now," Hoth said, giving Thealos a cruel look. "We don't need a Shaden in our band. Kill him and dump him in the river."

Thealos felt a surge of real fear, but his anger proved stronger. He wanted to throttle Hoth with both hands. Containing his rage and clenching his teeth, he sat silently, glaring at Tannon's Band. Tomn released the wooden spoon, his hand dropping on the hilt of a dagger.

"There's more of us who want him dead now," Cropper told Tannon.

"In the morning," Tannon replied. "No one touches him tonight. Got that, Cropper?"

"He's just a Shaden. He's got you blind now too."

"If you want your thirty days of leave," Tannon replied, "you'd better start doing your job. Now stand watch."

"Tie him up, first."

"He ain't going anywhere..."

Cropper shook his head. "Tie him up, or I'll kill him now." He took a step forward, jerking the mace loose in his belt hoop.

"It's all right," Thealos said, offering his wrists to be tied, trying to stifle the mounting tension. "I know the rules. And Beck," he gave the other soldier a half-mocking smile, "we dance in white silk socks. They have to be a certain color." It earned him a few chuckles from Hoth and Beck, helping to mollify the mood a little. "Come on," he said lightly. "We were only joking." Tannon and Cropper glared at each other. Finally, Cropper cursed and stalked off into the shadows.

Thealos decided that he'd better not be with Tannon's Band in the morning.

* * *

I'm sorry if they scared you tonight," Tomn said in hushed tones, scrubbing the pot again. Thealos didn't know why the cook bothered. Without scalding water, soap, and a chisel, he would never get it clean. Tomn sat next to Thealos where they could keep their voices pitched low so the others wouldn't hear. Tannon snored like a bladder horn. Jurrow twitched in his sleep, his arm cradling a wineskin. Beck and Hoth were also asleep. That left Cropper in the perimeter. From the corner of his eye, Thealos could see him in the darkness outside the rings of firelight.

Thealos studied Tomn. Finishing the pot, the cook plopped down and dusted his pants. His reddish-brown hair looked gold with the fire behind him. He had a splotch of freckles across his nose and cheeks.

"I am scared," Thealos whispered. "They almost killed me tonight."

Tomn looked over at him, concern wrinkling his brow. "I wouldn't have let them."

Thealos smiled sadly. "Four against two isn't very good odds. That's about how many humans there are compared with the Shae. You could say we're used to being outnumbered, but not against soldiers. I'm not a soldier, Tomn."

Tomn tugged at the rim of his boot. "What does your name mean, Thealos? In your language."

"Thealos means 'Spirited.' I wasn't the easiest child my Correl and Sorrel had to raise."

"Hmm," Tomn muttered, wringing his hands. "You said your father...I mean, your Correl, was a cloth barter, right? If I showed you something, you would be able to tell me what it's worth, right?"

Thealos nodded. While Tomn went over to his own knapsack, Thealos glanced back at Cropper. His head had started to sag down on his chest. Good. The cook returned with a large bundle wrapped in oilskin to protect it. He untied the leather thongs and gently unraveled the fabric. It was a fine wool gown, cut to fit a human woman, made from a rich shade of ochre with a blue and violet trim around the bodice. It certainly wasn't Silvan in style or pattern, but it was attractive.

"It's a nice gown, Tomn," Thealos said approvingly. "I'd examine it, but I can't like this..." He held up his wrists and shrugged. *Let him untie me, Vannier. Let him untie me.*

The cook made sure everyone was asleep and then untied the knots that bound Thealos. Thealos rubbed the circulation back into his hands. He took the fabric and quickly examined the seams. "They used the Silvan stitch-marking rules, good. Wool is a fine sturdy fabric, very popular in the city. The trim is also nice – I like the pattern here. Where did you get this?"

"I bought it in Sol."

Thealos nodded. "You probably paid over twenty pieces for it."

"Twenty-five."

"A good price. You could sell it in Dos-Aralon for thirty and make a profit."

Tomn shook his head. "No, it's for a serving girl I know. She'd look so pretty in it. She has dark hair and dark eyes. She said... she says she likes that I'm so quiet. Do you think she'll like it?"

"If you treat her as well as you do others. Sounds like she's a rare woman. 'Rare as a brown-eyed Shae.' That's what my people would say."

"That's right, I'm sorry I've been calling you a Shaden. You have green eyes, like mine. I didn't know Shae had brown eyes – I thought they were all blue or green or something."

"I've never met a brown-eyed Shae before either," Thealos replied. "It doesn't happen among my people. I have seen a few who are dark-haired, but that's also pretty rare. You're right. We have blue, green, or gray eyes, and sometimes a mix of the three. But I've never even heard of a brown-eyed Shae. That's why it's an expression."

"Ohh," Tomn said. He fidgeted for a moment and then pulled another bundle out of his shirt. "I wanted to give this back to you. I don't know what it is or what it means, but it wasn't right for us to take your things like we did. We'd get in trouble with the army if they found out. Here. I'm sorry." He handed Thealos the small leather bundle that held Arielle's hoppit doll. A pang of homesickness struck his heart like a dagger. Thealos smiled, a sad smile. He'd never missed his family so much in his life.

"Thank you, Tomn. It belonged to my sister. It's just a toy."

"Well, it's yours. You'd better get some sleep. It's my turn for watch anyway – you don't have to stay up with me. We'll be pretty busy in the morning, looking for the clutch. I think we'll find it this time."

It was time. "I don't think they'll let me help you find it," Thealos stated in a quiet voice.

"What do you mean?"

"You heard Cropper and Hoth tonight, Tomn." He dropped his voice even lower. "I think they're going to kill me tomorrow."

"I won't let them," Tomn muttered, his face pained.

"But what can you do? Even if I led them right to it, do you think they'd let me go? I could report you to the army commanders in Dos-Aralon. They know that."

"I think they'd let you go if you promised..."

Thealos shook his head. "No, Tomn. I don't think they will. I'm just a Shaden to them. If I help, then there's no reason to keep me alive. Don't you see? I lose either way."

"I could cut you loose," the cook suggested. "Cropper just hates Shade...the Shae because a barter tricked him and his brother with a contract and they had to spend some time in jail. But I don't think you're all like that. You're the first one I've ever really known."

"Then would you help me, Tomn?" Thealos pressed. "If I helped you?"

"How? Cut your ankles loose now?"

Thealos shook his head. "What if I took you to the clutch now. Tonight. After we've found it, you can let me go. I trust you, Tomn. I don't trust them. You'd get first pick of the clutch too. Do they ever let you get the first choice?"

Tomn's eyes lit with eagerness. "You think you can find it, Thealos? In the dark?"

"It would be easier for me in the dark," Thealos promised, knowing that his eyes were glowing white-gold with firelight.

IX

Thealos had lost count how many days he had spent with Tannon's Band. The night in Nordain's council chamber was a blur in his memory, a fragment of time rubbed away by the bonds he had worn with the Aralonian soldiers. The back of his head still had a tender spot from the first of Cropper's blows, but a knot had formed there. It would take at least another week to heal fully. Thealos glanced over his shoulder, watching as Tomn struggled through the screening trees in the dark. Pausing, Thealos grabbed the cook's arm and helped him duck beneath a clawing branch that would have scraped across his face.

"Ban, it's so dark," Tomn whispered, his voice edged with panic. He'd never been out in the woods at night before, not without a lantern or a torch.

"We'll be all right," Thealos assured him, maneuvering around a slanted boulder. Tomn stumbled, but Thealos caught him and helped him gain his feet. The maple trees were huge and twisted, their branches interlocking and blotting out the sky and stars. The blue glow of Eroth peeked through the gaps of leaves and branches providing just enough light for Thealos.

"Do you...do you think the Sinew dragon is dead?" Tomn asked worriedly.

"Yes," Thealos replied with confidence in his voice. "Stop here a moment. I need to get another bearing." He lowered

79

his cowl and heard the wind rustling the leaves, Tomn's ragged breathing, the shrill call of an owl. No sounds of pursuit. Thealos was grateful for every moment, though he was not truly concerned about their ability to find him in the dark. He just didn't want to hurry.

Kneeling in the damp earth, Thealos closed his eyes and plunged his hands into the gritty mud. Tomn huffed from the journey. Thealos listened patiently, feeling through the inky swirls of Forbidden magic staining the mud, a magic that had scarred the land and destroyed the trees and life within the small forest. If the Sinew dragon was dead, the land would finally begin drinking from the Earth magic again. Then it would regain its health. His fingers went quickly numb from the cold mud, but he probed deeper, trying to feel the right pulse. He wasn't searching for Earth magic or Forbidden magic. He looked for something else. He heard it then, faintly, beckoning him nearer to the river. Silvan magic – the kind that the Crimson Wolfsmen had. It was a chord of purity in the darkness. He smiled and opened his eyes.

"Did you find it? Is it...singing to you, Thealos?"

Thealos wiped his hands on his pants and nodded. "We're close, Tomn."

As they started into the trees once more, he caught movement out of the corner of his eye. It was barely a shadow, something blacker than the woods. Whirling, he slipped out his small hunting bow, an arrow at the ready. A feeling prickled on the back of his neck, going straight down his spine. He didn't see anything. But he knew something was there – watching him.

"What is it?" Tomn gasped, drawing a dagger from his belt.

"I saw something," Thealos said, certain of it. He studied the darkness, scanning the stretch of gnarled maple trees to his left and right. He saw Tomn as clearly as a camp fire in the middle of a field. Breathing slowly, he let his vision drift, trying to catch another glimpse of that puzzling movement. Where was it? He knew something was in the forest with them. Fear bloomed in his stomach.

"Maybe it's Cropper," Tomn whispered. "He's good at

sneaking around."

Thealos remembered this feeling. It had happened in the streets of Dos-Aralon. It was happening again.

"I don't think so. Follow me, quickly."

Thealos pressed deeper into the maze of gullies and washes. His bow was ready. In the distance, he could hear the gentle rush of the river. Risking a backward glance, he tried to see what was stalking them. Had it followed him all the way from the human city? Or was it just now finding him again? Thealos didn't know what it was. But he felt it, a presence in the darkness. Something living but that couldn't be seen by a Shae. It terrified him that something like that could exist.

"Ban it," Tomn cursed, stumbling in a rut and landing on his arms. He massaged his elbows and righted himself. They crossed a thin grove, hopping over a small ravine to the other side. Each step brought them closer to the churning murmur of the river.

Then Thealos heard the noise in the distance. Tannon's camp had been roused. A cry of alarm went up, followed by shouts and curses. Thealos squeezed his eyes shut and nearly swore in frustration. They were so close he could feel the Silvan magic beneath his boots. Without his money, without his dagger, he needed the weapon that the Crimson Wolfsman had trusted to save him from the Sinew dragon. The trust had failed, but he knew the magic was waiting, dormant. He could taste it in the air now, a coppery flavor of metal and fire.

"I told you! I warned you Tannon, but you wouldn't listen to me!" It was Cropper's voice, bitter and angry and distant.

"Find them," the angry leader roared. "Find them both!"

Tomn's voice was a frantic whisper. "Are we almost there? They're as mad..."

"We're close," Thealos promised, scanning the trees ahead. Rising from the gully ahead of him, Thealos caught the glimmer of cool blue light. It was dim – so faint it could have been the moon reflecting in a pond. But the light caught his eyes and held them. He crushed the urge to dash forward and approached cautiously. The glow did not change.

"There! Do you see it, Tomn?" he asked, pointing towards the light.

Tomn squinted. "See what?"

He smiled. "When you found the dead Wolfsman, was it this close to the river?"

"I...I think so. I couldn't find it in the dark. Not now. You know where it is?"

Thealos squeezed his arm. "Follow me."

They went forward and came to another gully. Peering down into it, Thealos saw the glow coming from the water of a small pond at one end. Bracken swirled on the surface and the gully water trickled slowly on the far side of it, passing around a thick mesh of mud and leaves that bulged from the pond. Something was damming the gully, creating the little pond. His eyes grew wide. Rising from the earth nearby, he heard the mournful sound of death before jerking his head. He saw the crumpled skeleton of a dead Shae not twenty paces away. Gripping the fringe of swamp grass for support, Thealos lowered himself down the gully wall. He landed with a little splash in ankle-deep water and his feet sank in the mud. He pulled the arrow back, bending the bow quietly with a broadhead arrow ready to fly.

Thealos walked a few paces. "The Wolfsman is over here," Thealos said, hurrying to the body. He breathed faster, listening to the sounds of pursuit in the woods. It would take Tannon and the others a little while to track them.

"How in Pitan did you find it?" Tomn muttered in astonishment. He followed Thealos down and crouched down in the mud. "This is it! Sweet hate, you found it!" His grin was triumphant.

Thealos examined the body quickly. It had been robbed of all value and recognition. Its bones moldered in the damp swamp. A small dusting of leaves and leeches covered it, and Thealos quickly brushed them off like roach moths on a cloak. He traced the bones with his finger, feeling the potency of the Wolfsman's agonizing death sting his nose like pepper. His eyes watered.

"We didn't kill him," Tomn promised, seeing the tears in

Thealos's eyes.

"I know. Looks like the Sinew dragon surprised him. Took his leg off." The bone was snapped and splintered, mid-thigh. "He must have dragged himself this far before collapsing." Thealos sighed. "He bled to death, Tomn. Quickly."

"Oh. Did he die...right?"

Thealos shook his head. Kneeling quietly in the mud, he crossed his hands before him. *"Keasorn in Eroth,"* he prayed softly, using the ancient tongue of his people, *"Welcome the soul of Jade Shayler back to your light and face. He died with your love in his heart."* He swallowed, steeling himself. *"Shenalle protect us from the Firekin. Shenalle protect us and keep us. Shenalle bring peace to the troubled..."*

A bobbing streak of light went through the trees at the top of the gully. Thealos could hear Tannon's band fighting the twisted maples, searching their direction. Cropper's voice was raw and furious.

Thealos clenched his teeth and hurried the rest of the prayer. *"Keasorn guide my arrows. Keasorn give me courage to strike my enemy. Vannier grant me luck. Vannier give me cunning. In the name of the three gods, grant my prayer."*

"Thealos," Tomn warned. "They're coming!"

Opening his eyes, Thealos swallowed his impatience. He left the broken skeleton in the gully brook and went back to the pond. From above, he hadn't seen it very clearly. From the bottom, he could easily see the mound blocking the flow of the brook. It looked like a tree had fallen into the gully, but its long shape was twisted and contorted. Raising the bow, he aimed for the bulge. He let it fly.

The arrow penetrated the mud, sticking into something solid. He waited and Tomn watched curiously. "The dragon is dead. Come on, Tomn, help me dig it out." He slid the bow around his shoulder.

Crossing into the pond, the two dug into the earth with their hands. Mud slid down Thealos' arms, but it also fell away from the stiff bony hide of a Sinew dragon. There was no Life magic pulsing beneath the shell-like scales. Turning, he plunged his hands into the mud at the bottom of the shallow pond. The water went up to his elbows and then up higher. Dropping to his knees, not caring how wet he got, he dug his fingers toward the eye sockets. The light grew brighter as he sifted through the water and debris. And then, between two bony knobs, he touched the hilt of a sword. Silvan magic screamed in his ears.

"They went this way," Jurrow panted. "See? Two sets of tracks. Can't be far, Tannon!"

"I'll kill that rook," Tannon roared. "I'll split his head in half!"

"Quit gabbing!" Hoth seethed. "Beck, over here. I think I see something."

Gritting his teeth, Thealos heaved at the sword. It wouldn't budge. He turned around, straddling where he thought the neck of the dragon was, and bent his knees. "Help me lift it," he urged Tomn. The water soaked his cloak and pants. Keeping his back straight, he clamped his fingers over the dragon's snout and lifted again. Tomn dug into the mud behind him and hoisted. Thealos felt the tendons in his neck bulge with the strain, and it started to move. The mud hissed and gurgled and it came higher and higher.

He let out his breath and then tugged again, feeling the strain on his calves and arms and back. "Keasorn, please!" he groaned. They came up suddenly – sword and dragon head, both with a splash. A glare of blue light stung his eyes as the blade shimmered in the night air. It was a Silvan short sword of such workmanship that he gasped. The hilt had the impression of a wolfs-head with two glittering green-blue gems as eyes. There was no rust or tarnish, and its blade was keen and sharp. The blade was aimed down, lodged in the dragon's skull right over the eye sockets.

"Sweet, holy Achrolese!" Tomn whispered in shock, staring at the Crimson Wolfsman blade. "Look at it!" His eyes shone with greed and astonishment. "It must be worth a thousand pieces...worth a kingdom!"

"Look!" It was Jurrow's voice, and then he heard the sound of boots dashing towards the gully. "It's brighter than the moon. Over there!"

Thealos stared at the weapon. There was probably other treasure around in the clutch, probably deep in the bottom of the swamp. He had led them right to it. But how could he give Tomn such a noble weapon – a weapon of fine steel and charmed with Silvan magic? Its power belonged to the Shae, not to the humans who desecrated everything they touched. The weapon looked almost hot to touch, so Thealos used the hem of his cloak and wrapped it around the blade. The light winked out as he folded the cloak around it. Then planting his foot on the dragon's snout, he yanked the hilt. It grated free and he could feel it tingling beneath the cloth.

"Give it to me!" Tomn insisted, his palm reaching. He trembled with anticipation. His eyes danced with emotion. "Sweet Achrolese, let me touch it! Give it to me!"

"Ban it!" Hoth screamed, "It's gone. Tannon – the lantern!"

"Tomn..." Thealos hedged. The cook lunged for it, but the mud-sucking pond slowed him. Thealos retreated towards the fallen Wolfsman, feeling the Silvan steel's reassurance. The blade belonged to the Shae.

"Give it to me!" Tomn roared, anger now sparking in his eyes. "You promised!"

"Tomn," Thealos hedged again. "This is a Shae weapon. I led you to the clutch. Please, the others are coming..."

"You banned liar!" Tomn shrieked. "You bleeding liar! Cropper was right! You knew...you knew about this all the time! I...I believed you!"

"Believed what?" Thealos demanded, his patience snapping. "You stole my money, my weapons! You held me against my will. Your friends were going to kill me. Listen to me, Tomn. A weapon like this doesn't belong with your people. You don't know anything about this kind of magic. It would destroy you."

"Liar!" Tomn cursed, holding his dagger out. "Nothing but liars. Tannon!" he screamed. "Over here!"

A beacon of lamplight shot across the trees overhead. They were at least forty paces away and charging. The gully was tight and would be easy for them to follow. He had to make it into the forest. By the time they found his trail, he would be out of the wood and running. If he could keep ahead of them, he would make it to Sol and then to the Shae in Jan-

Lee. Then he would be safe.

"I'm sorry, Tomn," Thealos said coldly. "But this is mine."

Rage twisted on the cook's face. He flailed at Thealos, swiping the dagger in the air before him, trying to stab the elusive Shae as he retreated deeper into the gully.

Boots cracked the twigs and roots behind him.

Spinning around, Thealos saw Beck and Hoth sliding down the gully wall, cutting off that way of retreat. They looked furious. Gripping the bundle under his arm, he unslung the short bow.

"This way! Over here!"

Thealos ducked to the outside of Tomn's thrusting dagger and swung the short bow around, cracking it against the side of his head. It dazed him, just enough for Thealos to slip by. He was halfway across the pond when Tannon's lantern reached the scene, throwing light across his back. He slogged through the pond, struggling to reach the other side where he could run.

"Cropper, get him! Hoth and Beck, he's right there!"

Thealos knew he'd never make it, not with that light exposing him. He let the bundle drop and slipped a steel-tipped arrow out of his quiver. Aiming, he shot at Tannon. The arrow hit the lantern, spinning it out of the soldier's grip, spraying oil and shards of glass as it sailed into the trees. As the flame hissed out, the soldiers hooted with dismay as darkness blanketed the gully. The glare of the Silvan short sword was dim beneath the waters of the pond. It sank quickly.

Scanning the edge of the gully, Thealos found Cropper running ahead of him and launched another arrow with a feeling of overdue vengeance. Cropper grunted with pain as the arrow tore into his ribs, and he fell to the gully floor in a heap.

"He got Cropper!" Tannon bellowed. "Kill him! Kill the rook!"

Plunging into the pond, Thealos used his cloak and wrapped the blade up in it again. He took time to stuff it into his belt before wading through the pond towards the other side, closer to the river. If he could make it to the Trident, he could lose them downstream. Dripping and soaking, Thealos scampered down the gully floor, away from Tannon and Beck and Hoth. They were close, but the dark would hide him. Passing over Cropper, he didn't see the knife waiting for him.

Pain sent fire up his leg as the wounded soldier dug a dagger into his thigh. The arrow had stunned and wounded him, not killed him.

"You Shaden whelp!" Cropper seethed, stabbing him again. "You stinking, bleeding Shaden!"

Thealos was bleeding. The pain crumpled his leg and he went down, dropping the bow. He felt the dagger sink into his leg again as he twisted to free himself. He kicked Cropper in the face, as hard as he could. He felt the man's jaw snap and it sickened him. Tannon and the others were hurrying over to help. Tomn shrieked like a madman, yelling that the blade was his.

Thealos grabbed the gnarled veins of tree roots exposed on the gully wall and pulled himself to his feet. The dagger stuck into his leg painfully. He wouldn't be able to run now. He had to fight them or die. He pulled the dagger out of his leg and tossed it.

Cropper had sagged down with the blow and shook his head, trying to rouse himself. Thealos twisted the Shae weapon out of the folds of his tangled cloak. He let the sodden weight of the cloak drop as he felt the Silvan magic explode inside him, reacting to his need. It made him gasp. Fire rushed through his arm into his chest. It was a beautiful weapon – with a leaf-shaped blade and silverwork hilt. The blade came down on its own, a living thing. The pain in Thealos' leg vanished, numbed by the rush of magic. Cropper howled with fear and agony as Thealos cut him down. Blood spattered on his hands and face, warm and wet. He tasted it on his lips. Trembling, Thealos stared at the dead man at his feet. The magic swept through him like a whirlwind. He felt no guilt.

Jurrow jumped down into the gully behind him. Thealos turned like a shift in the wind, meeting the cleaver polearm with a flash of Silvan steel. The metals clashed with a hiss of sparks. Then Jurrow went down, cut through by the power of the weapon, the blade of a Crimson Wolfsman. Thealos felt the rush of the magic intensify, felt his thoughts dance and tremble with joy. He loved it, the tastes and fears and deliciousness of it. Some part of his mind told him that his knee was throbbing, that he was bleeding, but he ignored it. The Silvan magic roared like a hearthfire inside of him. He no longer feared Tannon's band. He wanted to kill them all. He would enjoy killing them.

Beck and Hoth met him in the mouth of the gully, free of the pond at last. He saw Tannon in the heights above him and Tomn just beyond their shoulders. Four against one.

"Should have killed you yesterday," Hoth said, holding his sword defensively.

"Yes," Thealos agreed. "You should have."

"I get the sword," Beck announced.

Thealos charged him, ready to slice him from navel to throat. His leg collapsed beneath him, unable to support the weight any longer. Panicked, he struggled to free himself of the mud that hugged his shirt and pants. Hoth's boot stamped on his wrist – he felt his bone snap. Beck tried prying the blade from his fingers, but Thealos tightened his fist, screaming. He was losing control of the magic. Pain crowded into his thoughts. He didn't want to face that pain.

"Hit him! Kill him!"

On his knees, Thealos struggled against the two, but he felt his grip loosen. His leg screamed from the dagger wounds. Hoth and Beck were fighting each other to get the Silvan short sword away from him. Desperately, Thealos used his free arm to jerk a knife from Hoth's belt. Tomn screamed, shoving at Beck to grab at the sword. When Thealos raised the dagger against Hoth, he felt Tannon's knife in his back.

His grip slackened and the world crashed in on him, pain and agony and despair. His wrist was broken, his leg cut into ribbons. He'd never felt so much pain in his life, all charging in at once. He tried to grab the dagger out of his back, but he couldn't reach it. Slumping into the gully water, he watched in a daze as Tannon joined them from above. He was going to die. They would kill him for sure and toss his body in the river.

"My father...will pay you," Thealos whimpered, struggling to drag himself away from the soldiers who fought to claim the blade. "He'll pay you..." Nausea turned to fear, cold and silent in his stomach. Tannon scattered the others and turned them against him.

"Too late, Shaden. He'll never know what happened to you." Even Tomn's eyes were pitiless. Beck and Hoth glowered at him.

"No," Thealos whispered, too weary to move. He cradled his wounded wrist. Terror washed into him, deeper than any knife. Spots danced in his eyes as the shock settled into his bones. He was going to faint. *What have I done! What have I done!*

"Kill him," Tannon spat.

A subtle movement flickered in the corner of Thealos' eye. He collapsed as the killing began.

X

It was the pain that brought Thealos awake. Hungry, screaming, bone-throbbing agony. He shuddered and crouched beneath the folds of sleep and waking, fearful to slip too far to either side. The feeling of being alone, abandoned by the gods, was almost too much to bear. But he wanted to live, not die in the swamp like the Crimson Wolfsman had, his body left to rot with worms. Cautiously, he let himself drift closer to the source of his life, preparing for the damaged body he would meet. It hurt to move, to breathe. Light stabbed his eyes, and he wondered how he could be feeling the sun in the depths of a gully.

Something wasn't right. Instead of damp mud with poking roots and hard pebbles, he was lying on a warm wool blanket. He smelled fresh cinders and the tang of a wood fire. It took a moment of struggle to open his eyes.

"You're alive," the man told him in a gentle voice.

Thealos blinked. He tried to move his arm to scratch his face, but it screamed with pain and wouldn't move. It was bound tightly to his body by a cloth sling. Glancing around, Thealos saw a small grove of twisting oak, free of the death and ugliness of the scarred maple forest.

"Here, let me help you sit up," the stranger suggested from behind. He felt strong arms cradle his neck and lift him up. He wanted to sob with pain. Looking down, he saw blood spattered on his clothes.

"Sweet Vannier. The blood! Is it all mine?"

"No," the stranger chuckled, coming around in the light where Thealos could see him. With his tanned face and wider shoulders, the man was certainly human, but his eyes were classically Shae – grey with streaks of ice and green. His dark hair with gold tints was cut just above the shoulders. He was of medium build and had a handsome face with a cynical twist to his mouth. He was clothed only in black. A long tapered sword was belted across his hips with a curious symbol etched into the steel pommel. An identical symbol hung from the stranger's neck – a bronze medallion of an offset cross within the borders of an octagon. Thealos looked from the stranger's hands to his face. The cowl of the cloak was down. He gave off a comforting smell, something akin to a cedar chest and well-worked leather.

"Have you had a good enough look yet?" the stranger asked pointedly, aware that Thealos was staring.

"I'm sorry," Thealos stammered. Distrust welled up in him instantly. "How did you find me?" He didn't know whether Tannon's Band had left him for dead or not. Something nagged at his memory, but it was hazy now. They should have killed him. Why hadn't they?

Behind the stranger, near the fire, Thealos saw the polished blade of Jade-Shayler and the Crimson Wolfsman shawl. There was also the dagger, still stained with blood. He looked at the stranger warily.

The stranger followed his gaze. "I saved those for you," he said. "You may need them where we're going."

"I don't understand."

"I saved you from those soldiers," the stranger replied. "I think you owe me something for that."

"They took all my money," Thealos answered. His shoulder throbbed.

"It's over in that pile." The man pointed to another heap. He saw glittering Aralonian pieces, the hoppit doll from Arielle, even the gown that Tomn had showed him. "I don't have any need of those things. I have need of you."

"Who are you?"

The stranger smiled. "You ask that in the same way you'd

91

ask a pirate. I'm not going to hurt you or ransom you. My name is Jaerod." He looked deeply in Thealos' eyes.

"Am I your hostage then? You said I was going with you."

"I don't take hostages," Jaerod replied. "Have you ever been to the Shoreland?"

"Only to Jan-Lee. Is that where you are going?"

"No, I'm on my way to Sol." He smiled, but Thealos didn't trust him. "I'd like you to come with me."

"And why would I want to go with you to Sol?"

Jaerod's eyes said more than his mouth. He looked at Thealos as if he'd known him for a long, long time. It was a strange…familiarity. "Because I know something your Silvan queen would want to know. Information her council and the Sunedrion would value." He smiled wryly. "But I don't think she would believe it coming from a human, do you?"

"And why would I want to give King Silverborne a message for you?" Thealos demanded. "He's the ruler of Avisahn, not his daughter." He was grateful that the stranger had saved him from Tannon's Band. But he didn't feel any more certain that he was free.

The reply came in perfect Silvan. *"Silverborne is a doting old fool who can't even remember his name anymore. It's quite obvious to anyone with sense that his daughter is the one who truly rules. But you already knew that. They would listen to you if what you knew could save them. I'm doing this because I'm a friend of the Shae."* Jaerod's dialect was fluent. *"Or should I say, I'm a Shaefellow. What is your name?"*

"Thealos Quickfellow."

"Thealos Quickfellow," the other whispered. *"Now that is a proper Silvan name. Is it from your father's or your mother's family?"*

"If you know so much about my people, you should already know that," Thealos answered. The dialect was fluent, but that didn't increase Thealos' trust. *"Quickfellow. It comes from…"*

"Your Correl's naturally," Jaerod finished. *"But that's not how it was done before Ravindranath. Back then, the father's name split with the mother's – if they were both noble blood. Silvermere became Silverborne. Only between*

nobles though."

Thealos stared at him curiously. "You know the Shae well for a human."

Jaerod looked at him blandly. "I'll try and take that as a compliment." He squatted low in front of Thealos, examining the cuts and bruises. "If I'm finished impressing you with how well I speak your language, perhaps I can help you. You won't get to Sol very quickly in this condition, so we'd better do something about it."

Thealos hadn't promised to go with him yet, but he held his tongue. "Are you a healer?"

The stranger nodded and went to a damp pouch at his waist. Thealos watched the quick fingers untie the strings. He stared apprehensively, expecting to see the flat brown leaves of tobac-flower wet with stinging juttleberry juice. It made a salve that stung worse than hornets but it was effective in curing most wounds. Instead, the stranger turned over the pouch and withdrew a dripping clump of green moss. It was green with streaks of blue and even violet. Thealos had never seen moss like that before − not in the darkest forests of Avisahn.

"Are you ready, Thealos?" Jaerod asked, holding the clump.

"What is that?"

"Show me your hand."

Thealos leaned forward, grunting with the pain in his ribs. He extended his grubby palm towards the stranger, curious. Jaerod took the moss and pressed the cool wet mass into Thealos's hand.

Silvan magic. There was a whirlwind of sound and color that rushed through Thealos' senses like a storm. His back arched with the jolt and shock of it, as if tongues of soothing fire caressed him. It didn't burn his skin − it burned inside his heart hotter and hotter. He felt the Silvan magic penetrate him, seeking and twisting through his marrow and joints, playing across his back. It was wonderful, tantalizing. The buds of the moss smelled like flowers and fresh thyme. The crooked break in his arm fused itself whole, the gashes and stab-wounds of his back knitted closed. He watched with astonishment as the cut in his leg closed shut, leaving no trace, no scar. The chorus swelled in his ears, music unlike anything he had heard. He savored it. Relished it. Feasted on it! He could not have spoken his own name if he had wanted to. Gasping for breath, Thealos felt the magic heal him. Even the spot on the back of his head where Cropper had clubbed him. He no longer remembered the pain.

It lasted only moments. The savory rush winked out, banished back into the colorful moss. It shriveled with the efforts. But Thealos stared at it in his open palm, feeling the power hidden within its damp spores.

Jaerod uncorked a flask of water and poured it out over the plant. It was fresh river water, cold and icy. Thealos' fingers went numb, but he stared at the magic he cupped in his hand. As the water drenched the buds, they slowly quivered, sending out fresh little shoots. It was smaller than before, but it was still living, still growing.

Jaerod cocked his head. "Now are you ready to listen to what I have to say?"

"This is Silvan magic," Thealos said in awe, looking at him anew.

"I know. The Shae brought it here."

"Here?"

"To this world," Jaerod explained. "It is the strongest of the Earth magics from the world the Shae came from. And it thrives very nicely here too."

"What is it?" Thealos demanded.

"Its name is the same in both tongues. We call it Everoot."

"Everoot." He stared down at the colorful moss. It still tingled in his hand, whispering to his Shae senses comfortingly. "The magic is still there, I can feel it."

"I know," the stranger said with a nod. "And I knew you would." He opened the small sack and brought it closer for Thealos to look within. There was more of the Everoot inside.

Tilting his hand, Thealos dropped the small bud back inside. "Where did you get it?"

A wry smile passed over the stranger's face. "And just a

moment ago, you weren't all that interested in what I had to say. As I told you, I think your little queen would want to know about this. It's growing down in the Shoreland – west of Sol near the fortress of Landmoor. That's where I am going. And you, if you'll come with me." He twisted the knots and fastened it again to his belt. Rising, he brushed off his black pants and rested his hand on the pommel of the long tapered blade.

"Do I really have a choice?" Thealos asked, studying him. He untied the cloth sling and stretched his arm. The bone was completely whole.

"I won't force you, Thealos," Jaerod replied. "I'm not a mercenary. I'll not kidnap you and drag you after lost treasure. I am a messenger, in a way. And you are part of that message. The way I look at it, you owe me your life, but whether you choose to honor that debt...I will leave that to you. The gold coins and Wolfsman magic," he nodded to the leaf-blade short sword, "they mean nothing to me. If you do nothing else, tell your queen that you met someone who possessed Silvan magic and knew where a grove of it could be found. Maybe she'll find that useful enough to act outside of Avisahn for once." He shrugged. "But I don't think so. There is so much she doesn't know."

"If I follow you, what then?" Thealos asked. "I'm still not sure what you want me to do. You may use our magic and speak in our tongue, but I don't know you. I don't even know what you are."

"There is really only one way to find out then, isn't there? Why don't you come with me as far as Sol and let me explain along the way why I need you. Besides, you don't really think you can go back to Avisahn right now, do you?" Something in his voice told Thealos that Jaerod knew exactly how little choice he really had.

* * *

In the end, it wasn't the small loaves of spiced-apple bread that made Thealos follow him. Or the cuts from ovals of sharp cheese or even the small sack of dried apple shavings and salted almonds. It was how he put out the fire.

Jaerod didn't let the coals burn low and leave the ashes and stumps of charred wood in the middle of the glen. He dropped a fistful of sapple-dust on the flames to suck the heat away, and then he carefully used a small trowel to bury the ashes and debris in the earth. He did it conscientiously, leaving no disturbance to mar his passing. It was a practiced maneuver, quick and effortless, not one awkwardly rehearsed in order to impress a Shae. He was demonstrating a respect for the land and the Rules of Forbiddance. A respect that had been taught by the Shae for thousands of years. Some humans, it seemed, had learned it even after all this time.

"Who are you, Jaerod?" Thealos asked as they hiked along the tall ridge of the valley just before dawn. To the east, the familiar rumble of the Trident showed the green fringe of the wood. To the west, he could see only the broad prairies and beautiful stands of elm and birch. It was a vast land, flat and low with rolling hills and high-looping hawks. Thealos' clothes were still damp from a quick wash in the river, but at least the dirt and blood were fading stains instead of the vivid reminder of what had happened to him in the gully. They were memories he intended to banish as quickly as he could.

"What do you mean?"

Thealos looked at him curiously. "I want to know how you found me in that wood with those soldiers. Did you happen upon us during...or after?"

"You knew I was there when you were dallying with the cook in the dark."

"I didn't see..."

"You knew I was there," Jaerod cut in. "Of course you didn't see me, but I was there."

"That was you?" Thealos said softly. "I knew something was following us. But why couldn't I see you?" Something snagged at his mind again, and he caught it. "You've been following me since Dos-Aralon, haven't you?"

Jaerod smiled smugly. "You remembered. Good."

"Why?"

"Why indeed? A Shae leaving Dos-Aralon before the gate curfew. Very curious. A Kilshae then – one of the banished ones? Perhaps. A Kilshae would have drowned his sorrows in ale... or worse." He shrugged. "A runaway, then. But from what?" He gave Thealos an arch look. "It didn't take long to find out. The Council Elder of Vannier is as angry as a hornet swarm." He clucked his tongue. "I'm beginning to think you don't have any idea how to make friends."

"And how did you know about Nordain?" Thealos demanded.

"The news is all over Avisahn. Everyone is talking about it."

"You went to Avisahn?" Thealos asked in disbelief.

"Why should that surprise you?"

"It surprises me that you made it past the Crimson Wolfsmen! The city proper is guarded on every side. You can't cross the river without being seen by the watch."

"You seem to know a lot about what I can and cannot do."

Thealos could feel the mocking tone in his voice. "How did you get into the city then?"

"That's really not important. What's important is what they are saying about you in Avisahn right now. Nordain has kept your disappearance as hushed as possible, but everyone is talking about what you said in the council chambers."

Thealos cringed.

"You were wise to head south. They started looking for you in Dos-Aralon first, searching the places you might stop for money." He gave Thealos a wink. "It was clever of you to prepare so well in advance. But I already knew where you left and I had an idea where you were going. It didn't take very long to catch up to you. By then, of course, you had blundered into those renegade soldiers. The dregs of Dos-Aralon's army." He clucked his tongue again. "That wasn't clever. That was very foolish, Thealos. They could have killed you and left you for dead. If they had brought you back to Dos-Aralon right away, Nordain would have had you for certain. But," he added admiringly, "you handled yourself well until it came time to escape."

"Then Nordain is still looking for me?"

"Insurrection, Thealos. The Shae won't tolerate it. They've sent the Crimson Wolfsmen to bring you back. They're tracking us. Right now."

"I did not intend to start this," Thealos said defensively. He walked a little faster, digging his hands against his sides. "Sweet hate, I'm not going to be able to go back there for a Silvan year at the least." He glanced up at Jaerod. "And so what you are really saying, Jaerod, is that if I had not chosen to come with you, the Crimson Wolfsmen would have found me?"

Jaerod shrugged and kept walking. "Would that have been my fault? I'm confident we can reach Sol before they find us. And by stopping at Sol first, we confuse the trail. They might expect you to go by ship to another land or city. They'll certainly be watching the river for you. And if we head straight to Landmoor, they'll catch us before we make it to the Shadows Wood." He glanced at Thealos. "I can help protect you, Thealos. If you went on without me, the Wolfsmen might catch you at any rate no matter where you went. And then you'd be brought back to Avisahn for treason."

Thealos grit his teeth. "That banned Nordain goaded me."

"You shouldn't have let him." He gave Thealos a sidelong look. "Certainly not a Shae with your family name."

"The only thing Quickfellow means in Avisahn is gold," Thealos snapped. "I'm the son of a barter, and only distantly related…"

"Distantly," Jaerod chuckled. "You could be the crown heir of Shampanelle with less noble blood than yours." He shook his head, irritated. "Save me your pathetic Shae humility. You know who your father is, where the Quickfellow family came from. Your father and his fathers have protected themselves by obscuring their name in Vannier's faith. Until you," he added, giving Thealos a sidelong look. "The Silvornes have been watching your family for several generations. You were allowed prominence and station, but weren't officially considered royalty. All for a reason, Thealos. All for a reason. And now Laisha Silvorne thinks you're out to raise a rebellion against her right to rule. I tell you, she's a clever girl. I don't think she'll let you get away with it..."

Thealos looked aghast. "But that's not what I..."

"Not what you intended?" Jaerod cut him off. He turned and gave Thealos a hard stare. "Then why else did you leave Avisahn in such an uproar, Thealos?"

"Because I wanted to learn about this land for myself," he replied defensively. "I don't trust her advisors or what they are saying. And she has never been outside of Avisahn in her life! But I have." He folded his arms angrily. "If we keep ourselves behind the river, the time will come when the humans will be strong enough to cross. If we wait to get involved until then, it will be too late."

"So what you are really saying is that you came to help start a war on this side of the river?" Jaerod's gray eyes glittered.

It was then that Thealos realized that once again he'd said too much.

XI

The firelight danced and played in the intricate grooves of the finely crafted pommel. Thealos turned the blade over, examining the other side closely. The hilt had the fascinating impression of a wolfs-head with two glittering eyes that seemed to stare at him. He was amazed that there was no rust or splotches on the blade or hilt. But it was the blade that intrigued him the most. It was narrow, leaf-shaped, and sharper than anything he had ever touched. He was a little surprised at the heft and how light it felt in his hand. In the night air, it was cool to the touch, but he could feel the fire of its power buried deep within – sleeping. He remembered how it had felt when he faced off with Tannon's Band. Its power had numbed him to everything, even pain. That was so very dangerous, he decided.

Glancing up, Thealos looked at Jaerod. The human sat against a shaggy elm on the other side of the fire and cut pear slices with a small knife. Their evening meal had been shared in silence. Thealos noticed the tapered long sword he wore at his side. It was an elegant weapon.

"Was your weapon forged by the Shae?" Thealos asked, rubbing the blade of Jade Shayler with an oilcloth once more before slipping it back into his belt. Jaerod looked at Thealos with an amused smile and nodded. "And where did you get it?"

"Not from Avisahn," Jaerod replied enigmatically. "Do you

want to see it?"

Thealos nodded, and Jaerod set the fruit and knife down and leaned forward, drawing the weapon from the leather sheath. Firelight glimmered across the narrow blade. Jaerod held it up for Thealos to see. There was a strange marking on the hilt, the one that matched the amulet around Jaerod's neck. It wasn't a Shae symbol, at least not one that Thealos recognized. Yet he could feel the power in the blade even as far away as he was. Silvan magic thrummed in the air.

"It must have cost a great deal," Thealos observed, nodding respectfully at the weapon.

"Actually it was a gift," Jaerod replied. He eased it gently in the sheath. "You've been quiet today, Thealos." He took a hunk of wood and tossed it on the fire. Sparks showered up in angry snaps. "You're upset about our discussion this afternoon?"

Thealos hugged his knees and stared at the flames. He knew from Jaerod's vantage, his eyes were probably glowing. "I said more than I should have." He glanced up at Jaerod and smirked. "I do that, you know."

"The tongue is the hardest to tame – especially for the young. And I'm very good at prying out secrets."

"I'm older than you," Thealos countered. "But if you know my people, you already knew that."

He smiled. "The Shae live longer than humans. The Life magic in you is strong and it sustains you well in this world. This longevity is a gift, truly. It gives you a special affinity with the Earth magic, which is a form of Life magic too – if you don't mind me putting it that way."

Thealos was not offended. To the Shae, nearly everything was a living thing and had its own magic. But people were considered a higher order than animals and plants. Shedding the life of a man was never done on a whim, just as beasts were slain for food not sport, and his people preferred working stone for shelter than slaying trees. He continued to listen as Jaerod went on.

"You are more sensitive to the balance of magic than humans or even Drugaen. You have every right to be wary of those not of your race, Thealos. Experience and disappointment are cruel teachers. I still have to earn your trust. Just as you have to earn mine." He poked the fire with a stick. "I understand your anger at what the humans have done to the valley. It used to belong to your people – from the Ravenstone to the Kingshadow. Imagine it – a forest that stretched across the entire way, cut into little ribbons by rivers and streams. It was a vast, beautiful kingdom. The Crimson Wolfsmen kept preserves for the king's hunting, and no man could pass or cross without using the Great Highway."

Thealos eyed Jaerod. He could well imagine what it used to be like during his elcorrel's days, but how did this Shaefellow know all this?

Jaerod took the charred stick and ground the embers into the dirt. "There was Avisahn, of course – the king's city. But there were also watchposts built to unite the valley as one." He poked the stick around the dirt, leaving pockmarks of ash. "Jan Lee, Jove Stand, Citidellian, Novune, Sol, Kirae." Each black mark Jaerod pressed into the dirt showed a web around the main one. "And we can't forget Jenterhome," he finished, stamping another mark far south of the first one. "Only a few remain under the control of the Shae now. They were built to preserve the Silvan way." The gray eyes lifted at Thealos across the fire. "We're going to one right now. It was the first watchpost to be surrendered to the humans of Aralon."

"Sol," Thealos said, nodding. "The river city. We still control Jan Lee though."

Jaerod shook his head. "Sol was a Shae watchpost. But it was not the first to fall. We're going to Jenterhome. They call it Landmoor now." He prodded the farthest scorch mark.

Thealos leaned back and studied the human. Had he learned this from the Shae somehow or was it some Druid-priest teaching? "Only the older scholars know this much about Shae history. Where did you learn this? Parath-Anatos?"

He shook his head. "I've been to Landmoor, Thealos. The governor of the Shoreland commands the garrison at the castle. But Landmoor is built on top of an abandoned Shae watchpost. The old records of the city...they are still there. If you can read old Silvan, they talk about what it was like back then. What an interesting picture. Long before the Purge Wars. Back during the time of the Empire of Sol don Orai."

"Before the humans came," Thealos said, nodding. "I still don't understand why you are telling me this."

"Maybe because you were not being very talkative tonight," Jaerod replied with a wink. "I told you that I am a Shaefellow. I believe in your people. I believe that you were sent to this world to save it. Not many humans believe that any more. The Druid-priests of Parath-Anatos certainly don't preach it."

"And you don't think it's wrong to want to take the valley back?" Thealos asked.

"I don't think it is wrong to want to defend yourselves. The gods know you are hopelessly outnumbered," he added dryly. "But do you even know why the humans control so much of your homeland? The history behind it? Or that aside, do you truly believe in what your people came here for?" His eyes narrowed challengingly. "There is always a balance. Always a reason why things happen the way they do."

Thealos felt a little goaded, but he tried to keep control of his patience. "Do I truly believe in why we came here? Is that what you're asking? We came here to save you from destroying your world and to teach you how to heal it again. We saved you, all right, and we taught you...but you would not learn and remember."

Thealos stretched his legs out, looking up at the northern sky where he saw the smooth blue light of Eroth. "That has been the more difficult challenge for us, I think. We have tried teaching you about the dangers of fire, yet in nearly every human city it is abused. Every other year, a fire burns out of control in Dos-Aralon, ruining sections of the city and destroying homes and lives. Yet before the ashes can be swept away and the scorch marks painted over, another one breaks out, repeating the lesson. Over and over, it happens. We tried to teach you about ale and mead and other things Forbidden to drink, yet there is no limit to the breweries or

103

drunkenness. The deaths caused by back-alley stabbings, squabbling over who gets the last sip. We tried to teach that marriage is honorable, a commitment..."

"Perhaps the humans learned more from you than you think," Jaerod interrupted softly. "Hypocrisy is so easy to pick up and so difficult to put away."

Thealos gave him a dark look. "Are you saying the Shae are all hypocrites?"

"In one way or another, Thealos, we all are," Jaerod replied with a sardonic chuckle. "I'm not criticizing you. Just making an observation." He stopped, cutting another slice off his pear. Bringing it to his mouth, he chewed slowly and continued. "When you try to teach someone over and over again and they don't seem to be picking it up, maybe you should look again at how the message is being delivered. But why am I trying to convince you of this? Isn't that one of the reasons you left Avisahn? One of the reasons you couldn't go along as a chapel monk or join the Shae army or fritter your Silvan year learning an artisan trade? You wanted a taste of freedom, to experience life for yourself without every little action being prescribed by a Rule of Forbiddance. You recognized the hypocrisy of your nation and chafed under it. It only stings because I'm pointing it out to you. The Shae may admit that hypocrisy to themselves, but never to those outside their culture. To do so would be to admit that they've botched their quest rather completely." He smirked. "And most humans don't even know what really happened at Ravin-Dranath. When the Shae almost annihilated themselves."

Thealos listened quietly. He fumed for a moment before realizing that he couldn't be angry at Jaerod for speaking the truth. He had had those exact thoughts himself. Staring across the fire at Jaerod, he replied, "I'll concede your point, then. If you'll concede that you are using me to your own ends. I don't think it was random chance that brought us together – not in the streets of Dos-Aralon, and not by the river when you saved me. You found me for a reason, Jaerod. Let's not be hypocrites with each other. Tell me why you're really here and what you expect from me."

Jaerod nodded. "More than fair. I doubted I would have been able to convince you to go with me to Landmoor unless I told you why. Let me try a little bluntness. We'll see if it works. I need you, Thealos, but not for my own ends. What I mean by that is it's my responsibility right now to prevent a terrible destruction – a destruction that has happened in the past and will happen again if we don't try to stop it. This destruction will come about because of the Everoot, this plant that healed you. I need you because of who and what you are. You are a Shae, but not just any Shae. You are the descendent of one of the noble Silvan houses. The House of Silver rules in this valley, but the House of Quick ruled longer. I am here to bring you to Landmoor – to the Shae watchpost of Jenterhome – because a warding that guarded the Everoot has been destroyed."

Thealos froze in the midst of warming his hands by the fire. From what little he knew of the Shae warders, it took strong magic to break a warding – the strongest of magics. The words had come from Jaerod's mouth almost casually, but there was so much sincerity in his eyes that pierced Thealos' heart. He listened closely as Jaerod continued.

"If we do not act quickly, those unfriendly to the Shae will use the Everoot to dominate and eventually destroy this valley. But the Shae knew this when they set the warding over the Everoot. They knew that someday the warding might fail. They also created and concealed a talisman to defend themselves if the Everoot were ever used against them. But you see, only a descendent of the original Quicksilver family can retrieve that magic. Neither can any ordinary Shae who worships Keasorn, Shenalle, or Vannier. I will explain more of the history of why this has happened along the way. There are reasons why it has taken this long for the warding to be discovered. It was set in place five hundred years ago back when Sol don Orai was destroyed – yes, by the Everoot. And there are those who would kill you for being an heir of Quicksilver. That is why I came for you, Thealos. I am here to protect you as best I can and to bring you to the Shoreland to fetch that talisman."

Thealos stared at him, speechless for a moment. "What

are you?" he whispered, awestruck by the revelation. "If you're not a...a Wolfsman, then..."

"I am a Sleepwalker."

Thealos swallowed. He felt his heart hammering in his chest. He rubbed his eyes, trying to get control of himself. His emotions seethed inside his chest. Was this all true? Yet everything Jaerod had said was burning inside him. "I don't understand. The Crimson Wolfsmen are the guardians of the Shae. They should be the ones to..." He stopped, struggling with the thought. "Are only... humans allowed to be Sleepwalkers?"

"We are not the Crimson Wolfsmen. They are in similitude of my order. If you are really asking if a Shae can become one, then the answer is yes. Most of my peers are Shae. You refer to whether we use Forbidden magic?" Thealos nodded hesitantly. "As I told you, everything is in balance. Life magic and Earth magic can be used two ways. The Shae use them as they should, as they were meant to be used. To heal, to protect, to defend. One practices Forbidden magic by using these magics inappropriately."

Reaching at his waist, Jaerod quickly untied the string and withdrew a clump of shriveled Everoot. Uncorking his water flask, he poured it out on the plant. The tiny sprigs turned a rich green and the blue and violet winked back vibrantly. "And even this magic can become Forbidden if used the wrong way." He gave Thealos an arch look. "It is the same with Sleepwalkers. There are some who use what they are taught in Forbidden ways. But this amulet I wear and this sword at my side... these can only be used by those who have chosen to fight Forbidden magic in all its forms. One is a shield and the other a weapon against all forms of Firekin."

"Firekin." Thealos said it with a shudder. Just hearing the word made him afraid.

"It translates from Silvan poorly, doesn't it? The 'power of night' doesn't begin to describe its myriad of nuances. There are forces at work in this valley stronger than my amulet or my sword. But the talisman that was abandoned and forgotten in Landmoor is stronger than any Firekin. It was created by the Shae to be so. Strong enough to protect you... and your people."

Thealos nodded solemnly. "I've never...this has never happened to me before." He shook his head slowly. "I felt...compelled to leave Avisahn. That if I stayed there a day longer, I would lose myself. I thought I knew why, but now I'm not sure." He scratched his scalp and sighed heavily. "You know so much about us, Jaerod, about our ways, about what is happening down here in this country. You say you are a Shaefellow, and I believe you." He swallowed, wondering what he should say. "And I've heard that some humans are allowed to live in Avisahn. If they renounce Dos-Aralon and swear to abide by the Rules of Forbiddance. Do you worship one of the Shae gods?"

"Keasorn, Shenalle, and Vannier?" Jaerod's eyes twinkled. "No, Thealos. No, I don't."

Thealos was disappointed, but not surprised. "How can you be a Shaefellow and a Sleepwalker? You said many of your peers were Shae. Are they Kilshae then? Is our true way of life then just another culture to you? Something that fascinates you, like studying fire or listening to the wind?"

"Not at all," the Sleepwalker replied with a chuckle. Then his expression hardened. "I do not believe that the Rules of Forbiddance are truly commandments of the gods. I think they are rules made by men. And men, whether they are Shae or not, are full of hypocrisy. That is why I'm not welcome in Avisahn, Thealos Quickfellow. Or with the Druid-priests, or with the sundry religions of Dos-Aralon." The tongues of fire licked the cool night air. His gray eyes were deadly serious. "And maybe you and I are more alike than you're ready to believe."

XII

The conversation with Jaerod changed Thealos' entire point of view. He barely slept that night, thinking again and again about what he had been told. When dawn came, he rose early, washed in the river, and hurriedly prepared to leave. He had never felt such a pressing urgency, not even in his desire to abandon Avisahn. If he could make it to Landmoor and grab the talisman, he would have the proof he needed to thrust in Nordain's face. No – he wouldn't bother with Nordain. He would go to Laisha Silverborne and her high council or to the Sunedrion itself.

"How far is it to Landmoor?" Thealos asked as Jaerod patiently buried the fire ashes.

"We're stopping in Sol first."

"Why? We should go straight there."

"The Wolfsmen, Thealos," Jaerod reminded him. "You stirred up some trouble in Avisahn when you left. We can hide our trail better in the city. Now be patient. Don't let the importance of this rush your reason."

Near mid-afternoon, the fog finally dissipated and the colors and scents from the valley returned. Thealos could see the sprawling city of Sol in the valley lowlands, perched on a high outcropping on the right bank of the Trident river. The city itself wasn't as enormous as Dos-Aralon, but its size had always impressed him. The outer walls were easily thirty feet high, spiked with watchtowers. Small villages hunkered down along the shadows, close to the protective bastions. From his vantage in the highlands, Thealos saw the needle-like masts from scores of ships on the far side of the city – the docks of Sol. Seagulls filled the sky like hundreds of gray leaves swirling in the wind, mingling with the smoke from smithfires and chimneys. There was also a smell, one that grew stronger the closer they approached. It was the stench of sewage mingled with the salty aroma of the ocean. Even from several miles away, it bothered him.

They approached a gate and joined a branch of the King's Highway just east of the main road from Dos-Aralon. As they passed beneath the spike and rail portcullis, the comforts of the Inlands vanished. Sol was a giant hulk of a city, bursting furiously inside the tight walls. Buildings rose two to three stories on each side, with narrow jagged streets barely separating them. Down the alleys he saw that the top levels of the buildings hung out over the streets, close enough that someone could reach across and open a window on the other side. A dog urinated in the sloping gutters choked with grit and debris. The stench was awful, and Thealos covered his nose and mouth to keep from gagging.

"It's not this bad along the trading wharves," Thealos complained.

"Of course it isn't. The Shae wouldn't trade here otherwise. But you get used to the smell...eventually. And the Shae sense of smell is more highly refined after all."

"It reeks worse than a slaughter pen," Thealos muttered, trying to ignore the pervasive stench. "This makes Dos-Aralon smell like mint, and I thought it was ill-kept."

"Sol has been like this for a while. She has a great deal of laundry that hasn't been washed, so to speak." Pausing, he turned around, his black cloak whipping. "See the garrison tower over there? The symbols have almost faded, but you can still make them out. Those were part of the original watchpost. Most of the towers are gone now, but there used to be long catwalks connecting them." His fingers traced across the sky. "The Shae could pass quickly, while the humans lived down here in the squalor of the streets."

"The humans lived here even then?"

Jaerod nodded with certainty. "Sol has always been a trading hub. The towers were heavily guarded from below so that the Shae would be undisturbed by what the humans did down in the streets." He shook his head regretfully. "Imagine how it made the survivors of the Sol don Orai destruction feel. The Shae were always watching them, keeping them down in the grime and mire. Armed guards prevented any contact between the races. And you wondered last night why humans never learn. The refugees from the destruction were taught by the Shae's example." He sighed. "The towers are gone now, the catwalks stripped away to make things equal. Visitors from the East Kingdoms stop here to trade with Dos-Aralon, but this is all they can see."

"Do the Bandits trade here, too?"

"Of course they do. Whether don Rion is ignorant of it or not, who can say? The Bandits have connections with the League of Ilvaren – in fact, one of their battle commanders used to be an Ilvaren pirate. If you refuse to trade with a pirate, then you get attacked on the high seas. An Ilvaren gold piece is worth the same as Aralonian crowns to the merchants and moneylenders of Sol. A Sheven-Ingen blade costs the same regardless. The garrison is well provisioned, so the Bandit Rebellion does not cause much trouble within the city itself. They don't want to end up in the River Cellars, the old Shae prisons along the wharves." He wrinkled his nose. "And you thought the gatehouse reeked..."

Thealos nodded briskly. He was anxious to get their business done and leave, but he didn't want it to show on his face. He was much more comfortable in the open plains anyway. The walls and buildings pressed in on him, and the air was thicker than he was used to breathing. He couldn't feel the presence of Earth magic at all in the city. It was worse than Dos-Aralon. "Where do we go from here?"

"For now, you can wander about as you'd like. There are shops that sell new clothes," he added, giving Thealos a scrutinizing glance. Thealos had to admit it – he did have the look of a common wayfarer. "I have a visit to make before I join you again. Meet me at dusk at the Foxtale Inn, near the Sheven-Ingen docks. It is a well-kept tavern along the piers. Oh, and don't play Bones with the Drugaen there. He cheats."

"Why can't I go with you?" Thealos asked.

The Sleepwalker looked at him with a smirk. "I have my reasons. Which I doubt you would ever truly appreciate unless you became a Sleepwalker yourself. Now buy yourself some clothes and I'll meet you at the inn later. Watch for thieves. I'm trusting the son of a barter can handle himself in a city."

Thealos nodded. "I'll meet you at the Foxtale then." Pulling his cloak over the blade of Jade-Shayler to hide the glint of Silvan steel, Thealos rested his hand over the hilt. As he joined the main road crowded with horses, carts, sailors, and merchants, Thealos felt the press of bodies. He turned to look back and Jaerod was gone. He craned his neck, trying to see him. Pin-pricks of gooseflesh danced on the back of his neck. He had the feeling he was being watched, but there was no sign of the Sleepwalker. Sighing with impatience, Thealos continued in the press of bodies toward the docks. Occasionally, a hand whisked on his clothes, but he kept a firm grip on his things and stayed along an open furrow on the rear side of the crowd.

There were other Shae within Sol. He hadn't really been looking for any, but their pale skin and light-colored hair was alarmingly obvious. He frowned. Some were obviously well-dressed moneylenders or barters attending to business. Others had lanky hair, cheap earrings, and thin beards. They shouted at everyone passing by, tempting them with deals on Silvan wine, palm-reading, some even hawking jewels from the Silverborne treasures. Thealos saw one juggle knives for a capful of coins. Kilshae, he remembered darkly. The banished ones. Over the years, how many had left Avisahn as he had? Did they miss wandering through acres of twisting oaks when the first green leaves were budding? Or did they miss the languid, peaceful lifestyle even more – the music, the flavors of wines and cheeses, the clear voices of a trained chorale? Many of the Shae he saw were filthy. There were other races as well. Stocky Drugaen longshoremen with wizened eyes and tangled beards shoved their way through the crowds. The Drugaen were a slave race that had thrown off their masters centuries ago. From what Thealos remembered, they were shorter because they had originally been bred to mine ore. They could be found doing hard labor throughout the world, but only so long as they were paid for it. The best Sheven-Ingen blacksmiths were Drugaen-born, smiths who could hammer without tiring until the moonrise. The sights of Sol dazzled his eyes all at once, and he secretly wished he were with Jaerod, to see the city as a Sleepwalker did.

Closer to the piers, Thealos found a tailor shop called The Silver Needle. He did not want to be recognized shopping in one of the Shae businesses that his Correl had dealings with. The owner was a large human woman with tight arms and long fingers. She gazed at him, watching his hands. He chose a thick pale green tunic sewn with silver-threaded trim and dotted across with studs, a heavy wool travel cloak that was ash gray, and he even found a padded leather vest lined with wool. He paused where the gloves were, tried on a few sets, and then put them back.

"You planning on paying for those clothes, Shaden?" the woman said from the counter. "Or are you just hoaxing me?"

Thealos turned to her. "Is my gold not welcome?"

She didn't flinch. "Just as long as you plan on leaving some of it here. It's not easy selling clothes that a Shaden touched."

Anger seeped into his cheeks, and he clenched the fabric of the cloak and tunic. He knew his clothes were blood-stained and shabby. He was accustomed to being treated deferentially as a barter's son. But it was obvious she didn't trust the Shae.

"I'll take these," he said, setting them down on the counter top.

She eyed him and then unfolded the cloak and shook it out. After examining the other clothes that way, a trick to be sure he hadn't bundled anything inside them, she propped her hand against her wide hip and said, "Five pieces."

"Of what?" he demanded.

"Gold," she answered firmly.

"You can't be serious," he said, feeling the barter's game begin. "The fabric isn't worth one piece, but I'll buy it for that. One Aralonian piece."

"One piece?" she laughed. "Get out of my shop. I sew each of these by hand with a silver needle. It's worth five, and that's all that I'll accept. If you don't like the prices, complain to the Silvan King."

"I could buy a new sword for five," Thealos countered. He raised the cuff on the tunic disdainfully. "If this were made by Silvan Weavers, I would pay five. Look how the hem is creased and stitched. Two lines of thread, not three. These barely meet the stitch-marking guidelines."

"How do you know about the...?"

"Or about the loose threads here along the hem," Thealos snapped icily. "It's fair work, Madame, but I know quality when I see it. And maybe I'm not an ignorant Shaden you can cheat." He reached in his money purse and laid two Aralonian pieces. They glimmered with a clean Avisahn mint. "They are worth one piece, but I'm in a hurry. It's two or nothing."

She hesitated, staring greedily down at the coins. It was obvious he could afford to pay, and that he knew the true value of the items. In the end, she accepted the gold Aralonian coins, and Thealos left after changing into the handsome tunic, cloak, and vest.

"Come back sometime, Shae Barter," she declared as he walked out. "Maybe we can talk some real business."

He gave her a mock bow and shut the door. The new clothes made him feel much better. What he needed was a warm bath and a laver full of soap cakes to cap it off. Pausing briefly, he asked a passerby about the Sheven-Ingen wharf and was given some vague directions taking him to the southeastern part of the city. Seagulls perched on the tall masts of ships and shrieked. Even though the roadway tilted slightly, the footing was good. Taverns and inns and warehouses jammed and crowded the Sheven-Ingen wharf, but it wasn't difficult finding the Foxtale Inn. It had wide windows that opened to a sprawling main room glowing with a huge hearth in the middle of it. The chimney was wide enough to fit a man across. It butted out of the tiled roof, sending plumes of gray smoke into the leaden sky. The inn wrapped around itself, with two aisles of rooms that met in the back with a second level perched on top.

Thealos studied it, inhaling the tangy salt smell from the ocean. That was the smell he remembered from Sol, not the filth by the gatehouse. Several wooden steps led up to the inn's foundation, and the stone was covered with wash marks from where the tide had risen suddenly and overrun the pier. Looking straight down the dock, Thealos could see the churning gray-blue waters at the end. A cool breeze blew through his hair. Thealos climbed the steps and entered. A blast of heat warmed his cheeks and hands, and he realized how cold it had been on the dock. The hearthfire roared with huge trunk-thick logs. He scanned the thirty or forty tables for a sign of Jaerod, but the Sleepwalker wasn't there yet. The owner leaned over on the bar counter, sifting through a stack of docket books. The man paused long enough to look up, scowl at Thealos, and then go back to counting figures. The room was barely half full, and there were plenty of open tables, so Thealos took a far corner table near the kitchen doors and dropped into a chair.

The inn smelled like beer and pipe smoke, but also of fresh bread and roasted geese. The wood-planked floor was surprisingly clean, and the patrons seemed to be enjoying themselves. There were dozens of little touches that made the inside of the Foxtale a warm and inviting place. Wainscoting, vine ivy, and fat tallow candles – all of which helped add to its charm. It was definitely a woman's touch – the innkeeper himself seemed out of place in it with his unkempt hair and rumpled sleeves. Setting his travel bundle and bow on an empty chair, Thealos sat and slowly scanned the room. A Drugaen sat on a tall stool by the bar, clumsily shuffling a worn deck of cards. One of his boots tapped against the leg of the stool. He had a wicked double-bladed Sheven-Ingen axe in his belt and an iron-knobbed club in a hoop on his other hip. The club reminded Thealos of Cropper, and he shuddered with the memory. The Drugaen was young and a little ruddy, with reddish-brown hair and a combed beard. His chest was as big around as an ale barrel, and his stubby fingers tapped as they shuffled through the cards. He leaned over and whispered something to a serving girl.

The girl caught Thealos's eye and he stared at her. She smiled at what the Drugaen had said and shook her head, making her jewelry tinkle softly. Her hair was dark brown and long, and her blouse drooped lazily in front. She nudged the Drugaen with her elbow, said something, and they both laughed. Then she glanced over at Thealos, catching him in his stare, and gave him a smile that was friendly and very pretty. Thealos nodded back and continued scanning the room.

Along the far wall, near the rear corner of the inn, he saw a knight from Owen Draw. It was clear who he was from the scarred armor he wore. The knight pored over a thick platter of roast goose, dabbing gravy with a hunk of bread. He had rust-gold hair, long and loose – the Inland style. A mustache drooped down along each side of his mouth. Small crisscross scars knotted his cheekbone and neck, everywhere the fine-chain mesh and silver plate didn't cover. His hands were bare, his gauntlets loose on the table next to him. Even his hands and fingers looked as if they'd been smashed and healed repeatedly. He looked like a care-worn hickory tree, solid and steady. Thealos watched him eat, wondering what the warrior from the Inland duchy of Owen Draw was doing down in the Shoreland.

The door opened, and a howling sounded as the warm air rushed out. Thealos looked towards the door and watched four hooded men enter the Foxtale Inn. They quickly took a table near the doors, hunching forward. One tossed off a hood, and Thealos saw his silver-blonde hair scooped and tied back – tied with a red-dyed leather thong. Thealos stared at another and saw the rough sailor's garb. But it was the red dye that made his stomach lurch. It was the color...

Thealos wanted to shrink in his seat as his stomach coiled with fear. Sweet Vannier, it wasn't possible! Four men – a quaere. And they weren't human either. He could sense it from across the room as if someone had whispered it right in his ear. No. They weren't human sailors in for a drink of ale.

They were Crimson Wolfsmen. And he didn't think it merely chance that they had entered the Foxtale behind him.

XIII

Dujahn pulled the reins back and eased the gelding into a light trot. Scratching the sweat-dampened skin behind his ear, he gazed at the picket fires ahead. Before reaching the south sentries, he dismounted and led the horse towards the flickering nests of light in the sharp darkness. His shirt was soaked, and sweat dripped down his ribs. The ground was spongy, moist and smelled like bitter weeds and mud. The vine maple and cedar crowded in on each other and in between the ruts grew thick patches of witch-thorn. His boots crunched over slick-beetles and crickets. Clouds of gnats and mosquitoes buzzed around him. The road was barely visible that night, but he studied the dimly-lit ruts and tracks and maneuvered without stumbling.

A Kiran Thall hooted like an owl, three low bursts from the wall of trees on his left. An alert call, Dujahn remembered from the training Miestri had given him. Just thinking about the Sorian made him shiver. She and Dairron had tricked him into serving them, letting him eavesdrop until he knew too much and now he had no choice but to forsake Folkes and work for them. Miestri had said exactly what would happen when he reached the picket lines and told him exactly what to do and say. She was well-informed about military affairs – she knew all the right things to say. Just as she had promised, the Kiran Thall had spotted him earlier than he thought they would. Impressive, but still not enough. If he hadn't wanted to be seen, he would have left the horse and started around the camp on foot as soon as the firelight was visible farther back.

An answering whistle replied in short crisp tones. Dujahn knew it meant he didn't appear threatening and that someone with a crossbow was tracking him closely. Maybe more than one. He continued forward, dragging the horse after him. From the south pickets, a detachment of sentries carrying torches approached. Their mail vests looked insufferably hot. None of them had drawn weapons yet. There wasn't a need to.

"Hold there, friend," the sentry captain announced warily. "Shine some light on him, Vison. I don't see a uniform."

The torches were raised, and Dujahn squinted as the light stabbed his eyes. He held the reins out so they could see his hands, and he took a step forward. "Good evening. My name is Dujahn of the Gray Legion. I'm here to see Commander Phollen."

"You're Gray Legion?" the sentry captain asked skeptically.

"Is Commander Phollen here?" Dujahn repeated. He looked to the right and left and studied the soldiers. They wore simple tunics and makeshift armor, not the black and gold of Bandit officers. Wearing drab brown and gray clothes himself, Dujahn looked more like a peddler. The sentry guards edged closer. They were scrutinizing him, as were the two or three Kiran Thall lurking in the trees. He stared at the sentries calmly, waiting for them to get over the fascination.

"What is the pass?" the sentry captain demanded.

"It's the name of Commander Phollen's ship..."

"And what is that?"

"– the Khariidawn," Dujahn continued.

Three Kiran Thall appeared from the trees. Dark streaks painted their faces, making their mud-colored uniforms blend better. They were certainly more skilled than the soldiers in front of him. Each held a black-iron crossbow mounted on wooden stocks, but they raised them deferentially and nodded to him.

"If he's Gray Legion, escort him into camp."

Dujahn didn't recognize the Kiran Thall who had said it, but the soldiers obeyed him at once.

That was much better.

"Commander Phollen hasn't arrived yet," the sentry captain explained as they fell in around Dujahn, leading him into the warmth and firelight of the Shoreland Regiment. "We expect him soon. Our orders are to mobilize and be prepared to march on the fortress, but to wait until he gets back."

"Who is in command then?" Dujahn asked, handing a sentry the reins.

"Colonel Hallstoy."

"I need to see him immediately."

"Of course, we'll take you right there. Is there something the matter?"

Dujahn planted his hands on his hips. "Nothing I can discuss with you. Take me." He nodded to the ring of fires. Sentry soldiers were the same the world over, Dujahn thought. They were intimidating behind a picket line with twenty other soldiers pressing about them stupidly, but as soon as they realized you weren't impressed with their authority, they turned into sniveling weasels. The sentry captain ordered the rest of the watch to gather back at the pickets. Extending his arm, the captain pointed the way through the lines and started off at a brisk walk. The buzzing from the insects was drowned by the clank of pots and the hiss of campfires. Smears of mud and drying ruts made the ground uneven. Mashed bootprints were everywhere, marring the stone-cut road of the old Shae highway. The Shoreland Regiment hunkered across the only road through the Shadows Wood and stretched deep into the forest on each side. Dujahn shook his head, surprised that King don Rion hadn't heard about it yet – or sent one of his Dukes down with an army. His defense ministers deserved to have their eyes stabbed out. The Bandits wouldn't dare mobilize so close to the Inland! It's all a bunch of nonsense and frightened merchants trying to keep the roads clear for trade. He knew what they would be arguing. But they were wrong. So very wrong.

"As I said, we're expecting the Commander any day," the sentry huffed, dodging pit fires and mule carts. "Mage warned us to prepare to march, so we've broken camp and pulled onto the main road to cut off any riders to or from the north. We're building scaling ladders and bringing in grapnels and knotted ropes…"

"You should post more sentries in the darkness farther south," Dujahn suggested. "The Kiran Thall spotted me too late because I was riding without a torch. I would hate for the governor of Landmoor to find out you're blocking the Iron Point Road."

"That's true, I guess," the sentry captain mumbled. "I'll take it up with Hallstoy. Say, are you working for Commander Phollen or Folkes, or was it General Dairron?"

"Who I work for is none of your business."

The captain gave him a wounded look and walked the rest of the way in silence. The bulk of the force was still on each side of the Shadows Wood, but the command staff had moved into the center where the road was flat and wide and the perimeter guard around it was defensible. But vulnerable, too. Dujahn shook his head and muttered an oath. Without a strong leader, a regiment could easily fall apart all by itself. He couldn't understand why Commander Phollen would try to organize a siege without being there to direct it. And here he was, Dujahn thought cynically, to help Miestri rattle the regiment and make it even more ungainly. That wouldn't be too difficult…

"There's Hallstoy's tent," the captain announced, pointing towards the command pavilion. It was ringed with Kiran Thall and officers, each dispatched with the evening orders. The smell of roasting boar and black-feathered jackdaw lingered in the stale air. It was muggy and fetid – Dujahn hated the Shoreland swamps. He was introduced to the chief officer on duty and then escorted into the pavilion where he could hear the Bandit colonel swearing.

"I don't care that he's a banned merchant! Take his cart, lock him in irons, and tell him to join the Bandit Rebellion. If he doesn't, let him wear the chains for a few days! Get out. How are the supply lines? Are we ready for the march? Good.

It's banned time. Now what do you want, Bonner? Fetch me more ale."

Dujahn stepped past the tent curtain. It was stifling inside, and he tugged at his collar so he could breathe the air instead of swallow it. Hallstoy was just as tall as Commander Folkes, and he was built like a bear. A white scar went from his bottom lip down the side of his chin, and he had three more criss-crossing along his scalp where the hair had never grown back. Sweat glistened on his face, but he still wore the heavy chain tunic and black and gold-lined armor of the Rebellion. He argued with a colonel about where the Kiran Thall should tether their horses and muttered an obscenity. "And what do you want, Komsin?" he asked the duty officer, giving Dujahn a look of contempt. "Caught another merchant on the road? Did you hear what I told Captain Shokle? Arrest them all. They're fools, Sons of Fire, all of them! This is a war!"

"This is Dujahn," the duty officer announced, getting the colonel's attention. "He's Gray Legion."

Hallstoy's eyes narrowed and he grabbed a towering goblet of ale half a cask deep. Taking a long drink, he wiped his stubbled chin and squinted at the new arrival with more than a casual interest. "So you're Dujahn," Hallstoy breathed, obviously having recognized his name. That was flattering. "What does Folkes want?"

Dujahn shook his head and stepped forward. "Presently, I'm representing Miestri of Vale."

"You work for that tyke?" Halstoy smirked. "I don't envy you."

Dujahn shrugged. He leveled his gaze at the tall Bandit soldier. "In that case, you certainly won't like my news. She's coming to the Shoreland Regiment, Colonel. Tonight."

Hallstoy coughed as he tried to suppress a laugh. "Like Hate she is, Dujahn. This is Tsyrke's camp, and she has no right being here. And don't tell me she doesn't know that."

"You can tell her yourself when she gets here. I was sent to secure a pavilion for her and two companies of Kiran Thall."

Hallstoy's eyes went wild and he laughed out loud. "Sweet

Achrolese, you were sent to do what?" The scar on his cheek burned. "You can't come into my army and start giving orders. I don't give a ban who sent you. Only Tsyrke or Mage or Stroth Ballinaire can make orders in this camp over mine. And in that order, too. I don't care if she's a Sorian – this isn't her camp!"

Dujahn shrugged. The half-smile he gave the colonel was forbearing. "The Sorian can do whatever they want, Colonel. Honestly, do you think you can stop her from coming here tonight? Do you think this entire army could stop her?" He gave the colonel a wry look. "Be reasonable. She's not here to take over your command."

"Then why is she coming?" Hallstoy demanded.

"She hasn't revealed that to me. I need a pavilion and a few companies of scouts. She asked specifically for Kiran Thall. That's all."

Hallstoy kicked one of the table legs, sloshing the ale. "No."

"What did you say?"

"I said no. I'm not giving her a thing. I will not let Tsyrke or Mage come back and find out I've been catering to her. You tell that..."

Dujahn reached inside his tunic pocket and withdrew a red-glass orb. A queer orange fire burned inside of it. The other Bandit officers stepped back, recognizing the shape and color of the orb. He heard one of them mutter something about dark magic.

"Why don't you tell her yourself?" Dujahn said coldly.

Hallstoy froze.

"Come, Colonel. Explain to the Lady of Vale why you won't greet a fellow member of the Rebellion. One who certainly has more authority over you or your officers. Go on, sir. Tell her."

"I don't have time for this," Hallstoy grumbled. He stared at the orb fearfully.

"I really don't think she cares," Dujahn advised. "The Lady of Vale is coming tonight. You know how they can be when they don't get their way." The orb gave off a wicked flash and a red mist began to creep from its shimmering glass. The other officers started to back towards the tent door. "She'll take your tent, Hallstoy. She'll be here in a minute if I invoke her."

The Bandit colonel gave Dujahn a deep frown and looked as if he was about to draw a weapon, but he tightened his mouth and shook his head. He looked ready to kill if they had been alone. "She's only daring this because Tsyrke and Mage aren't here," he whispered. "I only hope -- by Achrolese! -- that one of them returns before she can disappear." Hallstoy straightened his sword belt, summoned a spoonful of dignity, and looked towards one of his officers. "Tell Grimme to get out of his tent." He turned back to Dujahn. "It'll have to do. Secrist is out roving with two companies of Kiran Thall right now. She can use them when he gets back." He gave Dujahn a delighted smirk. "I would truly like to see her try and threaten him."

Secrist's companies? Dujahn thought dryly. "Thank you, Colonel," Dujahn said with a small bow. The red mist retreated back into the orb and he stuffed it back into the pouch. "The Lady of Vale will be pleased at your obedience." Without waiting for a response, he turned and followed the officer out of the stuffy pavilion. He was a little disappointed. Miestri had said she might have let him use the Firekin to rip the skin off of Hallstoy's skull. It would have been fascinating to see that – and to see the looks the other officers would have given him when he did.

Colonel Grimme went into a fury when he was dispossessed of his tent, but the order had been given, and not even he was brave enough to challenge a Sorian for it after Hallstoy had backed down. Dujahn stepped inside the musty tent. It reeked of sweat and ale. The fabric blotted out some of the noise and he stood quietly for a moment, feeling his entire body race with the heat. He had felt the power in the orb as he held it in his hand. He could have done anything with it! He wiped his forehead and paused, listening to the sounds of the camp rumble around him. Reaching into the pouch at his waist, he withdrew the fist-sized sphere again. The smoky orange light pulsed inside it, giving the orb a throbbing dull red glow. It was like staring into smoking coals, but the orb was cool. There were shapes in the mist, but she had warned him not to look at them. It was dangerous to do so. Dujahn looked away and set the orb on the tent floor. He backed away from it.

The flickering magic danced in the orb and the shapes began to take form. The reddish light grew brighter, yet darkening the tent as well as it covered his boots and hands and then the tent wall all around. The churn of magic came inside the pavilion, and Dujahn felt it grip and twist his stomach. It was like dancing on a hill during a lightning storm. A cool breeze came from the red-hot orb, and suddenly Dujahn found himself shivering.

There was a rustle of velvet robes and Miestri stood before him, holding the sphere in her palm. She smiled and raised her eyebrow, as if asking him why he was shaking. Two Shae appeared behind her, gripping their ash longbows. As the red light jumped back into the orb, Dujahn saw gorgeous woven rugs and dangling crystals within the tent. It smelled like cinnamon and sage. A soft bed with three pallets filled nearly the entire space, but there were also stone animals – ravens, sparrows, and vultures – and wooden puppets suspended from leather strands coming from the tent poles. He stared at the dangling ornaments, but recoiled when he saw the leering and tortured faces.

"Well done," Miestri said approvingly, slipping the ball-sized orb into her robes. "You handled Hallstoy well enough. If he had balked, you would have used the orb on him as I showed you?"

Dujahn bowed his head and stepped back, nodding. He'd killed men before. But never with magic. Never like that. Even though it was cold in the tent, he hadn't stopped sweating. "What else do you need me to do, my Lady?" He tried not to look in her eyes, but he found he couldn't help it. They were dark, almost black, and he couldn't distinguish her pupils. Swallowing was a word he felt described them best. It was like staring down a cliff at night.

She stepped closer, making the velvet robes rustle. "I want to know what is going on here, Dujahn," she whispered in her low musical voice. "Where is the Shoreland Commander?

Where is Mage? When will they return? See what information you can gather and bring it to me at dawn."

"Of course," he answered and nodded. "Is there anything else?"

"Yes. Go find where the prisoners are kept. I want a young man, the youngest you can find. Bring him to me when you return."

He looked at her quizzically.

"Don't think, Dujahn," she warned. "Just bring him to me."

Dujahn felt something go black inside of him. Blinking, he thought for a moment he would faint. Stumbling, the Gray Legion spy left the tent, grateful for the soggy warmth that nestled into his armpits once he stepped outside. The buzz and the rumble of camp soothed him. There were men outside used to war and death and the thousand faces of pain in between. He understood them. He understood their motivations, fears, and desires. That was easy.

But Miestri of Vale? He shook his head, remembering what it felt like to be around her. Understanding a Sorian was like trying to understand what made the wind.

XIV

The only thing Thealos would have dreaded more was Elder Nordain walking into the Foxtale instead. He couldn't believe his bad luck. A Crimson Wolfsmen quaere! He knuckled his forehead, worry turning to panic inside his chest. There was no mistaking it. How long had they been following him? From the plains? Or had these been watching the streets of Sol for him to arrive? Desperation tore at him, making him want to bolt for the door. But they had already positioned themselves there. There was no escape that way.

Where are you, Jaerod? Thealos silently seethed, hiding his face in his hands. Hiding his face wouldn't help. If he could feel them, then they could certainly feel him. He risked a look across the tavern hall. They sat silently, waiting.

"In trouble with your friends?"

Thealos glanced up at the serving girl. He hadn't heard her approach the table. He swallowed. Looking into her eyes, he realized that worry shone on his face and she could tell.

She nodded imperceptibly, forestalling an answer. "I could send for the garrison. Or would that be even worse?" Her voice pitched low enough so that only he could hear.

Thealos watched the Wolfsmen over his knuckles. He shook his head, cursing his own foolishness. "Do you have a way out the back?"

"Yes," she nodded, holding a tray in front of her. "But the

last thing you want right now is a dark alley where they can get you alone. Doesn't look like they mean any trouble right now. Probably waiting for you to leave." She offered a pretty smile. "I'm Ticastasy."

"Thealos," he replied, nodding. It helped to be talking to someone, though he knew she wouldn't be able to do anything to save him. Not even the knight from Owen Draw in the corner of the tavern could defeat four Crimson Wolfsmen. It would take a whole company of knights. He doubted even a Sleepwalker could match that many.

"Are you hungry? Why don't I get you a plate while you mull this over."

He nodded gratefully, but his stomach was wrenching. The serving girl put a hand on his shoulder and gave him a gentle squeeze. "How about some Silvan wine, too. You look like you need it even more." She gave him a wink and looked back at the bar towards the Drugaen. The earrings she wore gave off a musical sound as she motioned for him to join them.

The Drugaen stared at her, nodded, and hopped off the barstool. He was a big fellow, thick around the wrists with big meaty hands. Approaching the table, he tossed the worn deck of Bones on the table and gave Thealos a warm smile. "Hello."

"Flent, this is Thealos," the serving girl said, folding her arms over the plate. "Play a round of Bones with him while I fetch his dinner." She nodded towards the table with the Crimson Wolfsmen, and Flent winked and pursed his lips, some silent communication passing between them.

The din in the tavern was washed lower when the owner raised his voice. "Flent!" the bar owner howled. "What are you wasting your time over there for? Fetch that grain bag from the stores like I told you to."

The Drugaen shrugged his shoulders and started tapping his boot on the leg of the chair. He gave Thealos a wizened look. "He'll forget I'm here in a minute. Nice to meet you, Thealos." He offered his big hand and gave Thealos a hearty shake. "My name's Flent Shago. You know how to play Bones?"

"I've never played," Thealos replied, watching as the serving girl approached the bar owner and whispered something to him. Thealos then glanced back in the corner of the room at the knight. He was leaning back in his chair, watching Thealos intently. He sipped slowly from a large mug of ale. Thealos folded his hands on the table. "Why don't you show me."

Flent started flipping the cards clumsily. It was a trick, Thealos recognized. The large fumbling hands, the ignorant pretense. Jaerod had already warned him. But Thealos kept back his own smile. He'd never played Bones himself. But he'd watched enough games played out in Dos-Aralon to know the rules.

* * *

Thealos lathered some butter on the rich slice of round bread. He took a few bites and set it down on the platter next to the stew. The Drugaen took a long sip from a mug of Spider Ale. He stared at the cards in his hands and then flipped over two, laying down a matching set.

Thealos nodded approvingly and flicked over an Aralonian piece. "Two shells in a row. You're pretty good at this."

The stocky Drugaen shrugged, finishing off the ale. "I play now and then. Mostly with sailors and Sheven-Ingen pirates." He patted the axe at his belt and gave Thealos a shrewd wink. "Did you come in down-river from Avisahn?"

Thealos nodded, taking another sip of Silvan wine. It came from the Radstill vineyards. A good name. Glancing over, he watched Ticastasy approach again with a fresh cup for Flent. Her jewelry tinkled softly as she sat down and joined them, sliding the mug over to her friend.

"Roye says no more games unless you're winning." She gave Thealos a playful grin and brushed the long dark hair over one ear. "I don't think your friends are planning to leave soon. It's dark outside now. Maybe Flent can help you sneak out back, unless a Shaden can see in the dark like a Drugaen can."

"I saw you over there talking to them," Thealos said cautiously, ignoring her suggestion.

She nodded. "They're definitely your race," she said, "Though they're trying to hide it. They have weapons. Like yours."

"Like mine?"

"The blade you're hiding in your cloak," she said, her gaze level with his. Her eyebrows arched. "Is that why they are after you? Did you steal it?"

Thealos shook his head slowly. "No, they want me, not my weapon." He rubbed his thumb along the lip of the wine cup. "I'm waiting for...a friend," he said delicately. "If you can get me out of here safely, I'll make it worth the trouble."

Flent nodded and shrugged without concern. "There are only four. We can handle it."

Thealos chuckled under his breath. "You have no idea who they are. One of them could turn that knight on his ear."

"I doubt that," the serving girl said, unimpressed. "He's a Knight of the Blade." Ticastasy looked at him probingly. "But if they're as good as you're boasting, Shaden, you must be pretty banned important. Who are you?"

Thealos clenched his fist, looking over Flent's shoulder at the Wolfsmen. "It would be better if you didn't know. You mentioned there was a way out through the back. Where does it go?"

She shook her head. "I have a better idea. It's dark out there tonight. You could get lost very easily and that wouldn't help your friend find you. Besides, what's to stop them from hurrying out the back after you? It might stall them longer if... they didn't believe you were leaving." She gave him a knowing look. Her hand rested on his arm flirtingly and then teased the hair along his ear. "I don't want you to get the wrong idea, Thealos. Any number of girls down in the Wash would sell themselves for a drink of ale. But not here, not on these docks. And certainly not me. But do your friends over there know that?" She gave him a scrutinizing look. "You said you would make it worth my trouble. Flent can get a message to your friend when he comes. And I know plenty of places to hide you."

A patron coughed roughly at the table next to them and

dropped a few coins on the table before lurching towards the door. The noise in the common room would have made it difficult for anyone to overhear them.

Thealos looked at her seriously. She was intelligent, for a human. He risked a look back at the Wolfsmen. If he made it away, what would they tell Nordain? That he'd been seduced by a serving girl in Sol? Nordain would believe it, and without any coaxing. But Thealos hadn't broken any of the Rules of Forbiddance since he left Avisahn. Without proof, what could Nordain really do? He looked into the serving girl's cinnamon-brown eyes. She was pretty, in a dusky way. An expensive gold pendant dangled down her throat.

"What will it cost me?" he hedged.

"Why don't you decide what it's worth to you? If you were a Silvan prince, the ransom would be generous. I think I'm your best choice right now," she pointed out. Her hand went lazily to his forehead, brushing his hair back. She gave him a flirting smile and then chewed on the corner of her mouth. "Come, my lord," she teased. "Who is your friend? What's his name?"

Thealos thought about it a moment longer and then quickly nodded. "I'm waiting for a Sleepwalker."

Her eyes widened with surprise. "A Sleepwalker?"

"Do you know how to recognize one?" Thealos asked.

"Jaerod," Flent said, staring at Thealos. "He plays Bones with me. Sweet Hate, if you're with him, you must be a Silvan prince." He looked at Ticastasy and gave her a solid nod. "Find him a nice hideout, 'Stasy. I'll pretend to fix the door, just in case they try and get out the front to follow you. Wait 'til I'm there before you move." The Drugaen pushed away from the table. He rubbed his stubby knees and started clomping across the tavern.

"Flent!" the tavern keeper called over the ruckus. "Another keg of Spider Ale! The tap is running dry. Don't scowl at me...get down to the cellar!"

The Drugaen held up his pudgy hands and waved the tavern keeper away. He wandered towards the front door.

Ticastasy took Thealos' hand and started caressing it with her thumb. "Let me see. Where should I take you? I could hide you at the Thumber Inn down the wharf. Or there's a tavern on the Wash called Riverwink." Her smiles were dazzling and flirting, but the eyes were calm and serious. It was all show. She leaned forward and kissed the corner of his mouth. "Or you could stay in my room until Jaerod comes." She leaned back, giving him an amused smile. She licked her finger and wiped the dab of rouge from his mouth.

Thealos sat still, speechless for a moment. He'd never thought flirting could make him feel the effects of the wine so strongly. He was a little lightheaded and giddy. He decided to play along. Taking her hand in his, he kissed her knuckles deftly. "Do you offer that to all the Silvan princes you charm?" She smelled wonderful, like apples and mint.

A tiny gleam flashed in her eyes and was gone. "Only to green-eyed princes," she said, giving him a warm smile – a real one. "Not gray, not blue, not violet. Never trust a gray-eyed prince. But you'd do better to be away from here. This city can swallow you if you're not wary. And I know it better than any lass around. Good, he's almost there. Come with me." Squeezing his hand, she started to tug him after her.

Flent had just reached the door when it burst open, letting out an angry rush of wind. Thealos hoped it was Jaerod. Instead, a band of soldiers entered. Each had a crossbow slung over his shoulder, the wooden stock sloping and well-crafted. Their hair was long and swept back in the Inlander fashion. The uniforms were light riding gear, a mail shirt covered with a leather tunic and open at the sleeves.

"Mother of Hate," Ticastasy whispered, looking at the newcomers. "They're Kiran Thall."

Thealos watched them enter, at least twenty strong. The mood in the Foxtale chilled. The leader was a tall, lanky soldier with a two-day growth on his cheeks. He had a hawk-nose and a long, hard face. He carried himself with arrogance, a self-possession making him seem younger. Swaggering in, he gave Flent a warning look to back off and marched over to the counter where the tavern keeper scowled.

"What can I do for you, Secrist? You don't stop by the wharves very often."

"My brother sent for me," the leader of the Kiran Thall

said. "Said to meet him here in a few days. You seen him this side of the Ravenstone? Been to port yet?" He grabbed another patron's mug of Spider Ale and gulped it down. He slammed the cup and gave the tavern keeper a menacing look.

"Let's go," Thealos murmured. They were causing enough of a distraction to escape.

She shook her head, her eyes never leaving the leader. "They would see us. You don't want them to notice you. Not a Shae this far from Avisahn. Trust me."

"Who are they?"

"You've never heard of the Kiran Thall?"

Thealos shrugged, angry at the delay. "They're a bane in the western half of the valley. They don't frequently stop in my kingdom. They look like Inlanders."

She nodded. "They're the cavalry of the Bandit Rebellion. Part of the Shoreland Regiment. Arrogant mules, all of them. That one is a colonel. Secrist Phollen." She looked at him with contempt. "Hate," she muttered again softly, watching the tavernkeeper, trying to get his eyes.

"Why doesn't the garrison arrest them?" Thealos demanded in a whisper. "Doesn't this city hold to Dos-Aralon?"

"You're in the Shoreland now. Sol is a port city. If the governor of Sol stopped trading with ..."

"Secrist, over there!" one of the Kiran Thall called derisively. Thealos froze, clenching the girl's hand.

But they were looking at the knight from Owen Draw who had slowly come to his feet. The look the knight gave them was so fierce that Thealos knew there would be violence. The leader of the Kiran Thall pushed away from the counter and started forward. An amused smirk crossed his bristled mouth. Several followed him, while others kept the door secure. The knight stood motionless, staring coldly at the soldiers approaching him. He unfolded his arms, setting a clove-pipe on his plate.

"You're a long, long ride from Owen Draw, you skulking rook," Secrist sneered.

"Are you so anxious to see a gallows, coward?" The knight looked at the twenty soldiers, sizing them up.

A mirthless chuckle came as the reply. Secrist glanced up at the rafters. "Well, this looks like it could do for one well enough in a pinch. Hang you like I did those fool knights who tried to route us in Iniva. They call it Blackwater now."

"We've all heard of it, boy. I arrest you for high treason in the king's name." He unsheathed a two-handed blade from a battered scabbard. "I arrest you for rebellion against your true king."

"Trobbe, fetch me a rope from my saddle bags," Secrist ordered, nonplussed by the knight's words. "I feel like hanging another knight."

"Secrist," the tavern keeper warned, "I...I can have some casks of ale ready for you right quick. Fetch 'em, Flent. Quickly, lad, fetch 'em! Won't cost you a thing. Come on, there's plenty. Don't kill him. Not here. This will ruin me..."

The knight stood unflinching. "You fetch that rope, little boy." He shook his head slowly. "But I just may use it on you."

Thealos' mouth went dry. He stared at the leader of the Kiran Thall, feeling nothing but distain for the man. He glanced around the room, counting them. The Kiran Thall had crossbows and light weapons. But there were at least twenty, and he didn't know how many more outside. The other patrons of the tavern bowed their heads down, not daring to look up. They outnumbered the Bandit horsemen, but only in numbers, not courage.

"I can't believe this," Ticastasy muttered. She let go of his hand. "I'm calling the garrison here."

"No," Thealos warned, but it was too late.

"You're not going to hang anyone tonight, Secrist Phollen, so quit blustering," the serving girl said, stepping away from Thealos's table. "You gamble with Fate every time you come to Sol. This is my tavern as much as it is Roye's. We've earned this place. But if you hang a Knight of the Blade, you're a bigger fool than I ever thought. And I think you're a banned big one."

Secrist turned and gave her an deprecating glare. His eyes went up her body, lingering at the soft curves. He wiped his mouth on a gloved hand and clucked his tongue. She stared at him defiantly, hands on her hips.

"Sporting with Shaden now, 'Stasy?" he jibed, giving a half-glance at Thealos. "I'm sure Tsyrke would love to hear that."

Thealos' eyes burned with anger.

"And you think he'd approve of what you're doing? You could spend a month in the River Cellars for a bloody nose, and he would let you rot. But killing a knight in my tavern – that'll earn you the gallows. And he'd hand over the rope. You'd better get out of here, Secrist. Before I call the garrison."

Secrist's eyes glimmered with fire. "And how are you going to call them?" he challenged. He looked around the room. "You gonna send that pudgy Druge?" He stepped towards her, his finger stabbing the air. "Call them. But you know they won't lift a finger. Not even if I hang that banned knight higher than cedar. When Ballinaire rules Sol, they'll be wearing the black and gold. Now be a good lass and fetch me a drink." She stood there, glaring at him. She didn't move. "I said fetch me a drink!" he roared.

Thealos reached down and rested his hand on the pommel of his Silvan blade. He watched her carefully, wondering how stubborn she was. If she would obey him.

Ticastasy took Flent's ale cup from Thealos' table and walked up to the Kiran Thall slowly. She looked him right in the eye. And splashed it in his face.

XV

For a moment, Secrist stared at her in disbelief as ale dribbled down his chin. His anger was sharp and quick. "You little whore..." he snorted, backhanding Ticastasy. She crumpled to the floor. Anger shot through Thealos, fierce and hot. Some of the patrons made a dash for the windows. Flent Shago thundered a blistering oath as he yanked the knobbed club out of his belt. He swung wildly at a soldier near him, dropping him with a shattering blow across the knees. The Drugaen howled, his gray-green eyes blazing as he rushed towards Secrist.

The knight didn't waste a moment. He also charged Secrist with his double-handed sword. Fighting erupted through the room as the Kiran Thall rushed the knight and the Drugaen. Other patrons of the tavern yelped with fear, ducking beneath tables to try and get out of the way, but some were trampled as the Bandit soldiers attacked. Two against twenty.

Thealos shoved his chair back, whipping his cloak out of the way as he grabbed the hilt of the Silvan blade. When he drew it, he felt the magic flare to life, sending a jolt of shock up his arm. The wash of magic rose through him as it had when he found the blade. It glowed a cool blue in the tavern hall.

Flent went down in the rumble, pinned and hammered from behind by three soldiers. The knight faced off against three others who feinted and lunged to get a blow in at him. He held them off with tight sweeps of the blade, giving ground slowly. The Kiran Thall attackers smirked wickedly, teasing their prey. It was only a matter of time before they had him.

"Fine weapon, Shaden," a soldier challenged, motioning a second soldier to come with him. "Should have hid under the table like the others. I'll take that blade and any gold you have on you. Now!"

Thealos watched the two Kiran Thall approach his table, weapons drawn. There were too many. He closed his eyes and fed the weapon's magic with his need. The feeling was there, a cool watery pleasure wrapping him in its arms. Silvan magic. The blade went from cool blue to white hot. Yet it was like cupping frigid seawater in his hands. When he opened his eyes, he saw the soldiers hesitate. He knew they could see his eyes glowing.

"If you think I'll be as easy to knock down as a serving girl," Thealos said acidly, "You've been riding those flea-bitten nags too long."

Thealos had to be quick. Standing off against trained soldiers was a fool's mistake – he'd learned that with Tannon's Band. He hadn't the skill or training to last long against them. But he was quick and unpredictable and hoped that would be enough to throw them off.

"Afraid of a lone Shaden?" Thealos taunted. "Maybe it's the Kiran Thall who wear silk socks and dance in the woods. Does your lady friend Secrist there ever let you lead?"

"Bloody rake, I get him first!"

Thealos lunged forward, slashing the Silvan blade at the soldier on his left, catching him by surprise.

The man saw the wicked glow of the blade and staggered back to avoid it. It gave Thealos just enough time to dart past them between another set of tables. He had to leap over a patron crawling away and duck around another table to where several Kiran Thall were kicking Flent. None of them saw him coming. The Silvan blade shrieked with magic, cutting through the tunic and mail and gashing a Bandit soldier's back. Swinging again, he cut another man in the side, watching with sick pleasure as the leaf-blade split him open. He felt the soldiers coming in behind him and whirled to face them, holding his weapon defensively. Flent lumbered to his feet with a roar, bleeding from his nose and mouth. He hefted his Sheven-Ingen axe in both hands.

"The magic," one of the soldiers whispered. "It's mine." It was just like Tannon's Band. They saw the blade and they craved it more than feared it.

Thealos tried to get control of it, tried to tame the bursts of delight that danced inside him. He couldn't. The blade was alive – a needing thing.

A dark-bearded soldier lunged for the weapon, trying to topple Thealos with his size. Thealos darted right and the blade seemed to slice on its own accord, scoring through the chain shirt like an axe biting into bark. It felt a little like borrowing someone else's reflexes. The soldier howled with pain as the blood gushed from his side. Another movement, and Thealos met it, snapping the long sword thrust at him like brittle glass, and kicked the man down. The Silvan magic roared through him, hot and icy at once. There were Kiran Thall everywhere, coming at them from all sides. Flent swung the axe furiously, trying to keep them from Thealos' back.

"Too many!" the Drugaen huffed, swinging his axe desperately. "Where's the banned garrison!"

Behind the mob of panicking patrons and Bandit soldiers, the air filled with the battle yells of the Crimson Wolfsmen. Four other gleaming short swords joined the fray, cutting through the ranks of the Kiran Thall. Toward Thealos. There were too many people, hardly enough room to avoid getting hit.

"The Shaden! Kill the bloody Shaden! Kill them all!"

Flent lost his footing in the slick blood-stained floor and went down. The Kiran Thall swarmed him, their tapered blades thrusting down at him. Thealos was alone.

Then the knight shoved Secrist through the huge window, shattering it, and the fight spilled into the streets.

* * *

The blow caught Thealos unprepared. Dark spots danced in his eyes, making it difficult to distinguish between enemies. His lip was bleeding from the stray punch, and he felt the sword gash into his side. He managed to flop to the floor as the soldier swept the sword down, trying to cleave his head in half. He tried twice to strike the soldier, but the man was too well trained. Thealos looked back at the window and tried to scramble towards it to escape into the street. He saw others taking advantage of the exit and fleeing into the side alleys.

"Give it to me, Shaden!" the soldier snarled, dislodging his weapon from the smashed wooden table and charged at him again. Thealos was dizzy with pain and fatigue, but he'd managed to keep himself away from the mob of Kiran Thall who had turned to fight the Wolfsmen. His arm went quickly numb from the shock of the blows. The blade of Jade-Shayler held the attacker off, but the weapon's magic couldn't match the skill of his foe. Thealos' rolled quickly sideways to avoid another stroke and hurried back to his feet.

Quickly, Thealos ducked away, trying to get out of the man's reach. He was almost to the window. But the soldier's lust for the magic drove him after Thealos relentlessly. "Give it to me! Ban you, Shaden! It's mine!"

A deathscream cut into the tavern and stabbed Thealos' ears and eyes like knives. The blade in his hand flared brighter than a torch, consuming him in a sheet of pulsing blue flame. The scream echoed in Thealos' mind, and the smell of death stung his nose. A Shae's death. For an instant, he felt death's kiss on his cheeks, then everything in motion stopped under a cracking of rich thunder. It wasn't thunder from a storm – it came from across the tavern and filled the leaf-blade in Thealos' hand. One of the Crimson Wolfsmen was dead. He couldn't see the body, but he felt the man's final gasp of pain. The blade had reacted to it like lightning, encasing Thealos in a ball of glaring light. Thealos stood helpless for a moment, feeling the strength of the magic intensify. It wasn't Earth magic – he'd felt that many times. It was different, stronger, more frenzied. Images of

138

the Wolfsman's life whipped past him, bonding him to the sword, to the memories. It was stronger than anything he had felt in his life. A bond. A communion with the dead. For an instant, all of the Shae in the tavern were one, Thealos with them. He could see things through their eyes and they could see through his.

When the shock of thunder was spent, the whirlwind of the tavern resumed.

The Kiran Thall stumbled away from Thealos, covering his eyes from the glare of the sword. Thealos could see the other Wolfsmen attackers in his mind even though they were still surrounded by enemies. They were just as aware of him as he was of them and charged forward, eager for the kill, whipping through the crowds of soldiers with lethal efficiency. There was no way they were going to let him escape. He was their charge, their mission. The Council of Elders in Avisahn wanted him in prison.

Thealos knew he had to leave. The Kiran Thall were strong, but the Wolfsmen were stronger now; the bond with their fallen comrade had renewed them. Thealos felt a pull, a windstorm against his back, an energy he'd never experienced. The soldier's eyes in front of him widened with shock as Thealos met him stroke for stroke, inch for inch. It was as if he'd handled the leaf-blade all his life. Thealos cut the man once, twice, slashing his armor open. Thealos pressed towards him, hungry for the kill. He couldn't stop himself. He didn't want to.

"The garrison!" someone shouted. "The garrison is coming!"

As the soldier turned to look, Thealos had him, driving the short blade all the way through, burying it to the hilt. Warm blood splashed on Thealos' hand as he jerked the sword up and out, letting the soldier crumple to the floor. He stared down at the body and then looked up.

The leader of the Wolfsman quaere was staring at him in fury. He could hear the man's thoughts. *That weapon doesn't belong to you!*

Thealos ran to the window and vaulted outside, cutting his hand on a shard of glass on the sill. He knew he was bleeding, but he barely felt it. If the Wolfsmen caught him, it was all over. His encounter with Tannon, this fight in the Foxtale – for nothing. They were distractions from his real goal. He had to get to Landmoor.

The sea wind on the pier whipped fiercely at Thealos' clothes. He saw the garrison jogging down the street, armor and weapons jangling. The Kiran Thall were making for their horses, falling one after another to the knight who defied them all. He cut them from their horses, spilling their bodies into the street. Hearing the stamp of hooves, Thealos turned and saw the charging gelding, almost too late. Thealos was hit from behind, shouldered roughly by the horse.

As he lay on his back in the street, just beyond the reach of Secrist's sword tip, he knew he had come very close to dying. The horse loomed over him, its foul breath snorting puffs of steam in the night air.

Secrist's eyes met his coldly. "You're dead, Shaden," he spat, giving him a look of hatred. "No matter where you hide!" Whistling, Secrist called the other Kiran Thall to ride and jerked the reins roughly, galloping into the night-filled streets. "Ride! Ride!"

Thealos got to his feet quickly. He wanted to chase the man and cut him down with all the others. The magic burned furiously inside him. He could still see through the eyes of the other Wolfsmen. Then he saw himself in their eyes. Turning quickly, he faced off as the leader of the Crimson Wolfsman emerged from the window. Holding the blade of Jade-Shayler before him protectively, Thealos backed into the alley near the inn. Wrapped in the thick night shadows, he retreated from the commotion of the inn-room brawl.

A moment later the Wolfsman leader was there. His eyes were flinty and blue, like a mountain framed against the sky. He joined Thealos in the darkness of the alley. Even in the dark, even at night, Thealos could feel the other Shae's presence.

"Thealos Quickfellow," the Wolfsman said angrily in Silvan. *"I am Xenon, Watcher Lor of Sol. You are under arrest by the Shae Council of Elders for high treason. You will come with me and stand trial before the Sunedrion."*

"I have not been charged with treason," Thealos countered in Silvan, backing away, keeping his distance. He felt the magic in his arm, but something was not right. It retreated back into the blade. Abandoning him to the wind and the pain at his side and hand.

"You defile that weapon by touching it! You are not a Crimson Wolfsman. You were not trained in the magic. You are nothing but an unskilled barter. A boy. Now set that blade down, or I'll make you."

"No," Thealos replied, shaking his head. He backed slowly towards an alley. *"I can't go back with you. Not now. There is danger for the Shae, I must..."*

"You have no choice, Quickfellow. This is not something you can run from anymore. You will answer for your crime, for the most serious of crimes! I have no respect for Kilshae, and oathbreakers are the worst. You are a craven and a rebel. Stand and face your crimes, boy. You've run far enough!"

Thealos felt a prick of awareness on the back of his neck. A whisper that someone was there, just behind him.

"I don't see him running from you, son of Keasorn," Jaerod said in perfect Silvan. His black cloak rustled softly. *"He chose to leave Avisahn. He chooses what he must."*

The Crimson Wolfsman studied the Sleepwalker for a moment. An instant. Then he came at Jaerod like a whirlwind.

Jaerod shoved Thealos aside, a hard blow that sent him off his feet and onto the cobblestones. Thealos twisted around, his shoulder throbbing, and watched the Sleepwalker evade the Wolfsman's blows.

Xenon was a trained Lor. He had been training since before Thealos had learned to read, and probably before Jaerod was even born. The short blade whipped around in dizzying strokes, slicing and stabbing at the black-clothed human. There was a frenzied haste to it, a hunger to kill so deep that Thealos recognized it in his eyes. The human would fall quickly. He was no match for the skill and training of a...

Xenon went over backwards, flipping, landing hard on his back. The Wolfsman blinked, stunned, and was on his feet instantly, slashing out again. The Sleepwalker waited for him. Jaerod moved like tidewater, his hands out and away from his body, his feet mercurial as he shifted his stances to avoid the hail of blows. He moved subtly, deftly, just enough so that the weapon passed harmlessly by him. The cloak followed his movements, snapping at the wind. Xenon struck again and again. He missed every time. In a quick reach, Jaerod caught the Wolfsman's arm, locking it painfully at the elbow and hurled him into the wall of the Foxtale. He struck it hard. Blood dribbled from a cut at the warrior's temple. Xenon didn't flinch, but flung himself at the black shadow, high low – high again. Every move and technique meant to bring his opponent down.

"Jaerod, behind you!" Thealos warned as the second Wolfsman joined the attack, coming out from beneath a dark awning into the alley.

The Sleepwalker didn't falter. He zigzagged around Xenon and put himself between them and Thealos. He faced two now, weaponless, his hands slightly apart as he studied them. Both came at him with a howl of fury and went down in a heap as the Sleepwalker ducked down, swept one down with a clip at the ankle and rose again, striking his palm under the other's chin. Xenon gasped with the jolt and reeled backwards, clutching his neck and struggling to stay conscious. Twisting sideways, Jaerod dropped down, hammering the flat of his hand against the other's neck. The Shae blacked out and slumped in the street.

The Sleepwalker rose slowly, his eyes never leaving the injured Lor. Xenon panted, clutching his throat and wheezing with pain. "The garrison," Jaerod reminded Xenon pointedly. The advancing soldiers had filled the street outside the Foxtale. It was only a matter of time before they flooded the alleys too. "The Shae queen would be furious to know that Crimson Wolfsmen were involved in a *ravinjon* in Sol tonight."

Xenon glared at Jaerod. He also replied in the king's common. "Then we will meet again, human. And when we do, you will die."

"All die in the gods' due time. And only then."

Thealos stared in amazement as the Crimson Wolfsman Lor heaved his unconscious comrade over his shoulder and stole deeper into the shadows before the first ranks of the Sol garrison reached them. Thealos looked at Jaerod, rubbing his throbbing shoulder.

The long sword dangled from the Sleepwalker's hip still enfolded in the slender leather sheath. Untouched.

* * *

The Foxtale was in shambles. Broken tables and smashed chairs littered the main hall. Posts that supported the ceiling were splintered and the cross-beams sagged. Blood and ale lay in puddles on the floor. Many of the patrons had been trampled or stabbed by the Kiran Thall attack. The dead were brought out to the wharves by the city soldiers, lined up, and covered with blankets to be taken to the garrison coroner. But those who had started the encounter had paid the heaviest toll. Barely half of the Kiran Thall had escaped with their lives. The tavern keeper, Roye, was furious and surly as he complained in guttural harshness to the captain of the damage that was done. Thealos watched them from a chair, tenderly massaging his shoulder. The cut on his side had stopped bleeding.

"If you were going to start a fight on this side of the river," Jaerod said, feeling the bone of Thealos's shoulder. "You should have waited for me to get here first." He took Thealos' arm and bent it, testing the soundness.

"But I didn't..." Thealos stammered and realized the Sleepwalker was only teasing him. His grey eyes glinted with amusement. He groaned as Jaerod popped his shoulder back into place. It hurt like fire, but at least he was alive. "I thought those Wolfsmen were going to take me back to Nordain. Thank Vannier you came when you did."

Jaerod nodded and rose, observing the damages. "You can thank him when you say your prayers tonight. Tell me what happened." He pulled out the damp bag of Everoot.

Thealos related the experience as quickly as he could, mentioning the Crimson Wolfsmen watchers and how the

Kiran Thall had provoked the fight by wanting to hang the knight. Jaerod's eyes darkened and he nodded, listening. He withdrew a bit of Everoot and pressed it into Thealos hand. The Silvan magic wrapped him in its warmth, healing the cut on his side and the gash on his hand, leaving him complete and whole once more. The feelings washed over him in warm waves, soothing and soft

"Fury, but that feels good," Thealos sighed, staring at the vibrant moss in his hand.

"I need to speak to the garrison captain so we can leave. Wait for me." The Sleepwalker approached the tavern keeper and the soldiers and began talking to them.

Thealos lowered his fist, savoring the dregs of the magic. He quickly looked around the room and saw Ticastasy tending the fallen Drugaen. The serving girl pressed a bloodied rag against his barrel chest in an effort to stanch the bleeding. Flent's face was paler than sapwax, and his breathing came in ragged gasps. Thealos was sickened at the sight. The soldiers had hacked him even after he'd fallen. He lay in a puddle of blood.

"How is he?" Thealos said softly, coming up behind the girl and squatting low next to her.

"Thirsty," the stocky Drugaen replied with a broken grin. He grit his teeth with pain. "'Stasy thinks... if I drink anything, it'll come spilling out on my shirt." He seized up in a cough and blood dribbled down his lip. "But I'd rather leak ale...than blood."

"Sshhhh," the serving girl muttered, putting a fresh cloth on his chest. "I sent Norrie running for a Zerite, Flent. He'll help you, just stay awake. Please, just stay awake a little longer!"

Thealos stared down at the Drugaen. He was in agony. How he'd survived the battle at all, Thealos didn't know. He wondered if he had looked this bad when Jaerod found him in the gully. His heart panged at the thought. "Let me help him."

The serving girl looked at him with a surge of hope. "Are you a healer?"

"My people are." He looked down at Flent and then at

144

the girl. Opening his hand, he showed them the stump of Everoot.

"What is that?" she asked, staring at it warily.

The Drugaen looked past Thealos, as if seeing something behind him. His eyes glazed over and his head drooped low on his chest. He was fighting to keep his eyes open.

"Flent!" she gasped, clutching his shirt front and shaking him. "Don't you give up on me. Stay with me!" Her eyes brimmed with tears.

With the Everoot in his hand, Thealos pulled the bloody cloth away and pressed the vibrant moss against the deep gash. He felt the magic surge, rush from the plant into the Drugaen's limp body. The Earth magic spread slowly from his hand. It wasn't the same reaction as when Jaerod had used the plant on him. It was weaker now, not as refreshed, but the results were the same. Flent gasped once, twice, his chest heaving – eyes wide.

"What...what are you doing?" the serving girl demanded, alarmed.

"Don't fight it," Thealos soothed. "It's all right."

Color returned to Flent's bloodless cheeks. His hand filled with strength as he gripped Ticastasy's arm, squeezing it so hard she winced. Her eyes widened with shock. His chest rose and fell, long and slow. A timid grin spread over his mouth. The bloodstained clothes were still there. But when Thealos lifted his hand, the gaping wound on his chest was gone. And so was the clump of Everoot.

"Thank Achrolese!" she whispered in surprise. "Thank Achrolese, you saved him!" She squeezed Thealos' hands fiercely. "Thank you, my lord. Thank you!"

Thealos' shoulders sagged with relief and he couldn't help but smile. He'd never saved someone's life before. With all the death that night, it felt wonderful.

"I'm sorry," she apologized, "What a wretch – I've got blood all over you!" Grabbing a fresh towel, she cleaned his hands.

Flent sat up slowly, letting out a deep sigh, and looked at his bloodstained clothes. Ticastasy tossed down the towel, looked at the Drugaen sternly, and then wrapped her arms around his neck. "Don't you ever do that again!" she said, half-choked with tears.

He smoothed her hair. "I've never let any man hit you, 'Stasy." His eyes narrowed. "If he comes back to Sol again, I'll split him nose to navel. I swear it."

She shook her head sadly. "I didn't know what else to do, Flent."

Thealos looked at her with a frown, remembering. "You provoked him. Deliberately. Why?"

Her eyes flashed. "So I could slip into the kitchens and send the cooks running for the garrison. I don't need to answer to you..."

Thealos touched her arm to calm her. "I'm glad you did. You surprised me, that's all. You knew that Kiran Thall?"

"Knew of him," she replied. "His brother is a merchant captain with the League of Ilvaren. I've known that. But Secrist is reckless. Ban him, trying to hang a knight from Owen Draw in the Foxtale. What in Pitan was he thinking!" She looked up at Thealos and flushed. "I'm sorry for my language. I do that when I lose my temper."

Thealos smiled. "I have that problem myself. I've said worse, and recently." He liked Flent and Ticastasy. They had both come to his aid. He owed them something for their trouble. "Neither of you are safe here." He glanced down at Flent, who nodded, listening to him carefully. "The Kiran Thall will probably come back. So will the men who were here for me."

He felt a prick at the back of his neck, but he saw Jaerod's reflection in the serving girl's cinnamon-brown eyes. The Sleepwalker stood behind him.

"He's right," Jaerod said, looking down at the two. "It will be dangerous for both of you to stay here. Especially you, Drugaen."

"Why?" Flent demanded, eyes cautious yet curious.

Thealos smiled. He put his hand on Ticastasy's shoulder. "You were willing to guide me to shelter. Let us do the same for you. Do you know a place where they can stay, Jaerod?"

Her brown eyes looked into Thealos'. "Who are you, my lord?"

"They'll come with us," the Sleepwalker said.

The serving girl wiped her eyes on her blouse and shook her head. "I'm not afraid of Secrist or the Kiran Thall. We'll have watchmen looking for them. And they'll all spend a fortnight in the River Cellars if they ever ride into Sol again."

"You must come with us," Jaerod insisted.

"This...this is our home, Sleepwalker. Roye depends on us. He can't run the Foxtale by himself. Flent, tell them!"

Flent stared at Jaerod. "It's dangerous because of the magic. Isn't it? The magic that healed me."

Jaerod nodded. "You are not safe here. Come with us."

"Flent! I can't believe you're considering this! We don't know who they are!"

The stubby Drugaen rose to his feet and slid the Sheven-Ingen axe in his belt hoop. He looked into her frantic eyes. "I should be lying here dead on the floor, 'Stasy." He waved his hand at the mess of blood on his shirt. The inn was rank-smelling as the serving girls brought out floor brushes and mops. "We leave tonight?" Flent asked Jaerod, and the Sleepwalker nodded.

"I won't let you go alone!" she seethed.

He gave her a frown. "Then grab some clothes, girl. Get moving."

The serving girl muttered under her breath and nodded, standing and folding her arms. "All right. But at least tell us where."

"Landmoor," Jaerod said, staring back across the tavern at something. A small smile flickered on his mouth.

Across the ramshackle tavern, the knight from Owen Draw slowly bound a wound he had earned in the fight with the Kiran Thall. He was watching them.

XVI

Thealos and his companions huddled around a small fire in a grove of elm near the Valairus shore. It was well after midnight. Fog swirled around the sheltering trees, chilling their cheeks with salty wetness. The fire snapped, its tiny flames whipped by the bone-cold gusts from the sea. Thealos pulled the new cloak tighter around his throat, keeping the hood from blowing off.

Flent Shago leaned against a stump of driftwood, munching on a handful of chickpeas. The cold didn't appear to be bothering him at all. He had a big travel sack next to him in the sand and grass, and a small round cask propped up his arm. He'd changed the bloody tatters for a fresh shirt and pants, a huge leather belt and buckle, and some sturdy walking boots. On his hip, he carried the double-bladed axe. He had boasted to Thealos earlier that he'd won it in a game of Bones from a Sheven-Ingen sailor. Ticastasy nestled close to the Drugaen, sharing his warmth. Thealos barely recognized her. Gone were the cheap tinkling bracelets and frilly green skirt he had seen her in earlier. She wore traveling clothes – sturdy brown pants with boots and a light loose cotton-twined shirt. A thick cloak with a wide hood draped along her back, and her dark hair was tied back with a colorful violet band. He noticed a thin knife in her belt. She shivered as the wind battered them again and stared into the fire, lost in her thoughts.

Thealos looked across the fire at Jaerod. The Sleepwalker crouched before the logs, prodding them with a stick as if to coax more warmth from them. The crash of the ocean waves on the shore was followed by a steady hiss as the tide retreated. The sound was comforting and brought back memories of his visits to Jan Lee with Correl.

"How many times have you been out to sea?" Jaerod asked Thealos over the dying firelight.

Thealos shook his head and folded his arms, shivering. "I was just thinking of that. I've never been to the East Kingdoms, but I plan to someday. Jan-Lee is pretty...and warmer. This fog is cold enough to freeze wine."

Jaerod smiled. "Oh, this is mild. Try crossing the Ravenstone during a blizzard."

"Cold is cold, Sleepwalker," Flent muttered sleepily, patting Ticastasy's arm with his meaty hand. She snuggled closer to him. "I was born in the Ravenstone but you get used to it, I guess." He wiped his nose on his sleeve. "This doesn't bother me much. But I'm never going back to those mountains."

"Why not?" Thealos asked. "Isn't that your homeland?"

"Nope. Sol is. During all those banned wars with the banned Krag in the Ravenstone, my parents died of tide fever. I wanted to fight, but they said I was too young, so they sent me to an orphanage in Astillon. I hardly remember what it was like any more. But I do remember it was cold."

"Astillon is pretty country though," Thealos said. "I like the highlands. Spruce and red-pine groves and fields of mustard clover."

Flent shrugged, not impressed. "You're talking about the scenery. It's not easy being the only Drugaen at an orphanage. Too young to fight in the wars, they said. Hah! Had plenty of fights at the orphanage. Nobody left to look after me." He gave Thealos a low smile. "Quite a few of your people there. The outcast ones – the Kilshae. Some of 'em, anyway. No one ever came back for me. You know, to bring me back to the Drugaen Nation." He chuckled mirthlessly. "So when I was old enough, I left and went as far from the mountains as I could walk. I love the sea." He smiled at the hiss of foam receding off the shores. "Ahhh, that's music."

"I can't believe we've known each other that long, Flent," Ticastasy smiled, jostling his leg. "What, eight years ago already? You were just a small lad back then. Look at you now. Too much Spider ale, and you've got scabby knuckles from all the fighting you do."

Flent chuckled. "And who are you calling skinny, girl? You were just a gangly little thing yourself, fawning over every sea captain coming into port. Never the first mates, either. She liked the captains best." He gave Thealos a wry smile, seeing the look on his face. Thealos had a difficult time reconciling the pretty serving girl's affection for Flent. "She's my sister, Thealos. We're kindred, no matter what anyone says. When Roye put me to work in the Foxtale, I started keeping my eye on her. Anyone got too close, and..."

"You left them bleeding out their nose on the back porch," the girl finished for him. "You'd think he was half-hen, half-rooster. Strutting like any freeborn Drugaen, yet he's as motherly as don Rion's queen. I'm surprised I've met anyone these last few years." She nudged him playfully in the ribs.

"Hush," Flent chided. He flushed with pride though. "Just kept the bad ones away, that's all."

"And how many bad ones were there?" Jaerod asked.

"Most of them," he shot back with a grin. Gazing over the fire at Jaerod, Flent looked him dead in the eye. "So we're going to Landmoor, Sleepwalker. 'Preciate you looking out for us. I just can't help thinking – wouldn't we run into more Kiran Thall down there than we would further north?"

"You're not the fool you pretend to be," the Sleepwalker replied with a wry smile. "I'm sorry for the little deception, but it was very likely that anything we said was overheard." Before the serving girl could object, he added, "Thealos and I are going to Landmoor. But we're stopping in Castun first. It's a little village on the north border of the Shadows Wood. I know the innkeeper at the Catpaw Inn, and I'm sure he'll have work for you until things settle down in Sol." He scattered some of the ashes with the stick. The earth was a mixture of dirt and sand. "When Thealos and I finish our business in Landmoor, you can go where you like." His voice trailed off thoughtfully, and then he looked at Thealos. "I learned some things in Sol tonight. Disturbing news. Things are happening much faster than I thought they would. I must leave you. Tonight."

"What?" Thealos sat forward with a start. He was aware of Flent and Ticastasy staring at them in confusion.

"If I leave now, I can be in Castun tomorrow. You three would only slow me down." His gray eyes glittered. "I need to make some arrangements before we head down to Landmoor. Before it's too late."

"Too late for what?" The thought of Jaerod abandoning him struck fear and anger inside him. He wanted to ask more, but he didn't dare voice his concerns. He had no idea where Castun was, or Landmoor for that matter. Jaerod had only asked him to follow, not to find his own way there.

The Sleepwalker snapped the stick in half and tossed it into the fire. He looked at all three of them. Flent and Ticastasy stared back. "There is danger on the road ahead as well as behind us. The Bandit Rebellion is massing an army outside of Landmoor. They plan to siege the fortress and provoke a war with Dos-Aralon." He looked at Thealos. "And possibly Avisahn too. We need to get into the city before it falls."

"And when might that happen?" Thealos asked.

Jaerod shook his head. "There is too much to explain tonight, and I don't have time. There are also too many factors that can affect the answer. When I left the Shoreland, the army was still gathering slowly. But I've heard otherwise tonight. I promise I will tell you the rest of it in Castun. Let me just say that if the Bandit army takes the city before we get there, a good many will die from an unknown sickness. This isn't a plague – it's something even worse. There are forces at work here you do not understand." He rose, his black cloak whipping in the harsh wind. "I must go on alone, Thealos."

"Why can't I go with you?" he demanded in a low voice.

"I can get there much faster alone," Jaerod replied. "You need to hurry. The sooner you can get to Castun, the better for us all."

"Can I talk to you?" Thealos pressed, motioning him away from the fire. He was furious, but held his tongue in front of the others.

Jaerod relented. Together, they left Flent and Ticastasy at the fire's edge and walked down the crunch of sand and stone towards the flat wash of the shore. The blue moon of Eroth was hidden beneath the shroud of Shoreland fog. They walked until the fire was just a tiny prick of light, though still not very far away.

Thealos dug his hands beneath his arms. "You didn't tell me you were going to abandon me with them," he seethed. "What am I? A wet-nurse? I don't understand why we're bringing them in the first place."

Jaerod gave Thealos a stern look. "Because you used the Everoot on the Drugaen, Thealos."

"He was dying!"

"I'm not faulting you for your compassion. But there are consequences with magic. You made a decision without knowing the effects." He sighed, giving Thealos another pointed look. "Using magic like this leaves an impression – a footprint, if you will. Just as there are trackers who can follow a deer through the scrub, there are those who can sniff out the trail of magic. We must bring them to protect you, Thealos. I spoke of powers at work in this valley. These people would kill you if they knew about you."

Thealos swallowed, his anger turning into water.

"The Wolfsmen were waiting for us, which means that the Shae also consider you a big threat. I've stayed with you this long to be sure they didn't follow us right away. We bought a little time slipping out of Sol tonight. The Wolfsmen will have to report the incident to Avisahn and wait for a reply before they will follow us. Speed is essential." He pointed to the firelight. "They will need you to guide them to Castun, Thealos. You're a far better woodsman than either of them."

"But I've never been to Castun," he answered, shaken.

"You'd never fought the Kiran Thall either. But now you have. I have confidence in you, Thealos. But I have no other choice. I need to see the progress of the army to know how much time we have left. If we have any at all."

"And the Crimson Wolfsmen?" Thealos asked. "I can't face one on my own, let alone a quaere if another is sent to track me. Jaerod, I think they can sense where I am through the sword. It is Wolfsman magic. Maybe that is how they found me."

"They can sense the Silvan magic as easily as you can – but only when they are near. We have a strong lead. If you hurry, you'll reach Castun before they find the trail and start after. I'll be with you if they catch us again."

"You don't understand, Jaerod," Thealos said, shaking his head. "In Sol, I could see the other Wolfsmen through the Silvan magic in the sword. It bonded us together...like brothers. What if they don't need to track me? What if they can see me right now?"

"One of the Wolfsmen was killed then."

"Yes." He paused. "How did you know that?"

The Sleepwalker nodded with understanding. "Because the blade uses both magics – Life and Earth magic. You felt the sword change when the Wolfsman died, didn't you? Life magic is ancient magic, Thealos. Very few of the Shae still know how to use it or invoke it. But when your people came to this world, they taught the Druids about the Earth magic and they taught a few about the Life magic. Only a few. Life magic is powerful, but it has a greater chance of being used in Forbidden ways." Thealos' eyes widened, but Jaerod soothed him. "The blade you have was forged with Silvan magic – meaning it uses its magic appropriately. You cannot kill another Shae with that weapon. The blade would reject and burn you if you tried. Now there is something about the Crimson Wolfsmen order that uses Life magic as well. When one Wolfsman dies, his Life magic is spent and given to strengthen his brothers. Not even Everoot could bring him back. You may never feel that bonding again. It happened because of who Jade Shayler was, not who you are. The blade channels it."

Thealos nodded. "How do you know so much about this?"

"I've told you that already." Smiling, the Sleepwalker put his hand on Thealos' shoulder. "I am a Sleepwalker. I've been to the Druid vaults of Parath-Anatos. Even to the Shae archives in Avisahn...and Landmoor. That's why I never make it a practice to kill a Crimson Wolfsman. The last man left of a quaere is strong and quick enough to kill even a Sleepwalker. Remember that."

"So you don't think the Wolfsman can follow me through the bonding?"

"If they could, you would share the connection. You would be able to see them as well. Do you?"

"I hadn't thought of that. Oh for Hate's sake – I'm going to have to start learning to trust you," he added with a reluctant smile. "I suppose you wouldn't abandon us deliberately, and it would be much harder to free me from Nordain's cell if you are wrong, and I won't be much help to anyone locked up." He saw Jaerod's smile and sighed. "Now how do I find Castun? We're on the shores of the Valairus and the Shadows Wood is west..."

"Follow the coastline, but keep near the trees. You won't mistake the Shadows Wood. It's too big to wander by, even with all the cover in the valley floor. Now be careful. The Kiran Thall have increased their patrols in preparation for the invasion. Don't let them find you. But they are looking north for trouble, not east. When you reach the forest, follow the north border until you reach the Iron Point Road. Castun is right there." He gave Thealos a warm smile. "I'll meet you at the Catpaw in a day or two. The owner will be watching for you."

"Do you have any more Everoot?" Thealos asked. "We might need it."

"You can hold it for now," Jaerod answered, reaching into his belt for the wet bundle. "Just remember to keep it wet with fresh water. Every day."

"I will. Be safe, Jaerod."

The Sleepwalker looked at him and nodded before turning and vanishing into the thick mist. Thealos stared after him, trying to pick him out of the haze and gloom. Clutching the moist bag, he stuffed it in his vest and started back towards the camp.

* * *

For hours, the wind surged across the slate-gray sea in the black of night, and shortly before dawn, the sky began to brighten – a little. Thealos awoke to a light pattering of rain from the leaden skies. He had only dozed lightly during the night, huddled beneath a cloak and blanket for warmth. Rising, he shook out his things and felt the stinging slap of brine on his hands and neck. The fog was inland now, reaching far into the valleys and troughs. He was anxious to reach the shelter of the forest, even one with as dark a reputation as the moors of the Shadows Wood.

"A bright and cheery morning has greeted us," Thealos drawled, jostling the sturdy Drugaen until he stirred. He chafed his hands to dull the sting of the cold. Flent awoke with a yawn and a belch. Thealos gently rocked the serving girl's shoulder and she awoke, her dark hair windblown and straying from its colorful tether.

"It's cold," she murmured, staring at the billowing mist.

"We don't have time for a fire, I'm afraid," he apologized. Thealos opened his travel sack and withdrew some provisions to share. "Not as good as the roast goose last night, but maybe we can convince Flent to share some of his chickpeas." They ate the meal in silence, chewing on the hard biscuits and salt pork without any relish. Flent washed his down with a cup of ale. As the Drugaen and the serving girl packed up their things, Thealos used sapple-dust on the ashes and buried them in the sand with a trowel. Dusting his hands, he slung his pack over his shoulder and strung his bow. He tested its pull and nodded, satisfied.

"It's a long walk," Thealos said, "But if we make good time, you'll soon enjoy a feathered mattress and cushions in Castun. We should reach the Shadows Wood before nightfall and Castun the next day if we hurry."

"Good enough, my lord," Ticastasy said, brushing her arms for warmth. "Let's walk."

In the dim dawn light, Thealos led them westward along the shoreline, following the trail of the ocean. Thealos walked slowly enough to keep from being separated from them. The fog shied away completely around noon. Colors lit the valley in shades of green and umber with dazzling fields of yellow wildflowers and blue snap-weeds. Thealos carried the bow on his shoulder, inhaling the fresh scents. He didn't let on that he'd never been here before, trusting in Jaerod's directions and the rumored size of the Shadows Wood.

After stopping for a meal at midday, they continued over a wide range of inland hills. Thealos' legs strained with the climb, but it felt good. Flent had the most trouble keeping up. His thick Drugaen legs were used to the flat streets of Sol. Beyond the third range of hills, a dense black-green forest swallowed up the prairie in front of them. The Shadows Wood. The only thing higher was the jagged outline of the Kingshadow Mountains behind it on the other side of the valley. Even from the top of the hill, they couldn't see the other end of the wood.

"And I thought the woods of Avisahn were big," Flent muttered, brushing his hands together as he panted. "We've bloody got to cross that?"

Thealos smirked and nodded. "It's broad and ugly, Flent. But it is much smaller than the forests of my homeland." The forests of Avisahn stretched the entire length of the Ravenstone Mountains. He felt a sudden pang of loss, remembering it. The Shadows Wood was probably half its size or less. Next to the bleached brown grass of the prairies and the green oak leaves, the dark tangled vine maple and cedar were ominous. Landmoor was somewhere on the southern edge of the forest, too far to see. He felt a small smile twitch on his mouth and wished he'd been able to send a courier to Nordain at that moment. *So sorry I couldn't respond to your summons yet, but the weather has been good and the scenery wonderful. The food isn't as choice as the baking guilds, but then…you already knew that.*

Pressing ahead, they reached the forest before sunset. In the Inland valley before the forest, Thealos had found drying mounds of horse droppings and long swaths of trampled grass. The trail led away from the forest. Kiran Thall horsemen, probably. Skirting the path, they came at a quick pace until they reached the tangled branches of cedar.

Trees loomed around them, punctuated by the angry clicking of beetles and flutter of ravens. Thealos let his heavy travel pack down next to a sapling. He gently crouched and touched the dry stabbing pine needles that carpeted the ground. There was a faint musty smell – the distant murmur of Forbidden magic. He had no idea how far away the sense was coming from, but it did not feel imminent. The forest was not friendly, and he could feel a certain hardness in the stiff crooked branches and the dead needles lying like a rug near the base of the trees. The forest was polluted. He wasn't sure how, but there was something dark afoot. It felt distant, vague.

"Are we going to camp here?" Flent panted. His boots crunched the twigs and needles.

Ticastasy leaned back against a tree. "I'm exhausted. I'm used to walking, but in circles around tables. You must be used to this, young lord."

Thealos brushed the scrub away and pressed his fingers against the dirt. Closing his eyes, he tried to sink into the Earth magic, to be one with it. The feeling was always stronger in the woodlands than in the cities. It nagged at him, familiar yet different. Breathing slowly, he tried to sift through his feelings, but they were too tangled, too conflicting. He tried to feel the presence of the Everoot, but something overshadowed it. Something Forbidden.

"Is he asleep?" she asked.

"Maybe he's praying," Flent muttered out of the corner of his mouth.

Thealos opened his eyes and glanced back at them. He rose and brushed his hands together. "A little further. I'm not sure I like the feeling of this place."

"Further?" Flent asked, dropping his sack. "We've been marching...all banned day! My feet have earned a few blisters and I've got rocks in my boots the size of walnuts."

Thealos glanced over at the serving girl. "Are you tired too?"

"I'm exhausted," she said, folding her arms. "I thought that fourth hill was going to kill me."

Thealos wiped his mouth and sighed. "We really should go on, but I guess we can stop here. This whole forest feels wrong. Now, do either of you know how to build a fire without giving off a lot of smoke?" They looked at him blankly. "Set a snare for a rabbit?"

The serving girl cocked her head. "We may be from the city, my lord. But we're not fools. Flent, learn how to light the fire. I'd like to learn how to build a snare."

* * *

A ring of stones crowned the small cooking fire, and Thealos adjusted one with the toe of his boot. Thin sheets of smoke wafted up through the trees, obscuring the scattered specks of winking stars. He adjusted the rolled up blanket behind his head and rested his hands on his chest. Flent unstopped his little cask and poured himself a mug of Spider Ale. He grinned and started savoring the sips. It was his third, and from the sloshing sound, the cask was nearly empty. The serving girl sat next to the Drugaen, brushing out her tangled hair with a stiff-bristled brush. Thealos watched her, feeling a little jealous of their companionship. He felt like an outsider.

"I'll never get these pants clean," she murmured to Flent, brushing the dust off. "And I only brought a quick change of clothes with me. I hope they have a decent tailor in Castun."

"And a bath," Flent added. "You smell like a sailor, girl."

She butted him in the ribs and gave him a scolding look. Thealos grinned wolfishly. "Don't tease her, Flent. I've been gagging since you took off your boots."

Ticastasy let out a burst of laughter. It made her eyes crinkle pleasantly as she smiled. He gave Flent a wink to apologize, but the Drugaen took the drubbing good-naturedly.

"Castun is a trading post," Thealos explained, "But even if they have good wool from the Clothweaver Guild, it'll still cost four times more than it's worth. Here," he said, sitting up and rummaging through his travel pack. Down in the bottom, he wrestled out the bundle wrapped in oilskin that Tomn the cook had bought in Sol. "This doesn't quite fit me anymore," he teased, untying the leather thongs and reveal-ing the rich fabric. He hadn't looked at it since he'd escaped from Tannon's Band. As he lifted the folds, he stared down at the fine wool gown, a rich shade of ochre with a blue and violet trim around the bodice.

"Sweet Achrolese, it's beautiful!" Ticastasy said with delight. She crossed around the fire and sat next to him, staring at it in amazement. "This came from the Green Weaver in Sol, didn't it? How much did it cost?"

"Twenty pieces, if I remember right," Thealos replied dryly. "It's yours."

"I can't take this," she replied, shaking her head. "It's too beautiful. A barter's daughter might wear it, but not a serv-ing girl."

"What am I going to do with it?"

She looked at him in disbelief. "Well, you don't really have the right coloring for it. But why did you get it? Did you mean it for someone? Was it a gift for the Princess of Avisahn?"

Thealos shook his head. "No, Shae women prefer silk or damask. It's a good quality gown though, look at the stitch-markings. Three, see that?" He showed her the seam and the stitch. "It's worth at least thirty in Dos-Aralon. If you ever wanted to sell it."

Ticastasy eyed him warily. "And you didn't mean this for someone, then?"

He shook his head. "I think it would suit you well."

She folded the fabric reverently and tied it up in the oilskin again. When she finished, she scooted up closer to him. Flent's head was starting to droop down on his chest. The beginnings of a very loud snore were starting to rumble in his throat. She seemed a little more comfortable sitting near him, and he could see his own glowing eyes reflected in hers. Her eyes were an interesting color in the firelight. Cinnamon. He liked that. Rare as a brown-eyed Shae...

"Who are you?" she asked, picking at the scrubs of pine needles.

"What do you mean?"

She nodded. "Back in the Foxtale, you said you were Thealos. Don't the Shae lords have family names too?"

He understood now. "Quickfellow," he answered, watching her eyes. Did she know anything about the noble Silvan houses? Would she know that Silverborne or Silvershire or any dozen other names meant royalty in Avisahn? Not Quickfellow – never Quickfellow. He wanted to tell her he was only the son of a barter. He should tell her.

"Quickfellow," she said. "I like that better." She gave him a teasing look. "Thealos is so heady. Doesn't come off the tongue very well. But Quickfellow has a nice sound. Would it offend you if I called you that? I just can't call someone 'my lord,' not if they can tease Flent about the smell of his socks."

He smiled. "It wouldn't offend me. And what should I call you then? Ticastasy is a mouthful as well."

"Well, Flent calls my 'Stasy. He's the only one who can get away with it." She winked at Thealos. "Up until now. You can call me that too if you want."

"It has a nice sound," he said, smiling. She sat close to him, making him a little uncomfortable. He felt blood rising to his face. Their hands were almost touching. Why had he noticed that? She wasn't Laisha Silverborne by any stretch of Silvan standards. Brown hair and brown eyes, about as human as she could get. Her skin was rich-colored, not pale like the Shae. Her cinnamon eyes would have been unfashionable in his homeland, but they looked well on her.

"You were wearing a pendant last night. Can I see it?"

"Your glowing eyes see too much, Quickfellow." She tugged at her collar and pulled up the gold chain and sparrow, cupping the pendant in her hand for him to see. It glittered in the firelight.

"Pretty. Who gave it to you?"

"Someone I thought was very special to me." She pursed her lips. "He was supposed to see me last week, but never came to port. I've thought about taking it to a goldsmith to melt down and turned into earrings instead." She shrugged and huffed. "Maybe I'm not as important to him after all."

"He's a fool then."

"You think so?" she replied. She sidled up a little closer. Her fingers grazed his. She scooped the pendant down her shirt again and shook her head. "You surprise me, Quickfellow. Most of the Shae I've met aren't nearly as well-mannered. I appreciate your kindness in looking after us."

The blade of Jade-Shayler flared awake at his hip. Tingles of Silvan magic sent a warning thrust of heat through his body. Then he smelled it, seeping into the small camp, coiling in the air like smoke. Not from their campfire. The smell was strong. Forbidden magic. He knew it instinctively.

"Something is wrong," he warned, putting his hand on her shoulder as he rolled into a defensive crouch. He slid the blade from his belt and felt it lick at his hand hungrily. He began to draw its magic inside him, preparing himself.

"What is it?" she whispered, staying perfectly still.

"I don't know," he replied in a low voice, trying to get a sense of how close the danger was. He could feel it, thick and alive. And coming closer. He turned around and scanned the treeline. Not there.

Looking over the serving girl's shoulder, Thealos saw a dark-armored Drugaen just outside the full light of the campfire.

XVII

There was no battle cry or hiss of warning, just ice-white eyes. A Drugaen warrior stood in the shadows, clenching a tapered short sword marked with strange runes. The slender blade glinted in the firelight, and the chill of Forbidden magic swept over the grove. His eyebrows twitched with fury and an unmistakable expression of hate contorted his mouth. He came at Flent and raised the weapon up to kill.

Thealos sprang forward. He whipped his Silvan blade around, the magic sending shocks of fire up his arm. The armored warrior was different than any Thealos had seen, but he had heard similar descriptions coming from frightened barters out of the Ravenstone. The warrior had pale eyes, a soot-colored beard, and slender eyebrows. His armor was the highest quality steel, sculpted with designs of twisting vines and skulls. A huge buckle made of white gold was emblazoned with an upside-down oak leaf.

The weapons sparked and jolted as they clashed, arcing with power and magic. Forbidden met Silvan. Thealos felt his arm go numb with the shock of power, and the stench of the offending magic burned in his nose. The Drugaen reeked of it.

With reflexes of a trained warrior, the dark Drugaen stepped in and backhanded Thealos with a gauntleted fist. The short sword whipped around and would have sliced him open from navel to throat, but the magic of the Silvan weapon saved him again. Flickering memories from a Crimson Wolfsman's life swarmed in Thealos' mind. The Drugaen hammered on him ruthlessly, the white eyes deadly and hateful. Thealos held him off, dazed by the quickness and ferocity of the attack. The fleeting images of the dead Wolfsman overpowered what he knew about sword-fighting, but it was just enough to parry the blows. Even with the magic, he was outmatched – and he knew it. Backing away, he nearly stumbled in the wooded glen. He saw Flent rise up behind his attacker.

The Sheven-Ingen axe bit into the Drugaen's armor from behind. Thealos ducked to the side, trying to save his own life. The Drugaen shrugged off Flent's blow and wheeled around to face him. He snorted, grinning with loathing and hate, and lunged forward with the dark magic. The short sword spit sparks as it slashed and glanced off the axe. Flent held his ground, using the flat of the blade to parry the attacker's strokes. He swept at the armored foe's neck twice but missed as his opponent ducked the blow and countered.

Thealos had a clear shot at the warrior's back. He saw that Flent's axe had split the armor open, leaving a black mesh of tangled mail. The armored Drugaen seemed to sense Thealos' approach and whirled on him, keeping both men back. Thealos swore under his breath. A Krag Drugaen from the deep Ravenstone. They were the enemies of the Shae and the Drugaen Nation. What in Vannier's name was he doing this far south? They never left the mountains – at least, not that he'd heard of.

The Krag feinted with a sword thrust and then kicked Thealos in the stomach. The air rushed out of Thealos' lungs with the force of the steel-shod boot. He couldn't breathe. The Krag slashed his wrist and the Wolfsman blade thumped to the ground, the magic abandoning him as soon as it left his touch. Pain and nausea smothered him and he crumpled, grabbing frantically for his weapon.

"You white-eyed craven...!" Flent roared, tackling the Krag from behind. The two rolled in the carpet of dead needles, thrashing and fighting. Flent was young and strong, but the armored Krag was a trained warrior. He flipped the stocky Flent over his shoulder and dropped heavily on the ground.

Thealos grabbed his blade with his left hand, felt the Silvan magic rush to fill the void it had left. He struggled against the surge of power, tried to tame it and control it, to feed it with his need. The blade burned with blue fire, invoking a rage and hatred Thealos had never felt before. But that was dangerous – he had learned it with Tannon's Band. Giving in to the anger made him careless. The Krag wouldn't be brought down easily. He had to remember that. Thealos's stomach still hurt, but the pain was washing away beneath the waves of surging power.

Thealos wiped his eyes and blinked, then nearly shouted out a warning as he saw Ticastasy sneaking up behind the Krag with her knife.

The Krag slammed Flent's face down into the ground. Then he withdrew, wheeling on the girl. She looked frightened but kept a firm hold on her dagger. Gripping the blood-smeared blade, he stalked her, shifting the weapon from hand to hand. He swiped at her twice, but she managed to dodge it, luring the warrior away from Flent.

"Leave him alone," she warned, her voice trembling.

Thealos staggered forward, clutching his stomach. Blood dripped from his wrist. Abruptly, from beyond the firelight, he heard the clatter and crunch of hooves in the forest. *Sweet Vannier, no! Not the Kiran Thall. Not now.* He gazed off into the dark woods. How much time did he have? Glancing back at Ticastasy, he hesitated. Flent was unconscious, his face a mess of blood and scratches. He would not be able to help. But Thealos had other magic. Magic the Krag didn't have. Reaching into his vest, he withdrew the sack of Everoot and untied it. He snapped off a stub of the plant and chewed it, feeling the rush of relief as it healed him. It was a different feeling this time, adding a rawness that thrilled him. He knew the Krag wouldn't be able to hurt him now, not with the taste of the Everoot in his mouth. He straightened, feeling his energy return. The cut in his wrist vanished, and he switched the blade to his other hand.

Ticastasy shifted her grip on the knife. She watched the Krag as Thealos drew up behind him. She gave him a quick glance and a deft nod.

"You're a little short for her kind," Thealos said, calling the Krag after him. "I haven't finished with you yet, Krag."

The warrior turned and glared at him. He said nothing but started towards Thealos again.

Thealos tightened his grip on the blade. He felt strong and alive. "You don't wish to discuss terms first?" He saw her heft the dagger, ready to throw it. The Krag stalked closer. Thealos nodded back.

Ticastasy threw her dagger at the Drugaen's head.

The Krag reacted instantly, raising his arm to deflect the blow. The dagger struck off the arm bracer, spinning into the trees. In that moment, Thealos attacked him from behind. He felt the power of a Crimson Wolfsman. The tip of Jade-Shayler's blade screeched against metal, slicing through the steel with twisting shrieks of blue magic. The Krag's chest exploded in a spurt of fire and scorched steel. Thealos clamped his arm around the Krag's throat and drove the blade in up to the hilt, feeling the Silvan magic overwhelm the Forbidden, crushing its spark and power. Smoke chafed from the wound and the Krag sunk low, twitching with agony before dropping dead at Thealos' feet.

The horse hooves came at a low ride, snapping through the twigs and fallen branches. Thealos motioned for Ticastasy to get behind him as he prepared to stand against the intruders. He was confident he could take them all now. Firelight glinted off the polished armor as a huge roan lumbered into the camp. A knight, not a Kiran Thall. Ticastasy breathed in quick gulps and sighed with relief.

"It's Sturnin Goff," she said. "Thank the stars. I thought Secrist had found us."

The knight reined in and shed the stirrups, landing with a jangle of spurs and armor. Thealos stared at the Wolfsman blade in his hand. The metal was clean of blood, glimmering a blue shade in the darkness.

From the saddle harness, the knight unslung a heavy double-handed sword. "Where's the Sleepwalker?"

Thealos studied his face. "What do you want?"

"Don't fuss with me, lad," he snapped. "The Krag never travel alone. Kick out the fire. Quickly, just do it!"

Thealos stared at the knight. "Who are...?"

"We don't have time to argue about this, lad. Killing a Krag is a foolhardy thing to do. Now put out the fire. The others will be close behind."

Thealos' confidence in himself guttered out. There were more? He listened, then obeyed, throwing a handful of sapple dust to quickly snuff out the flames. He kicked in the ashes quickly, and closed the stones over the embers. Darkness washed over the camp. The whispers of the forest were haunting. He tried to sense more Forbidden magic, but the Krag's weapon gave off such a stench he could not smell past it.

"Flent? Can you hear me?" Ticastasy knelt by her friend.

"Yeah," he muttered angrily, sitting up. He mopped the blood on his face with his sleeve. "Banned Krag. As ugly as I'd heard they were. Never thought I'd get a chance to fight one."

"Here, take some of this," Thealos said, breaking off another stub of Everoot. "Chew it quickly. It will take away the pain." It was dark now, blacker than ink.

The knight crunched through the pine needles. "So the Sleepwalker abandoned you out here, did he?"

"We weren't abandoned. The Krag stumbled onto our camp. The fire was still pretty bright, so it wasn't that difficult to see us. Foolish to light one in the first place."

"You know what they say about a Drugaen's eyesight. They'd have seen you in the dark just as well. There will be at least five or so more." The knight took the charger's reins and patted its neck. It grunted and snorted, stamping its hoof. "A Sleepwalker would have avoided the whole company." He swore under his breath. "Never had to fight off more than three before." He looked over at Flent. "But you're a sturdy lad, and the Shae has a decent weapon. That might count for something."

"Why did it want to kill Flent?" Ticastasy asked. "He...he just came into the firelight and attacked us."

"The Krag hate other Drugaen," Thealos said. "They've been fighting in the Ravenstone for years. I thought they were just a political faction trying to take over the government. I had no idea they'd be involved in something this far south." He watched Flent approach the body of the Krag warrior. The tapered short sword lay nearby.

"Don't touch it," Thealos warned. "It's Forbidden magic." He walked over and crouched near it, feeling his stomach revolt. "I don't see any ornamentation. They must have used blood in the tempering." He shook his head with disgust. "I can't just leave it here."

"You can do all the rites you want later," the knight said. "They'll kill you and the Drugaen lad without so much as a whisper."

"Why?" Ticastasy asked, her voice fearful.

"We supported the Drugaen Nation at first," Thealos replied, "But the fighting is fiercest deep down in the mountains. That's not our best ground. The Drugaen resent us now for not helping them drive the Krag out, and the Krag hate us for selling weapons and armor to their enemies." He glanced over at the knight. "I wasn't aware that Owen Draw even knew about the Krag."

"There are caves in the Kingshadow too, and they openly support the Bandit Rebellion. That makes them our enemies too, doesn't it?" Using his boot, he kicked the Krag over on its back. "Shadowoak," he muttered. "Their best." The white gold symbol on its buckle glimmered. "But you're right, Shae. They shouldn't be this far south. Unless Ballinaire is drawing in all his forces."

Thealos stared at the knight in the darkness, his vision good enough to see the lines on his face. He remembered the man from the Foxtale Inn in Sol, and how he had challenged Secrist and the company of Kiran Thall. Obviously, the knight had been tracking them across the coast. The oppressive stink of Forbidden magic wafted in the air again, coming from the woods. Like cinders and spoiled meat. "You're right. More are coming." Thealos stared off into the dark folds of the forest. The smell of Forbidden magic wavered in the air like smoke, difficult to tell which direction it came from. He did not want to leave the body and the weapon untended, but he did not have time to dispose of them both properly. "We'd better leave."

"Oh, it's too late for that," the knight answered, yanking the tether and dragging the horse towards Ticastasy. "Mount up, girl. We'll hold them here. Better be away from here in case we can't."

"What?" she demanded.

"No time to argue with you," he said, hoisting her by the waist onto the saddle. "The Shadowoak fight in sixes. There are five more coming. Maybe more. Got to find out why they are down here and you'll only get in the way."

"Get in the way?" she seethed. "You don't have to..."

"Wait a minute. If we hurry..." Thealos interrupted. He didn't like the way the knight had charged in and started ordering them around. "We might be able to gain ground. They're short and can't match our stride."

"Is this the first Krag you've faced, Shae?" the knight asked, pointing at the dead one.

Thealos swallowed and met his stare. "Yes."

The knight shook his head and muttered impatiently. "You've got to kill all six," he warned. "You leave one alive, and they'll hunt you down to the last man with as many Krag as it takes. They drink revenge like Spider Ale. We've killed one – their point scout. Even if we tried to run, they would catch us before the night is through. If we have to fight, I'd rather it be on our terms. Not theirs."

"I'm ready to kill a few," Flent said, patting his hand with the axe. He spat on the ground.

"Good," the knight approved. "Now get your bow out, Shae. I can't handle five on my own. You've got to bring a few down. Have any bodkins?"

"A quiver full," Thealos replied, sheathing his blade in his belt. "Are you sure we can't outrun them?"

"Can you fly? Only have one horse."

"Why are you even here?"

"Because of you, Shae. You know something about what's going on in the Shoreland. You and the Sleepwalker. Now get going, girl! I didn't follow you here to get killed by

Shadowoak."

Thealos looked up at Ticastasy and gripped her hand. "Ride to Castun," he told her.

"But..."

"For the love of Shenalle, just do it!" He squeezed her hand. "Find Jaerod. We may need him."

* * *

The Shadows Wood was aptly named, Thealos thought as he hunched forward in the dry carpet of needles and scrub. He pulled his shooting glove on snug and then stuck four arrows in the ground nearby within easy reach. He readied a single bodkin arrow in the thick linen string of his bow. A bodkin could go through plate armor more easily than broad heads. Just like hunting an elk, he tried to remind himself. But his stomach did not accept the lie so easily. Flent knelt next to him, staring into the darkness and resting his arms on the Sheven-Ingen axe. The wind rustled through the treetops, sending a few pinecones crashing down. The knight from Owen Draw propped himself behind a thick twisted cedar.

"There they are," Flent whispered, peering into the blackness. Thealos didn't see anything yet, but he followed the Drugaen's stubby finger. He'd always heard that nothing could beat a Drugaen's eyes in the dark.

Thealos hunkered down low, smelling the hidden reek of Forbidden magic drift closer. He felt the presence of the Krag moments later as they emerged from the depths of the undergrowth. There was another scent in the air, something more familiar. Straining against the night, he tried to see what it was.

"Three...four....there – there's the fifth. Looks like he's dragging a prisoner." Flent pitched his voice as mild as a whisper. "Yeah, they're pulling him along by the wrists. Thin fellow." He cocked his head. "Heading straight to our camp. What do you want to do?"

"Ambush from the flanks," the knight said softly. "They can probably see as well as you can. Aim well, Shae. You've got to take a few down before they reach us."

Thealos wasn't listening. He saw them now, weaving through the black trees in small number, marching with a determined pace. "They have a Shae prisoner," he murmured.

"How can you tell?" Flent asked, squinting. "He's got a hood on..."

"Trust me," Thealos answered. He nodded to the knight. "I have an idea."

"Make it quick."

"Flent, duck low and hurry over there. When I bring down the first two, yell in challenge so they can see you." He looked up at the knight. "When they charge him, strike from the trees. I'll slip around and free the Shae before they can kill him."

The knight thought a moment and nodded. "You think like a battle commander. Get moving, Flent. Hurry now, go!"

Flent scurried off, keeping low in the brush. Thealos gathered his arrows and veered into the trees, stepwalking silently and carefully to avoid the needles and dried twigs. He kept low and dodged from tree to tree. Taking cover behind a gnarled cedar choked with moss, he peered around, watching the Krag Drugaen warriors approach the remains of their camp. He set the arrows in the dirt in front of him. Taking a deep breath, he raised the hunting bow, sighting the leader.

Glancing to the side, Thealos made sure the knight and Flent were in place. He wiped the sweat from his forehead and watched the leader again. He repeated the lie again in his mind, trying to quell the nervousness and fear inside him. Many times, he had brought down deer and even elk at a distance. The Krag were even closer. He would not miss. The memory of Tannon's band haunted him, and he bit it back, squelching it. How many arrows would he get in before they scattered and sought cover. Three? Maybe four? They marched single file, a row of armored warriors with the peculiar white gold oak-leaf buckle. Trailing with the last man. the slender Shae walked head down, ducking beneath the low-hanging boughs and branches. He was the smallest man

Thealos had ever seen, almost gangly. He wore a dark cloak and long skirting robes. Or maybe it was a woman?

Raising the bow, he let his vision fade – feeling the connection between himself and the lead Drugaen. He pulled the arrow back to his ear. The space between tied them together, a single point of time and distance. He forgot his fear. The arrow hummed, finding its target with a thud and shock. The Drugaen went down, clutching a shattered knee. *Ban it, too low!*

Before his second arrow took flight, four tapered short swords glowed in the darkness as the Krag reacted to the attack. Thealos let another arrow fly and struck the second in the chest. He heard the armor ping, and wasn't sure if the sharp head had penetrated the steel or not.

Flent roared the rallying cry of the Drugaen Nation, brandishing the Sheven-Ingen axe. "For Faradin and Eroth!"

The trailing Krag slammed the hilt of his short sword against the captive Shae, dropping him like a stone and probably killing him. Thealos seethed a curse, unable to fix the man quickly enough. The Krag scattered four different directions, but they charged Flent in a swarm.

Flent let out a throaty challenge. "Come as one or take your turns! I've got a whooping for each of you."

Thealos fixed another arrow and let it loose, catching the nearest Krag in the arm. The arrow transfixed his arm, but it didn't slow the attacker. Grabbing another, he let it fly. The Krag went down, the shaft buried in his neck. Only three left. From the huge cedar tree, the knight from Owen Draw swung around, knocking another flat with his double-handed sword. With no room to press the advantage with his bow, Thealos sprinted around the side, hurrying to the fallen Shae.

When he reached the still body, Thealos felt for a pulse while tugging the bag of Everoot loose from his tunic pocket. Blood trickled from the wounded Shae's pale forehead, matting the silver hair with a dark stain. The Shae's heartbeat was a dull throb, growing slower and slower. Cursing himself for not being quicker, Thealos removed a handful of Everoot and pressed it against the bleeding scalp. Silvan magic shot through him, exploding in his ears like the purest strains of music. He looked over his shoulder, watching as Flent and the knight fought off the remaining two Krag. Both fought back to back, hammering at the wicked glint of the short swords.

The Shae at Thealos' feet stiffened, blue eyes wide with shock. He was handsome with long, silverish hair, but so thin he was almost gaunt. Had the Krag starved him? The Shae looked up at Thealos in amazement and then raised his hand, as if he were going to choke him. Thealos recoiled when the rush of Earth magic swept from the Shae's hand. It came out as a streak of blue light and swept past him, catching the Krag with the shattered knee as he struggled up behind Thealos to kill him. The light hammered into the white-gold marking, throwing the Krag like a windblown leaf into a huge pine. He impacted violently against the bark, and when he collapsed to the earth, his armor was nothing but a smoking black char of twisted metal and gaping ash. The blue light sizzled, spreading across the armor, consuming it whole.

A Shae Warder!

Thealos stared at him in awe. The bloody gash in his head was gone, folded over and healed. On his feet quickly, spreading his robes, the Shae stepped around Thealos and raised both hands. Twin bolts of blue light flashed out again, smashing the other two Krag Drugaen from behind. Both shuddered from the blast and roared with pain and horror as the blue light ate their armor, charring their skin and swallowing them. Then the fire was gone, leaving only smoking gray ashes. The Shae looked down, breathing in heavy gulps. He nearly collapsed in a faint as if he'd run ten leagues. Using the magic had exhausted him.

"Thank you," the stranger whispered to Thealos in Silvan. *"Thank you for saving me."*

"I know you're a Warder, but who are you?" Thealos demanded, steadying the man.

The Shae clutched his head, shaking it. *"My name is..."* He winced and shuddered. *"My name is...I am..."* His face contorted with anger and desperation. *"I am the Warder*

Shae of Jenterhome. My name is…" He looked at Thealos in a panic. *"By Shenalle, why can't I remember it?"*

XVIII

They gathered the remains of the Krag and their weapons into a heap, and the nameless Warder Shae summoned the Earth magic again. He opened his hands and seemed to draw the power into the mound of the dead as he breathed in. Blue fire consumed the remains of the Krag Drugaen, leaving a black scorch mark on the forest floor. The sharp tang of dross stung Thealos' nose as he watched the embers gutter out. Flent snorted and scuffed his boot in the ashes. The Krag Drugaen and their dark magic were no more. The Warder Shae lowered his hands. His eyes glowed in the firelight, speaking of his heritage as much as the pale skin and silver hair.

"Will there be others?" Thealos asked as he began covering the scorched earth with sapple dust and forest debris. The other Shae shook his head.

"There was only this company," he replied. *"The rest returned to the Ravenstone earlier."*

Thealos nodded. He still hadn't determined the stranger's age. He was young, but certainly well into manhood. Ten or twelve Silvan years old perhaps. He glanced at the knight from Owen Draw. "He said that this was the only company of Krag. I wasn't expecting your arrival, master knight, but I wanted to thank you for your warning and your help." Thealos extended his hand. "I am Thealos of Avisahn. If you hadn't warned us, we all would have died tonight."

"No need for thanks, Shae." His grip was iron. "You raised your weapon in a tavern in Sol, don't forget. Consider my debt repaid."

"Flent Shago," the Drugaen introduced himself, cocking his thumbs in his belt. He nodded to the knight before looking at the Shae stranger. "What's his name?" he asked Thealos.

"He doesn't remember."

"Why'd they take him prisoner?"

Thealos asked the question in Silvan. The Shae's eyes were a bright azure and they glittered with fury. *"They were taking me to the Ravenstone to work the mines."* He gritted his teeth at the memory. *"I had planned to escape near Avisahn."*

"I thought you were their prisoner?" Thealos said.

"I let them believe that, rather than wander the valley alone. Had I not found you first, I would have destroyed them near the Trident River. I seek the help of the Shae King."

"Why?"

The Warder Shae looked at the others warily. *"We will speak later, my brother."*

Thealos nodded. Trust was not easy to earn. "They wanted to bring him back to the Krag Nation. He's grateful we found him first." Rubbing his hands together briskly, he looked back at the other Shae, wondering why he didn't appear to understand the king's common. He had looked completely baffled as Sturnin and Flent spoke. His robes were certainly a different style than any Thealos had seen in all his years in the house of a barter.

Flent nodded and sniffed. "Well, he needs a name. Can't go around calling him a stump or a stone as they say. How about Justin." Thealos looked at him curiously. Flent shrugged. "I knew a Shae lad in Astillon. Sickly boy – kind of reminds me of him."

Thealos looked at the frail Shae thoughtfully. *"The Drugaen would call you Justin. Would that offend you?"*

"No," he replied. *"This one is a fool, but harmless. Tell him that I thank him for the new name."*

Thealos smiled. "Looks like you've made a friend, Flent.

Justin will do." Flent beamed and gave the frail Shae a quick nod. Turning to Sturnin Goff, Thealos gave him a level look. The night air rustled as a heavy wind shook the upper limbs of the pines. "Now... why don't we clear a few things up? Why have you been tracking the Sleepwalker?"

He shook his head and chuckled. "Can't track a Sleepwalker, lad. I've been tracking you."

The quirk of a smile twitched on Thealos' mouth. "You still haven't answered my question."

The knight gave him a hard look. "You prefer bluntness. Very well. You're green, lad. Green as fresh cut wood. I don't say it to insult you, but I watched what happened back in Sol. And tonight. You carry a blade you barely know how to use. Your hands tell me you're a rich man's son. And you dress like any number of Shae barters I've seen across the river. Maybe I was a little too curious what you are doing this side of the Trident with a Sleepwalker. Either you're paying him a lot of coin for some kind of work, or he's pulling you along by the ear." His green-gray eyes flashed. "I think it's the latter."

Thealos stared at him, at a loss for words. He felt anger rising in his chest, but he kept it under control. "Dragging me by the ear you say?" he replied with an edge to his voice.

"I'm a plain speaking man, lad. I've seen a Sleepwalker or two in my days. One could have killed all six Krag before your friend there got whumped on the head. Sleepwalkers are dangerous. Now, I've heard that the Gray Legion has spies working in the Rebellion. But if they're paying for Sleepwalkers too, that means trouble for Dos-Aralon. We wouldn't want the king slain in his bed in the middle of the keep by some black-clothed life-thief. But they cost a great deal, and only the Shae have that kind of money. Again, maybe I'm too curious. Either way, I will have answers from you." His voice was soft, his eyes accusing.

"You tracked me across the Shoreland to ask if I hired an assassin to kill your king? And if Jaerod had been here would you still have approached the camp?"

"Of course. I thought he was with you," the knight replied. "Don't get me wrong, I have a healthy respect for Sleepwalkers. Just as I have a healthy respect for the Crimson Wolfsmen." He gave Thealos a small chuckle. "But I sent a warning to Dos-Aralon in any case about the two of you with word that I'd try and follow along. Whatever the Bandits might be paying for something like that, you can be sure Dos-Aralon can counter any offer."

Thealos folded his arms. "I won't speak treason against your king, Sturnin Goff. I may not like the king of Dos-Aralon, but I have no reason to want him dead. Besides, we're not exactly going that direction."

"Then why are you in the Shoreland? Those Wolfsmen in Sol weren't looking for me."

Thealos felt a little exasperated. "You expect a confession? I'm not a fool, nor am I part of your country. What were you doing in Sol? That's a long way from Owen Draw."

"I was in the Foxtale for a reason, lad. The Duke of Owen Draw was given a message that the Bandit Commander of the Shoreland Regiment wanted to meet the Knight General in Sol. We've heard there have been some conflict between the leaders. The message didn't say anything about Kiran Thall." He cocked his head, his eyes boring hard in Thealos'. "The Knight General sent me to see if this was a Gray Legion ruse or not. And for my trouble, I got attacked by a company of Kiran Thall. Now I'm asking you again, boy. Do you have any idea what you're dealing with out here? Sleepwalkers don't just wander the Shoreland. Was it chance we happened to be in the same tavern that night? Out with it."

"So you were sent to meet with a Bandit Commander?" Thealos hedged, feeling his stomach tighten in knots. He remembered that Jaerod had left him on the streets of Sol to meet with someone. Confusion welled up in his mind. He needed time to sort this out and not look like a fool in front of the others. "You are suggesting that Jaerod is involved with the Bandit Rebellion and want to know if the Shae are as well?"

"Can you give me any reason to believe he isn't?"

At the moment, Thealos could not and was glad when Flent interrupted.

"Hopefully your duke didn't pay in gold to hear those Gray

Legion lies," Flent said. "I've been working at the Foxtale for eight years. I know all the regulars." He waved his hand and chuckled. "A Bandit Commander? In Sol? We get Sheven-Ingen pirates, drunken wrecks from Copperyon and even farther. But the Foxtale ain't a Bandit hideout. That was the first time the Kiran Thall ever came into our place."

"What about the Sleepwalker?" Sturnin challenged.

"Sure he is a Sleepwalker," the Drugaen answered with a shrug. "And what law in Dos-Aralon is there about being a Sleepwalker? The man has stopped by over the last few months, but only to talk and play Bones. Maybe he's a spy, but he's no Bandit general."

"Then maybe he knows where I can find him," the knight replied. "You sent the girl riding to Castun. I'm assuming he's there."

Thealos felt trapped and cursed himself. "He said... he would leave a message for us there."

The knight smirked. "You're a bad liar. Surprises me, coming from a Shae. But I suppose we'll see soon enough when we reach the trading post. You see, I'll find out one way or another." He cocked one of his eyebrows. "Now why don't you tell me why those Wolfsmen were after you?"

"You don't really think I'm going to tell you, do you?" Thealos countered, meeting the knight's stare with his own.

The knight paused, feeding the air with tension. Finally, he muttered something under his breath and shook his head. "If you were drowning in a river and I was on shore, I'd toss you a rope." Sturnin's voice softened. "Don't haggle that it's too coarse. If your intentions are good, I'd like to help you get out."

Thealos sighed. "I appreciate the gesture. I know more than I can say right now. But I'm a good swimmer despite what you may think about my swordsmanship." He paused and stared down at his boots, steeling himself. He looked up at Sturnin again. "And maybe you and your king are in the river and haven't realized it yet."

* * *

178

Thealos and the others marched up and down the undulating hills just within the borders of the Shadows Wood. Sweat streaked down Thealos' face, and he mopped it up with his sleeve. He glanced backwards, watching Flent struggle to keep up, his thick legs leaving him slightly behind. The Drugaen had tried early that morning to teach Justin how to play Bones, but the game was lost on the older Shae, who smiled bemusingly at him and made all the wrong moves. Sturnin Goff walked with his sword strapped across his back. He was sweating heavily in the glinting armor, but he was stronger and more fit than any of them and marched without complaint. They stopped to rest at midday, savoring the break from the humid, scorching air.

Sitting on a crooked stump, Thealos withdrew his water flask and carefully doused the sack of Everoot with it. Then he splashed some of the river water on the back of his neck and savored the coolness. As it dripped down his back, he watched the Warder Shae draw near.

"You have it," Justin said.

Thealos cocked his head curiously, cinching the bag strings and stuffing the bundle in his tunic. *"Have what?"* he replied in Silvan.

"A connection with Earth magic." His pale face was the only one not dripping with sweat, and he looked almost cold in his dark blue robes. Thealos studied his long, narrow fingers – bony and elegant – then opened his cloak wide to reveal the blade of Jade-Shayler. The Shae's eyes gleamed and he nodded, looking at the weapon respectfully.

"Last night, I felt the magic nearby," he said. *"I knew you were there, before you attacked. Are you one of the Shae Guardians?"*

Thealos shook his head. *"No, I am not. I found this magic, and I feel some of it working in me when I use it. What do you know of it?"*

The frail man squatted near the stump Thealos sat on. *"I have kinship with the ones who forged it. It was made with the skill of my kind. The Shae Warders."*

Thealos looked at him curiously. *"I know of the Sian Council in Avisahn, but I did not know there were Warders*

179

living down here..."

Justin shook his head, forestalling him. *"I am not from Avisahn. Tell me – who is the Shae King today?"*

"What do you mean, today?" Thealos asked, confused. *"King Silverborne has ruled for nearly sixty Silvan years; surely you are not that old."*

Justin smirked. *"He was a young man when I last knew of him. Does he have any sons? Who is his heir?"*

"But that doesn't make any sense. You are scarcely older than I am!"

"You do not understand the nature of the Shae Warders. We do not live as long as the rest of the Shae as a price for the powers we invoke. I, myself, have lived out twenty Silvan years. No more. But I have not seen Eroth's light for many years...I have slept in the Earth magic protecting the Warding that I was called to defend."

Thealos stared at him in disbelief and leaned forward. *"And what Warding were you called to protect?"* he said in a soft voice, but he thought he knew already. Justin was talking about the Everoot. He was certain of it.

"I cannot tell you," Justin said. *"It is a secret I must guard until I can remember my charge. I know what I am, but not who I am. I remember snatches from the past, back before the great wars. When I awoke, I remember being caught by the Krag in the ruins of my watchpost, not knowing what had transpired to bring about its desolation. My memory has been...razed. Whether it is due to my long sleep or not, I do not know. I was summoned back to my Warding. But I do not remember when or how. You must take me to the Shae King."*

"Why?"

Justin shook his head. *"I do not know. But I'm sure the answers I seek are in the archives of the Shae King. I ask again, my friend. Who has survived these many years? Who leads the Shae now?"*

Thealos slung his travel pack loose and set it down next to him. He mopped his neck and throat. *"Silverborne's daughter, Laisha. She rules the Shae in her father's name. He had a son, a great one. When I was a small boy, he was killed during the Purge Wars."*

"The Purge Wars?"

Thealos looked at him in amazement. *"When the Shae and the King of Dos-Aralon drove the Bandit armies out of the Shoreland..."*

"Dos-Aralon?" Justin asked, confused. *"'Dos' means there was another before it. When was the other?"*

"You truly do not know what happened?"

"I swear by the goddess Shenalle, whom I serve."

Thealos was baffled by the Shae Warder's ignorance. He was certain Jaerod would know what he was talking about. But too many years had passed. The humans and the Shae were allies instead of enemies. He could see Justin's hatred for humans in the way he glared loathingly at Sturnin Goff. Tensions between the races must have been even stronger back then. How was he going to convince him to speak with a Sleepwalker?

"I will tell you what I can, but there is a man you should meet. A man called Jaerod."

"A human?" Justin said, wrinkling his nose.

Thealos sighed. *"He knows the ways and history of our people. He has visited many of the Shae watchposts and studied from their archives. He may know who you are."*

"The language of man has changed too much over the centuries. I can barely understand the Drugaen tongue that the Krag spoke."

"Jaerod speaks Silvan."

The Warder Shae paused, uncertain. *"I do not think this is wise. Perhaps I should go on to Avisahn alone. I will find my answers there."*

"The village we travel to isn't far. Go with us that far. Perhaps more of your memory will return with time."

"If you think it is wise, my friend," he answered with a nod. He rose with a slight trembling. Staring up at the dark tangles of trees, the Shae pulled the hood tighter and waited for Thealos to stand.

As they started walking again towards the village of Castun, Thealos wrestled with his thoughts. Sturnin had given him too many conflicting words, making him doubt

181

Jaerod's loyalty a little. He did not like feeling that way. But what did he really know coming from a realm of rumors and gossip? How many of the pieces actually worked together instead of conflicted? He thought about it a moment. A Bandit army was preparing to siege Landmoor – he had learned that from Jaerod. It seemed that Sturnin Goff was aware of some of the Bandit movements as well. There was a grove of Everoot somewhere nearby, and the Bandits had discovered it. Only Jaerod had known that. The Shae were needed to retrieve a lost talisman that would protect them from the dangers inherent in Earth magic being used in Forbidden ways. That was the secret he could not share. And Justin – or whatever his true name was – had been the guardian of a Warding, a work of magic created to protect something. The talisman or the Everoot itself?

As he walked and crunched in the matting of pine needles and shrubs, Thealos felt something pulling at his heart, tugging him inextricably south. He hadn't seen it before, not when he was in bonds with Tannon's Band. Or when he escaped the Crimson Wolfsmen in Sol. But he could see it now, as clearly as the sun's hot smile. There was something pulling him south.

To Landmoor.

He knew for certain that the events unfolding in his life had not been random encounters. No, it was all too cleverly worked out for that. The gods were at work. And they were using him.

XIX

Roye scrubbed a trail of sticky ale from the wooden counter with a damp cloth. Three customers were passed out at the bar, and one snored with a throaty growl. The hearth fire snapped, keeping the chill of the sea's wind outside the Foxtale. Rubbing his bleary eyes, Roye stepped around the bar and cursed the name of Flent Shago. Normally, Flent would have carried the drunks to the porch and let them sleep until the street dogs woke them up by licking the ale from their faces. But the Drugaen was gone and no amount of complaining would bring him close enough to cuff. And since Ticastasy had vanished too, it had been murder running the tavern that night by himself.

"Ungrateful Drugaen," Roye muttered to himself. He shook his head. "Girl...you better not be working for anyone else. I swore I'd counter any offer you got." He poked the nearest man with his thick finger and grumbled for him to get out. The man stirred, said a few slurred words, and Roye grabbed his shirt and helped him stand. It took a few moments before all three were either lying cozy off the porch or stumbling half-blind into the fog-misted streets. The garrison watch would find them, Roye thought, wiping his hands. Then they would be *their* problem.

Jingling a few coins he had snatched from their pockets to pay the tab they owed, he pulled the crossbar over the door and limped over to a stool to rest. *Old bones getting tired*, he thought, rubbing his swollen fingers over his scalp. He finished off the left-over drink from one of the patrons' mugs before reaching for a well-used deck of playing cards. He flipped through it and smiled, remembering how good the Drugaen had become playing Bones. The dull expression on his face had lured unwary gamblers into playing high stakes. Added to the gracious way he lost and how he appeared to win by mistake, it made him a reliable source of income. Roye frowned. He hadn't paid the Drugaen what he should have, but what had he ever asked for? A place to stay, some stew to eat, and all the drink he could swallow. Not a shabby trade, Roye thought, in a world that had little a Drugaen could trade his muscles for.

Roye dumped the cards on the counter and began picking up the empty mugs and plates. He wondered how long Flent and Ticastasy would be gone or if they would ever come back. How many days had it been? They were the reason behind the success of the Foxtale. Ticastasy had a way of making the place shine. Not just her personality, but how she arranged things in the place. He'd paid her well, but maybe another innkeeper had finally lured her away. The Drugaen could be replaced, but it would all be very costly.

A thump sounded at the door. At first Roye thought the wind had shaken it. But it sounded a second time, rattling the crossbar. Roye huffed and walked towards another table.

"I'm closed!" He turned his back to it, not waiting for a response. "Why is there always someone thirsty right before sunrise?" he muttered. "It's so banned late I can hardly see."

"Roye. It's Tsyrke."

The tavernkeeper stopped. He knew that voice. Even worse, he knew what the voice wanted. Fear knifed him in the ribs, and he took a cautious step backwards. *Oh, for Hate's sake! Why did he have to show up tonight!* "Everybody's gone," Roye stammered, his mouth dry and hot. "Just cleanin' up, Tsyrke – why don't you come back in a few hours..."

"Roye," the voice warned. "Open the door."

The owner of the Foxtale dropped the plates on the nearest table. Limping forward, he unlatched the door and pulled it open, fighting against the wind. The sudden chill from the sea cut into his skin and made his teeth chatter. It was Tsyrke Phollen, the sea captain who had taken a liking to Ticastasy. One of the richest men in Ilvaren – and one of the most dangerous.

I should have closed up an hour ago, Roye thought angrily. *If I'd been in bed, he wouldn't have found me here. Ban those two! Ban them to Pitan!*

The musty smell of the ocean clung to the man's clothes and armor. Roye did not think it strange at all that he wore a long hauberk under his thick salt-stained tunic. A man with his reputation was a target for thieves and worse. Tsyrke had a tousle of sandy brown hair that was cropped short like most Shorelanders preferred. The hauberk clinked and rattled as he entered the Foxtale, swinging the door shut behind him. A tattered red cape hung lop-sided down his back, discolored by soot and blood stains. Deep brown eyes glanced over the empty tables and rested at last on Roye. His wind-burned face was hard and showed the faint tug of a frown. He was not happy. Roye's mind raced for a way to start the conversation.

Tsyrke Phollen stole the chance. "Just be quick, Roye," he said. "She's not at home. She's not in the back. She's not anywhere in Sol that I could tell. Now where is she?"

"W..who? Oh, 'Stasy – yes, she's not in the back..."

Tsyrke scanned the bar, eyeing a keg with hunger in his eyes. "I don't have much time. Where is she?"

"Would you...like something to drink?" Without waiting for the answer, Roye hurried to the bar and dribbled two cups of Spider Ale. "Come have a sit and let's talk – you been sailing long? How is your ship?"

The thud of Tsyrke's boots came across the planked floor and the callused hand closed around the mug. His thumb rubbed across the rim for a moment before he took a deep swallow and savored it. Raising his angry eyes to the tavernkeeper, he said softly, "You don't care about my ship. You don't care about me. But you'd better start speaking the truth, Roye – or by Achrolese, I'll beat it out of you! If she went off with another man, you'd best hurry and tell me."

Roye saw the huge broadsword strapped to the man's back and swallowed a few gulps of the ale to steady himself. He didn't know for certain where Ticastasy had gone, but he thought he had enough of an idea to get Tsyrke out of his tavern.

"Don't jump to conclusions. She left just the other night, after a huge scrape your brother started in here. The damage alone cost me nearly a hundred Aralonian pieces. And since he's your brother, I was thinking that..."

The man's eyes narrowed with contempt. "Secrist came here? Already? Sons of fire, he never arrives in time. He was supposed to be here tomorrow." He gave Roye a hard look. "I'm not paying you a single piece until I know more. Now where would Ticastasy go? You know she has no family left and no place to stay but here. Who did she go with? The Drugaen?"

"I think so, but I can't be sure...it's Hate's own truth. I swear, she left that night. I think they both went with that Sleepwalker, I don't know..."

Roye grunted as Tsyrke grabbed his shirt and hauled him up on the counter top. "What in blazes are you talking about?" he thundered. "A Sleepwalker was here?"

Roye winced and panicked. "Calm down, now! Calm down! He wore all black, like I've heard they do. Even 'Stasy thought he was a Sleepwalker." He tried to shrug but couldn't in his position. "He started coming to Sol 'bout the same time you left on your last run."

Tsyrke released him and he collapsed on the counter. He gripped the ale mug so tightly that Roye was certain it would shatter. "His name?"

Waving his hand, the tavernkeeper said, "Oh, Tsyrke, how was I supposed to remember? She always got to know the folks..." Tsyrke grabbed the fistful of Roye's shirt again and jerked him closer. "Oh Hate, Tsyrke! Calm down, now. Jamin? Jorim? Something like that. How should I know who he really is? Only 'Stasy could tell you for sure, and she's not here."

Tsyrke shook his head, unclenching the cloth shirt. He

stared at the counter top, his fists balled up tightly and he breathed out slowly. "And you think she went with him? You suggest she went away with this Sleepwalker?"

"I don't know," Roye said, sinking his face into his hands. "I swear to you by the king's crown, I don't know anything more. They both left me. The Drugaen and her. Like a privy stall in a high wind!"

Tsyrke pushed away from the counter, looking once more at the cup of Spider Ale before him. He started to reach for it and then closed his hand. "You can't even remember the man's name. Blustering idiot. Do you know where they went – where they were headed? You don't remember anything at all? Why did Secrist start a fight?"

Roye shook his head. "It's ruined me. There was a knight…"

Tsyrke bowed his head and muttered a dark oath. "No wonder there was a fight." He rubbed his forehead. "Secrist would attack a knight from Owen Draw on sight. Ban it, ban it, ban it."

Roye suddenly remembered. "Oh, and there were Shae here too! Never paid for their drinks either, the rooks. There were four of 'em – no! The four came looking for this young one. There were five! He sat over there and slipped out when the fighting started. I don't remember it very well."

"You were probably hiding under a table," Tsyrke said acidly.

"But then the Sleepwalker came in at the end and took the boy away, and 'Stasy and Flent went with him I think. They were all huddled up in that corner over there, talking at that table." He lifted his head and pointed.

Roye blinked with surprise. There was a man in black robes sitting at the table that had been empty all night. His bowels turned to ice. "Who in Achrolese's name are…?" His voice snipped off mutely and he stood frozen.

Tsyrke straightened and turned. He peered into the dark corner of the tavern. "Mage," he said simply. The Sorian met him in the center of the tavern where the center beam looked as if an axe had gone to work on it.

The Sorian's voice was soft. "There was enough blood

spilled here to tell a great many stories. They're going to Landmoor."

Nodding, Tsyrke went to the door and pulled the crossbar up. He tugged the door open. A gust of wind careened into the tavern, tossing Roye's hair wildly, but he stared at empty space. They stepped back into the mist-shrouded city and passed over a snoring drunk lying in the street.

When the door shut behind them, Roye awoke suddenly from the daze, startled. He slowly lifted his head, blinking. His eyes went from the booth in the corner to the front door rattling with the wind. Scratching his throat vigorously, he thought a moment. "Who was I talking...?"

He wiped his mouth and started shuffling across the floor. He dropped the crossbar into its cradle, securing the door, and rubbed his scalp. "Could have sworn I'd locked it already," he muttered to himself, taking a swallow from Tsyrke's half-sipped cup.

* * *

It was a searing pain inside his heart, growing more unbearable with each step. She was gone from Sol – beyond the reach of his protection. She was heading towards the most dangerous region of the kingdom. He swore softly to himself, cursing the winds that had blown against the sails. He was late. Too late.

Glass lanterns hooked on tall iron poles lit the misty cobblestone street. The quavering howl of a sewer mutt echoed from an alley across the way. The air smelled like an old wharf – a familiar, comforting scent to a man who had spent nearly his whole life at sea. The sound of Tsyrke's boots scraped on the gritty stone before thumping on the soft wet wood of the docks. "How long have you been waiting for me?" he asked the Sorian.

"Stop a moment, my friend. You need to steel yourself for what's ahead. The cravings will be strong tonight."

Tsyrke nodded and stopped, leaning back on a dockpost. He wanted a drink so badly he could hardly think. He rubbed his eyes, trying to banish the images of Ticastasy's smiles. He was tempted to yank out his sword and try splitting the dockpost.

"I was surprised when I did not find you here already, Commander. Bad weather? The fog?"

Tsyrke shook his head. Mage was trying to help. Trying to focus him on his responsibility. He was the Commander of the Shoreland Regiment, not an Ilvaren sea captain. Focus on the title. Always focus. "The business in Harper Ket delayed me. I bought the homestead in Ishtol."

"A place for the girl?" Mage asked with a voice void of judgment.

Tsyrke knew he could hide nothing from the Sorian. It wasn't possible. Yet the green-eyed old man still asked questions – even ones he knew the answers to. They were as different as a breeze and a gale, but something had always kept them blowing in the same direction.

"Did you pester my grandfather with questions about his women?"

"Always."

Mage had helped Tsyrke's grandfather establish the League of Ilvaren. A famous man, his grandfather – Kiran Phollen. His grandfather's red cape had survived the ferocity of the Purge Wars. It had outlived the man who had worn it. Now, after so many years, skirmishes, and petulant seas, Tsyrke found himself commanding one of Ballinaire's regiments. Ballinaire – the hero of the Purge Wars turned traitor and rebel himself. Ballinaire – the man who had persuaded him to join the Rebellion. And hate every banned day of it. Tsyrke was tired and quickly moving past the fire of his youth, but he still had the stubbornness of a galleon shoving its way through a tempest. Becoming Lord of the entire Shoreland region was tempting. But it was just not worth it anymore.

He swore under his breath, realizing he had ignored Mage's question. "I'm sorry. Lost in my thoughts. Yes, you know I bought the homestead for her, Mage. Not quite the same as making her a queen, but that probably wouldn't have happened anyway. I'm stunned that she's not here. But she can't be at Landmoor. Not this soon. Did she go with the

Sleepwalker?"

"I don't know."

Tsyrke snorted as if Mage were joking. "What do you mean you don't know? I doubt there is anything on this banned world you don't know."

The Sorian gazed at him and smiled. "We've known each other too long for flattery, Tsyrke. Let us just say I am not totally certain of his whereabouts. He is certainly more than an average Sleepwalker because I wasn't able to read his past."

"He's warded then. Pretty good ward, too, if a Sorian can't break it."

"I didn't bother," Mage replied. "I'm familiar with the wretches of Pitan and all the mutations that Firekin can create from it. Like the Drugaen. If the Sleepwalker used Firekin, he would have been under my dominion. He kept himself hidden in Silvan magic, which is why I hesitate to label him anything."

"Shae magic? Not stronger than a Sorian?" Tsyrke pointed out.

Mage shrugged. "I'd rather not have to find out, Commander. In the old days, the Shae held dominion. But this man wasn't a Shae."

Something cold went down Tsyrke's spine. He let out a low whistle. "For all our sakes, I hope not. Show me what happened that night? Did my brother truly come barging in like an oaf?"

Mage nodded, his eyes glinting with anger. He withdrew an orb of orange fire from his robes. "The Firekin will show you everything. Look into the flames and see the past."

Tsyrke did. He watched the flickering pattern of light reveal the Kiran Thall, his brother's company, disturb the Foxtale. He had come early, responding to Tsyrke's orders, but had chosen to bring the entire company instead of leaving them outside the city. A knight from Owen Draw was there also – not the Knight General, but one sent by him. Even a few Crimson Wolfsmen had joined the fighting.

Tsyrke seethed with disbelief when the light winked out. "Ban it, the knight probably thought he was baited into a

trap. There is no way he's going to trust me now. Ban it!"
He rubbed his eyes. "A bloody quaere too. Why were they
here?"

"For a young Shae who came in before your brother. He's
warded too, so I don't know who he is, but he went with the
Sleepwalker and Ticastasy. The Sleepwalker said very little
– but he did say they were going to Landmoor." His eyes
glittered with amusement. "And when he said it, he looked
right at me, as if he knew I would be watching him from the
Firekin later."

"Then the Sleepwalker is a fool for baiting a Sorian,"
Tsyrke snapped. "He can die just as the others have. But
somehow he found out about Ticastasy." He shook his head
angrily. "He's kidnapped her. But who hired him? I've heard
Folkes is using the Gray Legion."

"I don't think Folkes could afford this one. Come, let's
return to your ship. We need to return to the army as quickly
as we can."

They started walking again.

"Who hired the Sleepwalker? Dairron?"

"It's difficult to say," Mage replied. "But that was my first
thought."

"Why?"

The Sorian gave him an arch look. "Because the
Sleepwalker gave the Shae a bag of Everoot."

Tsyrke stopped and gripped Mage's arm. "Everoot?" he
said in a strangled whisper. "How in Hate's name did he get
a bag of Everoot? There isn't any Everoot any more. It was
all destroyed when Sol don Orai burned! That was five hundred years ago. You told me it would never return."

"I did say those things. But I was wrong. Do you remember the meeting with Lord Ballinaire you missed?"

"I don't give a ban about Ballinaire or his meetings,"
Tsyrke snarled. He wanted a drink again. He muttered a
few more choice curses and turned down the pier where his
ship was docked. The sound of creaking boats smothered the
noise of his steps. He was furious. Things were tumbling out
of control. Their carefully laid plan – their most secret plan
– was about to be ruined. He risked everything, not least of

all his own life.

Tsyrke closed his eyes and tried to steel himself. When you play high stakes in Bones, you trust in your luck. Too many players. Too many risks. Mage walked patiently next to him, waiting for him to master himself again. The Sorian was all ice inside. He had been playing this game for centuries with nations poised as the bet. This little affair with Dos-Aralon was probably too insignificant to get excited about.

"I tried to be back for Ballinaire's meeting," Tsyrke explained, more calmly. "But the homestead took longer than I thought and I had to hurry here to meet the knight. You went to the meeting to represent me. Is Ballinaire going to sit still down in the Shadows Wood long enough for the knights to nab him?"

A wan smile flickered across Mage's mouth. "He's not planning to sit at all. He's starting a war with Dos-Aralon. Just like we persuaded him to do."

"He's starting it now?" Tsyrke asked. "If the knights of Owen Draw can't summon their troops quickly enough, they'll never engage. They keep sitting there, waiting for Dairron's army to come out of the Kingshadow. I need those knights down here!"

"I know this doesn't suit your plans, but it suits Ballinaire's. You cannot change the coming of the tide, Commander. He's ordered you to bring the Shoreland regiment and occupy Landmoor. You only have a week or so to do it. I told Hallstoy to start mobilizing when I passed through your regiment."

Tsyrke let the air slowly out of his lungs. "My regiment is not enough to stop Dos-Aralon. When they bring down the Amberdian Army and those fools from Cypher – they'll crush him. Our plan isn't going to work if he destroys my regiment by using it as bait and leads a counter-attack from the Kingshadow."

"It's the other way around," Mage explained. "He intends to use Dairron's regiment as the diversionary one and he'll attack Dos-Aralon with yours. He plans to do it personally."

"Is he mad? They'll see us coming and have plenty of warning!"

"You're missing the point, Tsyrke. The tides have changed. The waters are deeper now. Miestri found a grove of Everoot in the Shadows Wood and turned it over to Ballinaire. He showed it to us at the meeting. He has cartloads full of it. I've seen an army use it before, Commander. Dos-Aralon could send twenty times its number and it would still fall. Every Bandit soldier wounded will be totally healed and strengthened the next day. Some will even come back from the dead. You can't stop an army like that. And remember, the Sleepwalker had a sample himself. That is why I suspect Dairron is behind this. I don't think he wants Ballinaire to succeed any more than you do. He's always wanted to make a pact with the Shae. And it looks like he's lured this young man out of Avisahn."

Tsyrke bowed his head as he walked and rubbed his temples. Anger boiled up and steamed inside of him. "Yes, this rings true. Dairron found out about Ticastasy. He sent the Sleepwalker to abduct her and a Shae." *It was just like him,* Tsyrke thought bitterly. With Dairron plotting to succeed Ballinaire, he would go to any lengths to be sure that Tsyrke served him or had good reason not to interfere. Tsyrke knew that if he pretended Ticastasy did not matter to him, Dairron would kill her for spite.

Mage nodded. "He mentioned something to that effect at the meeting. He has had eyes on your regiment for a while now. After all, his isn't nearly large enough. And how else would the Sleepwalker know that I would be here later?"

"Only a Sorian would know a Sorian," Tsyrke replied. "You people are too devious, it's hard to keep up with your games. You are right. It's as obvious as spring after the thaw. Dairron wants Lord Ballinaire dead as much as I do. But for the wrong reasons. The banned wrong reasons." He knew Dairron wanted to bring the Rebellion to a boil. But not Tsyrke. Tsyrke wanted it finished. "He wants me out of the way, and he would stoop to use a banned Sleepwalker to do it. Of course Miestri would ward him against you. He'd never leave a clear trail. Tell me the rest, Mage. I doubt it could put me in any worse a mood." He looked up the dock and saw the ramp to his ship just ahead.

"Folkes will bring his regiment across the Yukilep in support of yours," Mage answered softly. "Dairron was ordered to attack from the north to draw don Rion off, exposing his rear – the city of Dos-Aralon itself."

"I'm not a fool," Tsyrke said with anger. "It's like asking two thieves to watch your back. Does Ballinaire really trust them to obey?"

"Does he have reason to trust you?" Mage asked wryly. He paused a moment, letting the words sink in. "He's convinced he will win. As I said, there is a grove of Everoot in the swamps and Lord Ballinaire has it. He has an army surrounding it and harvesting it. He has two Sorian to advise him. There is nothing but open plains between the Shadows Wood and Dos-Aralon. He still needs you, my friend. He still needs you. If we are quick and clever, we can turn this around. If we can get to that Shae lad before the Sleepwalker brings him to Miestri..."

Tsyrke clenched his fist in frustration. The hinting taste of failure was bitter in his mouth. He could lose it all, slipping right between his fingers like water. He sighed and shook his head. "The knight was the key, Mage. The key to our plan. I can't fight Dos-Aralon *and* Ballinaire *and* the Shae."

"You're not listening to me," the Sorian soothed. "The tides change with the moon. I've seen them change long enough to see the pattern. Listen to my counsel. Miestri is the youngest Sorian among us. This is her first real conquest in centuries since she seduced a Shae watchpost. I've juggled dozens more complicated than this. Hear me out. Dairron's intention is to bring the Shae into this, but maybe we can forestall him. We need to understand who this Shae lad is. He was warded for a reason. He is the linchpin, Tsyrke. Find him, and we can turn this around to our favor."

"And how do we find this Shae boy?"

"The same way we find the woman you care for," Mage answered. "She still has that pendant you gave her, and she's only in Castun right now. And with my powers stirring the wind, we'll be in Landmoor by dawn."

XX

It must always be hot in Castun, Thealos decided. Nothing protected the hamlet from the scorching prairie winds of the lowland plains. Both the eastern and western edges of the land had rivers to draw in the mist and chill the air, but the Shadows Wood blocked all of that, leaving the northern borders of the forest to swelter in the heat.

"Only fools live in Castun," Sturnin Goff muttered. "Neither side cares to fight over it."

Thealos agreed with the assessment, though he wondered if the people were truly wise for living in a place that no one wanted. He frowned as they walked into the dusty streets. The only buildings that had survived were the ones made of stone and thatch. Sweat dampened his clothes and skin, and the dust clung to him like chalk. They were all weary from the hard walk, and from a distance the town seemed like a chance to escape the heat of the plains. But the refuge was only an illusion. Lopsided cabins hugged a central main square of tall taverns, trading posts, and a few smith-yards that looked as if they would sigh and collapse into dust. A line of splintered fences surrounded the hamlet and divided it. Smoke drifted from the thick chimney of the nearest forge, and the grunt of horses and mules broke the stillness. There were an uncommon number of graveyards, Thealos noticed – some fenced and sheltered, others open and overgrown.

"This is the only trading post this side of the Shadows

Wood," Sturnin said with a weary tone. "A way-station that brings Sol and Dos-Aralon to Landmoor. There's only one road cut through the forest, called the Iron Point Road, and there are more thieves and Bandits than trees."

Thealos nodded. With the Bandit Rebellion so powerful in the south, he wondered just how many still considered it safe to travel. He glanced over at the knight. "The town is small, Sturnin. Why so many graveyards?"

The knight shook his head and shrugged. "Some plague years ago. Blamed it on the Shae, I think. You'll be fine as long as you keep with me."

"The Shae were down here?"

"During the Purge Wars."

"Never been to Castun," Flent said, hooking his thumbs in his buckle. He walked between Thealos and Justin, keeping a watchful eye on both of them. The Warder Shae kept his head bowed and said nothing, but Flent had chattered enough for both of them. "Heard there wasn't much to see here." He snorted and spit on the ground. "Guess they were right. Hope they have some ale barrels, that's all I have to say."

Thealos glanced over his shoulder at the Drugaen. Flent seemed a little unsure of himself. He was probably missing Sol more than he cared to admit. "I thought the same thing when I first went to Sol. It's a wreck of a city, Flent. Even Dos-Aralon has gardens and flowers."

"Who cares about bloody gardens. I miss the ale! The best ale in the world comes from Sheven-Ingen, and it costs a fortune up north or out this way." He sighed. "Sol may not be pretty on the outside, but the beaches! Loved walking those beaches." The Drugaen sniffed and shrugged. "But if I was going to move, I'd go find a shack in one of the Shoreland cities farther south, or maybe an island. Windrift is nice enough, I've heard."

"If you're an outlaw," Sturnin muttered under his breath.

"The Shoreland?" Thealos said with a wince. "Sun, rain, and mosquitoes. It's awful. Why not move to Dos-Aralon? It's expensive, but the wages are better. There are even a few Drugaen settlements up there. Those that don't want any part of the war with the Krag."

Flent shook his head in disgust. "Can't stand Inlanders." He glanced at the knight and his eyebrows rose apologetically. "No offense, Sturnin. No offense. Every kind of folk passin' through Sol has stopped by the Foxtale once or twice. But it's the sailors I like. They've got stories and things to sell. The ocean is always cool – none of this banned sun baking your brains." He glared up at the sky. "I'm not always going to unload barrels and toss out troublesome folk. Gonna buy my own ship some day." He chuckled. "Won't that be a first! A Drugaen galleon."

Thealos grinned. He searched the taverns and brothels for a sign of the Catpaw Inn. From the slanting porches of homes, he saw a few curious and some angry stares. "The Port of Jan Lee has a beautiful harbor. Puts Sol to shame."

"Never been there," Flent said with a sniff. "But I guess that's because your people won't let others in."

Thealos shook his head. "They let *some* people in, but I'm sure the ale merchants find the business rather poor," he added with a grin. "It's beautiful to see, but you would probably die of thirst in there, Flent."

They turned the corner and started down the main street to the south, toward the entrance of the Iron Point Road. A dog stared at them, its sad eyes bemoaning the heat, and its tail wagged sluggishly. It yawned and then dropped its head back down on the deck. They stopped to rest by a wooden post near a chandler shop, and Thealos wiped the sweat from his neck. He scanned the street and discovered a well-painted sign bearing the name of the inn they were searching for.

Crossing the street and shoving open the door, Thealos blinked, letting his eyes adjust to the shade. Thick stone walls kept the main parlor cool. The smells of baking bread and lamp oil greeted them. The common room was half-empty, filled by a few loggers and a solitary woodsman in the far corner of the room, sipping from a cup. The woodsman nodded to them and went back to his meal.

"Not bad...not bad at all," Flent mumbled, nodding with appreciation. "Better than Roye's place."

"Get us a table, Flent," Sturnin said. "I'll talk to the inn-keeper and ask about the girl." He brushed the dust from his upper arms and approached the man behind the bar counter.

Thealos quickly caught the knight's shoulder and stepped around him. "I can do that, Sturnin."

The knight paused, giving him a steady look. But he backed off. "I wouldn't try slipping out the back, lad," he said quietly. "I mean to see the Sleepwalker here."

"I hadn't forgotten," Thealos replied with an even tone. "But I doubt he would have left you a message, would he?"

The innkeeper was a gaunt man with friendly hazel eyes and a receding hairline that was well salted and wispy. He had crooked teeth but a warm smile. "You're a long way from home, my friend," he greeted with an easygoing grin. "If home is Avisahn."

"Are you the owner?" Thealos asked, leaning against the counter.

He affirmed it with a nod. "My name is Talbin. You must be Thealos." He kept his voice low. "Why don't you join your friends and I'll bring out some dinner for you. The girl you sent ahead has been fretting since she rode in."

"She's safe." Thealos sighed with relief. "And Jaerod?"

"Ssshhh," Talbin replied, wiping a mug clean with a towel. He glanced over Thealos's shoulder and looked at the woods-man in the far corner. "He should be back tonight. I've got two men out looking for him."

"Why?" Thealos said, concerned.

"Because that man over there is waiting around to kill him."

* * *

The woodsman watched them with open interest. Thealos felt the man's eyes probing their table. The Warder Shae sat like a recluse, withdrawn into silence because no one but Thealos knew Silvan. He merely asked for a cup of hot water and proceeded to make an herbal tea. Flent bit into the greasy pork platter and trencher bread and washed both down with a huge mug of Spider Ale. Sturnin chewed at his meal, his eyes straying more than once to the woodsman so intent on them.

The woodsman's hair and beard were pale brown with a few grizzled edges. What surprised Thealos was the man's clothes and weapons. He was clearly an Inlander, like Sturnin, with long hair and sunburnt face and hands. But his long bow was distinctively Silvan, a strong yew bow. A sheaf of steel-tipped arrows hung from a quiver at his waist with the styled markings of Silvan fletchers. He also carried a tapered long sword with fine hilt work, possibly made by the Shae as well. His cloak was a mottled color of greens and browns. When he caught Thealos staring again, he nodded respectfully.

"Do you know who that is?" Sturnin Goff whispered to Thealos between bites.

"No," Thealos answered. "Do you?"

The knight nodded and dabbed his bread in the thick gravy. "I'd bet a month's pay he's Allavin Devers, probably the best scout in the realm." Sturnin nodded with confidence. "He's loyal to the Duke of Owen Draw, but he lives with your people. Or so I've heard. Do you know the name?"

"No," Thealos replied, risking another look. "He lives with the Shae? Where?"

"The Riven Wood," the knight answered. "A small community. But he wanders up and down the Kingshadow, tracking the Bandits for us. I'm going to go have a talk with him."

"Finish your dinner first," Thealos said, stalling him. "He doesn't look like he's in much of a hurry to go."

The knight's eyes glinted with anger. "You're a pushy lad, aren't you? I'm not here at your command."

"*Or* my invitation," Thealos countered. His anger had flared too quickly, and he struggled to wrestle it back down. "I don't seek a quarrel with you, Sturnin," he said. "We came here for a reason. When Jaerod arrives, you'll get to ask your questions. Now be patient with me a while longer."

Over Flent's shoulder, Thealos spied Ticastasy emerge from one of the rooms at the top of the stairs. She looked straight down the hall at them and smiled. She was wearing the gown he had given her. It fit her well, its violet trim matching the ribbon that held her hair back. The hem was long, covering the tops of her soft leather boots. Descending the stairs in a rush, she came up behind Flent and gave him a hug.

"Flent, you smell like a gutter!" she complained, wrinkling her nose and giving him a hard hug. "It's good to see you." She gave Flent a little shove, but aimed her smile at Thealos. "Thank you for the gown, my lord. It fits better than I hoped."

Sturnin raised his eyebrows in between bites of food. Thealos hooked the chair leg next to him and pulled it out, offering her a place to sit. She slipped in it, planting her elbows on the table. Her hair was freshly washed and clean and her skin smelled of scented soap. She wore the tinkling jewelry she had in Sol, except this gown made her look even better.

"It actually fits a little snug, Quickfellow," she said in low voice. "Are you sure you didn't mean it for the Silverborne princess?"

Thealos chuckled at her banter. "I told you, it wouldn't match Laisha's coloring." At the mention of her name, Thealos caught Justin's surreptitious glance. "She wears green damask or blue silk and sapphires. It looks well on you, Stasy."

"Thank you," she replied, blushing. "Are you serious about her gowns? I've heard she has a hundred made each year."

Thealos smiled and leaned back, folding his arms. "An exaggeration to be sure."

"Really? Then is she as beautiful as they say?"

"Well... what do they say?" He couldn't help feeling a little guilty talking to her so freely. He did know Laisha Silverborne and her taste for fine cloth – which was served by the Quickfellow family among others, of course – but suggesting a degree of intimacy was more than a little misleading.

"They say," she replied with a saucy air, "that a man who catches sight of her will fall all sick in love and act like a fool until she's gone." She looked at him pointedly. "Did that happen to you?"

Thealos smiled. "If I remember right, she did make me forget my name. I was younger then, but does that count?"

"Now you're boasting."

He shook his head. "Boasting is clearly against the Rules of Forbiddance," he replied. "I don't want to give you the wrong impression, though. She likes her gowns well enough, but I wouldn't say I'm an insider as to the variety of her apparel. In Avisahn every year there is a grand ball at the palace. I've danced with her and exchanged pleasantries..."

"You and how many others?"

He grinned. "Two hundred, I think. She's a good dancer."

"Well I can cut a good caper too, Quickfellow." She leaned forward and rested her cheek on the flat of her hand. "You need a bath as bad as Flent does. Isn't it Forbidden to be this filthy?"

"I imagine it's written somewhere in the Rules," Thealos agreed, stifling a chuckle. He saw Justin's disapproving look and felt a stab of guilt. She seemed to notice him for the first time and raised her head. "Who's this?"

"After you left, there were five more Krag, and they were holding a prisoner." He nodded to the Shae Warder.

She looked at Justin. "And where are you from?"

"He doesn't speak the king's common," Thealos answered. "Only Silvan and a little Drugaen."

She nodded and looked more resigned. "I don't think he likes me."

"He doesn't like humans in general. Don't be offended."

"You don't seem to mind us." She gave Thealos a direct look.

"Most of the Shae in Avisahn have never left its boundaries." He brushed crumbs from the tabletop and gave her a sidelong look. "What they know about humans they've learned from the Council Elders. Many of your ways are Forbidden to us, and so they fear what they do not yet know." He hesitated, not wanting to lie outright. "I've...known a few barters, you see. The ones who trade with Dos-Aralon and other nations. There are many humans I wouldn't trust to hold a sterling coin for me. But there are others," he nodded respectfully to her, "who I would trust." He knew already that she thought him a Silvan lord. He didn't want to ruin that image, to confess that he was only a barter's son. He managed to keep it from his face, but the deception was starting to gnaw at him.

She took his compliment and tucked it away with a smile. "I like the Catpaw," she said, staring up at the rafters. "They have baths upstairs, if can you believe it. You are certainly a wealthy man. Talbin said that Jaerod spared the best rooms for us."

"Did you see him when you arrived?"

She shook her head. "No. But Talbin promised he would come back for us. I arrived this morning and must have missed him." Her eyes fastened to his. "I was... worried about you."

Thealos stared across the table at Flent who tore at his meal like a wolf. Sturnin also politely ignored her over the noise of his plate, but Justin's eyes were wary and watchful.

"*The human is coming,*" the Shae Warder warned in Silvan as the woodsman approached their table.

Thealos turned in his chair.

"Now this is about the oddest scene I've come across in a long while," the stranger said with a chuckle, planting his strong hands on the back of Thealos' chair. "A sturdy fellow from Owen Draw, a Drugaen, a pretty lass who must be the king's own sister, and two Shae. *Greetings to you both, in your language.*" He smiled as those who didn't know the Shae speech raised their eyebrows curiously. "Odd company for Castun. Hope you don't mind the intrusion. My name is Allavin Devers."

"There's an extra chair," Flent said, nudging one open. "Flent Shago. Glad to meet you."

Allavin nodded and sat down, his hand grazing the pommel of his sword. He had the low and confident stride of a cat. An odd-looking scar ran alongside his nose, deforming it slightly. "Thank you. If you don't mind, I will join you."

"*You speak our tongue,*" Justin said with a hint of disdain.

"*I do,*" Allavin replied without rancor, in flawless Silvan. "*And I live among your people as well.*"

"And what brings you to Castun, Allavin Devers?" Thealos asked, directing the conversation away from Justin and deliberately changing the language. "You are a man of reputation I understand."

"A small one, if any. I've spent some time in the Kingshadow, Iniva, Yukilep," He replied with a shrug. "Or anywhere the Bandit armies go." He nodded to the knight from Owen Draw. "This part of the country hasn't seen many of your rank since the Accords of Dos-Aralon were struck after the Purge Wars. What brings you this far south, Sturnin?"

The knight chuckled. "You recognized me. I thought I knew you, Devers. You tracked for us several years ago. We even hung some Kiran Thall because of it." He took a sip of ale from his mug and dipped the rim towards Thealos. "I've been following this Shae since Sol."

Thealos was getting more and more uncomfortable. He tried to nudge the conversation off course again. "Are there really Shae left in the Riven Wood?" Thealos said. He wanted to stave off any reference that might make mention of the Sleepwalker.

Allavin leaned back and folded his arms. "Maybe two hundred, if that. The village in the Riven Wood used to supply provisions for the watchpost of Jove Stand in the Kingshadow. They haven't had word from Avisahn in at least a hundred years. But my weapons are from Citadellian. That's another watchpost in the Kingshadow – the southern end. You heard of it?" Thealos nodded. He hadn't learned about them in Avisahn, but Jaerod had used a charred stick one evening to map them in the dirt. "No matter. A good group of Shae. All of them." Thealos saw pain in his eyes, a rush of emotion that seemed to burn.

"And what are you doing in Castun?" Thealos asked.

The woodsman's cheek twitched. His countenance fell and his eyes narrowed with some awful memory. He glanced at the faces around the table. "Not long ago, I went with a group of Shae scouts into the south borders of the Shadows

Wood. The whole banned Shoreland regiment is holed up there right now." Sturnin stiffened, and the woodsman nodded. "Hate's own truth, Sturnin. It was Tsyrke Phollen's regiment. Just sitting there, getting ready to siege Landmoor. Phollen isn't there yet, but word is he's coming."

Ticastasy's eyes went wide with shock. She glanced across the table at Flent who shared her expression.

Allavin shook his head in disgust. "But they're not just waiting to siege the fortress. They were digging up something in the swamp. A strange plant or root – looked like moss. Ballinaire himself was there overseeing it."

"Fury," Sturnin Goff muttered in awe, leaning forward. "Ballinaire himself is down here? We had heard he was still rotting in the mountains. I wish I had been there to cleave his head from his shoulders."

"No," Allavin replied, coughing. "No, you don't wish you were there. I was the only one who made it out alive."

Thealos felt his heart pinch in his chest. "What happened to the Shae..."

"Killed to the last man," Allavin replied grimly. He looked hard at them. "By a Sleepwalker."

XXI

I'm sorry to hear that," Thealos told Allavin earnestly, rising to his feet. He kept all expression from his face, though his stomach clenched with worry. "It's never easy losing our friends. Linger with us. I'm sure you and Sturnin would like to talk." Without waiting for a response, he retreated to a window seat and sat down. *What am I doing here?* he asked himself.

The Catpaw Inn was warm and comfortable. A cool breeze had finally dispelled the awful heat of the day. Thealos folded his arms, breathing in the rich smells of spicy stew and bread and feeling nauseated by it. He stared at the reflections in the window glass. It was too dark a night and poorly lit outside to see much more than the image of the common room painted on the glass by the lamps inside the inn.

Back at the corner table, Sturnin conferred with Allavin. They spoke in low tones, using the table in front of them as a map of the land. The tracker drew out where the Bandit armies had positioned themselves – or at least when he had last seen them. A Bandit regiment had gathered in the Shadows Wood. How far away?

Flent nudged Justin's elbow, flipping through a stack of Bones and trying to teach the game yet again to the Warder Shae. Justin sipped from his cup of tea, withdrawn and impassive, his eyes straying to the other patrons in the room. There were smiths and tanners and woodsmen at

205

nearly every table now, and the Warder Shae seemed to shrivel up as he glared at them all. Thealos decided to talk to him later and give him some measure of Shae companionship. He looked very miserable and edgy, though not as much when Flent spoke to him.

"Don't tell me you can see anything out there," Ticastasy whispered over his shoulder, her voice soft and mocking. She brought him his goblet of Silvan wine.

He cocked his head and gave her a weary smile. "No," he said after taking a sip. "But we like others to believe we have eyes as good as a Drugaen's."

She sat down next to him on the window seat, their legs brushing. She leaned back against the polished oak siding, regarding him. Her hair was slipping free of the piece of violet fabric, loose and combed.

"I feel a little out of place here tonight," she said, glancing at the common room and shaking her head. "Don't get me wrong, it's wonderful watching the other girls doing all the work. But part of me feels guilty – like I should be helping with the dishes or something."

"This place is a little slower than business in the Foxtale. I imagine ships dock at the wharves at all hours."

"Yes, but the mood is much nicer here. Talbin is wonderful. It would be easy working for him. See how he asks the girls gently, doing everything in the shadows. Even when that girl dropped a platter, he didn't fuss." She shook her head. "Roye would have started swearing."

Thealos nodded in understanding. "It's...quiet here."

"It's only quiet because it caters to men like you," she replied, giving him a pointed look.

He shrugged.

"I can't figure you out, Quickfellow," she said with a hint of a pout.

"What do you mean?"

She folded her arms. "I've known a Shae or two over the years, but never a Silvan lord." She smirked. "We don't see them too often on the Sheven-Ingen wharves, but I'm sure they visit Sol now and then. You have the looks of a barter's son," she fingered the fabric of his vest. "But maybe you just want to look like one. That's what I thought at first. But then the Crimson Wolfsmen came looking for you. I'd heard of them but had never seen one fight before. It's not that easy to cut down a horseman of the Kiran Thall. All of these things make you different. And then there's the Sleepwalker." Her eyebrows raised. "Your protector? Your...traveling companion? But I can't quite put the pieces together. If he's your protector, why leave to come here ahead of us?"

Thealos saw her frustration and couldn't help chuckling.

"Why is that so funny?" she demanded.

"Are you always this prying?" he asked.

She arched an eyebrow. "I don't make a habit of running off with strangers, Quickfellow. I've known you only a few days and suddenly I'm sitting with you in a respectable inn miles away from Sol with the strongest urge in the world to throttle the truth out of you." She smiled when she saw the shocked look in his eyes. "Oh, don't take what I say too seriously," she said, shifting the tone of the conversation. Her voice lowered. "What I'm trying to say – and probably not doing a very good job – is that you... intrigue me. And not many people in this forsaken kingdom do."

Talking with her helped settle the twisting feeling in Thealos' stomach. He saw the admiration and curiosity he was arousing in her, even though she was only a serving girl from Sol. He didn't want to tell her the truth, that he was a Kilshae in all but name, that Jaerod had saved him from being killed by a band of Dos-Aralon thieves. He could see the respect in her eyes for the enigma. Even Sturnin Goff offered a grudging respect and had remained silent about Jaerod in front of Allavin Devers thus far. Though Thealos didn't doubt for a moment whose side the knight would take when a confrontation finally came. He wasn't as sure of his own decision yet.

Thealos squeaked his thumb around the rim of the goblet. "I hope you're not too disappointed when you figure me out."

"Disappointed? You gave me a gown I'd never have spent money on for myself. You've put us up at a very nice inn to keep us safe. You've treated me like a lady, Quickfellow, and not a stupid human churl. I never forget a kindness."

"Or a debt or a good cask of ale from swill, I'm willing to barter," he joked. The street was hidden in the glare of the glass. Nestled in the window seat next to her, it truly felt as if they were alone in the world. "I'm from a different world than you," he admitted. "I miss Avisahn. I miss my family – especially my little sister. I'm also a long way from home. There's nothing like a walk through the city at night. The smells that linger in the air."

"I've never even seen Avisahn," she said, staring down at her hands. "I wish I could say I'd been as far as Dos-Aralon, but I can't. Flent and I...we live our lives from the memories of others. Sailors tell more lies than Shae barters," she gave him a wink, "But sometimes it's nice to imagine going there someday."

He wasn't offended. "Do you speak any Silvan?"

She shrugged. "Oh, a few words here and there. Some of the words are a lot like the king's common, but the words have different meanings. At least that's what I've heard. Like the word 'fire' – it means magic or power or light."

"That's pretty good," he complimented. "Words you use like *fire* or *silver* or *quick* have many meanings in Silvan. You've paid attention to some of the details. Being close to barters, I've known many humans myself. Mostly the cloth traders in Dos-Aralon. You can learn a lot from a cloth trader, though. You learn what people are wearing in the high court of King don Rion, or what colors the Duke of Amberdian fancies these days." He shrugged. "You also hear about the colors that are important to the Shoreland cities."

"Is this about money, Quickfellow?" she asked, her brows wrinkling with the hint of disgust. "War always raises the prices on everything. Not as much silk and satin are sold – soldiers need wool for blankets and capes and liveries." She regarded him coolly.

Thealos shook his head. He had learned in recent days how easy it was to give away too much. He was more guarded with Ticastasy. More deliberate. "I can see why you would think that, knowing my people as you do. I'm not after gold." He held up his hand when he saw she was about to interject something. "There are many in Avisahn who would like another war between don Rion and the Bandits. Doesn't matter who wins or loses, both sides will need supplies. I've no doubt that you've heard my people are, above all else, money-dealing thieves who can't be trusted."

"That is exactly what I was going to say," she replied. "But you're saying that's not why you're here?"

"No, I'm here for other reasons. That plant that the Bandits are digging up, the one that Allavin mentioned at the table. That's one of the reasons. There are others as well. But none of those reasons are about wealth. Believe me, my Correl is wealthy enough that I'll never lack for it. But when Jaerod comes, maybe then I can tell you the rest. Agreed?"

"Do you think he killed those men who were with *him*?" she asked, nodding her head towards Allavin and Sturnin.

"No," Thealos answered.

"Are you sure?" she pressed.

"Not unless he can walk faster than the wind," Thealos countered. "He's been with me."

"Oh," she replied. "I just heard somewhere that the Shae can tell when one of their kind is murdered. I figured that if he had done it, you would be able to tell."

Thealos chuckled. "Do you believe every rumor about us?"

"Well, I have yet to see you dance with the moon," she teased. "You're starting to change my mind about your people as a whole, Quickfellow," she conceded with a smirk and a nod. "I'd heard the Shae never give anything away." She smoothed the bodice of her gown. "That's just an another ugly rumor, isn't it?"

Thealos felt a cold prickle go up his spine and quiver on the flesh of his neck. A chill rushed through him.

"Are you cold?" she asked, nudging closer.

"No," Thealos answered, looking out into the darkness once again. "Jaerod is here."

* * *

The noise and gaiety of the Catpaw Inn hushed as Thealos gently shut the door behind him. He stood alone on the back porch of the inn, washed in darkness so thick that it took several moments before he believed he hadn't stepped off the edge of the world. As a Shae, he could see very well in the dark, but he wished he had the night vision of a Drugaen. The blue moonglow accented the rear street before revealing a tack and harness shop reeking of horses and leather. The heat from the day was replaced by a cold wind that knifed at Thealos' hands and cheeks. He stared down the street both ways, looking for the Sleepwalker.

"I'm over here." Jaerod's voice came out of the stillness.

Thealos nearly stumbled and his heart jolted. He calmed himself down. If Jaerod had wanted him dead, he would have let Tannon's band finish him in the woods. He had to remember that. The porch wrapped around the one side of the inn, and in the darkness Thealos had failed to see a small wooden bench with flat arm rests. Jaerod was a smudge in the shadows.

"You startled me," Thealos said, walking over to the bench. He folded his arms and hugged himself for warmth.

"It's always a pleasure doing that to a Shae," the Sleepwalker replied. "I see that we've picked up some stragglers after Sol. The knight followed you?"

"He caught up in the Shadows Wood. He was looking for you."

"And so is Allavin Devers, I understand." He paused. "What about the one playing Bones with Flent? Another stray from Avisahn?"

Thealos saw the Sleepwalker's medallion against the dark fabric of his tunic. "Flent calls him Justin, but he can't remember his own name. We found him in the Shadows Wood under escort by six Krag Drugaen. He said they were taking him back to the Ravenstone as a slave. He's a Warder Shae..."

Jaerod was standing. Thealos took a half-step backward without realizing it. The Sleepwalker had risen so fast, his motion was just a blur in the blackness.

"A Warder Shae," the human said, interested. "Or should

210

we say, *the* Warder Shae."

"You know him?"

"A Warder Shae was left to guard the Everoot," Jaerod answered. He paced away from Thealos. "When he wasn't down in the tunnels, I assumed one of the Sorian had disposed of him." He stopped and looked back at Thealos. "You don't understand a word I'm saying. Forgive me. His presence is a surprise, but one that will make a great difference in our favor." His voice whispered from the shadows. "Strange, isn't it, Thealos? It's as if the seasons have rolled on their wings, bringing summer, fall, and winter in the span of a week."

"You're not making any sense," Thealos said after a pause. His heart hammered in his chest. "Who are you...really? How did you know Justin was supposed to be there?"

"You're doubting whether you can trust me," Jaerod said. "Have I earned your trust so far?"

"Yes, but I don't know who you really are, Jaerod. You've already said that Allavin is waiting for you. I assume you also know why?"

"He thinks I killed a group of Shae scouts," Jaerod replied.

"Did Talbin's men tell you?"

"Yes. They were left to warn me in case the Kiran Thall chased you into Castun. Thealos, I don't have much time to waste convincing you of my sincerity in this matter. I've never shed the blood of a Shae. Take me at my word, or walk away from me. But I brought you here for a reason."

Thealos stood still, trying to feel if the man's words rang true. Vannier help him, but they did. "What do you want from me, Jaerod?"

"When I arrived in this land, I went into the Shoreland first. I was there long enough to search the ruins of the watchpost and to see what was going on in the Shadows Wood. From there I left for Avisahn to get you. Allavin Devers is also a *Shaefellow*. And so am I. This is all about the Everoot. Do you still have the portion I entrusted to you?"

"Yes," Thealos replied, patting the front of his vest.

"And you've been watering it?" the Sleepwalker pressed.

211

"Give it to me."

Thealos withdrew the damp sack and pressed it into Jaerod's palm. He felt the tingling prick of Earth magic leave him as he passed it over. The Everoot murmured to him soothingly, speaking to his Silvan senses of taste and sound.

There was silence between them. "You found it...useful?" Jaerod asked.

"It saved us against the Krag," Thealos answered, feeling the presence of the Everoot itch at him. Somehow, it didn't feel right – it didn't *belong* in Jaerod's hands. The magic belonged to the Shae, to those who would use it properly.

"Hmmm. You used too much of it," Jaerod muttered. "As soon as I took it away, you began craving it again, didn't you? This is how it begins, Thealos. This is part of the danger inherent in so strong a Silvan magic. It's the nature of Silvan magic to want to harness and control it. Be careful, Thealos." Jaerod's firm hand rested on his shoulder. "Be very careful not to heed those feelings."

Thealos stared up at the Sleepwalker. "I don't understand. I've used it as you showed me..."

"No, you didn't. I only use it to heal others. Never myself. I'm thankful I didn't leave you alone with it for too long. By morning, the craving will have faded and you'll see it for what it is. You remember Tannon's Band, don't you? How much they wanted your blade? It's the same thing. Only, it feels different when it happens to you. I've never let Everoot heal me. And for this reason, I never will. Let me safeguard it for now, Thealos. Whether you use it again, I will let you decide on your own. *After* you've heard what I came here to tell you – what I brought you here for."

Thealos clenched his jaw. He took a deep breath and then let it out slowly. "I'll have faith in you a little longer then."

"Thank you," he murmured sarcastically. "I am a man of secrets. My particular profession requires that. Yet what I have to tell *you* tonight, the others have a right to learn too. It affects all of us. But right now, I'm afraid Devers won't trust me if I just walk in there and say I want to talk peacefully. I don't want to fight him or the knight and cause a stir that will have everyone's tongues wagging. I move in secret where I can. Go back inside and call a *Shaefellow Pax*." His voice dropped lower, more distant. "We don't have much time before the Bandits move out of the woods. It may even happen tonight."

XXII

Xenon knelt in the dry scrub of dead cedar and turned earth and dug his fingers into the soil. His Shae senses were stung with fetid harshness, and the smell made him scowl as if he'd just breathed in the scent of a moldering corpse. Ashes and dross had been buried here – in the Silvan way. Yet beneath the corrupted soil, he felt in the distance the elusive presence of the Forbidden. The entire Shadows Wood reeked with it.

Xenon shook the stinking earth from his hand and muttered a quick prayer of purification to Keasorn.

"The Kilshae is keeping the traditions," Kitrey offered, bending nearby. The trowel marks were obvious beneath the layer of scrub.

Xenon looked at him. "Or pretending to." Kitrey was a little taller than Xenon, more willowy and graceful, but their skills were equal. Xenon rose slowly, seeing the glowing eyes of the brothers of two other quaeres with small lanterns. "There are too many tracks and confusing signs in this place," he announced, "but one thing is clear. Forbidden magic was used in this spot. This wayward child is swimming in deep waters. The instructions from the Sunedrion are very clear. He must be brought to justice."

Kitrey, Watcher Lor of the Inland, nodded in agreement. "Would you like us to find the boy and bring him to you in Sol, Xenon?"

Xenon shook his head curtly. "No, I owe him and his companion a debt for the brother we lost in Sol."

"But we've seen no sign of the Sleepwalker who was…"

"No one has," Xenon interrupted. He turned to another brother in the quaere. "Did you see sign or track of the man coming down from Avisahn when you followed the boy's trail?"

"No, Lor Xenon. It appeared to the very earth herself that the boy walked alone. There were no tracks from the gully to the campsight either. It's a Warder trick, I think."

Xenon nodded with satisfaction. "I do not know what powers he has, but the Sleepwalker is here, luring the boy into the Shoreland. It may take all three of our quaere's strength to find and subdue them. The Sunedrion is insistent. We hunt them."

The other glowing eyes narrowed with enthusiasm. Reaching to the pommels of their leaf-bladed short swords, they shared a communion of strength. Silvan magic welled up, making the grove glimmer with cool blue light. Xenon showed them his memories of the Sleepwalker and how he fought.

"He fights like us," one of the brothers from Kitrey's quaere murmured.

"No," Kitrey answered. "But it is similar. It is the old way. Who would have wasted such teachings on a human though? What a loss in…years. He'll be a withered leaf before long, Xenon. Then maybe you'll be able to catch up with him."

A murmur of laughter sung in the grove. Xenon smiled, sharing the savor of the joke through the magic's bond. It was not a taunt against Xenon as it was against the human he had faced. *He will not be so lucky when we next cross swords*, he promised himself.

"Should we send a hawk to Nordain?" another brother asked. "He's waiting word of Kil-Quickfellow's arrest."

Xenon shook his head no. "When we have the boy. *When* we have him."

He kicked at the mound of stinking ashes and the lamps around the grove dimmed into blackness until only the pale threads of moonlight were visible. The Crimson Wolfsmen

215

began to hunt again.

* * *

Thealos had never called a *Shaefellow Pax* on his own before, but he knew the ritual well enough from Correl that he was confident he could do it. He understood immediately why the Sleepwalker wanted him to call the *Pax*. It was the quickest and easiest way to call a truce between him and Allavin Devers. It struck Thealos as odd how Jaerod didn't put himself in the forefront of things. He seemed to go out of his way to give Thealos the opportunity to lead and to be recognized for it. Regardless of his motives, Jaerod's plan was a good one.

The warm blast of hearthfire air greeted Thealos as he entered the Catpaw from the rear doors. The humans called the *Pax* a 'Truce Bargain.' No weapons or magic permitted, only words. The results weren't as decisive or glorious as a battlefield victory – at least not to the humans – but the Shae preferred to conclude matters with peace if possible. Under the authority of Vannier, the *Pax* were used to create long-lasting ties between barters, partnerships and covenants that neither side would dare break – human or Shae. Thealos remembered one human merchant in Dos-Aralon who had broken a *Pax* with Correl. Both Shae and human stopped trading with him, and before the year was out, the man was ruined.

As Thealos entered the common room, he stared out over the tense faces. Ticastasy watched him from the table, her head cocked, her eyes intense. Flent was engrossed in a game of Bones, but Justin had raised his head when Thealos re-entered the room.

"Is everything all right?" Talbin whispered on his left, his eyes darting to the table with Sturnin and Allavin.

"It will all be fine," Thealos assured him. "Do you have a separate room in the back that is free?"

"Yes, do you need to use it?" When Thealos nodded, the innkeeper continued, "I'll get you the key. Do what you need to do."

216

Thealos stepped towards the table and called their attention to him. He swallowed, trying to remember all the words he was supposed to use. "As Thealos Quickfellow of Avisahn," he said, "I am calling a *Shaefellow Pax* – a Truce Bargain." As much as he didn't want to pronounce himself in front of strangers – where he was certain Nordain would find out about it – he had to follow the proper initiation. "The Pax concerns what has brought us here thus far and the Rebellion against the kingdom of Dos-Aralon. If you wish to attend, you must leave your weapons with the innkeeper and follow me to another room. If not, it is by your own choice." He gave Sturnin a level look. "Not even a dagger."

Their eyes were fastened on him. Thealos scanned his companions, judging for a reaction. He went over to Justin and whispered to him in Silvan that Jaerod would be meeting them soon and to follow him. The Warder Shae nodded suspiciously and scooped up his robes, following Thealos back to where Talbin waited with a key.

"*You're calling a Pax?*" Justin asked quietly in Silvan.

Thealos nodded. "*It's the only way we can all meet without killing each other.*"

Removing his hunting knife and Wolfsman blade, Thealos wrapped them in a blanket and handed them to the innkeeper. "Hold these for me." He took the key from Talbin and started towards the rear of the inn.

"You are truly calling a *Pax?*" Allavin called out from the table, his voice betraying his surprise.

Thealos stopped and nodded to the tracker. "You've been to one, haven't you?"

"To several," the tracker replied, rising from the table. "But never to one called in a human city. Or never without a Shae battle commander present." Allavin appraised Thealos shrewdly, then left his yew bow and quiver at the table and went to Talbin to turn in his Silvan-crafted sword. Thealos crossed the hall and unlocked the door. He lit the lamp and motioned for Justin to take the nearest seat. He leaned near him and promised to do his best to translate what was said. Arms folded, Thealos waited and watched as everyone came in. Allavin Devers, Ticastasy, Flent Shago, and Sturnin Goff.

There were still plenty of chairs, but the room was cool and silent. They all stared at him.

Thealos trimmed the lamp oil, making the shadows richer. "I am not a Shae battle commander," he said, giving Allavin a wry smile. "But the Pax is appropriate tonight considering the dangerous news I need to share with you. I called this Truce Bargain because you will all learn something that affects the peace and safety of this valley. It does concern the Bandit Rebellion. And it concerns the Shae as well." Thealos carried the lamp in front of him and set it down on the table so that they could all see the glowing in his eyes. He stared at each one of them, as part of the Pax tradition, but only Justin's eyes were also made to glow by the lamplight. "My people are not often trusted in this valley, though it is our homeland. I won't contest whether it's a reputation we've earned or not. The danger which threatens this valley threatens my people as well." He looked at them seriously. "And so we're involved. From Owen Draw to Sol." A prickle went down his neck, and he knew Jaerod had entered the room even though he hadn't heard him.

Allavin's eyes widened with shock. Thealos glanced over at the door and saw Jaerod standing there, his sword belt gone. The medallion gleamed against his black tunic.

"*What have you done?*" Allavin whispered in horror, staring aghast at Thealos. It was the worst sort of treachery imaginable to murder at a *Pax*.

"*I came without weapons,*" Jaerod said in perfect Silvan. "*I will abide by the Pax.*"

Allavin scooted backwards, his chair screeching across the wood floor.

"Wait," Thealos said, giving the woodsman a hard look. "I have not broken the Pax by calling this man here. He is a *Shaefellow.*"

"This man is a Shae killer," Allavin whispered, a look of anger and fear wrestling for control.

"No," Jaerod replied, shaking his head. He walked closer. "Never have I shed the blood of a Shae. Not once, in all my years." His gray eyes glowered at Allavin. "What you faced in the Shadows Wood was not a Sleepwalker. I can promise you that."

"How?" Allavin demanded. "How in the banned abyss can you promise me that?"

Thealos glanced at Sturnin and saw the look of determination on his face. The knight was judging whether he could take Jaerod without a weapon. The anger and tension in the room was sickening. Thealos stepped forward, cutting the quiet with his voice. "He has proof, Allavin. I asked him here to show it to us – to you. But I called a *Pax*. Do not forget that. The *Shaefellow Pax* forbid that any weapon be drawn in anger. There will be no fighting here. You must hear him out first. After you have listened, you may leave and do what you will. But not in here. If you profess to understand the culture of my people, you know you accepted it willingly." He stared at Allavin. "You cannot violate it and remain a Shaefellow."

Jaerod looked over at Thealos and nodded. He stepped back, letting some of the tension ebb from the room. He gave Thealos a commending smile. "If I didn't know who you really were, Thealos, I'd have assumed you to be a member of the Sunedrion."

Flent wiped his forehead and breathed out in relief. "Have a chair, Jaerod. There's enough for us all."

Allavin leaned back in the chair, his expression still coiled and tangled with doubt, but he gave the Sleepwalker a begrudging nod and held his tongue.

Sturnin spoke up. "I came to Castun to find you, Sleepwalker. But I won't dishonor the Shae by condemning you before hearing you. Tell us what you know." He leaned forward, resting his arms on the table.

Jaerod glanced across the room, going over each of their faces. "I'll stand, Flent. Thank you. My name is Jaerod of Safehome," he began in the formal tradition of the *Pax*, but the name *Safehome* caused Allavin and Thealos to stare at him as if he'd uttered blasphemy. "I am known by your customs as a Sleepwalker, though that is not what we call ourselves. I do not work for the Gray Legion or have ties to generals or emperors. My loyalty is to the Shae of Safehome. My order is the guardians of Safehome, the Shae city that first came to this world a long time ago."

"Came to this world?" Sturnin asked. "Or do you mean settled?"

"He means *came*," Allavin answered with a look of disbelief. "I've heard the legends. The Shae say that they came to this world on a city in the clouds and that it will return and bring them away when their work here is finished."

Thealos nestled back against the wall where he could see everyone clearly, including Jaerod. He folded his arms and listened. He knew of Safehome. But Allavin was right – it was a legend to even the Shae. How could he say he was *from* Safehome?

Jaerod sighed. "The Shae traditions you know tell a portion of it, not all. Safehome is not a city in a country or bordering the woodlands as you might expect. It is a city of peace. It did not leave the world with a promise to return. It never left. It abides here still."

"I don't understand," Allavin said. "There are many Shae anxiously waiting for Safehome to return again."

"I do not have much time tonight." Jaerod's expression was one of sadness. "Not enough to explain all that would be useful to you. Not enough to explain a hundredth of what I know about our enemies. And I am not here to tell you about Safehome and argue with you about what you may know of it. I am here because of your valley and what is happening here. I am not part of the Bandit Rebellion. Any part of it. War is beginning again in this land. A Bandit regiment has massed just south of us – about a day's march away – in the heart of the Shadows Wood. It is the Shoreland regiment, one of Ballinaire's three. The other two still threaten, but are not close enough to interfere yet. What threatens us this time is that Lord Ballinaire will not fight his war merely with weapons of steel and protect himself with armor. He has discovered in the Shadows Wood a remnant of Silvan magic – magic the Shae once controlled."

Reaching into his black tunic, Jaerod withdrew the damp sack of Everoot. He tugged open the strings and emptied the sack into his palm. The green moss looked almost black in the shadows, except for the buds of blue and violet. Thealos heard it sing to him and felt its craving stir his blood.

The Sleepwalker's eyes were unsettling. He looked at Allavin. "Is this what you saw in the Shadows Wood?"

Allavin nodded. "Yes, but we couldn't get close enough..."

"No, of course not. Ballinaire has a Sorian to guard it. There is no way you would be able to sneak past one. But a Sleepwalker..." He let the thought dangle in the air with another wry smile. "We have ways of getting past even them. This plant...this powerful bit of Silvan magic –" He looked over the faces of those in the room before stopping and staring at Flent. "It can heal any wound. No matter how mortal." His voice dropped to a soft whisper. "Do you remember how it healed you, Flent Shago?"

The Drugaen's eyes widened. "That's how Thealos healed me in Sol?"

Thealos met Flent's look of surprise and nodded. He looked at Ticastasy. "You've seen it work too."

"How does it heal?" the knight asked brusquely, stroking his mustache.

"It heals by touch," Jaerod replied. "Press it against an injury. Chew on a stub for poisoning. Make it into tea for a fever." He shrugged. "It heightens the senses, makes you keen and focused with Earth magic. But it needs water to rejuvenate itself. Simple, clean, water. As I said, the strongest of Silvan magics. It's name is the same in both king's common and Silvan. *Everoot.*"

Justin's eyes widened at the word, and Thealos leaned over and quickly told him what Jaerod had been saying.

"How much does Ballinaire have?" Sturnin asked. "Just healing alone, it would benefit any army."

"He has wheelbarrows full of it," Allavin said, shaking his head. "They're scraping it off the trees and rocks. There was a waterfall there, a...a grotto in the woods. They were shoveling it into crates. But when they washed away the mud, it speckled just like that," he said, pointing a finger at the Everoot. "Just like that." The memory seemed to haunt his eyes.

"The army of Dos-Aralon will not be defeated easily," Jaerod warned, shaking his head. "The king can send ten legions if he musters his full strength and abandons the borders. But the Shoreland regiment is enough to bring it to its knees. Imagine it. A Bandit soldier – wounded in battle – only to rise again and keep fighting, strong and whole, the very next day. You could face the same army for days, for weeks. They never tire. They never die." The Sleepwalker sighed. "Round after round of bloodshed and destruction, the smaller force whittling down and outflanking the stronger. But it does not stop there. It does not stop with Ballinaire defeating Dos-Aralon. No, the lure of the Everoot is strong. After they win, the Bandits will fight against the Shae, then the Drugaen. They will bring down the Yukilep and Iniva and force the Shoreland cities to combine. And then as it happened before it will happen again. They will turn on themselves, leaving ghosts to walk the valley."

The banquet room was as quiet as ashes.

"It will happen again?" Ticastasy asked, her eyes intense and sad.

Jaerod scooped the Everoot back into the pouch and tied it up, concealing it back in the folds of his tunic. "I have been inside the Shae vaults in the city of Landmoor. It was once a mighty Watchpost, many centuries ago. Back during the days when this valley was one enormous forest that stretched from the Kingshadow to the Ravenstone." He looked at Ticastasy. "Your ancestors came to this valley seeking refuge from a great devastation. They pleaded before the Shae king with bitter tears to grant them sanctuary from the destruction and hate that was afflicting their nation." He smirked. "To be more exact, the humans had an Empire. The Empire of Sol-don-Orai." Thealos saw confused looks from others in the room, except Justin, who started and gazed at Jaerod intensely. "Sol-don-Orai was one of the greatest, if not *the* greatest, human empire. They tamed magics that shadowed the power of the Druids of Parath-Anatos. There was a Sorian there, one who could invoke the greatest possibilities of Earth magic and Firekin. The records in Landmoor, they speak of riches and wealth and power beyond the greatest Shae king's court. An age of wisdom and opulence, the historians called it. But that wisdom was overcome by their own lust for power and magic. Yes, the Empire of Sol-don-Orai had tamed kingdoms and principalities with dazzling flying cities that could plunder and destroy, carrying armies great distances without fatigue. With a Sorian who could command nature and cause crops to yield the richest grain and fruits, this empire was unstoppable. But when they tried to control the Everoot, when they tried to seize what they had no right to control, it destroyed them. As magic always will when handled improperly."

"You're speaking too quickly, Sleepwalker," Allavin said, shaking his head. "We've heard of Sol-don-Orai. At least I have. My understanding is that a great drought destroyed it five hundred years ago."

"No," Jaerod said. "Those who remember what happened to her were too ashamed to speak the truth." He looked over at Thealos. "Except the Shae. Obviously Thealos is too young to have ever known of her. But your *elcorrel* knew Sol-don-Orai, and the Quickfellow name was known there." He looked back to Allavin. "In the Watchpost of Citadellian, there are records dating back dozens of Silvan years. They describe the empire, though briefly. Landmoor was closest to Sol-don-Orai." He stepped around a chair, his back towards them. "This Empire discovered too late what happens when Earth magic is controlled that should not be. As strong a gift as the magic is, it is also a curse. You see, if you deprive Everoot of water for more than a few days, it withers and dries. Its husk becomes a poison." He turned back, his eyes dark with anger. "Deathbane. As vicious in death as any poison to be found in nature. Metal is powerless against it. The rust and decay it causes make an armored horseman a casualty more than a strength." His eyes flickered to Sturnin Goff. "Arrows were made of the stuff. And entire legions of cavalry were hewn down like grass.

"Imagine how appalling it was!" Jaerod went on in a near-whisper. "The struggle when two armies wielded Everoot and Deathbane against each other. It was murderous. It was devastating. Refugees fled Sol-don-Orai. The borders were closed, trapping those who remained inside to meet the fate of the Empire. The Sorian who had guided them and preserved them – who had built them up from a small trading nation to the greatest power on this continent – they no longer listened to him. They were trapped by their need for the magic. When war consumes a kingdom, reason and hope gutter out first. And so the Sorian who created Sol-don-Orai destroyed it."

"Sons of fire," Thealos whispered under his breath. He couldn't believe all that he was hearing. His ears burned and his throat clenched tightly. They had never taught the full story in school.

"The Sorian killed them all?" Allavin asked, his brow wrinkling.

Jaerod nodded, clasping his hands together. "He stopped the rains. With the awful power they can command, the Sorian caused great winds to blow over Sol-don-Orai out into the sea. The clouds formed but were cast over the sea before the rain could nourish the land. He invoked the drought and the Everoot dried up. The healing and regeneration stopped. And while the remaining armies fought over water, the motes of dust swirled in the air and began killing everything in the path of the winds. Within a few weeks, the Empire of Sol-don-Orai was no more. And the land became uninhabitable. The greatest, richest nation, crumbled into dust."

"The Dust Plague," Thealos said, nodding in agreement. He looked to the others in the room. "We are taught that it was Forbidden magic that destroyed the humans there."

"Indeed," Jaerod replied. "Deathbane is Forbidden. And that is one Rule of Forbiddance that I would certainly agree with."

Thealos stared at the Sleepwalker. "The rest of it then, Jaerod. Tell them why we must go on to Landmoor. Is it too late yet to stop the Bandits from controlling the Everoot?"

"It is too late to stop them from seizing it," he answered. "But not from keeping it. The Shae witnessed the destruction of Sol-don-Orai from afar – from the safety of the trees. But even then there was fear that the war would spill over the sea and into this valley and drown the Kingdom of Avisahn in its wake. The Shae did not want to destroy the Everoot like the Sorian intended to do. It is Silvan magic

– Earth magic from their home world. It has a proper place and must be used appropriately. Deathbane was Forbidden to them. That had to be destroyed. And so the Shae appealed to the Mages of Safehome for an artifact. One that would defend them from the smallest motes of Deathbane or the great evil of the Sorian. They requested this artifact to keep the struggle of the Everoot away from the valley." Jaerod pursed his lips, silent now, pondering. "An artifact was given to them. They called it the Silverkin Crystal. It was never used. It is still in the Shoreland – still at the Shae Watchpost in Landmoor where it was intended to be the first line of defense in case the struggle came here." The gray eyes sought Thealos'. There was more – Thealos knew there was more. The door creaked open.

"Jaerod!" Talbin warned from the doorway. "A company of Kiran Thall just rode into Castun!"

XXIII

C ould be Secrist's men," Sturnin Goff said, looking at Jaerod. "Or maybe from the Shadows Wood. I think I'd like my sword back now."

"They won't be from the main regiment," Jaerod answered, glancing back at Talbin. "There were no orders to march on Castun. It must be another company."

Thealos stepped forward, his stomach twisting with the shock of all the news. He felt an urgency to get to Landmoor, before the Bandits could take the city. "How long should we stay?"

The Sleepwalker frowned, angry at the sudden interruption. "I don't want to be penned in here with so much happening near Landmoor." He scanned the faces of those around the table. "What I told you all tonight is not common knowledge in this valley. The Silverbornes of Avisahn would have records of the Everoot and the destruction of Sol-don-Orai. The older members of the Sunedrion might even recall the deal they struck with Safehome. The humans of Dos-Aralon have forgotten why they came here, or where they came from." He crossed over and put his hand on Thealos' shoulder. "I cannot fetch the Silverkin Crystal. Only a Shae can retrieve it. And there are those in Avisahn who will speak against getting involved, unless there is proof. The Crystal will be that proof. I am a *Shaefellow*, Allavin. Now you all see why Thealos and I must go to Landmoor – we would stop this kind of destruction from happening. But I can't do that alone. And Thealos shouldn't have to carry the burden himself." He looked to the others. "We need you. As many as are willing."

A hush fell over the room. Thealos felt everyone's eyes on him – there was newfound respect and admiration for what he was doing. He liked the taste of it, though his heart hammered with fear inside his chest. An artifact of Silvan power to stop the threat in the valley. Only a Shae could get it. Again it struck him that Jaerod was using him as the focal point instead of himself. He swallowed his own nervousness.

Thealos gripped the edge of a chair and faced the others. "I would be grateful for any help you offered," he said, looking them each in the eye.

"I fear if we don't get to Landmoor before the army reaches it," Jaerod said, "The destruction that happened in Sol-don-Orai will start all over again."

Sturnin rubbed his mustache. "The fortress will hold for a few weeks, I think. Don't underestimate the city's defenses."

Jaerod shook his head. "It will fall in a day, Sturnin Goff. I just pray that day is not tomorrow."

* * *

Secrist Phollen jerked the reins of his lathered gelding, drawing a snort and a shuddering backstep from the beast. He studied the face of the inn – the hazy glass of the windows, the high roof supported by huge timbers and stonework. It was a marvelous thing – would be a pity to torch it. He chewed on the Everoot, feeling the flavor dance in his mouth. It tingled inside him, making his senses knife-keen. He saw better than he ever had. He was stronger than he ever was. Faster. Dangerous. He loved the feeling the 'Root gave him.

Checking down the lines of the cavalry gathered next to him, he watched the puffs of steam rise from their breaths. Lantern fire splashed across the Catpaw, illuminating the crevices and stonework.

"She's a beauty, just like they've said," Bralt said with wonder after letting out a loud whistle. Secrist glanced over his shoulder at his chief lieutenant, who was admiring the inn. For men who lived in the saddle, marauding the lowlands day and night, nice inns were a luxury.

"What else do they say?" Secrist said sharply.

Bralt rubbed his black stubble and shrugged. "Only that a Sleepwalker watches over the place. Friends with the innkeeper...I think."

"I don't give a ban about a Sleepwalker." Secrist snorted, feeling a rush of the 'Root inside him. "You ever seen one?"

"Nope. Known a few fools who said they did...but they were drunk at the time." The hardened lieutenant grinned smugly. "This is where your brother's girl and the Shaden went. Give the orders, sir."

"Carnten and Roth – make sure the rear is still secure. I don't want Jhef and Brendin asleep back there. Kill anyone who tries to slip out."

Carnten nodded and went one way, while Roth took the other, joining the few in the back. Secrist wasn't worried. He had enough horsemen to raze the town if he wanted to.

"What about the knight?" Bralt said in a near-whisper from behind. "He's bound to be with them if we read the tracks right."

"I'll hang him. We're here for my brother's girl and that Shaden. And if we're lucky," he added with a sly smile, "A Sleepwalker too." The 'Root made him giddy and he chuckled, not feeling the bite of the cold at all. "Let's get in there, Bralt."

Kicking free of the stirrups, Secrist left the gelding prancing in the street. He unsheathed the tapered blade belted on his hip. The pommel felt cool to the touch. He wanted that Shaden's weapon, though. The short, leaf-bladed sword. That would fit so nicely in his hand. He'd cut the boy's throat with it. Ear to ear.

Secrist tested the handle of the door and it opened, letting out a torrent of hot, clotted air. He inhaled the smells of the room like fire searing his lungs and scanned the tavern hall for signs of his quarry. The woodcutters and miners gathered at the tables looked up at him and then went back to the decks of Bones and dice cups. No knight. No Shaden. No Ticastasy.

Secrist felt his anger snap and flare up, surging inside him. They were supposed to be here.

"Good evening, rider," the innkeeper said, wringing out a towel and drying another tumbler. "What can I get you tonight?"

Secrist glanced at the fine iron-work of the chandeliers. His men filed in behind him, taking measure of the place. Too pristine. Too orderly. It lacked a sticky floor and clove smoke. Not the kind of tavern Secrist liked. The innkeeper kept staring at him.

Secrist approached the bar. His boots thudded on the hardwood floor as he walked. He looked at the innkeeper's nose, fighting off the urge to crush it against the counter top. He wanted to kill someone tonight. It itched inside him. Bralt and the others filled in the room, bringing the crossbows out to menace the bystanders.

"I'm here for the Shaden whelp," Secrist announced, staring straight into the innkeeper's eyes.

The innkeeper didn't flinch. "Which one?"

Secrist scrutinized him closer, his forehead wrinkling.

"I asked which one?" the innkeeper continued, setting down the tumbler and towel. "I had two here tonight. One in robes, very sickly. The other was better-dressed. Looks like he had some money. You looking for that one?"

Secrist stared at the man. "You Talbin?" he asked.

The innkeeper nodded.

"I hear a Sleepwalker watches over your place. That true?"

Talbin stared at him, his expression guarded. "What can I do for you?"

Secrist didn't like the innkeeper's tone.

Grabbing a fistful of the man's shirt, he yanked Talbin up on the counter top and pressed the naked steel of his sword against the slope of the man's throat.

"You think a Sleepwalker's going to save you?" Secrist

seethed. He sliced into the man's neck so that blood dribbled down from the cut and stained the table. Talbin blinked quickly, flinching, but he didn't move.

"Never presume with a Sleepwalker," Talbin warned, his eyes flinty and stubborn. "Not a wise thing."

"Not a wise thing crossing a Kiran Thall either," Secrist countered. "I thought you fools in Castun would have heard that by now." He looked around the room, watching for anyone to challenge him. Nothing. He felt Talbin swallow, his eyes turning white with panic.

"Just a rumor then?" Secrist taunted. "A fool's rumor?"

Talbin said nothing.

"Then it's too bad for you," Secrist chuckled, jerking the sword back to sweep the innkeeper's head off.

Secrist's arm locked behind him and he felt a rush of wind as he was thrown backward onto the floor. Shouts of surprise rang in his ears. He was stunned by the blow and waited for the 'Root to bring him around. Crossbow strings twanged and bolts thudded into wood. Opening his eyes, Secrist saw the Sleepwalker standing over him, twisting and dodging as bolts slammed into the counter space and wall. He moved like quicksilver. Dropping down to one knee, the Sleepwalker hammered his fist into Secrist's nose and wrenched the sword from his hand, tossing it away. Secrist felt himself being lifted and then he was in the air, crashing headfirst against the far wall where he collapsed with a thump. It should have killed him.

Secrist bit deeply into the 'Root, sucking the juice down his throat to stave off the fits of pain from his crushed skull. Shouts and yells erupted from the Catpaw as the rest of the Kiran Thall attacked. Secrist struggled to open his eyes and then watched in horror as the Sleepwalker brought his men down, one by one. Bralt, Cremno, Dagger, and Tomn. They went down — just like that — with a whisper of death in the air. The Sleepwalker had a long, tapered blade of his own with an odd-shaped pommel, some strange design carved into it. It flashed against the glare of the lamps, spraying blood across the room. Another surprise, the knight appeared from the side hall, brandishing his double-handed blade. He struck at the Kiran Thall from the other side, slashing three before the others whirled and fled. Already the horsemen were retreating, howling in dismay, cowering before the strength of the Sleepwalker and the knight. The blades danced in the air, zigzagging here and there, leaving fallen soldiers in puddles of blood. Secrist stared at the Sleepwalker through half-lidded eyes, feeling his strength return and his thoughts cool into ice. The 'Root healed him. His broken nose fused back together, his smashed lip stopped throbbing. His skull fused whole again. Secrist didn't have enough 'Root left to keep going against the Sleepwalker alone. Not yet.

It was over.

The Sleepwalker stood silently over the dead Kiran Thall, looking for any movement of life. The knight had followed the fleeing men, determined to hack down as many as he could. *The craven rook!* Outside, the horses were galloping away, rushing down the street into the protection of the night. They had left him to die. *The banned cowards.* Secrist stared at the Sleepwalker through half-lidded eyes. *I'll kill you myself, you black-robed rook.*

* * *

It's over," Allavin Devers whispered in the blackness, appearing out of nowhere. Thealos eased the tension from his bow. The woodsman's boots didn't crunch in the scrub and pine needles. It was the softest stepwalking Thealos had observed in a human – except for Jaerod. He joined Thealos at the edge of their small camp nestled in the quiet of the Shadows Wood.

"Where are they?" Thealos whispered, resting the bow on the toe of his boot.

"Can't say for sure. But they scattered the Kiran Thall to the four winds, I can tell you that much." He clucked his tongue. "Ban, Jaerod is faster than any man I've seen. The knight is a howling fury himself. I'll keep watch for them. You should try and get some sleep."

Thealos patted Allavin's shoulder. "Sleep? After all this?" He rose and joined the rest of the camp. The moon barely penetrated the thick net of branches and needles. But down the slope of the hill, he could see a few of the glimmering lights from Castun. Thealos moved past the towering trunks and found Flent and Ticastasy grumbling in the dark.

"Here comes Thealos," Flent said, his sharp Drugaen eyes catching him in the shadows.

Thealos blushed, noticing that she had just finished changing into her traveling pants and boots. She shivered in a thin chemise and quickly tugged on her shirt, tucking it in. "Where's my cloak?" she asked, rubbing her arms.

Thealos saw it crumpled nearby and unfolded it before draping it over her shoulders. "I didn't mean to walk in on you," he said. "The gown you were wearing was pretty, but it would have only tangled you where we're going. Allavin is back. Talbin and the others at the Catpaw are safe."

"Good," she muttered, tugging the cloak about her. "But I was really looking forward to sleeping in that bed tonight. You should have seen the stuffed mattresses, Flent. Roye never would have paid for those."

"No he wouldn't have," Flent chuckled, rubbing his meaty hands together for warmth. He packed the gown into her traveling sack and cinched it closed. "Haven't had a good sleep since Sol. Hate, I sure miss the smell of the ocean."

"I don't mind the ocean, it's the bird droppings and dead fish I don't miss," Ticastasy quipped. She cocked her head. "What about you, Quickfellow? Wish you were home instead of down in the Shoreland like this?"

Thealos sighed. "I told you I miss my sister a lot...but this is where I'm supposed to be. I'm glad you were able to hear what Jaerod had to say tonight." He thought about the feeling of safety he had grown up with, believing that the Crimson Wolfsmen kept intruders out. But it was only illusion after all. Their defenses wouldn't work against a threat like this. "It's not easy being so far from home, is it?" He gave Flent a firm pat on the back. "You don't have to come with us," he said. "You could go back to Sol or head north to Dos-Aralon from here."

"What for?" Flent muttered. "There's nothing in Sol worth going back for. So Roye can yell at me and call me some stu-

pid rook again?" He shook his head. "No, I don't think I'm
ever going back there." He looked up at Thealos. "I would
have died that night in Sol, if you hadn't healed me. I owe
you for that, Shae." He paused then grinned. "What, thirty
pieces or so? My life's gotta be worth about that."

"Ten and you're pushing it." Ticastasy gave the Drugaen
an affectionate hug. She also looked up at Thealos, giving
him a smile. "He's my best friend in all the world. That made
you my friend when you saved him."

Thealos dropped to a low crouch, feeling his cheeks burn.
"I haven't forgotten that both of you offered to help me in my
time of need. I don't forget my friends either." He touched
his hand to theirs. "If we make it through this, I promise you
won't have to work in Sol ever again."

"A while ago, we used to talk about opening our own
place," Ticastasy said. "What did we want to call it, Flent?
The Ragged Staff? We decided to be the owners, so we'd get
to keep all the Aralonian pieces. Maybe we should open it
up in Dos-Aralon, what do you say? After this foolish war is
over. I'm...never going back to Sol either," she said with a
hint of regret in her voice. She looked at Flent knowingly. He
nodded and patted her hand.

Thealos stared at her in the darkness. He knew she
couldn't see his face, and he was glad. She had lost her
meager belongings leaving Sol. He felt responsible for that
– for all of them. She was the first human – except Jaerod
– who had stood up for him after leaving Avisahn. He owed
her something.

"The Ragged Staff, is it? It'll be the nicest tavern in all the
realm," Thealos promised, giving her shoulder a comforting
squeeze. "Nicer than the Catpaw. Nicer than the Foxtale. I
can get you a good price on Silvan wine."

"And Spider Ale?" Flent asked hungrily.

"You silly Drugaen," she laughed. "The Shae don't touch
ale." She leaned back and rested her head against Flent's
chest. "Maybe it won't be Dos-Aralon. Maybe we'll build it
down here in Landmoor. Promise to visit us, Quickfellow?"

Thealos smiled and gave her a little hug. "Of course I will.
I have plenty of Aralonian pieces Flent hasn't cheated from

me yet." He butted Flent with his elbow. He envied their friendship and the years they had known each other. But it was something more. Maybe it was the fierce loyalty of friendship Ticastasy had for Flent. All his life he had struggled to make his own way, and he had struggled alone. Those he had grown up with had chosen callings like they were supposed to. He alone had defied the Shae hierarchy. He saw a little of that defiance in Ticastasy. He stared at her in the dim moonlight and felt a mixture of feelings, both tender and strong. Flent and Ticastasy were his only friends outside of Avisahn. His only real friends. Jaerod was a mentor, but he had motives Thealos couldn't begin to comprehend or relate to. These two accepted him the way he was.

Or who they think me to be, he thought darkly. A Silvan prince.

Glancing across the shadows of the camp, Thealos saw Justin watching him with a frown and a look of disgust. Thealos met Justin's disapproving stare and held it. "Try and get some sleep, both of you," he said to Flent and Ticastasy before moving away from them to join Justin.

Justin huddled in his dark robes, his features almost indistinguishable in the darkness. As Thealos drew near, he felt heat emanating from the other Shae and saw that he was comfortable in the coolness. The tiniest wisp of Earth magic flavored the air. Justin's blue eyes glimmered in the dark.

"You are too familiar with the human girl."

"I have not broken any of the Rules of Forbiddance," Thealos replied, dropping into a low crouch before the other. *"They are my friends. I deserve no reproach for that."*

Justin smirked contemptuously. *"The Drugaen is harmless. A child. He covets her friendship and nothing else. But the girl is dangerous. She cares for you, and you know that love between our races is Forbidden."*

"You mistake her affection," Thealos countered. *"There is another she has given her heart to. She wears his regard on a chain around her neck even now. But who I chose to make my friends isn't your business."* He gave the other Shae a level look. *"Now, I did not have time to translate everything Jaerod*

told us tonight. But you seemed to recognize some of what he said. You know of Sol-don-Orai?"

Justin nodded. *"I've been there."*

His statement didn't startle Thealos. *"And the Everoot?"*

"It was the cause of her destruction." Justin's eyes flashed with anger. *"I do not trust the human who holds it. His loyalties are divided, I think. He prances and speaks like a Shae, but he is still a human to the core."*

Thealos frowned. *"Jaerod is the reason I am here. He wants to stop the sickness that plagued and destroyed the Empire. He doesn't want it to happen again here in this land."*

"And are you Vannier, who can read the true intents of a man's heart?" Justin asked mockingly. *"How do you know he isn't using you for his own ends?"*

"He isn't."

"But how do you know?"

Thealos stared at Justin. *"I don't think..."*

"It does not matter what you think," Justin interrupted. *"You trust the humans – it is as obvious as lightning in a rainstorm. But I do not. I have known too many to ever trust them. They twist our ways and profane our gods. They mock us, my friend."* He shook his head. *"I am not a Banished One. I cannot abandon our heritage that easily."*

"Is that what you think I've done?" Thealos challenged in a harsh whisper. *"Abandoned our faith? To trust them? Do you know what has happened to the Shae since the days of Sol-don-Orai? Sweet Vannier, they have taken nearly the entire valley from us as a result of our 'trust'! The eastern river is the last boundary they haven't dared cross. The rest is theirs. We've been pushed and cramped up against the Ravenstone mountains where the bloody Drugaen have been fighting since I was born!"* He noticed that Flent and Ticastasy were looking at him with concern. He calmed his voice, grateful they didn't speak Silvan. *"I did not allow that to happen to our people. I am here because I believe the Sunedrion will finally involve itself in this war if they know what is happening down here. And if we get involved, we take back some of what was ours. The leader of the Bandit Rebellion is our enemy, not Sol-don-Orai, not Jaerod. The leader's name is*

Ballinaire and he has taken the Everoot, and he is using it without instruction on its dangers. That is Forbidden." He glared at Justin. *"But I must have proof when I return to Avisahn. If I'm to convince them that the humans have found and are spoiling Everoot, I must have proof. They will not move without it."*

Justin leaned forward and gripped Thealos' arm. *"Then make me your proof! The records at Avisahn, they will tell me what I need to know – what I cannot remember because of my long sleep. The records of my watchpost are ruined. Everything has sunk and fallen into the bog. But they kept all the records in Avisahn, in Silverborne's palace."* His eyes were eager, intense. *"Come with me, Thealos. Come with me to Avisahn. Let us find the truth and tell the Sunedrion together. The witnesses of two Shae are worth more than all of these unbelievers combined."*

Thealos shook his head, frustrated. *"I can't."* He rubbed his eyes, not wanting to explain about Nordain. If he went back without any evidence, he would spend the entire war in a Shae prison. *"The only defense we have against the horrors of Sol-don-Orai is a Silvan artifact – the Silverkin Crystal. The Crystal is ours if we can get there first. Jaerod knows where it is..."*

"He knows nothing."

"I know more than you think," the Sleepwalker said from the darkness, Allavin Devers in tow behind him. They joined the two Shae. Justin's eyes glittered like dagger tips.

XXIV

*S*peaking *Silvan well does not make you a Shae,"* Justin mocked.

"I suppose it doesn't," Jaerod replied, sitting on the carpet of pine needles. *"But not even Shenalle can make a human into a Shae. The best we can do is act like you. And try to do better,"* he added with a barb. Before Justin could rally a retort, the Sleepwalker raised his hand. *"I was taught by the Shae. As was my friend here."* He nodded to Allavin. Jaerod looked Justin in the eye. *"I understand the source of your distrust, Warder. In your day, the Shae cowered here in the valley, praying that the Empire of Sol-don-Orai would leave them alone. It would have taken more than Warder Shae and Wolfsmen to call off the Empire's flying cities and you knew that back then."*

Justin tensed. *"I was there, human. Do not pretend to know what it was like."*

Jaerod smirked. *"Too many years asleep in the Earth magic has its consequences, Warder. You don't remember as much as you wish you did. But the devastation that the Empire brought on itself was enough to cause your watch-post concern. Concern enough to seek the aid of the Mages of Safehome. When they grant the desires of the Shae, there is always a price. And the coin chosen is never the same. What do you remember of your Warding when the Mages chose you to defend it?"*

Justin's mouth dipped into an angry curl, but he kept his temper wrapped up in his robes. *"Why should I reveal any-thing to you?"*

"Because I know more than you think I do. Maybe I can help you remember who you are."

Justin didn't look convinced. *"I will say what I can, human. The Mages chose me for the Warding because of my youth and expertise in taming the Earth magic. It was not certain how long the war in Sol-don-Orai would last. I protected the Everoot that was taken from Sol-don-Orai and planted here. To preserve and cultivate it that its magic would not be lost from this world. If the Warding was disturbed, I was to intervene."*

Sturnin Goff appeared out of the darkness. He'd left his roan in Castun, but he was wearing his traveling armor, which was dented and spattered with blood. He nodded to them before nestling against a crooked cedar tree nearby.

The Sleepwalker nodded to him before turning to face Justin. *"Do you remember when the Warding was breached?"*

Justin shook his head no. *"When I awoke, I was in the tunnels of my watchpost. Everything was in ruin. I thought that the Solarian war had already ended, that we had lost and the Warding had failed. But the humans I discovered in the tunnels did not speak Silvan or the tongue of the Empire. I came to realize that they were not Solarians at all. They were descendants with a garbled language. The watchpost hadn't fallen, it was abandoned, covered with earth, and being sub-sumed by the moors."*

Jaerod rubbed his mouth. *"What was your directive if the watchpost was to fall? Do you remember?"*

The Warder Shae folded his arms. *"I cannot tell you that. All I can say is that I am to seek the Heir of Quicksilver."*

Thealos looked at Jaerod in confusion, and the Sleepwalker held up his hand to forestall any questions. *"Why?"* Jaerod asked.

"I...I can't tell you."

"Do you remember? It was part of the Warding," Jaerod insisted. *"They were linked – the Everoot and the Silverkin*

Crystal. If the Warding was breached, the Silverkin would call for help."

Justin looked disgusted that Jaerod knew so much. *"Then I won't bother lying to you,"* he said archly. *"You are right. There is another magic in the tunnels. But it was Warded as well. Only the Heir can reach through this Warding. I do not know what the talisman is or how it was supposed to work."*

"What did the Warding look like?" Jaerod pressed.

"The other Warding?" Justin shifted and tugged his robes around himself. *"An Otsquare,"* he answered.

Allavin Devers whistled.

"You know of an Otsquare?" Justin demanded incredulously to the woodsman. *"By the gods, is nothing sacred in this era?"*

Allavin raised his hands defensively. *"I've seen the Otsquare, but I thought they were only found in the Riven Wood. They are Forbidden to humans. I do not know what they mean, but I know they are held sacred."*

Justin gave Jaerod a challenging look.

Jaerod replied with a calm smile, *"You are right, Allavin. An Otsquare forbids any human to pass. Not even a legion of Bandits can cross it. Not even a Sorian."*

The Warder Shae raised an eyebrow. *"So the Sorian are involved in this."*

Jaerod nodded. *"Two, this time. One you will remember from Sol-don-Orai. The Emperor's advisor, Mage."* Justin nodded in recognition. *"The other made her home with the Shae in the Kingshadow – Miestri of the Vale."*

Thealos shook his head, not understanding. *"Who are these Sorian?"*

Allavin rested his bow in his lap and rubbed his thumb along the riser. "Jaerod just finished explaining to me about the Sorian I met in the Shadows Wood. The one that killed the Shae scouts I was with. The one I thought was a Sleepwalker."

Jaerod gave Allavin a reassuring nod and joined the story. *"The Sorian were part of the original religious order when the Shae first came to this world. My order have been taught and trained by the Shae to counter and oppose their work. I must tell the rest in the king's common, Warder. They do not yet understand the enemies we are up against."*

Jaerod called Flent and Ticastasy over to join them. The knight was cleaning his blade with an oilcloth, but he listened as the Sleepwalker spoke. "The Kiran Thall are fleeing, but some will flee to the army to warn them. That is unfortunate, but it doesn't change my plans. I was intending to go through the middle of their camp, not the edges, anyway."

"Why go through the middle?" Ticastasy asked, confused.

"It's the thinnest part of the line," Jaerod replied. "I scouted to the east and west to see if there was a good point where we could slip through. If we tried to go around either side of the regiment, it would take days. And we do not have that long. The narrowest point, the least defended, is the center. Because no one would be so foolish to do what we will do."

Sturnin Goff shrugged. "What about the sentries? I'm sure there are Kiran Thall watching the road."

"I know where they are," Jaerod answered. "Allavin and I will deal with them. The Bandit officers will be watching for us to slip around the army. They do not realize our goal or our intentions. The command pavilions in the center are their most vulnerable point. Before we continue south, I wanted to tell you more about the dangers we face in the Shadows Wood. Specifically, the dangers of the Sorian."

Thealos looked at Ticastasy and Flent and saw the somberness in their eyes. Jaerod continued. "The Sorian order has lived on this world for thousands of years. Since before the Shae came. They do not age – at least not noticeably – and they rarely die. This medallion I wear is of the order of Safehome. My work is to oppose the Sorian wherever I can. Their intentions have proven throughout history to be...very destructive. I am not the only one who wears this medallion, but there are only a few of us left, and many who were taught no longer remember why the order was founded. They use the skills and training for their own ends. You know them as Sleepwalkers, and so we share a reputation, not a cause. Let me explain what I told Allavin earlier. The Sorian involve themselves in the affairs of kingdoms and generals. They seek to control and manipulate crowns and principalities to increase their power." He looked at them seriously. "They do not do this directly themselves, but manipulate through others. As I mentioned, it was a Sorian who took a small trading nation and turned it into Sol don Orai. It was a Sorian who founded the Druid priesthood of Parath-Anatos. There is a Sorian who advises the Emperor of the Shieldlands to the north. And there is a Sorian who created the East Kingdoms."

"Why?" Sturnin asked. "If they are so powerful, why bother with underlings? I've never even heard the name before."

"You're from Owen Draw, Sturnin. You've heard of the Witch of the Vale, haven't you?" Sturnin nodded, understanding. "Rulers come and go, humans age and die – but the Sorian can only be killed by their own kind. The reason they don't become the kings and emperors is because of the attention they would get. They don't fear man or Shae, but facing an army would be foolhardy and come at great cost to their powers. In such a weakened condition, they can fall prey to other Sorian. It's a game they play amongst themselves. And empires have fallen because of it. My order has battled their influence since the beginning. And many of us have died for opposing them. The founders of my order were Shae." Thealos stared at him in disbelief. "But they trained those who were willing and prepared to carry on the fight. Some Drugaen were taught. Humans were also. My grandfather, father, and uncle were all part of this order. We have a deep respect for the ways of the Shae. But the Shae no longer involve themselves in the struggle as they once did. They have turned within themselves. They have forgotten why they came here."

Jaerod paused, looking from Thealos to each of them. "I have never taken the life of a Shae. This is how I convinced Allavin that I could be trusted. This is why he is choosing to come with us to Landmoor."

Allavin nodded. "Tell them the rest, Jaerod."

"What else?" Thealos demanded.

The Sleepwalker looked at them and sighed. "When I visited the Bandit camp earlier today, I discovered a Sorian there. Maybe there is another guarding the Everoot, too. What I mean to say is crossing the army will be more difficult than I first thought."

* * *

Dappled sunlight poked through the web of tree-limbs and towering branches, bringing a surge of warmth to the new day. Thealos came awake when Jaerod passed through the camp, telling them that it was time to leave. A few hours of sleep was all they were given. But timing, Jaerod had said, was important. Thealos felt sluggish, but he roused himself, rolled up his blanket, and tugged on his boots. The rest of the group finished gathering their blankets and hurried down a quick meal before Jaerod broke away from Allavin to join them.

"You look weary this morning," Jaerod announced with a sad smile. "I wish I didn't have to tell you that sleep will be precious in the days ahead. Would that we could have stayed at the Catpaw for a night – your rest would have been better there." His gray eyes went to each of their faces. "But we need to reach Landmoor quickly, before it falls, and there is a Bandit regiment and a Sorian blocking the way. Thealos and I can go on alone. You need not risk your lives. If you wish, Talbin will allow you to stay in Castun until we return."

He waited, but no one had changed their minds. Thealos was grateful. Flent and Ticastasy seemed nervous, but determined. Justin scowled, anxious to be on his way to Avisahn instead, but willing to postpone the journey until they had accomplished the task. But he had only promised to go with them in return for Thealos' word that they would bring the Silverkin to the Shae once they'd claimed it. Sturnin studied Jaerod skeptically, and it was clear by his expression that he was still convinced that the fortress of Landmoor would hold for several weeks and determined to prove it.

"I've talked with Allavin and Sturnin, and we feel the least dangerous time to attempt to cross the army is at night. They will be watching for us, so it will not be easy – but I would rather try to slip through than fight my way through...if at all possible. If the Sorian decides to get involved, leave that to me." He gave them all a confident smile. "I know a few tricks the Shae scouts didn't. You are to go on without me if I'm delayed. Thealos' mission is the linchpin. He must get to Landmoor at all costs. He must claim the Silverkin Crystal and bring it safely out of there. Allavin, would you give the marching orders?"

The lean woodsman nodded and stepped forward. "The Iron Point Road is well-traveled and clear. Not many rough spots until we reach the Shoreland swamps. This half of the forest is dry and flat, but the southern half is jagged and wet. That's where it will be difficult, but it will also help us dodge the regiment and Kiran Thall. It will take at least two, maybe three days to cross the Shadows Wood. It's thicker to the east and west – that's why they cut a road here. Wide enough for an army to march. Jaerod asked me to scout ahead, to warn us of ambushes and approaching horsemen. Sturnin Goff will take the front, then Justin and Ticastasy. Flent will linger in the back, and Thealos, I want you to bring up the rear. You will help keep anything from sneaking up behind us. I always want a bowman in the front and the rear." He put his hands on his hips. "Good enough?"

"You are one of the best," Jaerod complimented. "Take the lead, Allavin."

Allavin smiled and went off ahead of them. His lean body had a long stride and puffs of dust came up from his boots. He moved quickly, in the Silvan stepwalking pattern.

A few moments later, Jaerod led them down a short embankment in the trees and onto the road. The Sleepwalker walked ahead of the rest. Thealos watched Ticastasy's hair bounce and Flent rub his ale-bleary eyes. Justin hugged his rustling robes. Sturnin looked menacing in his splotched armor, and Thealos was glad to have him in front.

Huge trees stretched their shadows across the Iron Point Road. A blanket of low-hanging clouds wore away by mid-morning, and only then the sun touched the road. The noontide sun bathed them with light for only a quarter-hour before the other wall of vine maple and cedar obstructed it. The Shadows Wood smelled of dust and cottonthistle, and there was scarcely a breeze. The road had been cleared of dense scrub and pine — just wide enough to permit wagons and travelers. Clumps of witch-thorn and wildflowers choked the sides of the road.

Thealos was lost in his thoughts as he walked. He remembered what Jaerod had told them that morning if the Sorian decided to confront them. *Leave that to me.* Thealos was impressed with his confidence, the way he accepted the danger and determined to face it anyway. Sleepwalkers had been killed by Sorian. Jaerod had intimated that much. But was this Sorian good enough to kill Jaerod? Thealos swore under his breath. He hoped to Keasorn not. In his mind, he remembered his last night in Avisahn when Nordain demanded that he choose a calling. Thealos now knew what he wanted most. He wanted to be a Sleepwalker. He wanted it more than anything. The benefit he could be to the Shae – and especially to Laisha Silverborne as she assumed the throne when her father died. A Sleepwalker could go anywhere and not be seen – could face down Crimson Wolfsmen without weapons. Jaerod had scattered a group of Kiran Thall – nearly alone. It was Sturnin who had insisted on fighting alongside him. And hadn't Jaerod gone to Avisahn looking for someone like Thealos? Hadn't he said that they were more alike than Thealos realized?

He stared down the road at the Sleepwalker, amazed that he left no trail of bootprints to follow.

XXV

Dujahn of the Gray Legion took a quick gulp from his cup of lukewarm ale. He set it down and rubbed his bloodshot eyes, listening to Hallstoy tear into him again. It was the middle of another sweltering night, and he'd only gotten a few hours of sleep the previous evening.

"You tell that banned woman I want her out of my camp!" Hallstoy bellowed. "Sorian or not, she's caused enough problems. Tsyrke will be here in another day or two, and another Sorian with him! If that bleeding harlot is still here by then, she'll rue it for sure. Do I make myself clear, Dujahn?"

Dujahn looked up at the Bandit colonel. "If you're too afraid to say it, I can tell her whatever you wish, Hallstoy. But she will leave when she is ready. Not before."

"The men were just fine until she came. Now every other man has the gut-sickness and a bout of tide fever is hitting us!"

"You're camped in the middle of a swamp!" Dujahn said, exasperated. "Of course there is going to be tide fever!"

"We were here before she arrived," Hallstoy said. "And we have all the tobac and juttleberry to handle a campaign. But now half the army is sick and in need of a healer. The whole banned Zerite cult couldn't cure all of us! You're a blind half-wit if you don't believe she's done this. I want her out of my camp."

"Tell her yourself."

They glared at each other. Dujahn watched fear and anger battle across the colonel's face. He didn't care. If he never set foot in the Shadows Wood again, he'd consider his life blessed. His voice was low so that the other duty officers wouldn't hear. "You're afraid of her, colonel. That's healthy. There are worse things than gut-sickness."

Hallstoy's expression went flat. "Get out of my tent."

"Gladly," Dujahn replied. He pushed away from the table and started for the opening of the tent door when shouts of alarm rose up in the camp.

"Sweet hate, what now?" Hallstoy said.

Dujahn opened the flap and was nearly knocked over by a Kiran Thall barging in. "Colonel! We're under attack!"

Dujahn blinked with surprise. "What did you say?"

A horn blurted in the darkness, several long heavy blats that caused a collective groan from the mass of writhing men. Yells and shrieks from the camp spurted up all around.

"The pickets were breached," the Kiran Thall gasped. "A dozen dead already. Some say the knights of Owen Draw – others claim they've seen the Shae. Half of the dead are from arrow wounds, Colonel. They're moving through the camp too quickly. Must be Crimson Wolfsmen – it's the only thing that makes sense!"

Dujahn staggered outside, watching the mass of teeming soldiers coming awake in the middle of a midnight raid. His heart slammed against his ribs, catching fire with the smell of smoke and fear in the air. The soldiers were panicking. If Hallstoy didn't quell it, they'd start attacking each other before long.

"Colonel!" Dujahn said, turning back into the tent. "It's a small force. Less than a dozen, no doubt. Maybe Wolfsmen, maybe they want us to think that. They're going to hit the south pickets. Send your forces there – quickly!"

"How do you know?"

"This is my profession, you fool," Dujahn snapped, rushing from the tent to warn Miestri.

* * *

Thealos had never felt so afraid in his life. Forbidden magic. Everywhere. The smell of it was thick and putrid in his nose, overwhelming in its intensity. The stain of it was throughout the Bandit camp, laced in the mud and cinders and groaning coughs of the sick. He felt its effects leeching the life out of the camp. As they had entered the army, the men were stronger. But near the center of the Shoreland regiment, the presence of true Firekin was thicker than the mud clinging at his boots.

He was amazed that no one had challenged them yet. Maybe it was the stinging smoke from hundreds of campfires. Maybe it was sleep and ale. Getting past the Kiran Thall at the perimeter was almost too easy. Jaerod had taken Allavin along with him, and both had returned moments later, beckoning them on in silence. Thealos had never felt so much tension in his life. At any moment, someone would call out in warning and the chase would be on. Waiting for that moment was agonizing. Thus far, Jaerod's plan had been flawless. They walked quietly through the camp, stepping around the sleeping soldiers and steering wide of the command pavilions in the center. Jaerod had been through the camp himself and picked out the path he had chosen earlier.

"Who in blazes…?" a voice rang out before an arrow whistled and dropped the man with a grunt. Allavin had another arrow ready instantly.

"Over there! Do you see them? Intruders!"

"Run!" Jaerod ordered, and the chase began. Arrows lanced out at the soldiers who had spotted them, but the alarm had been raised at last. As a group, they started a quick jog together. The Sleepwalker's advice burned in his memory. Create chaos and confusion in the darkness. The Bandits would start fighting themselves. Thealos turned and shot an arrow into a smoldering firepit as he had with Tannon's band. A shower of sparks erupted, causing curses and shrieks from the soldiers sleeping nearby.

"Right flank! Thealos!" Allavin shouted out, dropping another soldier with an arrow to the man's throat.

"Got them!" Thealos shouted, swallowing to keep from

vomiting. He gripped the riser of his hunting bow and drew another bodkin arrow back, sighting a Bandit commander's mail shirt before letting it fly. He reached for another arrow and dropped the other soldier with a solid shot to the leg. The man stumbled and cursed, grabbing the shaft that crippled him.

"You Shaden rook!" a Bandit yelled from behind him, and Thealos whirled, using the bow to block the sword thrust. Before he could grab at his blade, Thealos watched Flent score the man across the back, sending him crashing into the churn of Shoreland mud. The Drugaen nodded for him to follow, and Thealos pressed behind him into the camp.

The alarm went up like wildfire as they ran. All around them, the soldiers were waking, emerging from tents and hurrying to fix their hauberks in place. It was madness. And if that wasn't enough, the reek of Forbidden magic was so strong he could barely think.

Sturnin Goff and Jaerod cleared the path ahead, their blades scything through the Bandit sentries who opposed them. Allavin held back with Justin and 'Stasy, keeping a steady rain of arrows on whoever charged at their flanks.

Thealos gasped, staring at the dead Kiran Thall sprawled in the wake of the Sleepwalker and the knight. Command pavilions came alight with lanterns and torch-fire. Thealos wanted to look everywhere at once, but he couldn't. His courage wilted under the danger, and he felt like dropping his bow and sprinting with all his might.

"Come on," Flent said, tugging at Thealos' arm to keep him from losing the rest of the group. The Drugaen's face dripped with sweat. His hazel eyes narrowed as another rush of Bandits came at their rear. Swinging the axe up, he prepared for the fight.

Thealos felt a prickle of Earth magic just before the ground turned into a stinking black morass and trapped the attackers. The Bandits let out startled yelps and sunk into it, and they were soon covered in black, tarry mud. Thealos glanced over his shoulder and saw Justin looking at the Bandits, his thin arms lowering.

"Quickly!" the Warder said, waving them after him. Naked

fear blazed in his eyes.

Thealos and Flent caught up with the group. Thealos breathed the humid air in gulps, trying to quell the fear and nausea in his stomach. He had never witnessed the carnage of a battle before. The blood-spattered wretches writhing in the mud didn't hint at the glory and honor that had always been his perception of war. And he had never felt so abandoned or so alone, so at odds with the peace and tranquility of Avisahn. In all the hard business dealings in Dos-Aralon, he had felt the absence of the Earth magic. The din of commotion always muted it. But the depressing blackness of thought and feeling that suffocated him was a hundredfold worse than anything he had experienced. Even the bitterness of the Krag they had faced was nothing compared to this. No, the Forbidden magic being used in the army was anathema to any Shae. And the wielder of that magic knew he was there — silent, thoughtful, and fully aware of his presence. A shiver of comfort ran through him, and he turned to see Jaerod behind him.

"We're almost through," Jaerod said, and the words brought Thealos back from the cliff of his fears. He could feel the man's presence tingling on the back of his neck. The Sleepwalker had doubled back, leaving Sturnin alone in front. Thealos glanced at each side of the camp, watching the trembling masses of men rise from their bedrolls, struggling to overcome the lethargy of sleep. They were too slow, too sick and disorganized to stop them. Jaerod's voice pitched low by his ear. "If we're separated, go on to Landmoor. Let nothing stop you."

In the bowels of the camp, Thealos felt a presence stir – a whisper of magic that stung his nose and brought tears to his eyes. His knees buckled. He stopped and stared, blinking quickly, and tried to steady himself. The presence was unmistakable and chilling. Squinting in the darkness, he saw a single pavilion, separated from the rest. Thealos went cold to the bone.

"Keep moving!" the Sleepwalker said, rallying the group around him. "Close together now."

Thealos stood paralyzed.

"Come on, Thealos," Jaerod urged. "It is only fear. I will protect you."

"The Sorian," Thealos stammered, all blackness and chills.

"Yes, the Sorian. The magic in Landmoor can stop this. Remember."

He listened to the Sleepwalker's voice and grasped onto his words. Fighting down the panic, he gripped his own blade's pommel for reassurance and followed Jaerod into the last row of pickets. Dead soldiers littered the ground.

"What now, Sleepwalker?" Sturnin demanded, mopping the sweat from his forehead. His mail shirt was cut in several places, showing glistening snags of chain. He had several nasty wounds. The breastplate was smeared in blood, giving the knight a menacing look in the dim light.

Allavin clutched an injury on his side and scanned the treeline. "Kiran Thall are roaming on the south bend. Ambushes everywhere. We should leave the road and strike into the woods. I can get us south around them. The road will be too dangerous now with their horsemen."

Jaerod nodded. "The Kiran Thall will follow us into the woods. Lead the way, Allavin."

Thealos felt a whisper of death in the air and froze again. He smelled the Forbidden magic even stronger. Justin shoved up his sleeves, revealing thin arms prickling with gooseflesh. The Warder Shae was as tense as a bowstring.

"*It's here,*" Justin whispered with dread.

Out of the darkness of the wood before them came a shape sharing the colors of the night. Soft velvety robes swished and moved apart, revealing a woman holding a glowing orange orb. Her eyes were depthless and black and sent shoots of fright down to Thealos' toes. He couldn't breathe.

"Get behind me," Jaerod warned, moving before the band to face her. His tapered blade was up defensively, gleaming with a cool white light. He jerked his head to Allavin. "Take them, now!"

"Go!" Allavin barked, jerking Ticastasy by the arm and breaking off away from the main road and the two combatants. The Sorian and the Sleepwalker faced off in the reddish light of her orb.

For a moment, Thealos panicked. He didn't want to leave Jaerod alone, yet he felt helpless where he was.

Justin did not.

The Warder Shae stretched out his long thin arms and sent a blast of Earth magic at the woman. Thealos inhaled the acrid smell of flame and cinders that brushed against his face as the light exploded on them. Heat and flames licked at her robes, but the orb flickered once and the fire guttered out, leaving nothing but haze.

"Go, Warder!" Jaerod said, advancing on her. "She is more than your match."

Justin's body tensed as he stared with hate at the Sorian. She stood still, studying Jaerod with an impish smile on her mouth. She wasn't interested in the Shae at all.

"Welcome to the Shoreland, Sleepwalker," she said in a teasing voice. "I've been waiting for you to come back."

Thealos covered his eyes as scarlet flames jumped from the orb and rushed at Jaerod in a blast.

Again Justin intervened, bringing up his arms and sending a jolt of blue lightning at her. With a casual pass of her hand, the jagged arc deflected away, slamming into a huge cedar with a shattering crunch of splintered wood and ash.

"Go!" Jaerod yelled, swinging his tapered blade and slicing through the red curtains of flame. The polished edge cut through the magic, absorbing its heat and rush.

Thealos grabbed Justin's arm and pulled him away, darting into the forest after the others. The Shadows Wood swallowed them in its blackness, and Thealos had to slow down as the branches cut his face and hands. He cursed under his breath, struggling through juniper bushes and over mossy slopes. Justin lagged behind, panting for breath. The Warder Shae's robes were stained with mud and his eyes glittered with emotion.

"*She is a Sorian,*" Justin huffed, pausing against the slope of a tree. "*And the Sleepwalker will die.*"

"*Don't say that!*" Thealos gasped. "*Jaerod knows how to protect himself.*"

Justin shook his head. "*Sorians are immortal. She cannot*

die."

The feeling in Thealos' stomach deepened. He looked back the way they had come. The forest was dark, but the light from the Bandit camp was getting brighter. Already the sounds of pursuit could be heard. Their sprint had taken them far from Jaerod and the Sorian, but they had also lost the others in the darkness of the woods. He didn't have Flent's Drugaen vision to see well enough in the night. He rubbed his mouth, listening to the sound of the Kiran Thall whistles getting closer.

"*Go with me to Avisahn,*" Justin said and then coughed. "*We cannot face her without the Heir.*"

"*And what about the others?*" Thealos said, praying that Jaerod would emerge from the trees, following them. He clenched his fist. *Don't leave me alone to do this, Jaerod. I need you!*

"*There is nothing they can do,*" Justin replied. "*There is nothing any of us can do. We must go to Avisahn and warn the Heir. That is our duty. The duty we owe our people.*"

Thealos shook his head. "*I don't believe that. Jaerod knew...*"

"*What could he know?*" the Warder whispered. "*He said it himself – they have fought and died against the Sorian. We need the Red Warriors here. We need the Silvan army. For the love of Shenalle, Thealos, you must believe in the Shae! If we die here, who will carry word of our failure?*"

From the Bandit camp, a blinding white streak of lightning lit the night. Thunder shook the trees and dropped them both to the ground. The force of it caused dry needles to rain down throughout the woods.

"Sweet Vannier," Thealos gasped in shock, knowing by a sick feeling of sudden emptiness that Jaerod was gone. The thin prickle of gooseflesh that had followed him since Avisahn had winked out, abandoning him.

XXVI

Dujahn had encountered a Sleepwalker once before. When he was advising the City Duke of Trivaedi years before, one had entered the palace grounds and abducted the Duke's daughter. Dujahn was the only one who had seen the man dressed in the darkest black walking the halls at night with unselfconscious ease. His heart had stopped for fear and he did nothing, not even when he saw the Sleepwalker carrying the girl out over his shoulder, bound and trussed. He would have died. He knew it then as clearly as he knew how to breathe. If the Sleepwalker knew he had been seen, Dujahn would have been killed. He never told the City Duke of Trivaedi. He'd never told any man.

Dujahn kept to the trees, watching as Miestri faced the Sleepwalker with an air of indifference. She was the most powerful person Dujahn had ever met, but he knew the reputation of the Sleepwalkers better than most.

This one was a medium-sized human, but fast as a cat. The black clothes disguised his movements, helped him blend in with the shadows and smoke. He had a wicked-looking tapered sword and handled it like an expert swordsman. There was no denying the Sleepwalker's abilities. Dujahn didn't get a good look at his face – the hood prevented that – but he saw the style and graceful movements, like a bird gliding just over the ripples of a lake. Effortless. Graceful. Deadly.

The sword whipped around again, catching the tongues of red fire and snapping them off before the flames could touch him. The sword was Silvan. There was no doubt about that. The blade glowed white, as if hot from the constant blasts of the Sorian's power, but it stayed firm and hard. Tempered steel would have shattered by now.

Miestri smiled teasingly, advancing another two steps. The Sleepwalker didn't run from her, but he shifted his position, always keeping her in front of him.

She spoke something in Silvan, a taunt. Dujahn struggled with it, trying to translate. *Do you know how many of your brothers have begged me for a quick death? They wept, Sleepwalker. They wept for it.* The Sleepwalker said nothing, focusing on the blade, ready to move when she attacked him again.

He's good, Dujahn thought, clucking his tongue. A few Kiran Thall had gathered near him, keeping a safe distance. The camp was still reacting from the attackers, but the rest had gone into the forest. Dujahn had seen the two Shae slip away, but he had heard there were others. A knight, a woodsman, a Drugaen, and a woman. Strange company. Strange night.

A dazzling white flame jumped from the orb in Miestri's hand, catching the Sleepwalker in the middle. He grunted with pain and swept the blade down, shattering the magic with the sword. Smoke burned from his chest and Dujahn's eyes widened. Was he hit? He thought nothing could hit a Sleepwalker! He only saw the smoke drifting from the man's chest. But as the Sleepwalker turned again, pacing in a half-circle around Miestri, Dujahn saw the smoking amulet. It had absorbed the blow. It had a strange marking – a cross set in an octagon. It matched the symbol on the pommel of his sword. Interesting...

"Must be the Sleepwalker from Castun," one of the Kiran Thall whispered. "Ban..."

"Killed Secrist's company, I heard," another muttered. "Sent the rest squealing like pups."

"Ssshhh!" Dujahn hissed, eyes intent on the battle in the edge of the woods.

The Sleepwalker and the Sorian faced off again. This time, Miestri bowed her head. Dujahn could feel the prick of magic in the air, the burnt smell of fire. The Sleepwalker tensed as red glaring flames exploded all around him. It came rushing at him from all sides like a sinkhole. The blast of heat and air singed Dujahn even at the distance and he covered his face.

"Sweet fury!"

From a cloudless night sky, a shaft of white lightning crackled down into the camp, swallowing everything in its dazzling glare. Thunder shook the trees, spilling pinecones and dead branches down. The clap knocked everyone to their knees.

Blinking quickly, Dujahn wondered in a panic if he were blind. He clenched his fists and stared at the ground until the white smear in front of his eyes cleared and he could see again. Looking up, he found Miestri standing alone, staring at a spot of scorched earth.

"She...she bloody killed him!" one of the Kiran Thall gasped.

Dujahn watched her in disbelief. But something was wrong. There was no look of triumph on her face. She stared at the smoking earth, studying it with cool fury. Dujahn stepped away from the others and advanced. The grove had been burned clean, leaving ash and soot everywhere. Only a smoldering pile of ashes in the middle showed the Sleepwalker's last stand.

He stopped. A black sigil twice the size of a barrel lid scorched the earth where the Sleepwalker had stood. It was the same mark – an offset cross set into an octagon. The air smelled sharp and sour.

Miestri sniffed at the wind and leaned forward, studying the mark. Dujahn scratched his head and watched her. Her smooth pale skin was soft in the dim firelight, and her eyes were thoughtful and intrigued. She prodded the black ash with the toe of her padded slipper. Closing her eyes, she inhaled a long deep breath through her nose. She opened her hand, revealing the orb. It gave off that strange reddish light that continued to haunt Dujahn. "Tell them to stand back," she said. The colors in the orb began to weave and convulse.

Dujahn swallowed, taking a short step back. "Back!" he said in a sharp voice. "Get back!"

The soldiers who watched were already abandoning the grove like waters receding after a rock is dropped in a pond. Dujahn couldn't move. He stared at the sphere, drawn like a moth. The reddish light made the ground dim and hazy, like an early morning fog out at sea. Miestri's hand tightened about the sphere, the tendons in her hand growing hard.

In an instant, the Sleepwalker stood before them, gripping his blade furiously, swarming red flames all around him. Dujahn felt the heat of the flames, felt the magic rush through his body as it attacked the Sleepwalker. He tried to cough and scream, but the flames didn't burn. It was only an illusion. Miestri's eyes grew hard and intense. The images slowed as if in a stupor. The flames looked like jagged knives, the colors slow and torpid. Everything seemed to happen like a slow, steady breath. Dujahn blinked with wonderment. He was watching it all over again.

Just as the flames reached the Sleepwalker, there was a burst of light, blood red and horrible. Shielding his face, Dujahn struggled to see through the glow, and then he saw the Sleepwalker move. Gripping his medallion, he stepped through a tear in the lightning and was gone.

"Interesting," Miestri murmured.

The crimson hue vanished as she tucked the orb back within the folds of her robes. The magic fire and lightning disappeared, swallowed by the sphere. Dujahn turned to her. She laughed softly at him. All of his training, all the diplomacy and composure he was taught was rendered mute by the Sorian. He gaped at her, seeing the orange light still flickering in her eyes.

"Did you drop your voice in a well?" she asked.

He nodded foolishly. She had reached into the past, twisted her fingers around it, and yanked it back to watch it again. It horrified him. "Who...who was that?"

"Only a Sleepwalker," she replied.

"And the others? Who were they?"

"One is a Knight of the Blade," she murmured. "The woodsman is from the Riven Wood."

"How do you know?"

She shook her head waved her finger. "Never doubt what I speak. Just believe. I've been in this valley for a long, long time."

"Yes, my Lady."

"The Shae," she mused, rubbing her lip. "You saw them, didn't you?" She stared past the wooden picket lines, oblivious to the masses of frightened soldiers watching her.

"You know them?" Dujahn demanded.

"One of them, yes. But I did not think he would return so quickly."

Dujahn looked at her, confused. "The one who tried to hurt you?"

"Hurt me?" She laughed. "Really, Dujahn, you have no imagination at all. He cannot hurt me, for he is mine."

"Then who was the other Shae?" he blurted out.

"Obviously the key to the lock," she answered. "And I thought it would be Silverborne's little one. Oh, this is getting very interesting indeed. If only General Dairron were here to enjoy it, too. Come, Dujahn. We have work to do."

* * *

Dujahn coughed as he parted the tent flap. The room was full of officers wearing the black and gold of the Rebellion. He saw animosity on their faces, but he didn't care. The Sorian gave him authority. They might glare and they might posture, but her threat was enough to keep their swords in their sheaths. "Excuse me, Colonel Hallstoy – the Lady of Vale would like to see you. She has your orders."

Hallstoy looked at the officers surrounding him. Anger sparked and flashed in his eyes. Dispatch papers were littered on the only desk in the room and stacked in a heap on the floor. He had rosters and reports to prepare – knowing that his head was in jeopardy if he didn't come up with explanations and answers for Ballinaire. "Get out."

Dujahn stepped inside confidently. "Do we have to go

through this again?"

The Colonel turned on Dujahn, his face red. "I don't like repeating myself, Dujahn! You tell Dairron's witch that I'll take no orders from her. I lead this camp when Tsyrke is gone. And if she doesn't like it, she can eat a warm bowl of trope!"

"Indeed," Miestri said, slipping through the tent flaps behind Dujahn. A chill went through the tent. "Do let it be horse trope, Colonel. Cow trope wouldn't fit in a bowl."

Hallstoy's eyes widened with shock. Scratching his balding scalp, Hallstoy spit on the floor and narrowed his gaze at her. "You have no authority in this camp, Miestri," he said. "Tsyrke is on his way, and Mage with him. This is my command tent...."

Miestri lowered her cowl and her raven hair spilled out.

Hallstoy frowned, seeing her ivory smile. "Get out," he hissed. "Take your banned magic and get out of my tent. We've just been under attack, and I don't have time to be wasting on your whims, I don't care..."

"My, we are brave," Miestri said as she raised her fingers and closed them together. Hallstoy's voice trailed off into a squeak and his eyes glazed over with fear. He might talk and bluster, but she was in control – even over his voice. Dujahn shivered. She stared into Hallstoy's bloodshot eyes and flashed a wicked smile. A current of magic trembled in the air, and Dujahn stepped to the side. The other officers backed away from Hallstoy.

Hallstoy's face started to twitch. A look of horror and pain twisted his expression, but he couldn't speak. His hands flew to his face as rips and tears began splitting across his scalp and cheeks. Choking with agony, Hallstoy fled the tent, trying to keep the skin on his face. Several of the officers coughed, nearly gagging with disgust. No one stepped in to confront her.

"Officers," Miestri said gently, spreading out her hands. "You disappoint me. It only took seven to make you all into fools." Her mouth flashed a dangerous smile. There was something in the air, a tingling feeling that spread as she spoke. "Lord Ballinaire will be furious when the dispatch reaches him. Commander Phollen will be equally outraged. How could you let seven Inlanders humiliate you? These were Iniven farmers and Shaden with pruning hooks and straw arrows who defied the armies of the Rebellion!"

Dujahn swallowed, not daring to let the surprise show on his face. He watched the colonels cringe and twist with rage and anger. He stared at her in awe at how she used her powers to manipulate them.

"Could you not hear them laughing at you as they walked through your watch fires and posts? They were laughing at you!"

"There was a Sleepwalker..." one of them mumbled.

"Shut up, you fool!" another snapped, cutting him off.

"The greater disgrace," she hissed, her eyes glittering with feeling, "Is that you were taken so easily. Like children caught napping. I've seen General Dairron's brigade. I tell you that they would not have been surprised so easily." She shook her head, making her dark hair flutter. "If Commander Phollen were here, do you know what he would do? Do you know what Kiran Phollen would have done?"

As her voice rose in pitch, the tension in the room increased. Her magic swept through them, her voice instigating it, drawing in the soldiers like candles eating light from a single flame.

She sneered at them. "I remember the days of Kiran Phollen. His courage was fierce and his cunning quick. He'd repay this insult a thousand fold. He'd be a scourge to Dos-Aralon. How long has it been since Lord Ballinaire commanded us to be at war? How long will you stand here, begging for a leader who will act? If Commander Phollen were here, he would strike don Rion in the belly and twist his knife deeper."

There were grumblings of assent.

"You are not dogs tied to a stake," she said, her beauty and magic stealing into their eyes and hearts, razing the memory of Hallstoy or any obedience owed him. "No master stands over you with a stick. Rise and bite! The village to the north is weak. Destroy it! Landmoor is unprotected. Take it! If you are men of courage, then show it! If I were a general, I would not let this mockery go unpunished."

"What should we do, my Lady?" Colonel Davys shouted. Dujahn looked at him. He was taken with her. It showed on his face. He would have done anything for her.

"War," she declared. "Let it begin. Your soldiers are not sleepy — why make them rest? March tonight – this instant! Send the horses of the Kiran Thall to scourge and the soldiers to reinforce. Landmoor – she is ours!"

The Bandit officers started drawing up the new orders, their faces livid. They were barking out orders, calling on duty rosters. The Kiran Thall would go first, followed by the first ranks of soldiers. They wouldn't wait for dawn.

Dujahn watched the small smile twitch on her mouth.

* * *

Dujahn didn't like the Kiran Thall leader the moment he saw him. This one swaggered like a man with too much to drink, and by the mutton on his breath, he hadn't drunk in a while. The man's resemblance to his brother was tell-tale. Both Phollens had a dark brooding expression, but this one had a half-snarl on his mouth as well. Tsyrke Phollen was a head taller, though, and wore his grandfather's tattered red cape. Secrist Phollen was trim and lanky. But his eyes were desperate. Living in a brother's shadow could be a consuming itch.

Dawn crept into the Shadows Wood, showing a camp that was in the final stages of deployment. Most of the command pavilions were down and the wagon wheels churned the mud and manure into thick dark cakes.

"You ruined Hallstoy, Miestri," Secrist spat, pointing in the direction of the woods. "I don't think even a Zerite could heal that face. No man will ever follow him again. Not remembering him like that. Tsyrke's gonna be in a Fury when he sees what you're doing to his army..."

Miestri gave him a contented smile. "You do not have time to worry about him, Secrist. You have other matters that need your attention. There were two Shae involved in the attack on the camp. They are heading to Landmoor. You must stop them."

The Kiran Thall halted, his eyes narrowing. "How do you know?"

"Because I know what they are after."

"The Everoot?"

She shook her head. "What they seek is in the city itself. Ballinaire has enough strength to protect the Everoot. And while this army is stumbling blindly in this swamp, the two Shae are hurrying south alone."

"If you did not already know this, you should," Secrist announced. "They have one of the best banned trackers in the valley with them. One of the wounded men saw him – swears it's Allavin Devers. Haven't had any luck hunting his band down yet."

She nodded. "Yes, but the Shae are no longer with him or the knight. They went by themselves."

"How do you know?"

"I know a great many things, Secrist Phollen. They are going to the tunnels beneath the city. They will enter through the shrine ruins. Down in the tunnels, there is a twisting maze at an archway supported by two stone gryphons. They must not enter that maze."

Secrist gave her a narrow look. "I could be killed for serving you."

The Sorian smiled knowingly. "But with this, you won't die," she replied, holding out her hand. A batch of the green moss quivered there. Dujahn watched the reaction on Secrist's face. He stared at it desperately, a look of hunger so raw on his face that it was painful to watch.

The Kiran Thall wiped his mouth. His hand was trembling. "What do you want me to do?"

"One Shae is a Warder. He will deliver the other into your hands."

Secrist smirked. "How convenient."

Miestri nodded. "He has a weapon you desire, I think."

Secrist frowned and rubbed the stubble on his jaw. "What do you want me to do with him? Bring him back to you?"

"Kill him."

Secrist smiled. "What about the Sleepwalker?" He nodded

to the Everoot. "If I have to face another one, I'll need more of that."

Miestri shook her head and reached into the folds of her robes. She withdrew a dagger with a copper hilt. A piece of leather wound around the grip. The blade was not any metal that Dujahn had ever seen. It had a grainy texture that looked like black sand. Had she poisoned it?

Miestri passed the dagger to Secrist, who studied the blade in the lamplight. He looked at her and raised his eyebrows. "Deathbane," she answered and watched the Kiran Thall grip it, mesmerized by the blade's dark texture. "If the blade so much as glances the skin – even a Sleepwalker would die. And no amount of Everoot will bring him back. Now go, Secrist. Use it against the Shae. Nothing can stop you."

A dark smirk crossed Secrist's face as her magic wove through him. He couldn't take his eyes from the dagger. "Where will you be after I've killed the Shaden?"

XXVII

Allavin Devers slouched against a cedar, resting a moment. He squeezed his yew bow, gritting his teeth. Anger and fear wrestled inside him. Only the Rebellion made him this angry. He was angry that a pig-headed knight rebelled all those years ago and caused so much suffering because of his ambition. And very few things in the valley frightened him anymore. Except the Sorian – the Witch of the Vale. He shook his head and steeled himself. The knight wasn't afraid. Those from Owen Draw had lived too long on the borders of the Kingshadow near the largest nest of Bandit regiments. They had learned to master their fear long ago. But he knew the magic of the Sorian would affect the Shae even more. Distant shouts whispered through the woods. He had come back to see why Thealos and Justin had not followed and discovered the Kiran Thall clotting the forest and following two sets of trails. He muttered an oath. The girl would be worried about Thealos. So would the Drugaen. Allavin had to admit it to himself. He was too.

Leaning away from the tree, Allavin quickly climbed the small rise, careful in every bootstep. Clearing the tracks as he went, he listened to the sounds of pursuit. The Kiran Thall were furious at being eluded, even though it was still the middle of the night. They had the advantage of horses and lanterns, but the Shadows Wood was thick and nearly impenetrable by horse in some points. Allavin knew enough tricks to shake the horsemen loose. But he wasn't confident either of the Shae did. He hoped Thealos was competent enough to elude the Kiran Thall. The difficult part would be crossing the lowlands to Landmoor without being seen. The edge of the forest was several miles from the city walls. And he had his suspicions that the Kiran Thall would be watching from the trees.

Grabbing a branch, he swung himself up and over a huge juniper bush and landed deftly. He glanced both ways, trying to pick out the path in the near blackness by touching the earth, letting his fingers read the signs instead of his eyes. Not much further to where he had left the others. The earth was mushy in spots, which he tried to avoid. Clearing tracks from mud was very difficult. But unless the Bandits did full circle sweeps every hundred paces, they wouldn't find his trail.

"It's Allavin." Flent's rough voice was distinctive in the darkness.

Allavin smiled. He'd forgotten about the Drugaen's sight. Bounding the last few steps up the steep rise, he joined the others in a small clearing surrounded by rock and crooked cedar high up the slope. A thin shaft of blue moonlight invaded the clearing, glinting dully off of the knight's armor.

"Where's Quickfellow?" Ticastasy asked.

Allavin settled down in a crouch, laying the bow across his lap.

"Captured?" the knight asked.

Allavin shook his head. "No. Not yet." He eyed each one of them. "I think she got the Sleepwalker though."

Stillness fell over the group.

"Are you sure?" Sturnin sounded skeptical.

Allavin shrugged. "I don't know enough about Sleepwalkers to be sure. But she called up this red fire to surround him and then a flash of lightning from above..."

"We saw it," Ticastasy said, nodding.

Allavin shook his head. "But he knew that when he faced her. No, what I worry about more is the two Shae." The girl's eyes flared with worry. Allavin held up his hand. "I double backed to fetch them but they ran another way. You've got to understand something about the Shae. They can smell Forbidden magic at a hundred paces. The kind that she used – this Sorian woman – well, that's the most Forbidden kind there is. When I got back, the Kiran Thall were everywhere." He frowned, the memory of Tiryn's death still bitter in his soul. "When she came, it reminded me of our ambush here in the 'Wood. Like I was living it all over again. The same sounds, the same looks. I thought none of us would make it out."

The serving girl nodded and squeezed his arm. "Was that near here?"

Allavin gave her a level look and sighed. "Other side of the Iron Point Road. I came here because some Shae scouts were flying overhead on alerion for a routine visit to Avisahn and saw some sort of magic storm in the Shadows Wood not far from Landmoor."

"They flew a what?" Ticastasy asked

Sturnin answered. "They are like large birds, but their wings have scales that cut like knives. We call them Dragonshrikes in the Kingshadow, but the Shae named them alerion. They love sheep."

Allavin nodded in agreement. "You won't see them in the Shoreland because they hate the heat. They prefer the cliffs and the snows. The watchposts of Citadellian and Jove Stand breed them to serve as mounts. Beautiful creatures. Their plumage is like the fire of a candle."

Flent and Ticastasy both stared at him in wonder.

"The Shae fly the alerion to keep information traveling to Avisahn," Allavin continued. "As I was saying, the scouts I knew were going there, but they saw magic being done in the Shadows Wood. They saw a waterfall and wooded glen. The forests were swarming with Bandits. They'd never seen that much activity before and wondered at the source of the magic. That's when we found Ballinaire digging up the Everoot. That's when we were attacked. I thought it was a Sleepwalker, because I couldn't get a good look at it. The reputation – that's what I'm saying. But the thing that hunted us down killed all four Shae and would have killed me if I hadn't stumbled into quickmire."

Sturnin leaned forward. "I'm sorry about your Shae friends, Devers. But right now we're missing two of ours. Did you see where they went?"

"I saw where the Kiran Thall were hunting them, but if Thealos has any sense, he'll start cutting crossways to make the trail difficult to follow. My fear is that they might double back and try and find ours, and I don't think either is good enough to out-track these Bandits. The Kiran Thall will catch them pretty banned fast if they tried."

Sturnin seemed to agree. "Would they be smart enough to go on to Landmoor?"

Allavin rubbed his chin. He picked a twig out of his beard. "I think so."

The knight rose. "If the Sleepwalker's dead, then we only have one option left. You go after the two Shae. You've got to catch up with them before the Bandits do."

"There's a Bandit regiment in between us, looking for all six of us," Allavin reminded him, shaking his head.

"I heard about that time when you led a company of Bandits around in circles for three days, giving the knights enough time to get there. We hung the commander when we caught him." He chuckled gruffly. "If anyone can, Devers, it would be you."

Allavin grinned, embarrassed. "All right, it's not that hard. But finding two Shae in the middle of the night without getting caught by the bloody Shoreland regiment is not as easy as you'd think. I'll need help, Flent."

"Me?" the Drugaen spluttered.

"You saw me at thirty paces in the dark and I was trying not to be seen. Besides, I can't handle a company of Kiran Thall on my own."

"Then why don't we all go?" Ticastasy said. Her arms folded and her eyes flashed defiantly.

Sturnin shook his head. "No, lass. We need to warn the governor of Landmoor and ready the fortress for a siege. Jaerod thinks she will fall in a day. But I think we can hold her longer and maybe even muster a sally against these craven rooks. You saw that army. They've got tide fever and dysentery. Hardly half would be fit to march." He looked at

Ticastasy. "You're coming with me."

She shook her head. "You warn the city, then. I'll go with Flent."

Sturnin gave her a rock-hard expression. He wasn't about to be countermanded by a serving girl. "You do not want to be caught by a Bandit army in the middle of a war. You'd be serving more than Spider ale."

Her face went ashen. "Maybe you're right."

"Good, lass. We'll have our own troubles. But leaving you out here in the woods isn't a good idea either."

She shook her head. "No, I'd rather be in a city."

Sturnin smiled wryly. "A city under siege isn't much better, but we'll make it through this." He looked at Allavin. "If you find them, bring him to us in Landmoor."

Allavin rose. "There's a good inn on the north side of town. The Wee Kirke. Owner is Blain Kirke – he'll know me."

"Hopefully you paid him last time you were there," Sturnin said and rose, gripping Allavin's hand and giving him a hearty shake. "Good hunting, tracker."

"You be careful, Flent Shago," Ticastasy said, her eyes burning. She gave him a tight hug.

"I will," the Drugaen promised in a whisper. She squeezed him even harder.

"You'll always be my best friend," she said, giving him a light kiss on his bearded cheek.

He smiled and gave her a squeeze around the waist. Nodding to the knight, he hefted his Sheven-Ingen axe. "Meet you in Landmoor, Sturnin."

"Before you go," the knight said, pausing him. He held out his hand and motioned for the axe. Flent handed it to him, confused. "I saw you in the Bandit camp. You swing this like you're cutting down a tree, which is good if you're fighting trees. Leaves you vulnerable when it's too wide, see? Swing it down like this, high to low and low to high. That's how you kill a man with it." He smiled and gave the axe back to Flent.

"You sure about that?" Flent asked, turning the double-bladed axe over in his hands. He looked back up at the knight and winked.

* * *

Ticastasy tugged the cloak tighter for warmth. Her ankles throbbed from all the walking, but she kept up with the knight without complaining. He wasn't a talker, not the kind that she enjoyed at the Foxtale. No, he was the kind who sat in the corner, quietly ate his supper and drank his ale, and then went for a bed with nothing more than a grunt or two of acknowledgment. Dawn had greeted them several hours ago, yet they still could not see the sun past the steel-gray clouds overhead. Fog swirled at the top of the trees, settling down over the Shadows Wood like a quilt.

Sturnin Goff reached the edge of the small embankment and stopped, peering through a thick curtain of scrub and pine. She walked up behind him, barely as tall as his shoulder.

"What is it?" she asked.

"The banned Valairus fog," he cursed. "Can't see Landmoor. But she's out there."

Ticastasy looked at the deep banks of thick clouds that had settled over the Shoreland moors. She heard bullfrogs croaking, the steady buzz of jupeflies, and even the whistle of swallows. There was definitely a creek or stream nearby, but the lapping waters were lost in the haze.

"And you were wondering how we would cross without being seen," she said. "The fog roams up here every night. Should have counted on that, Inlander."

"It's a blessing and a curse," the knight said. "If the Commander of the Shoreland regiment is half as clever as a grub, he'll march the army down in the early morning. He can get pretty close to the walls without anyone noticing. Come on, lass. Let's go."

Ticastasy followed him down the rugged slope, leaving the thick forest behind them. The marsh grass was soft and squishy beneath her boots and soon cakes of mud clumped on the heels. She paused to shake them off, but Sturnin kept marching. Walking in the mist was like getting little wet kisses on her face. They had to stay close to each other, for the fog swirled so thick in parts that neither could see past a few paces. She watched the dew collect on the tips of her hair and soon felt as if she had just emerged from a dripping bath. She wiped her face, surprised at how much moisture was there. Sturnin's armor looked absolutely frigid. Little streaks of watery blood trickled down the breastplate, making her shudder with disgust.

She thought about Quickfellow as she walked. She knew she shouldn't, that it would only make her worry more. Knowing that Flent was with the best woodsman in the entire realm helped lessen her anxiety for her friend. Allavin would keep him alive. But she couldn't help wondering where Thealos was. Were he and Justin crossing the mists at the same moment? Walking two hundred paces from each other and not knowing it? Wouldn't she be surprised if he emerged from the fog ahead of them. She wanted to laugh. Would he even care if she did...?

A thrush fluttered from the tall reeds ahead, flapping its wings and cooing after being startled. Ticastasy's heart thundered in her chest, but she calmed down, watching Sturnin Goff shake his head and mutter something. It had startled him too.

Suddenly, he stopped and planted his fists on his hips. She joined him and stared down the edge of a small rut into the icy waters of a creek. The waters were at least knee deep, and probably deeper in the middle.

"Wait," Sturnin advised and stepped down into the cold creek. He sank a little in the mud and then held out his hands. "Let me carry you across."

She stared down at the frigid waters and shivered in spite of herself. She didn't want to appear weak, though. "I can...I can make it," she said, nodding.

Sturnin gave her an amused smile. "The cold can hurt you faster than you'd think. I've seen men die of the cold after crossing rivers. Big men. Now come here."

Hesitantly, she lowered herself down and let the knight carry her. His armor was hard and biting, but she didn't fuss as he waded through the wide creek. On the other side, he boosted her up the embankment. Reaching down, she tried to help pull him up, but he was far too big and heavy to be much help. If she had been with Quickfellow instead, they probably would have crossed it and then shivered together. He certainly wasn't big enough to carry her across the creek. She smiled at the thought. Why was she thinking about him? He was too pale, too rich, and a stubborn Shae to boot. But he had a charming smile – that was certainly in his favor. He was generous in a world that did not nurture generosity, especially among a people noted for their bartering and deceit. Yet he fit neither description very well. That intrigued her. It always had. Quickfellow was...unique. So different than Tsyrke.

The memories sparked to life again and she shivered with anguish. That was why she was thinking about Quickfellow so much. She had been trying to forget Tsyrke Phollen. Lies, all along. She had fallen in love with Tsyrke months ago – or who she thought he was. A rich sea merchant from Ilvaren who wanted to take her away. She was blinded by the gold coins, his roguish smile, and the possibilities of what it would be like to be called his wife. But then he had left and never returned, leaving her with a small pendant to whisper those promises in the dark. But they were lies! He was a Bandit commander. It was his army she had just crossed. She couldn't help but wonder if he had been there. She would never forgive a betrayal. Not one. She'd warned him of that. She was one man's woman – wouldn't share him with anyone else. Well, he'd had his chance. Now all she had left was Flent. And Quickfellow.

It felt like she had been walking for days when they finally reached the base of the hill leading to the city-fortress. The fog had receded a little, but the moisture clung to their skin and clothes. Ticastasy was exhausted. The traveling pack dug into her shoulders, and she was tempted to leave it behind in the rushes.

"We're almost there," Sturnin said, following the base of the hill until they joined the Iron Point Road that wound its way up to the summit. Her legs groaned in protest, but she plodded forward, shaking the mud from her boots as they climbed the stone road up the side of the hill. Her breath came in quick gasps and the muscles in her calves knotted up.

"Are...are they going...to listen...to us?" she panted.

Sturnin nodded, his face drawn with fatigue. His pace never wavered. "When the Accords of Dos-Aralon were passed, the knights were given authority to command any garrison to defend the kingdom. We've had more training against the Bandits than most, so the Governor may just turn over command to me. He probably has a retired battle commander in the city for token duties," he added. "But we're facing a full regiment out there. He'll need experience."

Ticastasy nodded, wondering how Sturnin kept his breath after marching all night and all morning. She couldn't wait to reach the Wee Kirke and a hot, steaming bath.

The city rose out of the mist like a forest made of stone. The watchtowers loomed overhead, breaking up the even blue of the sky with stark gray lines and ridges. It was enormous, and she gasped in awe. Noises rose from the city proper, along with smells from a hundred places. Dumplings frying in tallow, smoke and cinders, stews and cheese vats, curing oils and dross. They were all welcoming smells to a girl who had spent her whole life in Sol.

The main gate lay open, but the portcullis was down, its huge timber frame blocking the way. Sturnin Goff advanced and greeted the gate captain on the other side.

"Well, sweet bleeding Achrolese," the man said in a thick Shoreland accent. His hair was trimmed down to the roots in the fashion of the south. "It's a bloody knight of Owen Draw. Take a look here, would you. By the Druids, I can't believe my eyes."

"You're using the porter doors?" Sturnin asked. The captain nodded, and the knight nodded with relief. "Good. I need to speak to the garrison commander. Send for him."

"Will do, sir," the gate captain said cheerfully. "Hey Hollom, open the porter door. Got a knight here. Hurry up, now! I don't have the banned key, I gave it to you this morning." He gave Ticastasy a low bow. "Sorry, your queenship. We'll have it open in a moment."

The porter door lock clicked open and they were met by

271

some of the garrison wearing the colors of Dos-Aralon.

"You're the first word we've had from the north in a long spell," the gate captain stammered, shaking Sturnin's hand. "I've sent for the garrison commander. You want to speak with the governor, too? Do you need to stay at the barracks?" The gate captain's men crowded around to get a good look at Sturnin and the huge sword strapped across his back.

"No, I'll stay in town. But send a man with her to the Wee Kirke if you would," the knight replied, nodding towards Ticastasy. "She hasn't slept all night. Go on, lass, I'll join you later." Then ignoring her completely, he turned to the gate captain and started hammering out his requests. "I'd like to see your stockyard and armory. Then you can show me the battlements and the cisterns. We need to start carrying in water right away."

The gate captain motioned for a soldier and spoke to him in a near-whisper. The escort nodded and offered to take Ticastasy to the inn. She followed, but something wasn't right. The gate captain looked nervous and kept glancing back at the barracks. Frowning, she followed her escort away from the knight. She scanned each of the sentries, trying to figure out what was wrong. As they passed the heavy battlement walls and entered Landmoor, she passed by the window of the barracks. She glanced a second time, just to be sure.

Standing in the window was a Bandit officer wearing black and gold.

XXVIII

Blain Kirke sliced into the hot roast goose with his knife and burned his fingers as he stripped a piece of the salty meat away. He savored the taste, enjoying the blend of ground sader and peppers that flavored it. Kirke was a plain-looking man with big shoulders, rust-colored hair, and a thick mustache that made him appear to frown. His hair was cropped short in the Shoreland style, but he still hadn't lost his Inlander way of speaking. Scooping up a hunk of bread, he dabbed it in the stew and chewed, wondering how long the stores in the basement would last.

Allavin Devers' last visit had not been very encouraging, and for days after he'd left, Blain had wondered if the woodsman was right. He shouldn't have wasted his time thinking about it. Allavin knew the Bandit army's movements better than anyone else. If he said there was trouble coming to the Shoreland, there would be trouble.

Travelers from the north had all but stopped in the last fortnight, causing no small amount of worry to the local innkeepers. Blain had enough Aralonian pieces to hold out for a lot longer than that. He was able to eat his dinner without the gut-gnawing worry of a man about to lose everything to the Shae moneylenders. But still, the lack of word from the north worried him.

Taking a sip from his tankard of ale, he watched the slow pace of the kitchen as they prepared early for the evening

273

meals. He shook his head. He didn't want to let any of the serving girls go. It was too soon for that anyway. They were good girls, but he'd lost Nerissa to some seedy pub in Windrift not many months ago. The others just weren't as good as her and struggled to bring in the share of coins that Nerissa's smile had brought them.

Dabbing a hunk of bread in the stew, he continued eating, wanting to be finished before the real crowds started. He always liked to wander and observe during the mealtime, to see what dishes worked and which didn't. It wasn't an easy business, and complaints spread faster than sewer fumes.

Tanita approached him from behind. "Blain, there's a girl here to see you."

He glanced over his shoulder. "I can't hire anyone," he answered. "Who let her go? That sneering wretch Bissom?"

She shook her head. "She said Allavin Devers sent her."

Blain brushed his hands together and then wiped the crumbs from his mustache. "Bring her on back. Be quick about it." He'd finish the goose later.

Leaning back in his chair, he folded his big arms and stared at the door. Tanita brought the girl into the kitchen and pointed him out. She nodded, smiled a quick thank you, and then hurried over to the table. Her boots were muddy, her clothes a mess, and her hair was tangled and damp.

"Sit down, lass," he said, pushing the other chair over with the toe of his boot so she could join him. "Looks like you're in trouble."

She nodded, leaning forward and looking at him with the nicest brown eyes he'd seen in a long time. A good scrubbing with soap, and he could imagine what she would look like underneath. A pretty girl, no doubt about that.

"I've a warning to give you," she said, keeping her voice low enough so that only he would hear. Her hand rested near his plate. "A warning for my friends. Please, they're in danger and don't know it."

He frowned. "Are they bringing trouble here?"

"It's not their fault," she promised. "But Allavin Devers said I could trust you."

"We've known each other a long time, lass. Is he coming

back to Landmoor?"

She nodded with exhaustion. "He'll be coming this way looking for me...for us. But he's not safe here. They'll be looking here, too."

"Who are you talking about?" he asked, feeling a protective urge awaken. He was a big man and never relied on hired hands to remove rowdy customers.

She bit her lip and her shoulders sagged. "I came here with a knight from Owen Draw. He's been arrested by the guard at the gate. And I saw a Bandit officer there, in the barracks."

"Sweet Achrolese," Blain murmured. "In the city?"

"Yes. One of the guards was supposed to bring me here, but I could tell we weren't going the right way. He was taking me into the western quarter, and I knew your place was by the north gates." She looked down at her hands. "I left him in an alley with a bruise on his forehead. When he wakes up, they'll look for me here. I can't stay. But Allavin will be coming with friends of mine. Two Shae and a Drugaen. You've got to warn them that the Bandits are already in the city."

"I can do that easy enough, lass." He leaned back and rubbed his mouth. "How long ago did you hit the guard? You came right here?"

"It took me a little while to find your inn," she replied. "Longer than I'd hoped. They could be walking in any moment."

"Don't fret about that. You look hungry...here, finish this." He scooted the plate over to her and watched her tear into it ravenously. She licked her fingers and gulped down a few deep swallows of ale.

He rose from the table and waived Tanita over. "Keep watch for the city guard. Let me know if anyone comes. Stall them. Keep quiet about the girl." Tanita nodded and slipped away, spreading the word in whispers to the other serving girls.

Blain looked over his shoulder and saw her stuffing the last of the bread in her mouth while coming to her feet. He went over to her and shook his head. "You're bone weary, lass. Rest a moment and let's talk."

She shook her head. "I didn't come to bring you trouble. I...I just didn't know how to get them a message. I've got to hide, find a place where they won't look..."

"Sit down," he said, guiding her back to the chair. He sat down and rested his elbows on the table. "I don't know if the governor is involved or not. I'm sure he'd want to know, but I don't dare risk telling him myself. Allavin warned me about this the last time he was here. And there have been rumors that the Bandits are thick in the woods these days. Two of my suppliers haven't been back from Dos-Aralon as scheduled." He rubbed his forehead. "I haven't seen Allavin Devers since his last warning. When did you leave him?"

Her eyes looked haunted. "Allavin joined us in Castun. The Bandit army is on the edge of the Shadows Wood. Right now, not ten miles from here. We crossed it last night to get here."

"Sweet Achrolese," he muttered again.

"They're coming to Landmoor," she said seriously. "Ban it, they're already inside!" She sunk her head in her hands. "We were too late. Too late."

He put his hand on her shoulder. "You're safe here, lass. I won't turn you over to the guard."

"But I can't just wait here," she said, clenching her fists. He saw the raw tenacity in her eyes.

"I've got a room upstairs that overlooks three streets down. Why don't you go up there and rest a bit. I can get you out the back in case they come. But if they don't come for a while, you'll need the rest. Just look at you." He sighed and then remembered his poor manners. "I'm Blain Kirke, as you already knew. What's your name?"

She looked up, gave him a weary smile, and told him.

* * *

Ticastasy blew the tiny lamp flame out and the room was smothered in darkness. Putting the warm brass lamp on the small table by the bed, she crossed to the curtained window. The bustle of the inn jutted against the walls. After listening for several moments, she parted the curtain. The back street was dark. Once the sun had set it was shielded by shadows from the city walls that the street lanterns did not penetrate.

Letting the curtain fall back in place, she went to the plush bed. Blain Kirke had put her in one of the nicest rooms, and she looked at the soft, stuffed mattress longingly. She stared at herself in the mirror at the foot of the bed. At least she looked like herself again, instead of the mud-spattered waif who had wandered in hours earlier.

Moving back to the window, she parted the curtain again, glancing for signs of anyone in the alley beyond. There had been no word all afternoon. Nothing from Allavin. Nothing from Sturnin, though she expected he had been put away quietly. Not even the city guard had come by the Wee Kirke. That made her worry even more, but it also gave her direction. She wasn't a threat to their plans. Anger boiled inside of her. Not a threat? She'd lived in Sol long enough to know how a city garrison worked. There would be a guard change not long after dusk. That was when they moved prisoners to the main jail. If anyone had been captured at the gate, they would be brought there then. And the only way to find that out would be to watch and follow. Ticastasy was good at both.

Finding the street empty, she tugged at the metal window brace. It unfastened with a faint creak, and she pushed the window open. The chilled night air blew past her cheeks and she inhaled through her nose. Stuffing the small iron room key deeper into her pockets, she hopped up on the sill and slid her legs over the edge. She jumped the little distance from the corner of the roof to the ground and scanned each end of the street. It was empty. Lifting the hood of her cloak over her hair, she walked to the rear of the inn.

Landmoor was quiet, except for the fragments of song that drifted by on the breeze. Would they be drinking themselves into oblivion if they knew an army camped a few miles into the forest? The smooth cobblestone felt hard compared with the soft dirt and grass she had trampled walking through the fog. She shook her head, remembering the day Quickfellow had come.

The day her life had gone upside-down.

After reaching the end of the inn, she turned and hurried until she found the northern wall of the city. It was huge and towering, and she brushed her hand against the cool stone. She followed the wall to the west, hidden in a slice of its shadow. Her keen ears picked out the steady footsteps of the soldiers patrolling the top of it.

She walked slowly, avoiding the tall patches of weeds that popped through the edge of cobbles. She was not sure how well the sentries could hear and didn't want to risk the stalks whisking against her boots. A few buildings sagged against the wall and she had to skirt around them, but she kept going west until she reached the huge northern gatehouse. Wisps of mist crept from the south streets, and she quickened her step. The Valairus fog would help her hide, but she hoped she didn't get lost in it. Mist thickened around her, roaming the gutters first, swirling around her ankles until it was part of her. Those from the Shoreland were intimate with it. She greeted it like a friend.

She reached the junction of the north gate. Tugging her cloak close, she stood at the crossroads of the gatehouse and watched. Torches glared from the wall sconces. The portcullis was still closed, and so were the inner doors. The fortress was clamped shut, just as it happened in Sol every night.

Ticastasy waited, shivering in the night air. Before an hour had passed, she saw the barrack doors open in the rear. In the light of the doorframe, she saw the same Bandit officer glance outside and then motion for the guards. Emerging from within, she watched twelve soldiers wearing the colors of Dos-Aralon escort Sturnin Goff away. His armor had been stripped from him and he wore a stained tunic and trousers. His hands were locked together in irons, and chains around his ankles dragged and scraped against the stone. There was a determined and angry look in his eyes, but he followed in the midst of the soldiers and disappeared down a street to the west.

The barrack doors closed. Counting the steps in her mind, she followed. She padded on cat's feet, anxious not to be heard but hurrying to catch up to the watch. They kept an even pace and joked amongst themselves. She was relieved that Sturnin was all by himself. Maybe Allavin and Flent were huddling outside the walls with Justin and Quickfellow. Maybe they would try and enter Landmoor in the morning. When the guards turned abruptly, she kept pace. They were off the main road now, heading down a twisting alley. She kept her distance. They walked for several miles before reaching a walled garden. This was unusual. The city jail would be near the center of town at the bottom of the town's keep. The guards had taken Sturnin to the western quarter. She swallowed worriedly. She was near where the guard had tried to take her. At the end of the alley, they passed beneath a wrought-iron arch. A lock and chains secured the gate, which they re-fastened behind them after passing. After waiting a few moments, she scrabbled up the corner of the gate and jumped down onto the soft grass. Shadowy trees appeared through the fog on each side, and the soaked grass cushioned her boots. Silently, she wove between the trees inside a walled park.

The mist fell away around a stone well in the center of the park. There was a large pillared gazebo nearby with stone benches and small footpaths spreading away from it like wagon spokes. The cool sigh of trickling water came from the deep stone throat of the well. A rusted steel rail encircled it. At two ends, tall stone blocks rose about eye-level, fixed across with a metal rod and a crank. A heavy chain sank into the well's mouth.

The guards approached the well and one looked down inside it. "Someone's been down and forgot to let it up," he mumbled. He grabbed the crank and gave it a hard jerk. The groan of metal scraping against stone sounded and something deep within the well shuddered.

Ticastasy heard the groans of chains quicken and then slow, ending with a click. Six of the twelve men stepped over the metal rail. Her eyes widened further when they didn't fall. She watched as Sturnin was hefted over the stone rim. One of them jerked on the crank again and the six began to sink into the well shaft.

As they disappeared below, the six remaining guards

waited until they were down before abandoning the park. They passed by her in the shadows and fog. She waited until she could no longer hear the sound of their boots. The creaking gate closed, and she heard chains drag and a lock clamp and click. Where had they taken Sturnin Goff in the middle of the garden? There was something below the city – tunnels or passageways. Ticastasy emerged from the trees and hurried to the edge of the well. The warm orange glow from a lantern slowly disappeared down a tunnel at the bottom of the shaft. She looked deep into the park. Where did the tunnel lead? She was pretty good at tripping a lock. If she could free the knight, they would be able to get out together.

She clenched her teeth, trying not to be afraid. Climbing over the rail, she grabbed the cold chain and climbed hand over hand down the well shaft. She dropped down to the floor of the well and waited, listening.

Voices.

Ticastasy looked around, hearing men approaching from a tunnel coming the other way. Fear danced in her blood and she tried to swallow. There was nowhere to hide, and these men were carrying torches. *This is foolish*, she decided. She gripped the chain and started climbing back up, listening to them approach. Torchlight flickered down the bend. Hand over hand she climbed the chain.

"Who are you?" a man demanded, grabbing her by the fringe of her cloak as she reached the top of the well. She saw his tunic and recognized the man as a Kiran Thall. Hauling her out of the well, he shoved her to the ground. "Speak up, boy!" Jerking the cowl away, he looked down at her face.

"You're a bloody girl!" he swore with surprise.

Ticastasy kicked his legs up from underneath him. Grabbing her small knife, she backed away as he scrambled for his feet. She kicked him in the mouth, knocking him over with a flop. Four more men emerged through the mist ahead of her.

"Hate," she swore, her stomach clenching with fear.

"Who's that over...?" The voice changed with alarm. "By the well!"

She ran.

The Kiran Thall shouted and went after her. She ran through the gazebo, bounding over the rail and ducked from a low-hanging tree branch. She cut north immediately, not wanting to lose her direction. The gate was locked. She needed time to climb it. The Kiran Thall sprinted hard after her. The fastest came like a barking dog. She turned left, cutting so hard she brushed against another tree. The soldier grunted as he smacked into it, but he recovered and quickly cut her off.

"This way!" he called over his shoulder to the others.

She twisted around another tree to try and lose him again in the slick grass. But the Kiran Thall grabbed a fistful of her cloak and jerked her towards him. Colliding against her body, he pulled her in with his other arm and tried to hold her as she flailed.

"Hold tight there," he said and then yelped with pain as she stabbed him in the hollow of his thigh. Ticastasy broke free and ran, but he caught her boot and tripped her. She struck the ground hard enough to see spots explode in her eyes. With a grunt of pain, she scrambled to her feet.

The Kiran Thall pressed his wound and hobbled after her, catching her arm as she tried to escape. She kicked his ankle up from under him and swung the dagger around, cutting his chin. Her tunic ripped at the shoulder as he fell, but she jerked her arm free and ran as the other three soldiers joined the first.

The fog swallowed her. She heard them swearing and calling after her, but she didn't stop. Reaching the gate, she pulled herself up and over the ironwork and jumped onto the cobblestones below. She kept running as fast as she could. A needle of pain in her side made her slow, but still she jogged until she could no longer hear their voices. She hid in a side alley and waited. Chattering with cold, she chaffed her bruised arm and bit her lip to keep back the tears. She made it. She made it. Her heart felt like it was a bird wriggling to escape her chest.

She breathed more slowly. Pulling the cloak tighter, she raised the hood to cover her hair. Where were the Kiran Thall? How close behind? Her ears strained for sounds of pursuit, but she heard nothing. She stood and started walking away. The soft brushing of the cloak against her hair was the only sound as she walked towards the main street where she could find the Wee Kirke again. The streets were nearly barren, but there were a few who had been drinking who sang and staggered down the way. Turning down a major street, she walked north until she recognized the weaponsmith shop. From there, she hurried around it to the alley it shared with the inn. The noises of the inn were still loud and boisterous. Letting down the cowl, she stepped up on the small stone ledge on the wall and pulled herself up on the roof. Carefully, she went to the window. It creaked softly. She paused, listening.

All was silent.

Planting her palms on the window sill, Ticastasy jumped up and sat on the edge. Sliding her legs inside the room, she dropped to the floor. Her hands trembled as she lit the lamp and trimmed it.

There was an old man in black robes standing against the door, regarding her with interest. She froze.

"There is someone waiting to see you, my dear," he said. The window swung shut by itself and the latch fastened.

XXIX

Allavin Devers dropped to a crouch and touched the thin outline of a bootprint in the soft hillside dirt. He traced two of his fingers along the earth and then pointed to a bent clump of stettleweed and another bootprint. He smiled up at Flent. "Thealos is banned good at stepwalking. I almost didn't see these."

"What about Justin?" Flent asked, folding his arms. He looked off into the mist and scrunched up his shoulders.

"His trail is hard to follow too, but he's still with Thealos." Allavin gazed into the mist. "The tracks are about two hours old. We've made good time catching up."

Flent dropped down on his knee and studied the print. "No Kiran Thall?"

"No Kiran Thall."

"That's good." He wiped his nose.

Allavin kept low to the earth and followed the set of prints he had re-discovered. Kiran Thall had crisscrossed the trail several times since the two Shae had left the Shadows Wood, but they didn't appear to have picked it up. Allavin was careful and had to keep reminding Flent to step on hard clumps of moor grass rather than the soft mud of the slopes. The trail led them towards the river, curling around the western face of the hill where Landmoor sat. With all the mist that morning, their movements were hidden.

"Doesn't make any sense," Allavin mused, scratching the

back of his neck. "Looks like they're wandering around the base rather than trying to find the Iron Point Road."

Flent stared up at the thinning mists. "Maybe they're lost."

"It's possible. The mist was thicker when they were here, and they don't know the valley that well. Hmmm. Look over there, now that's...those are horse tracks. Hate!"

Allavin and Flent hurried over to the tromping mess of hoofprints and smashed grass. "At least a dozen riders. Maybe more, it's pretty messy. Sons of fire, they caught the trail right here."

Flent withdrew his heavy axe and patted it against his palm. "Can you tell what happened?"

"Give me a moment," Allavin replied, bending near the earth and studying the web of tracks. He was careful to skirt around the mess of churned mud and grasses and waved Flent over to join him. "No, they just found the trail. Lucky fools, just stumbled onto it. Ban!" Allavin fumed. He and Flent were still two hours behind the two Shae, and the Kiran Thall tracks were fresher than that. They were still too far from the city's northern gatehouse. He couldn't understand why they weren't looking for the road.

"Come on," Allavin said, preparing his long bow. He bent forward, not bothering to conceal his own tracks, and followed the trail of tracks around the side of the hill.

The mist thinned quickly. Allavin jogged, slowing his pace evenly so that Flent could keep up with him. The Drugaen stared ahead into the mist, searching. The mist and the sharp angle of the hill slope concealed sounds very well.

The noise of hooves thudding in the dirt came from directly ahead just moments before a riderless horse cantered out of the mist, its reins dragging in the moor grass. Allavin dropped to one knee and almost brought it down with an arrow, but he saw that the animal wandered aimlessly. A quiver of crossbow shafts hung from the saddle horn along with riding supplies and a blanket. Frowning, Allavin looked at Flent and motioned to follow. What was going on?

Just around the next outcropping of rock, he had his answer.

The Kiran Thall lay dead. The horses had already scattered, but the riders lay in their blood. Flent looked at the mess with stern eyes, gripping the axe haft, ready to fight. It had been over for a while. Allavin spied a cave in the side of the rock. An inlet of some kind. The Kiran Thall were in heaps all around it. He approached one of the fallen horsemen that had an arrow protruding from his ribs. Stepping on the man's chest, he yanked the arrow out. A broadhead. One of Thealos'. He quickly scanned the number of dead. Eleven in all.

"How in Keasorn's name..." the tracker stammered and then saw another of the dead. The words caught in his throat.

The air smelled sick with blood and charred flesh. The flies were just finding the spot. By noon, they would be swarming. But what turned the tracker's stomach wasn't the blood. Staring down at another fallen horsemen, he saw a man with a smoking black hole in his chest. The man's face was transfixed with terror. Allavin blinked, vividly remembering the look on Tiryn's face when he died – the same frozen expression of agony. Seven others were dead, struck by some fiery magic. Judging from the tracks, it looked as though one Kiran Thall had made it away alive. The others were downed by arrows.

Allavin crouched next to the body. In his mind's eye, he saw the flash of blue lightning as it struck his Shae companions one by one. Such awful, terrible magic. The blue light still burned behind his eyes. Then he remembered something else.

"Justin," he said in a near whisper.

"Justin did this?" Flent demanded, prodding the dead man with his boot.

Allavin stared into the inlet of stone and felt a coldness in his bones. Maybe Jaerod was wrong about the Warder Shae being an ally.

* * *

They're close!" Thealos hissed in Silvan, struggling to keep up with the Warder Shae. *"I can't tell how many horsemen."*

Justin never slowed. *"They mean nothing to us. Quickly now. We are near the entrance."*

"Are you sure?" Thealos asked. His lungs heaved from the run. Justin didn't even appear winded. He glanced over his shoulder, expecting to see the Kiran Thall come bounding out of the mist. *"If we run towards the river, we can lose them again."*

"They are nothing!" Justin snapped. *"Here we are. Follow me. We will deal with the humans here."*

Thealos followed around a large outcropping of rock. The hill angled steeply on this side. He couldn't see the walls of Landmoor – at least not yet. But he felt the shape of the hill rising up like a mountain into the thick whirl of fog. Justin stopped at a small stone inlet at the base of the hill. The Warder Shae rubbed his hand along the smooth rock covered with thick moss. Tangled weeds littered the base of the hill, some nearly as tall as the reeds by the river.

"This is the hidden entrance?" Thealos asked, studying the thick ruff of moss. It was rust-colored and slick. Certainly not Everoot. He put his hand on it, feeling the wetness and tickling texture of the moss.

–Son of Quicksilver–

Thealos jerked his hand away.

"Yes, one of the hidden ones," Justin explained, looking up at the archway. *"It leads to the tunnels beneath the city. That is where you will find your proof. The humans roam the halls, but we will not be seen by them."* He scowled. *"This is what is left of my home,"* he added with bitterness.

Thealos stared at the wall. He felt a presence, a whispering through the earth that spoke to him. It was like sensing Silvan magic, except the feeling was so strong that it emanated from the rock itself. Like feeling the heat from a flame on his face – he knew it was there, but for some reason he couldn't touch it. He glanced at Justin, but the Warder seemed oblivious to it.

The stomping of horsemen approached in the thick swirling mists. Thealos brought up his hunting bow and nocked a broadhead. *"They usually have crossbows."*

The Warder Shae stood at the entrance of the tunnel, his back to the hillside. His arms were loose at his sides, his head bowed. Thealos felt the prickle and smell of Earth magic rise up from the moorlands, drawing into Justin like water. The first horsemen appeared out of the fog, the rider a Kiran Thall. The horse shied and the rider controlled it. His crossbow leveled at them. Others appeared, forming a half-circle, pinning them against the inlet. Thealos swallowed, keeping his bow ready, watching the lead soldier.

Justin raised his head and looked at them. His eyes were glowing.

"Put down the bow..." the soldier started when a streak of blue lightning sprang from Justin's hands, throwing the rider off the horse. The gelding shrieked, flailing hooves madly in the air. Kiran Thall shouldered their crossbows and triggered the releases. Thealos shut his eyes and flinched, but the bolts spattered harmlessly against the rocks behind them. The blue lightning struck again, smashing into another soldier, killing him.

The rush of Earth magic in the air smelled like taper shavings. Justin channeled the magic, bringing it to being inside him before loosing it on the humans with crackling swiftness. Thealos let the arrow loose, dropping a rider. He took aim again and again, catching more as they whirled to flee. Justin brought down the rest. When it was finished, a haze of acrid smoke lingered in the air.

The Warder Shae lowered his hands and the Earth magic settled back down into the grass and mud. Thealos stared at him in awe. *"I thought that only worked against Forbidden magic,"* he whispered, remembering the Krag Drugaen in the Shadows Wood. He watched Justin's shoulders slump. He looked even frailer. *"Does it...hurt you?"*

A half-smile twitched on Justin's mouth. *"It's not without a price,"* he answered. *"It never is."* He examined the field of the dead and then turned dispassionately to Thealos. *"There is no time to bury them. I do not have the strength for it. Follow me."*

Thealos joined him at the inlet of stone. He stared at the sculptured walls, squinting in the shade. There was a feeling beneath the scrub of moss. A familiar feeling. Mud and debris littered the stone floor. Thealos looked around, gazing at the structure. *"This was a holy place?"* he whispered.

"The ruins of a shrine," Justin explained. *"The humans have already desecrated it. They use it to bring the Everoot into the tunnels. So many of them."* He shook his head and glared contemptuously. *"It would destroy me to kill that many. Come, this way."*

Thealos paused, feeling a whisper of magic beneath his boots. Calling to him. A prickle of apprehension went down his spine. Not a Sleepwalker – but the presence of Silvan magic.

–Son of Quicksilver–

"Do you hear anything?" Thealos asked, catching up with Justin.

The Warder Shae cocked his head. *"No."*

Thealos nodded and followed him down a narrow path carved into the rock, leading to a stretch of stone steps. They started up towards the ruins of the Shae watchpost buried within the hillside.

* * *

It was difficult for Thealos to concentrate on anything except the constant murmurings of the magic. A presence in the broken tunnels, the magic twisted loose his feelings and thoughts. Thealos recognized Silvan symbols carved into the rock. The markings were centuries old, detailing the layout of the ruined watchpost. The floor was broken and uneven, which made the journey difficult. Portions of the tunnels had collapsed, exposing hunks of stone from the upper floors. Thealos folded his arms for warmth in the clammy passageways. Moonstones glowed faintly on the floor and walls, offering just enough light for their Shae eyes to see. Muddy puddles collected in cracks and seams, and corridors split off from the main one the deeper in they went. It had the feeling of a tomb and sent cold chills up Thealos' arms.

—I am the Silverkin Crystal—

Thealos listened and felt another shudder of apprehension. It was a voice no louder than the softest whisper, but it sent shivers through his skin and a burning feeling inside his chest. It invoked feelings so strongly that he blinked back tears. He was terrified of what it was doing to him. It knew he was there. It called to him soothingly, yet the power beneath it was frightening. It wanted to be freed from the warding. It sensed Forbidden magic and wanted to destroy it.

—Come, Son of Quicksilver—

Thealos squeezed his eyes shut, trying to banish the voice inside his head. He knew where it was. Just touching the stone wall, he felt its pulse, its life. The magic was alive, there was no doubt in that. It was awake and needful. The Silverkin needed him as much as he needed it. Thealos didn't tell Justin what he was feeling. The way the Silverkin spoke to him was private and personal.

The slope of the tunnels rose at a steep angle in several stretches, bringing them higher up the hillside. Thealos had no idea how far they had traveled or how high up they were, but deep ahead in the tunnels he heard voices. Justin paused for a moment and then motioned for Thealos.

"There are side passages to avoid the humans," the Warder said. *"Follow me."*

Turning to the right, they circled around the main tunnel and followed the twisting passageways. The tunnels were full of rooms without any doors. Moisture dripped from the ceiling tiles, splunking noises that irritated Thealos. The sound of the Bandit soldiers grew sharper as they went, but it came from the main passageway. Reaching the end of the new corridor, they stopped to investigate.

At least fifty men carrying heavy oak chests worked their burdens down the main passage. Even from afar, Thealos could feel the Silvan magic contained within the chests. They were full of Everoot. Justin scowled, studying the humans with disdain. The soldiers walked away from the main corridor, up a path lit with brilliant torchlight. Justin's eyes reflected the light and glowed in the darkness.

"That tunnel you see – it is the main crossroads on this side of the city," Justin whispered. *"It leads to the rest of the tunnels in the center. The humans have made different entrances to the tunnels from above. I have not explored them all, but it is sufficient to say that they can enter the ruins of this Watchpost easily."*

Thealos pressed his hand against the wall and felt the magic sing to him. *"Where is the warding?"* he asked.

"Down the corridor we were on – this one," he said, pointing. *"But it is guarded by an Otsquare. You may not be able to enter it."*

Thealos nodded, but he didn't doubt it for a moment. The whispering voices in his mind gave him the confidence that he could. *"Show it to me."*

After watching the Bandits disappear down the side aisle leading towards the center of the city, the two Shae left their shelter and took to the main passage again.

–I have been waiting for you–

Thealos clenched his teeth, feeling the presence of the magic grow stronger. The tunnel became less disturbed the further they went. Fewer muddied tracks littered the floor, showing that the halls were seldom patrolled. Thealos felt the kinship with the Crystal more keenly, its need growing even stronger. How far away was it? It felt close.

It was like walking into an ice-crusted pond. The tunnel hadn't changed, but a biting wash of dread struck Thealos in the pit of the stomach. Justin hesitated, too.

"What was that?" Thealos whispered. The reek of Forbidden magic curled around him like smoke.

"We just breached a warding."

"What did it do?"

The Warder Shae frowned. *"I don't know. It wasn't here before."*

Thealos looked back the way they came. *"I don't like this."*

Justin nodded. *"It was put here by someone for a reason. But not to stop us. A Death Warding would have been instant. This one is...different. As if to warn someone we were here."*

Thealos gripped the hilt of his weapon. *"Are we almost there?"*

Again Justin nodded. Together, they started jogging down the rest of the tunnel. The presence of Forbidden magic grew stronger and stronger. A cold sweat began to form on Thealos' forehead. The smell of the Forbidden magic drowned out everything but the Silverkin's voice. It only intensified.

—I will protect you from the Firekin—

Faster!

The broken floor tiles tripped him, almost spilling Thealos to the ground. He kept his balance and pressed onward. The smell of Forbidden magic made him want to retch. He nearly did. Justin also looked queasy, and he brought up his hands into a defensive position. Earth magic swelled around him, but it was pale compared to the intensity of the power ahead. He couldn't speak. Where was it? How much further? Far down the corridor, Thealos saw a blue light.

—I will protect you—

He knew what it was. Just ahead, amid the broken stones and putrid rock, he saw a stone archway suspended by two pillars sculpted like massive gryphons. The light came from within the archway. It was as blue as the moon Eroth, except the light was painful to look at. Like staring at the sun at noonday.

Squinting, Thealos approached the pillars. The light drowned out details, blurring the pathway to follow. He felt the Silverkin screaming to him, louder and louder. He could not make out the words, but he felt the impact of them. Something wasn't right. It was warning him, beckoning him to rush to seize the magic entombed inside. Thealos wanted to scream.

Something moved in the blue light.

Both of the Shae stopped, trying to get a look at it. The raw shadow of Forbidden magic knifed into them.

"No," Justin said, his eyes bulging with panic.

Thealos recognized the presence. He had felt it during the night in the Bandit camp. The awareness that he was there, that he was a Shae. Thealos froze. It was a Sorian.

The Sorian stood before the stone pillars, cold and aloof.

He was medium-sized for a human, with jade green eyes. His black robes seemed to smother the blue light shrieking behind him past the portal. Thealos couldn't move. Fear guttered out any resolve to run.

The Warder Shae raised his hands, but his thin arms were trembling.

The Sorian stepped forward, his green eyes locked on them both.

"*Go,*" Justin whispered to Thealos.

Thealos couldn't move.

"*Go!*"

Magic exploded from Justin's hands, rushing to close the gap between them and the Sorian. The blast had destroyed the Kiran Thall one by one, but the Sorian held up his hand, revealing an orb the color of fire. The orb simply swallowed Justin's attack. He continued forward.

Justin sent a stronger wave of magic, trying to stall the advance. The magic hammered at the Sorian, but the orb deflected it, sending it spraying away from the green-eyed man, shattering rock and sending shudders through the tunnels. The orb flared once and the Warder Shae's magic winked out, tamed and controlled. Justin's face twisted with horror. The Sorian gave him a small glance, and Justin slammed into the rock wall before crumpling to the floor.

Thealos' breath came in quick gasps. Fear weighed on him like a heavy mantle. He was going to die. His legs were still rooted to the floor. He slid the Wolfsman blade out of his belt and felt the cool tingle of Earth magic swell in his arm.

The Sorian gave him an amused smile. The orb flared once and suddenly the blade was white-hot. Thealos gasped with pain and dropped it, soothing his burned hand. The blade clattered to the floor, twisted and warping as the magic destroyed it.

Glancing down at Justin's still body on the floor, the Sorian looked up and gave Thealos an arch look. "*You can walk or I can drag you,*" he said in perfect Silvan, his voice soft and subdued. "*But either way, you are coming with me.*"

XXX

The hall torches hissed and sputtered, making Thealos squint as he passed them and turned the corner. He was flanked by a dozen Bandit soldiers, each one wearing a sword at their belts and tunics of black and gold. Ahead walked the Sorian with his green-fringed robes whispering across the paving stones. The Bandits said nothing, neither to Thealos nor to the Sorian. He wondered whether he was quick enough to slip past the guards behind him. He wondered, but he didn't dare. Two soldiers followed, dragging Justin's limp body.

The tunnel rose in a steep slope that ended at a large iron door, its hinges embedded into the rock. It creaked and Thealos was ushered into a cell block. A few sallow faces stared at them from the shadowed corners. Rats peeked down from the rafters while roaches skittered across the floor, only to be crushed underfoot by the guards. The corridor ended at a sharp stairwell leading up. Thealos kept going, but he retraced the steps in his mind as to how they had reached that point. They were far from the whispering magic of the Silverkin Crystal. The soldiers dragging Justin didn't follow him up the stairs. Instead, they took him towards another passageway deeper within the tunnels.

Entering the waiting chamber at the top of the steps, Thealos saw a row of low-hanging iron chandeliers. They were as wide as wagon wheels with thick black chains suspending them from the web of arches above. The air held the aroma of kitchen smoke coupled with the smells of bread, cheeses, and salted meats. Deeper into the hall, they passed the kitchens, and Thealos spied large hearth fires with roasts twisting on the skewers. Bread ovens were open, revealing oval loaves of golden bread. The cook slid them out with a long wooden paddle. Further down the hall, two well-fed dogs skirted away from the advancing guards and then watched them take Thealos away.

The guards stopped at a lacquered oak door bound with iron hinges and decorated with fluted gold work. It was certainly Silvan in design, reminding Thealos of Elder Nordain's private chamber in Avisahn. The Sorian faced the guards. "Go to the kitchens for something to eat. You'll be called when you are needed."

Thealos watched them nod in respect before retreating back down the corridor. The Sorian motioned for Thealos to enter first and then followed, shutting the heavy oak door behind him. The smell of Forbidden magic clung to the Sorian's skin like smoke, but the overwhelming feeling of terror was not as strong as it was near the Silverkin. Perhaps the Sorian had to invoke the dark power to protect him while being so near the ancient talisman. But just because Thealos wasn't gagging with terror, he was not all that relieved. He had no idea who he was about to meet. Lord Ballinaire perhaps? The governor of Landmoor?

Entering the room, Thealos stood face to face with Secrist and stopped suddenly. But it wasn't. He frowned, instantly wary, and felt fear bloom in his stomach. The man who sat in the large chair had the facial features of the Kiran Thall, but his cheekbones weren't as high and his forehead a bit broader. The resemblance was unmistakable though. Who was this man? Seeing Thealos enter, the man rose from the chair and planted his hands on the fat table in front of him. He was taller than even Sturnin Goff and his shoulders were broad and strong. A thick red cape hung over his rich tunic, but Thealos could see the glint of a hauberk beneath it. The cape was smoke-stained and tattered along the fringe.

"He was alone?"

The Sorian walked past Thealos, his arms folded. "She is still outside the city, but should be reaching the gatehouse within the hour. The guards are waiting for her." The Bandit leader nodded slowly. "This one," the Sorian continued, "was with a Warder Shae near the forbidden section of the tunnels. Apparently they separated after slipping through the regiment last night. His identity is no longer concealed by the Silvan magic. His protector failed in the Shadows Wood."

Thealos watched the exchange, not sure what to think. He thought they might be talking about Ticastasy and Jaerod, but he wasn't sure of the context. "And what about the Warder I came with. Is he still alive?" Thealos asked.

The Sorian smiled with amusement. "Oh, he'll recover. But I'm having him secured in a special cell. Old dungeon bars would not hold him very long."

Thealos nodded, relieved that Justin would survive. His worry for Ticastasy and the others chafed at him. "Who are you?" he asked the man standing behind the table.

"You crossed my army last night," the man replied with a grim tone. "And a dead Sleepwalker is hardly an even trade, if he is truly dead." He gave Thealos a narrow look. "I'm Tsyrke Phollen."

"You have a brother," Thealos said, trying to keep the loathing from his voice.

The Bandit leader's expression didn't change. "I understand you met him in Sol."

Thealos nodded. He felt sick to his stomach with fear but was determined to hide it from the other man. He prayed that his negotiation skills would help him. "We were...introduced. I understand you wanted to see me?"

The Bandit straightened and paced away from the table, clutching his hands behind his back. Thealos nearly flinched when he moved, but he kept himself steady. The man stared at a tapestry hanging from the wall of the study, but his eyes weren't fixed on it. "We'll start with the simple questions and go from there. Do not bother lying to me, Shae, as hard as that may be to resist. My friend over there will know if you do. If you try to conceal the truth, he will compel it from you.

Believe me – he can. The first question – why did you take her?" Turning his head, he gave Thealos a hard look. "The girl from Sol. Why?"

Thealos felt a bite of panic inside his chest. His mouth went dry. "Ah, you're still looking for 'Stasy, aren't you?" It was a guess, but it felt right. This was the man she had fallen in love with. *By all the gods...*

Tsyrke's eyes were cold and angry. "It's an easy enough question, lad. And you'd banned well better answer it. I've dealt with the Shae before. Evading comments won't work with me."

"I wasn't intending to evade you, sir," Thealos apologized. His mind worked furiously. "We brought her with us to protect her from your brother." He did his best to keep his face calm and untroubled. He knew he was at the disadvantage, just as he was when Nordain had summoned him before the Council Elders. This time, he would guard his tongue. For although Nordain might want Thealos in prison, this man would probably not flinch to see him dead. "Did you send your...brother to the Foxtale to bring her to you or to hang the knight? Or both?"

"Fury, no!" Tsyrke barked, his brown eyes sharp and glaring. "I arrived in Sol just after you left. Secrist was acting on his own, as he usually does. I haven't seen him in weeks."

Thealos steadied himself. He was trying to piece it all together. He remembered from the Foxtale that Ticastasy had known Secrist. Or known about him. She had told him once that she was waiting for someone – someone who was special to her. He had given her a pendant that she had worn after leaving Sol. Thealos felt his heart clench. He doubted she knew who he really was. Not this man. Not a Bandit leader.

"You arrived just after we left?" Thealos asked. "What a deplorable sense of timing then. She told me she was waiting for...someone. But he never came. I'm assuming now that she meant you."

"Oh, I came. Only to hear that she'd run off with a Sleepwalker, her Drugaen friend, and a pampered whelp from Avisahn. You – I'm assuming." He faced Thealos. "She wasn't in any danger from the Kiran Thall and she knew it. Why did she go with you?"

Thealos shook his head. "You expect me to understand how a woman thinks? My people are noted for our wisdom, but not even we have solved that riddle. Let me clarify something. We didn't *take* her from Sol. She chose to come with us. I believe she doubted that you were coming back. When have sailors or Shae barters been men of their word? She doesn't know the truth about you, does she?"

The Bandit glared at him. "And how much do you think you really know?"

Thealos gave the Bandit a level look. "It might surprise you how much I know. I know that the Bandit Rebellion is massing down here in the Shoreland. I know that you are using Shae magic for purposes that are clearly Forbidden. Digging up the Everoot and hoarding it is not how it is supposed to be used."

"Spare us your speech on morality," the Sorian interrupted. "Tell me, how do the Shae feel about murdering their own kind? Some of us know about the Kinslayer wars. About Ravindranath."

Thealos ignored the deliberate insult. If Tsyrke were not tainted with Forbidden magic, there might be a chance to reason with him. "Consider this, Tsyrke. If I am here and I know about the Everoot, then doesn't it stand to reason that so does Avisahn? I know what the Everoot can do and what it has done in the past." He gave the Sorian a hard look. "At least there were survivors of Ravindranath. More than Soldon-Orai."

"But if the whole banned Shae kingdom knew about this," Tsyrke said, "then why are *you* here and not the Wolfsmen? Were you sent to negotiate a Pax?"

Thealos rubbed his jaw thoughtfully. "Why indeed?"

"You are here because there is a Silvan artifact locked behind a Shae warding," the Sorian answered. Thealos felt a tickle of magic in the air and the brief smell of smoke. "Your Warder companion was not strong enough to cross it. What makes you think you can?"

Thealos looked at the Sorian with distrust. "I am not the

only one who can cross it," he replied. "There will be others. The Shae will not sit back in Avisahn while you destroy the land with Forbidden magic."

Tsyrke stepped forward. "And what happens if you get this artifact, Shae?"

"The Rebellion will end."

Tsyrke seemed to consider his words carefully. "How?"

"If I told you that, there would be no need to keep me alive. Would there?"

"Your death is hardly of any consequence to me."

Thealos shrugged meaningfully. He was gambling with his life, just as he had with Tannon's band. It took every bit of composure he possessed to keep his knees from trembling. "Of no consequence, you think? But you know how the Shae are," he said. "If I die here, they will send in the Shae legions. Of no consequence? Are you ready to engage the Shae army, commander? Kiran Phollen could not stand against them. Are you ready for the Crimson Wolfsmen in the city? You do know what a *Ravinjon* is?"

The Bandit commander looked at him coldly. "Maybe I'm counting on that."

* * *

The old man had let her bring her knapsack and cloak. As they left the Wee Kirke together that night, it felt to Ticastasy as if none of the patrons could even see them. She didn't trust herself to speak. But she'd managed to give her initial warning to Blain earlier that day. She'd done the best she could. For in her mind, Ticastasy knew that the old man was bringing her to Tsyrke. And she wasn't ready to face him. Not like this. They crossed the fog-shrouded city in silence and reached the governor's mansion before midnight. The manor guards never saw them.

"You're not going in?" Ticastasy asked as they stood before a large door in the south wing. She shivered just being in his presence and especially as his green eyes studied her. He smelled like cinders and clove smoke. He reminded her of a Sleepwalker.

"He will speak with you alone."

The enormous door opened smoothly on its gold and iron hinges. It was well oiled. She paused on the threshold and then entered. The smell of honeyed mead and tray wafers greeted her in the entryway. Mead – an unusual drink. She only knew one man who truly craved it. A single lamp burned on a polished wooden table across the room. Various rugs and tapestries hung from the wall and there was even a tall wooden dressing screen in one corner near a wardrobe.

Her eyes were still adjusting to the shadows before she smelled him.

"Tsyrke," she whispered as the door shut gently behind her.

"Sparrow."

The way he said it sent chills down her arms. He was a full head taller than she. In fact, she barely measured up to his shoulders. His hair was shorter than she remembered, freshly cut. The scent of the sea greeted her. He always smelled like seawater and mead. She shook her head, still not believing her eyes. In one corner of her heart, she longed to rush and hug him. In another corner, she wanted to reach for her knife.

"What in Hate's name are you doing here?" she whispered.

He gave her a crooked smile and drank deeply from a goblet. "I could ask you the same question. Landmoor is an odd place for a reunion. But there is something else I want to know even more." He eyed her seriously. "Why didn't you wait for me in Sol?"

She bit her lip and folded her arms, aware of how disheveled she looked. Her shirt was torn, her hair tangled. She was exhausted physically and emotionally. And this – meeting him in Landmoor was a kick in the ribs. Anger came easily.

"When sailors start keeping their promises, I'll have grown old," she said, walking in closer. She was intimidated by his size, but that only made her more resolved to stand up to him. Her fear glazed over with the sparks of anger. He had lied to her. He had said he was a wealthy seafarer, not a

299

banned Bandit general!

"Do you still have the pendant I gave you?"

She stared at him.

"You still have it…don't you."

She nodded. Why was he doing this? The pendant was a promise based on deception. She wanted to cry, but she knew that she alone had the opportunity to rescue her friends.

Tsyrke set down the goblet and walked over to the table. He looked at her torn clothes and winced. "Did any of my men hurt you?"

Again, she bit her lip, cutting off the urge to curse at him. He seemed to be expecting it. No, she needed to poke at his guilt instead. She replied softly, "Not as much as you did."

He slammed his fist on the table. The look he gave her was full of anger and anguish. "Bloody Hate, I came for you, Sparrow! I landed in Sol after you had already gone!" He breathed out deeply and relaxed his hand, controlling his temper. She could see his eyes twitching towards the goblet of mead. He wanted it badly. "I came for you only to learn you had run off with a Shaden and a Sleepwalker."

She took another step closer, seizing the opportunity. "Quickfellow's here?"

He smirked. "A princely name isn't it."

"Ban it, stop using me!" she said. "You used me for companionship in Sol, and now you're using me here. Quickfellow is my friend and I'm worried about him." She already knew that Sturnin was locked down below. Where were the others?

"He took you away from me," Tsyrke pointed out bitterly. "He's your friend? That's a rich slice. When did the Shae start keeping their word?"

She shook her head. "No, Tsyrke. No, don't blame him for your grandfather's death. Kiran Phollen brought trouble to himself. You told me that you had a brother in the Rebellion. You told me about Secrist – that he would never hurt me." She laughed and covered her cheek. "He hit me in the mouth. He knew who I was and he hit me. His men destroyed the Foxtale. If you truly did come, then you saw the ruin he caused. The Shaden…" She stopped, calming herself. "Quickfellow took me with him to Castun to protect me from them. But I still trusted you. I still believed what you had told me." She shook her head in amazement. "You lied to me. You said you were a ship captain. You had money and contacts. You said you cared for me. I warned you never to lie to me, Tsyrke. If I can't trust you, I can't be with you. I said that. I meant it."

He gave her a hard look, wrestling to control his emotions. The look on his face was haunted with some twisted irony she could not see as he took a step closer to her. His voice was husky and raw. "And what was I supposed to do, Sparrow? Tell you I was going to betray Ballinaire to the king and end this war? Tell a bloody serving girl in Sol? Do you know how ridiculous that sounds? The risk?" His frown was hard, intense – honest. "The promises I made you...I meant every one of them. I still mean them. I'm bone weary of this army. I'm bone weary of this Rebellion." His voice was so soft she barely heard it. "You are right. My grandfather wasted his life fighting Dos-Aralon and when the Shae joined in, it finished him. He wasted his whole life over his ambitions." He paused and studied her. "I'm not going to do that. I was the one who called for the knights. I was the one he was supposed to meet in Sol, not my brother." His look softened. He shook his head as if suddenly aware of how close he was standing to her. "Sweet Achrolese, I feel bad enough. Look at you. Let me fetch you some fresh clothes. You look bone weary as well. Are you hungry?"

She wanted so much to believe him. That the dream he had taught her might actually happen. But she could not trust him. Not without proof. And not before rescuing the others. She held up her hand. "You could be lying again."

"Why?" he asked. "I've just risked my life telling you the truth. The whole of it. I couldn't share this with you in Sol. I have to now."

She stared at him and swallowed. "Are Quickfellow and the others alive?"

He nodded and raised the goblet to his lips. "I haven't decided what to do with Prince Quickfellow yet, though." He chuckled darkly. "You know he's lied to you as well?"

"What do you mean?"

"He handles himself very well, doesn't he? Who do you suspect he is?" Tsyrke asked, his face cruel. "A Silvan prince? The son of a Sunedrion councilman?"

"He's a Shae," she answered. "And more honorable than most."

"Oh, he's a Shae, Sparrow. As glib as they come. And as common as they come. He's only the son of a barter."

Ticastasy stared at him. A spasm of pain and betrayal went through her. "I don't believe you."

"We had a nice little discussion about him earlier today. He's been banished from Avisahn. The Wolfsmen who caught up with him in the Foxtale were going to arrest him for treason. None of this is sounding familiar to you? I imagine not. I don't think he would have told you this about himself."

She had no idea whether Tsyrke was lying to her or not. He had lied to her before, despite his excuses, but he seemed to have strong details. He knew about the Shae who had come to the Foxtale. Was it all an elaborate ruse? Angry but uncertain, she decided that before she would condemn Quickfellow, she would hear it from his own lips first. Maybe she'd wanted to believe it too much. Maybe she'd fooled herself twice. *Ban you, Quickfellow, if you've lied to me too...*

"You swear it, Tsyrke?"

"He's in the dungeon below the mansion," Tsyrke replied, motioning towards the door. She gave him a wary look. "Hate, if you want to see him breathing, I'll let you!" he snapped. "I told you my reasons, Sparrow. I told you the truth about why I'm here. I want this Rebellion to end."

She gave him a skeptical look. "Yet this is your army. You hardly look like you're quitting."

"I can't exactly manage that with Ballinaire rustling in the woods. One of the other generals has been watching my movements. I've had to be very careful. But consider this. I am in the governor's manor in Landmoor. He knows and stands to profit greatly from this. I told you that I sent word to the knights to meet me in Sol. And I see you brought one with you." She bowed her head and nodded. "I haven't met with him yet, but I will and then you'll see. I plan to let him go back to Owen Draw. I don't want his blood on my hands. But what about Quickfellow? Do you know what he is after?"

She gave him a wry, sad smile. "You said it yourself, Tsyrke. I'm just a serving girl from Sol. No one tells me anything."

Tsyrke didn't seem surprised. "I didn't think he did. Well, I doubt he'd tell you the truth of it anyway. You want to see him then? At least let me get you some fresh clothes. Do you need a healer? I can fetch a Zerite. There are a few here in the city."

She glanced over at the changing screen and saw Tsyrke's two-handed sword hanging from one of the posts along with some of his clothes. An idea sprouted in her mind. "I have something here," she said, twisting the travel sack from her shoulders. "Can I...?" She nodded to the changing screen.

Tsyrke nodded deftly and walked around the table, easing himself into the big chair. Ticastasy hurried behind the changing screen and quickly untied her sack. She removed the gown Quickfellow had given her and unraveled the bundle.

"I swear that I'm going to kill Secrist when I see him," Tsyrke chuckled blackly. She heard him fill the goblet of mead. "This is all really his fault, isn't it? Ban it all, he's never been early in his life..."

Unfastening the lacings, she smoothed out the gown and then hung it from a peg. Tugging off her shirt, she slipped into the gown quickly, feeling gooseflesh prickle up her arms. "You know your brother," she said, trying to quell the nervousness in her stomach. "He's a mule in need of a good whipping. Make sure he feels it." She pulled off her boots so she could get the pants off quickly. There was a mirror on the inside wall and she studied herself, swiping at stray tufts of her billowy brown hair. She tugged on her boots again and straightened the gown. Reaching behind her, she did up the lacings as quickly as she could.

"I've missed you, Sparrow," he said. "It was a long winter. Too long. The seas were wretched – straight from Pitan. But I bought the homestead I told you about. It's mine."

Ticastasy looked at herself. Then reaching into the travel sack again, she withdrew the sparrow pendant he had given her in Sol and fastened it around her neck. She quickly slid on her bracelets and earrings from a small velvet jewel pouch. Her shoulder throbbed, but she ignored the pain.

"What are you doing?" he demanded, rising from the chair.

"I'm almost done," she said, stalling him. She furrowed through the pile of clothes left on top of a chest near the wardrobe. It was mostly comprised of his armor, settled nicely on the tattered red cloak. A relic from his grandfather, he had said. She fingered the fabric while slipping one of his daggers in her boot. Where were those keys?

There was a loud rap on the door and she froze. Tsyrke muttered something under his breath. "Enter!"

The oak door opened and Ticastasy saw a Bandit officer between the slits in the screen. "Lord Ballinaire is on his way to see you, Commander."

"Doesn't the old man ever sleep?" Tsyrke said. "Where is he?"

"He's in the tunnels, sir. Will be here soon. I thought I'd warn you." The soldier sounded worried.

"I'll deal with him, Trent. Go find Mage and tell him to meet me here."

"I will, sir."

Ticastasy stepped away from the screen as the soldier left the room. She watched Tsyrke's expression change as he looked at her. It was hard to keep a smile from her face, but his look was flattering.

"Sweet Achrolese," he murmured, "but you are fair."

She approached him and looked up into his eyes. "I'm glad you like it," she said, enjoying the expression on his face. She fingered the pendant. "There have been changes, Tsyrke. Surely you realize that. I...I need time, to see how I feel about you, about what you are doing here. I'm not your prisoner, am I?"

"Hate, no!" he sputtered, folding his arms.

"I'll see Quickfellow then. If that's all right. I don't want to be here when the leader of the Bandit Rebellion comes in to talk to you," she said. "Sweet Achrolese, I wouldn't know what to do. Pretend I'm your serving wench? But I do want to talk to you. After he leaves?" She gave him one of her most promising smiles.

Tsyrke thought about it, trying to seem reluctant. She read right through it and arched her eyebrows. "Let me stop by the kitchen and make sure he's eaten. Please, Tsyrke. He's my friend, a barter or a prince. I'd fetch you a bowl of stew if you were rotting in the River Cellars in Sol."

A smile finally broke on his stormy face. "I've missed you, Sparrow. I've missed you more than I can say." He turned around and raised the goblet. "We'll talk later. We have a lot to talk about. Fetch the Shae lad some buttered rolls. Tell him to get some sleep. He'll live through the night – because of you. Tell him that."

Ticastasy gave him a warm smile. The small iron key pinched in the bottom of her boot.

XXXI

Heavy iron manacles clamped against Thealos' wrists and ankles, making his fingers and toes tingle with the lack of blood. The manacles were connected to a short length of chain fixed to an iron ring hammered into the stone wall. He rested the weight on his lap and tried to find a comfortable position on the floor. Clumps of dry straw littered the cell, and he scooted some over with his boot to see if it might cushion him a little. But the straw stank of urine, and he kicked it away.

Thealos sat in the main holding cell at the head of the hall. He could hear other prisoners in cells further down, locked behind huge iron doors. The door on his cell was made of long iron bars, fastened together at the top and bottom with steel slats. The hinges were rusty and made a grating screech when the soldiers had opened the door. Torchfire sputtered outside in the corridor, and without any windows he was unable to tell whether it was noon or dusk. Twice since he had been locked up, the Bandits had brought in other people, chained them to the wall near him, and then returned later to take them to another cell. He was alone at the moment, but he could hear the others. Some muttered and grumbled. One man, far down the hall, hadn't stopped whimpering since Thealos arrived.

Sitting in the shadows of the holding cell, Thealos thought about his encounter with Tsyrke Phollen. He remembered it over and over, wondering what else he could have said. He wasn't sure whether they intended to kill him or not. Fear bloomed inside him again and he loathed the feeling. He was weary of his fears and shoved it down inside himself. He was alive at the moment. If they had wanted him dead right away, there was nothing to stop it. He visited the conversation again in his mind. Tsyrke's words had been plainly spoken: *Maybe I'm counting on that.* Had he meant it only as a threat? That they intended to kill him in order to lure the Shae down into the Shoreland? Or was it something to cow him and make him more willing to bend and tell them what they wanted to know? Thealos shook his head in the darkness. They knew about the Silverkin. Well, they didn't know what it was, but they knew *something* was there. A wry smile crossed his mouth. He was hoping that they would send him in after it. Did they know that the Otsquare prevented any human from passing into the chamber? They would not be able to follow him in. Better still, if he could only manage to slip out of the cell, he knew he would be safe within the warding. But how? How was he going to get that far?

Thealos' stomach grumbled with hunger. How long had it been since he'd eaten? He remembered the savory food at the Catpaw and wished he had finished eating all of the stew in the trencher bowl. He was fearful – who wouldn't be in his place? – but he'd manage to skirt trouble all the way from Avisahn. Granted, having Jaerod as a protector did have something to do with that.

A roach roamed across the floor in front of him and he crushed it under the heel of his boot. He missed Jaerod. He thought back on the flash of lightning coming from a clear night sky. No rain, no storm. Just a single streak of crackling white. He hoped against hope that the Sleepwalker had somehow survived, even though he no longer felt that prick of awareness, that second sense whenever he was nearby. If anyone could face a Sorian and make it through alive, Jaerod could. He wished he knew for certain whether Jaerod had.

The door at the end of the hall opened and the sound of marching steps came down the corridor. Another prisoner? Thealos could hear the clinking of chains. He didn't have any idea how long he'd been locked away. Was it morning yet? Had the Bandit army reached the walls of the city?

A group of guards shoved Sturnin Goff down the way.

Thealos nearly blurted out the knight's name, but he caught himself. He sat up quickly, coming into the light so the knight could see him.

Sturnin Goff noticed him, but he also kept silent. He wiped his nose on the back of his hand, but not before making a quick gesture to Thealos not to say a word. The guard stopped and stared into the holding cell.

Thealos kept his expression blank and his eyes fixed on the guards, not Sturnin.

The guardsman hesitated a moment and then withdrew a ring of keys and unlocked the door leading to the holding cell. Four of them muscled the knight inside and locked him to a ring on the other wall. Brushing off their hands, they left, locking the door once again. Howls for food started up as soon as the soldiers continued down the hall.

"Well, you are the last man I expected to find down here," Thealos whispered in amazement after the soldiers had left.

Sturnin settled down on the floor with a slump. "I didn't banned expect to find you here either," he answered. "When were you caught?"

"That depends," Thealos replied. "I don't know whether it's day or night. I've been in the tunnels since the morning after we lost you."

The knight nodded. "That would have been this morning. Sunset was an hour ago."

Thealos looked at him seriously. "Where are the others?"

"Faring better than we are, I hope. Allavin and the Drugaen went looking for you two. Where's the other Shae?"

"They took him to another cell." He nodded vaguely down the hall. "I think he's alive, though. And Ticastasy?"

"They've probably got her by now too. When we came to the gates, I sent her ahead to an inn Allavin told us about. They'll probably have some Kiran Thall in disguise waiting to drag in anyone else who comes along." He shook his head angrily. "Banned foolish of me. Banned foolish."

"It's probably too late to point out that the Bandits control the city, isn't it?" Thealos said it with an ironic edge to his voice. The knight nodded, festering with anger. "Don't worry yourself, Sturnin Goff. There is no way you could have known."

The knight gave him a black look. "I am only one man. I just take heart knowing that the Governor of Landmoor will die when this is over. That he could betray the king like this..." He shook his head. "Well, justice will come due. And it will ride with hooves of thunder."

Thealos cocked his head. "I didn't know the knights were poets. What in Pitan makes you think that justice is coming?"

The knight regarded him and a cool smile lit his face. "I sent a message from Castun. A woodcutter agreed to carry it to Owen Draw for me. I paid him well enough to get the job done and promised him more if he could get it there in three days."

"And will they answer it?"

"I sent it to the Knight General of Owen Draw. He *should* be the banned Champion of Owen Draw. Maybe he will get the title once Ballinaire is under the shovel."

Thealos scooted back against the wall, letting his chains rest on his lap again. "And why won't there be a Champion until Ballinaire is dead?"

"Ballinaire was the last. He destroyed a tradition of honor that had been with the knights of Owen Draw since we were established. You know we trace our origins to the Shae, don't you?"

Thealos shook his head. "No, I didn't."

The knight leaned forward. "We do, Thealos. We patterned our order after the Crimson Wolfsmen. They were dedicated to protecting the Shae people and to defending the life of your king and his family. The knights of Owen Draw are the protectors of the kingdom and the life of don Rion and his family. It is our single duty. Our honor. In the past, there was one knight chosen as Champion of the realm. The one who had perfected his skills, the one who every other knight deferred to. He had power to lead the king's army on his behalf, to stand in his place should the need arise. The next most powerful man in the realm, except maybe the heir to the throne."

"Ballinaire," Thealos said with a nod, remembering a little of Dos-Aralon's history. "I knew he was originally a knight from Owen Draw – and that he did not lack for wealth or power. He fought during the Purge Wars, if I remember right."

Sturnin Goff nodded savagely. "He won great honor for his courage. He was young back then, but already a great leader. No one ever questioned his loyalty. He was popular among the people and even won the respect of the Shae battle commanders. He was one of the few who defined the Accords of Dos-Aralon, giving the knights of Owen Draw power to command any garrison in the realm."

"I did not know he had done that," Thealos said, impressed. "So Ballinaire became Champion of Owen Draw after the Purge Wars. But when he rebelled against don Rion, it probably cast doubts on you all. It is easier to believe the evil in men than the good."

"In no small way," Sturnin Goff added with contempt. "There were many knights who remained loyal to the man and rebelled with him. It shouldn't have lasted this long. The rebellion should have guttered out the moment he forsook his honor. For if a man would betray his king how could you ever trust him again?"

"Didn't he rebel because he was not named the Duke of Owen Draw?"

Sturnin Goff nodded. "A right petty grievance, if you ask me. I guess it shows how far and deep hate and pride can go together."

Thealos listened as Sturnin told him about the knights and their order. He had always wondered why the man was so aloof and distant, so unemotional about living and dying. He'd never thought to compare him to the Crimson Wolfsmen and their single-minded determination to protect the Shae. To the end, Sturnin Goff was a soldier who lived and breathed a life of trouble. His parents had both been killed during a Kiran Thall raid in Owen Draw. At first he wanted to be a knight to avenge them. But as he trained and studied the arts of war, he discovered that his pain was not the only pain in the valley. Many others had lost their homes, their families, even their lives because of the lightning attacks of the Bandit Rebellion. The Rebellion wasn't strong enough to topple don Rion's government. But it was too prideful to admit that, to try and soothe the wounds between an embittered Ballinaire and his king. Too many had died for there to be any forgiveness.

Thealos smiled fondly at Sturnin Goff. He was not a man with flowery words or fragile sentiments. Though hardened by years of war and training, he was still a man who wanted nothing more than the Rebellion to end so that peace could return and ease the suffering done to hundreds of shattered families. His duty would not allow him to quit until that end was accomplished. He knew many knights who had been killed by the Kiran Thall or trapped and outnumbered by companies of Bandit soldiers in the Kingshadow. In their memory, he continued to fight.

The door at the head of the corridor opened, bringing smells wafting down from the kitchens. It was enough to drive Thealos mad with hunger. He glanced at the knight and shook his head. "That smells like a roast hog and cider, doesn't it? They built this place near the kitchens to torture us. I'd rather face the rack about now."

"You're right. Smells like roast with onions and sage. The Governor is supping well tonight. I'll remember that when I hang him," he added as the clamoring within the other cells rose up around them.

"They haven't fed me all day," Thealos said. "Maybe it's time now."

Sturnin shrugged. "You think you'll get the governor's scraps, do you? Don't let it bother you, lad. You get used to hunger in the saddle."

"Don't talk about horses, you're only making me more hungry," Thealos quipped, cocking his head, hearing the sound of bootsteps approach. One guard followed by someone with low-heeled boots. It was a soft step, almost a...woman's?

Thealos nudged closer to the door as a guard approached

and unlocked it. He tugged it open with a grating squeal, and Thealos gaped with surprise as Ticastasy walked in bearing a tray loaded with food.

She wore the gown he had given her. For a moment, he was paralyzed. He could see her clearly in his mind's eye serving tables at that tavern in Sol. The image clashed with a dank cell full of roaches and stinking straw. He blinked, trying to be sure it was her and that his eyes weren't deceiving him.

"I've always thought it strange how your eyes glow like that," she said with the twist of a smile, bringing the tray over and dropping down in a crouch. She glanced back at the guard in annoyance, and he fumed and walked away, grumbling at her to shut the door when she finished feeding them.

"Let's see, we have some spice stew here in a loaf trencher, some buttered wafers and apricot halves." She glanced over at the knight. "Hello, Sturnin."

"Hello, lass," he said, studying her. "How did you end up serving tables down here?"

"Eat up," she insisted, grabbing a wafer and tossing it to the knight. He caught it and started chewing. "I made sure the stew wasn't scorched before dipping in the ladle, and let's see – I even brought some Silvan wine because ale and mead are also both Forbidden. I can't understand why that's true, but then I've never pretended to know everything about the Shae."

"What are you doing here?" Thealos demanded, sensing that something was wrong. Her bantering was forced, uneasy.

"Saving you both, it would appear," she whispered, smiling with satisfaction at his bulging eyes. "Quickly, eat! That guard won't wander down the hall for very long and I've knocked out plenty for one day. Here, have some fruit." She tossed Sturnin an apricot.

Thealos tore a hunk from the loaf and dabbed it in the stew. It was steaming hot, but he ate it ravenously. The meat was a little tough, but he wasn't about to quibble over how rare it was supposed to be. He took a long sip from the wine cup, soothing his parched throat. It was an excellent vintage, probably from the governor's wine cellars. She bent close to him and stared into his eyes. He felt his stomach shrivel.

"How is your wine?" she asked coolly.

He set the goblet down, wiping his mouth. "Why are you looking at me that way?"

"Because I need to ask you something. And I want the truth. You can always tell if a man is lying – it's always in his eyes. Is that why your eyes glow, then? I've wondered that a long while about the Shae."

He stared back at her. "I don't understand." He swallowed, feeling her presence so uncomfortably close. She shifted nearer, her face so close he could feel her breath on his cheek. It was as if they were lounging on a cushioned window seat, not a filthy cellar floor.

"Are you the son of a barter?" she asked.

A shaft of guilt went into his stomach. He closed his eyes, feeling the irony slap him behind the guilt. He knew there was no point denying anything. She wouldn't have asked if she didn't already know.

"Yes," Thealos replied, not daring to open his eyes.

She was quiet for several moments, but he could feel her breathing, feel her stiffen. He opened his eyes. It didn't matter how guilty he felt. This was the only chance he had to escape. He had to convince her to help him.

"I don't need to ask how you found out," Thealos said, staring into her face. "You've seen him, haven't you?"

She nodded curtly. "Don't change the subject, Quickfellow. Is that really your name, then?"

Thealos nodded. "I should have clarified this earlier. Let me try to explain it quickly. Many, many years ago," he said, feeling suddenly exhausted, "my father's family were heirs to the Quicksilver throne. This was back when the Shae lived over in the East Kingdoms. There was a revolt and a civil war over the succession of the throne. My Correl's family chose to follow a Silvan prince to this land and renounced their rights of inheritance. In another land, I might be considered a Silvan Prince. But not here, not in this place."

"You let me believe a lie, Quickfellow. What else have you

led me to believe?"

He frowned, feeling his frustration strain against the tethers of his self-control. "Do you think I came here to buy wine?" he demanded, leaning forward. "There is an army beyond the city. You've seen it. You've also seen the Everoot and you heard what was done with it by your forefathers."

"Yes, but how do I know you aren't hear to buy the Everoot, barter? Think for a moment, Quickfellow! Why else would you be here?"

He gripped her arm. "Because although I am the son of a barter," he said in a low voice, "My birthright gives me access to another magic that is down here, in the tunnels. I do not know why that is. I don't care. But the magic is real and it will stop this madness from continuing any further. It will stop the Rebellion. Think of all who will die if we don't get the Crystal. Think of all we stand to lose if Tsyrke and his fellows win. Remember the Kiran Thall in Sol? Remember how they behaved? Think what will happen to the valley if they win!"

She frowned, obviously angry and disturbed by what he had told her. "Then the Crystal *is* real?"

"You said you could tell if a man was lying. I have told you the truth. I swear it."

She was quiet for several moments. "I believe you. Maybe I'm the world's greatest fool for trusting a Shae, but I pray that I'm not." Ticastasy hiked up her skirt and tugged off the leather boot. A small key ring plopped into her hand. She gave him a wink.

"Quit flirting lass and unlock us!" Sturnin grumbled.

She gave the knight a smile. "I came here to free you, Sturnin. I just needed to know whether I should let Quickfellow out too."

It took several tries until the key made a little snick in the lock and the manacles opened. Blood tingled in Thealos' feet and he smiled with relief.

"Thank you," he said, tipping her chin so that their eyes met. "We'll see you safely through this, I promise you."

She grabbed the chain between his wrists. "Here, hold still, Quickfellow. This won't take..."

The door opened at the far end of the hall and the marching sound of boots thundered into the dungeon. Ticastasy's eyes widened with shock as the clank of sword and armor rattled the stillness.

"In the shadows, lass," Sturnin warned. The serving girl stole deeper into the cell, hiding herself in the darkness. Sturnin leaned forward, blocking sight of her. Thealos took another hunk of bread and quickly chewed it, watching to see who was going towards the kitchens and the stairwell leading out of the dungeon. The advance guard wore black armor fringed with gold. They carried long-handled torches before them, showing the rats slinking in the ceiling rafters. The man in the middle looked about seventy years old, his face hard-edged and angry. His hair was long and gray, spotted with streaks of ice. His gait was strong and sturdy, his walk quick. He stunk of Forbidden magic.

"Ballinaire," Sturnin said in a near-whisper.

Thealos bristled as the soldiers passed, obviously on their way to meet with the commander of the Shoreland regiment. The clanking noises faded as they mounted the steps. The door leading to the kitchens slammed shut behind them.

"That should give us even more time," Ticastasy said, slipping in front of Thealos once again. She swiped some of her dark hair behind her ear. "I knew he was coming – hoped to get down here without having to cross him. Ballinaire is here to speak with Tsyrke. You've met him, haven't you?" Her eyes met his and then looked away.

"I know who he is now," Thealos said, squeezing her hand. "And I know that you didn't. I'm sorry."

She bit her lip and then slid the key into the manacles on his wrists. "It gets pretty complicated after that, as you can imagine."

Thealos nodded, feeling a surge of relief when the heavy iron fell onto his lap. He scooped up the chain and set it next to him on the straw. The feelings of relief surged within him. Without her, he would never have made it safely out. He owed her more than a tavern. He owed her his life.

Her eyes found his again.

"You wore that in Sol," he said, nodding to the pendant

around her neck. His touch grazed her skin. "You wore this as a promise, didn't you?"

She sighed and nodded.

Thealos shook his head slowly and tugged the pendant, snapping the thin chain. He tossed it into the straw "You don't belong to him, Stasy. Not him."

She brushed her hair back again. "I don't belong to you either."

"Quit staring at each other like smitten fools and unlock me!" Sturnin hissed.

Thealos didn't know why he did it. He couldn't stop himself. Leaning forward, he kissed her.

It surprised them both.

"Thank you," he said. "For saving my life."

A shadow blocked the doorway of the cell and she flinched, shoving away from him in a panic.

Secrist Phollen stood there, gripping a dagger.

XXXII

The reek of Forbidden magic stung Thealos' nose, bringing tears to his eyes. It seethed from the dagger. He should have noticed it approaching the cell, but the scent of Ballinaire passing through the tunnels still lingered in the air. Secrist's eyes locked on his, his mouth tightening into a snarl.

Ticastasy wiped her mouth, watching Secrist with naked fear on her face. He didn't even look at her. He stared at Thealos.

"Shaden," he said, swinging the cell door open with a rusty groan. There was an intensity in his eyes that was unnatural, a self-feeding hate that drained the color from his cheeks. The stench of Forbidden magic entered the cell even more strongly. Thealos looked at the grainy textured knife blade. His skin shivered.

Ticastasy regained some of her composure and reached under her skirt, producing a dagger from her other boot.

"No," Thealos said, holding up his hand to stop her. He backed away from the wall and watched as Secrist followed his movements. Fear threatened to overcome him, but he swallowed it down. One touch from the blade – one slice in the skin and he would die. He knew what it was, even though he'd never seen Deathbane before. He wished he were a Sleepwalker. But he wasn't, and wishing for it wouldn't change anything. He retreated several steps back into the cell, grabbing Ticastasy by the arm and pulling her behind him.

"Take this," she said, trying to give him the dagger.

Secrist lunged.

Thealos nearly screamed as the Kiran Thall slashed at him with the dagger. Ticastasy gasped, but Thealos managed to grab the Kiran Thall's forearm with both hands. Some flicker of thought went through his mind, faster than his own reflexes. Even though he was separated from the blade of Jade-Shayler, he felt a remnant of the magic still inside him. A Crimson Wolfsman's training – just enough to save his life. They both went down, arms and legs thrashing as Secrist jerked and heaved to break free of Thealos' grip. Twisting, Thealos tried to throw the man off of him, but he was too heavy.

Suddenly, Secrist arched in pain as Ticastasy drove her dagger into his back. Thealos saw a mess of chewed roots in Secrist's mouth, its juice dribbling down his chin. With his other hand, he reached back and pulled the dagger from his back.

"You bloody rook!" he roared, his body convulsing. Thealos watched his eyes glaze over in ecstasy. He was chewing Everoot. Thealos inhaled the honey-sweet smell from his mouth. He was thick with it. The Everoot was part of him now, a craving he couldn't quit. Thealos recognized it at once and knew that the magic had overwhelmed him.

Secrist's eyes went wild. Staring at the bloodied dagger in his hand, he looked down at Thealos. Then drove it down towards Thealos' throat.

Thealos bucked and shoved Secrist off of him. Ticastasy landed a kick to his ribs, but the soldier hardly grunted. Straightening, he pounced at Thealos again, both daggers whipping around. Thealos dove to the left, into the cell's cramped corner, trying to keep away from the attack. His mind whirled furiously. How long could he dodge Secrist's thrusts? He needed a weapon. He needed his Silvan sword, but the Sorian had destroyed it.

"I'll kill you!" Secrist swore, his voice slurred and thick. "I'll bloody kill you all!"

There was no reasoning with him. No logic to call on. Something was driving the Kiran Thall, pushing him to the fringes of reason and then a few steps further. The madness gave him strength, but it also clouded him. Thealos sidestepped to the right, not wanting to get trapped in the corner. If they could make it to the door and lock him in ...

Thealos sidestepped the thrust and nearly went down. Secrist was still quick. Having missed the Shae with the dagger, he slammed his elbow into Thealos' throat. It hurt like fury, but Thealos grabbed the man's arm and shoved him back, trying to win more space between them.

Sturnin heaved Secrist off his feet, his arms twisting one of the iron chains around the Kiran Thall's throat.

As the knight and the soldier whirled and wrestled, Ticastasy pulled Thealos toward the cell door. Her quick thinking had saved him again. The manacles no longer encumbered the knight, but he used the chains as a rope and slung it around Secrist's throat, slowly twisting it closed around his neck. The Kiran Thall jerked in spasms and cut wildly in the air. He still had Tica's dagger in his hand, and he struck the knight in the chest twice. Sturnin winced, but held his forearm over the chain, hoisting Secrist backwards, trying to snap his spine and choke him.

"Go!" Sturnin gasped as blood gushed from his side. He slammed the Kiran Thall into the wall a second time.

Indecision twisted inside of Thealos. He watched the knight struggle and then he saw the Deathbane dagger rise up and fall, stabbing Sturnin in the stomach. The knight let out a yell of pain – as if the scream had been ripped from his lungs. Thealos watched in shock as the knight twitched and convulsed as the flood of Forbidden magic swelled in eddies through the cell. Thealos saw Sturnin's life wink out like a snuffed candle. All his years of training, all the battles he had fought. Gone in the flicker of a moment. His skin started to shrivel and blacken.

"Sweet hate!" Ticastasy breathed in horror.

"Run," Thealos said, grabbing her arm.

He slammed the cell door shut behind them, hearing the lock click into place. But he knew somehow that the cell door would not hold Secrist long.

* * *

Tsyrke stared dispassionately at the aging Bandit leader. He didn't know how Ballinaire had survived so many years of war without his bones ending up snapped and broken, but here he was, with a stride full of stamina and vigor. *The man will bloody never die.*

Ballinaire held his white-plumed helmet in the crook of his arm. His face was hard aged skin, split by wrinkled crags. Even his eyebrows were flecked with gray. A thin white beard garnished his lower jaw. Five gold general bars and a golden star were pinned to his cape along the shoulder. It was all about rank. All about authority and position. As if anyone in Owen Draw or Dos-Aralon remembered anymore about the good he had done early in his life. Tsyrke wanted to chuckle. All they would remember was his angry defiance and the countless lives lost. Blackened fields and ashes, all of it.

"You look like Pitan," Tsyrke said, offering Ballinaire some honeyed mead. "Do you want a drink?" As a true Shorelander himself, Tsyrke never took the Inland customs of deference to rank seriously.

"I did not come here to get drunk, *Commander*," Ballinaire said with a clip and rasp in his voice. "You'd better pray to the Druid god Achrolese that you didn't come here for that reason either. Are you sober?"

"Very," Tsyrke replied, setting the goblet down. Mage sat in a chair to one side, watching them both. "Though after I heard what happened last night…" He took another sip from his large cup.

"You should have been here sooner," Ballinaire said, pacing on the other side of the desk. His eyebrow twitched. "You should have been here weeks ago!"

Tsyrke held the glare and matched it with one of his own. "I came when I could," he replied. "It is no easy task keeping a regiment moving and fed, not staying any place long enough to get pinned down by the brags at Dos-Aralon. Hiding in the mountains is one thing, but roaming the Shoreland without getting caught is totally different. I got my troops into the Shadows Wood for you. But what about Dairron and Folkes? Are they moving?"

The Bandit leader stopped and lifted his chin peremptorily. "Why wouldn't they?"

"Are they moving?" Tsyrke repeated.

"Commander Folkes' regiment is nearly to the Dayspring Rush," Ballinaire replied with full confidence. "Soon yours will be reinforced. I think you are too generous with their ale, Commander. The men can hardly stand up straight."

"It isn't easy to stand straight with tide fever. Mage and I will join the army in the morning to make sure Miestri has left. Was she acting under your orders, my lord?"

"You *all* act under my orders," Ballinaire seethed. "Do not take that tone of voice with me, Commander Phollen. Your army is in lamentable disarray. No discipline. No order. They should be in Landmoor by now, not perched at the brink." He held up his finger to stop Tsyrke's retort. "I want to know what you have done to move our cause along. Where were you?"

Tsyrke leaned back in his chair. "I was at sea, my lord. Securing supplies for my regiment. I can't likely buy my grain from Iniva, or raid it like you do. We'll need to be ready to withstand a siege, and likely a very long one."

"No," Ballinaire said, cutting him short. "You need to be ready to march. To march on Dos-Aralon itself."

Tsyrke shook his head and chuckled. "March on Dos-Aralon?"

"There is nothing at all amusing about my orders, Commander. General Dairron is swinging his army down from the north. We need to start marching to arrive at the borders of Dos-Aralon when they have left to attack him. We must not fail General Dairron."

"Do you know if his army has left the Vale yet?"

"Miestri informs me that it has," he answered.

"Has she also told you that the Shae know about this? Do you think they'll stay in Avisahn while we attack Dos-Aralon?"

"You do not appreciate the power of the Everoot," Ballinaire answered. "I see that you do not. It is no matter if the King of Dos-Aralon himself awaited us there with all the hosts of the Crown, for he *cannot* win. If the Shae send the Crimson Wolfsmen across the river, they send them to be slaughtered. I have seen what the Everoot does when it becomes like dust." He shook his head and fixed Commander Phollen with his finger. "If you lack full confidence in our cause, perhaps *you* shouldn't be leading one of my regiments."

Tsyrke glared at him, the grooves of his mouth frowning more. His blood ignited in his veins.

"I do not reward failure, Commander Phollen. You've forgotten your heritage. I fought against your grandfather during the Purge Wars. He was a vicious and a cunning general, and a skilled leader. That is why I desired you for my Rebellion. I hold you responsible for everything that has happened since the Sleepwalker shamed your troops in the Shadows Wood. I want no excuses, Commander. I *expect* you to exercise your full faculties on behalf of my army. If you do not, I *will* relieve you of command. Remember that, Commander!"

Tsyrke's hands tightened into fists as Lord Ballinaire swung around and left him alone with Mage.

Tsyrke waited for several long moments.

"You didn't tell him about the Shae we captured," Mage said.

"I did not," Tsyrke agreed. He rubbed his thumb on the rim of the goblet. He looked at Mage. "He's a little overconfident, isn't he? He's assuming Dairron left the Kingshadow."

"He hasn't. But Folkes is marching and the knights will collide with him if he doesn't turn back soon."

Tsyrke nodded confidently. "Just like we planned. Here – in Landmoor. The Rebellion ends *here*."

Mage nodded and rubbed his chin. "You did the right thing, letting the girl set them both free. Having the knight locked up with him was the most convenient way to do it."

"It was your idea," Tsyrke said with a sobered smile. "You planted the seeds in her mind."

"Yes, but seeds don't always sprout. She'll think it was her idea after all. And now we'll learn what the Shae have been hiding beneath the city all these years." The Sorian looked smug. "She must help him claim the magic and slip out tonight – before Ballinaire learns who he really is."

Tsyrke nodded. "Or Miestri."

* * *

The shock and warmth of the knight's death made him double over in ecstasy. The dagger. Oh, the dagger! The juice of the 'Root tingled inside his mouth, but that was salt compared to what the dagger made him taste. It was like licking tongues of copper fire. It sent swirls of feeling inside him. And pleasure! Oh, sweet pleasure! Secrist yanked the chain from around his throat. No bruises or even a gash. Whole and unharmed.

Invincible.

The Kiran Thall looked down at the dead knight. He was gone, a lifeless husk. His entire body had shriveled and blackened with the Deathbane's power. His memories and pain and triumphs were inside Secrist now. Harvested like grain for the winter. He felt the knight's skill and training whispering to him. The man's skin was already crumbling to dust. The feeling of power would not last long. Maybe a day. Maybe only hours. But for now, he was everything the knight was. The magic was locked inside him, ready to use. To kill again. To keep killing and to keep feeding the hunger. To kill the Shaden. To cut down the banned Shaden and drink his blood. It burned inside his mind, growing hotter and hotter. What would the Shaden's life taste like when he died?

Secrist didn't remember why he wanted to kill. Only that the need drove him. Like hunger or thirst. He went to the cage-like door of the cell. It had shut and locked. Secrist jabbed the dagger into the lock. The metal hissed and corroded, steaming as it burned away. The blade sliced through it as if it were freshly churned butter. Shoving the cell door open, he emerged into the hall. The whelp was not far away.

Hungrily, he started to run.

XXXIII

The sputter of torches lit the main hall of the tunnel in even increments, but further down emerged several soldiers carrying their own. Gripping 'Stasy's hand, Thealos pulled her into a side tunnel to hide. The Bandits were everywhere. He stopped in the darkness, waiting for the soldiers to pass and praying that he had seen them first. Sweat streaked down his face and his stomach clenched after the hard run. His legs trembled, out of fear – out of anger. He squeezed his eyes shut, trying to blot out the look of agony on Sturnin's face as he died.

"Quickfellow," Ticastasy whispered, and he clamped her mouth shut with his hand.

Four Bandit soldiers passed by and the light from their torches played in the grooves of the paving stones, just reaching the tip of Thealos' boot. He watched them pass, relieved, and then nodded.

"Is he...do you think he's still following us?" she panted. She wiped the hair away from her eyes.

"I don't know," Thealos said, breathing heavily. He was winded. "I thought we lost him at the junction, but he followed." Carefully, he went back to the main corridor and peered down. He watched the glare of the torches. The Bandits had stopped for something nearly fifty paces away. There was a grunt of warning and then cries of alarm. Secrist cut them down, his strange dagger glimmering with a greenish light in the distance. The four soldiers collapsed in a heap, their deathcries grating down Thealos' spine.

Ticastasy gripped his arm. "Come on," she begged.

Thealos nodded, and they slipped back into the main tunnel, heading away from Secrist. Four Bandit soldiers, down in hardly a wink. He shook his head. The Deathbane was powerful. The stink of Forbidden magic crept in the air behind him, getting closer. The sound of the boots warned him – Secrist was running.

"Come on!" Thealos said and bolted. Ticastasy looked bone weary, but he appreciated her determination. Her gown was damp with sweat and it hindered her stride, but she ran with a furious scowl, gripping his hand tightly to keep from stumbling. He would not let her go, no matter if Secrist caught them. He would not leave her to die.

"Shaden!" Secrist hollered. The voice was disembodied in the tunnels. He didn't sound tired at all. "Shaden!"

Thealos' knees groaned liked a rusted door. The constant pounding sent sharp stabs up his ankles, and his feet, swollen and tight, threatened to crack into pieces. He had to keep moving. Keep running.

"Quickfellow," Ticastasy panted. "I'm...I'm so...tired."

"It's okay," he said, squeezing her hand. "A little further." He wiped the stinging sweat from his eyes and tried to focus on the passageway ahead. They had crossed a good deal of the city already. Broken aisles and corridors split off here and there, but he didn't dare take any, knowing that it might lead to a collapsed tunnel that would trap them. Somehow the Kiran Thall still followed them, getting closer and closer the longer they delayed. It was more than hate and anger that drove him. No, it had to be something more. The look in his eyes – the madness. The reek of Forbidden magic.

The Sorian.

He shook his head, too tired to curse. If he could only get to the Silverkin. He knew that the magic would be able to stop them all. But he was so tired of running!

"Shaden!" The voice sounded much closer.

"Keep running. Come on, keep running!" Thealos' arm jerked as Ticastasy stumbled and fell, nearly bringing him down with her. She winced as her knees struck the ground. Chewing on her lip, she brought herself back up and looked into his eyes.

"A little further," he lied. "Please!"

She nodded, her shoulders sagging. She couldn't speak.

They started running again, though it was hardly more than a jog. His legs felt like mush and the stitch in his ribs was stabbing deeper with every breath. They had to keep running. He needed time to get the Silverkin and use it on Secrist. He could not leave her alone with him. Passing another sideshaft, they hurried to distance themselves from the Kiran Thall.

"Thealos!" a gruff voice hissed from the dark tunnel they had just passed.

Thealos stopped, whirling around. Ticastasy's eyes were wide. "Flent!" she said, her eyes widening in recognition.

Thealos's mouth opened with wonder when he saw Flent and Allavin emerge from the darkness into the torch-lit main hall.

"Thank Vannier!" Thealos gasped.

Allavin smiled with relief. "It's about bloody time we found you."

Ticastasy hugged Flent fiercely, nearly weeping on his shoulder with relief and panic. "We've got to run, we've got to run!"

He pulled her away, studying her face. "What's wrong, girl?" he demanded.

"Shaden!"

Allavin spun around, an arrow nocked in his yew bow.

Secrist slowed, his eyes full of fury. Blood spattered across his cheek. Thealos gulped and stepped back, watching the Kiran Thall advance. The dagger was poised in his right hand, its mottled tip dark with blood.

Allavin didn't hesitate. He let the arrow fly. The bowstring twanged and the shaft struck the Kiran Thall full in the chest. It jerked him back but didn't stop him. Secrist shrugged off the blow and kept coming, not bothering to remove it. The woodsman loosed two more on him. He was too close to miss. But the Kiran Thall's eyes leered in the torch light. He was looking at Thealos, not at any of the rest of them.

"I'll kill you," he said in a half-gargled breath. Spit dribbled down his chin. Wrenching the first arrow out of his chest, he flung it to the ground. The wound closed up on itself, perfect and whole.

Allavin drew another shaft, bringing it back to his ear.

"No," Thealos said, clamping his hand on Allavin's shoulder. "You can't kill him."

"We'll see about that," Flent snorted, swinging loose his Sheven-Ingen axe. "Get going," he snapped over his shoulder.

"No, Flent!" Ticastasy warned. "He killed Sturnin! No, we have to run!"

"Not very good at that," the Drugaen said. He approached the Kiran Thall, the axe haft tight in his meaty fist. "Come on, you rook. You still owe me a dance after what you did in Sol."

"Flent!" Ticastasy screamed.

Thealos felt his heart groan. Not the Drugaen too. Not them all.

—Son of Quicksilver—

The whisper of the magic came from the ground, swelling around him like mist. He opened his eyes, feeling the magic's need grow inside him. It was there. Behind an Otsquare. He jerked straight, remembering again what Jaerod had said. Where no human could follow.

"Come on," Thealos said, grabbing her by the arm. "Come on. Before he gets us all! Allavin, do you know the way out of here? I have no weapons, I can't protect us."

Allavin nodded, his face twisting with anguish. He watched the Drugaen face off with Secrist.

"Come on, you bloody rake!" Flent roared, bringing the axe up with both hands. He swung wide at Secrist, but the Kiran Thall ducked the blow and stabbed up at his ribs. Ticastasy shrieked and nearly tore away from Thealos, but he yanked her back. Flent dodged the blow and punched the man full in the face. The axe whirled around, up and over, slicing straight down Secrist's front. The gash dropped the Kiran Thall to the ground. But the magic of the Everoot revived him and he came right back up.

"Ban it! Let's go, lass," Allavin said, taking her other arm. "He's made his choice. Best to honor him for it. We're not far from the end of the crossroads," he told Thealos.

Thealos nodded and hurried down the length of the tunnel. He could feel the magic beckoning him. He didn't know how far they had gone, but the Silvan magic whispers grew louder.

—I will protect you—

A half-dozen torches appeared in the corridor ahead, carried by Bandit soldiers.

Allavin called out in warning, bringing up his bow. The arrows loped from it swiftly, dropping two before they even knew who was there. Thealos heard 'Stasy sobbing with grief, and he felt tears swim in his eyes. *Not Flent. Please, Keasorn, don't let him die!*

The Bandits attacked, bringing out their swords as they rushed the hall. Allavin had just enough time to toss Thealos his own sword before the soldiers were there. Allavin swung his yew bow around, stabbing the tip into a soldier's throat. Thealos unsheathed the Silvan-made blade and crossed swords with the next man. The blades rattled, but Thealos slipped around the man, kicking his boot up from under him. Thealos finished him with a stab before the next man was there in his place. Thealos felt his arms go numb with the shock of trading blows. He ducked, feeling his opponent's blade whip past his ear and crash into the wall next to him. He drove his blade into the soldier's gut and shoved him back.

Allavin had a knife in his left hand and finished slitting the throat of the last man. Thealos looked at him and nodded, wiping the sweat from his eyes.

Ticastasy had a knife in her hand now and stared back down the hallway. "Flent," she mumbled. "No!"

Thealos spun around and saw Secrist. As soon as the Kiran Thall set eyes on Thealos, he let out a hiss and started running at them.

"Run!" Thealos shouted. The Kiran Thall was close enough that they could hear his ragged breathing. "Keasorn help us. Run!"

They bolted, abandoning the dead Bandit soldiers.

"*Shenalle protect us from the Firekin,*" Thealos prayed, scrambling down the corridor. "*Shenalle protect us and keep us. Shenalle bring peace to the troubled. Keasorn guide my sword. Keasorn give me courage to strike my enemy...*" Poor Flent!

"He hasn't caught us yet!" Allavin Devers snarled in anger, grabbing Thealos' arm and pulled him towards the crossroads ahead.

—Son of Quicksilver, I have waited for you—

At the end of the tunnel was a junction leading two ways. They stopped, gasping for breath. One path led down to the foot of the hill beneath Landmoor. It opened up to the moors and the streams and darkness where it was still night beyond. The darkness would aid an escape.

The other path led to the Otsquare and the Silverkin Crystal.

Thealos looked back and watched Secrist appear out of the gloom, not thirty paces away. The Silvan magic of the Crystal was so strong that he felt it tremble beneath the stones. He looked down the corridor towards it, seeing blue light shining from a distant set of pillars. The Otsquare. He licked his lips, nearly able to taste the magic.

"Take her to Castun," Thealos whispered, squeezing Allavin's shoulder and giving his sword back to him. "I'll join you there."

"Where are you...?" Allavin demanded as Thealos pushed Ticastasy into his arms. She turned around, her face stricken.

"I'll join you there!" he promised.

"Wait, lad!"

"I'll be safe here," Thealos said, staring into Allavin's eyes. "He won't be able to follow me. Take her and go!" He risked a look at Ticastasy. "I'll come for you," he promised.

"Shaden!" Secrist's voice rasped and he ran at him again. Thealos retreated into the corridor with the Otsquare and watched as Allavin and Ticastasy fled the other way. His heart burned. So many dead. But so many others would die if he didn't get to the Silverkin. He felt the light of the magic caress his neck and shivered from the thrill of it.

—Come—

Secrist turned down the hallway after him. A sick grin came over his mouth when he saw Thealos alone. His boots plodded forward, almost like a hoppit doll. Thealos moved slowly, bringing the Kiran Thall after him – deeper into the tunnel's throat. The stench of Forbidden magic was mild compared to the rush of Silvan magic caged behind him. Glancing at the walls, he saw where the chunks of stone had been broken away after Justin had turned the Earth magic loose on the aged Sorian. He did not feel the warding anymore. No, the Sorian had set one trap to warn him of intruders. And they had sprung it earlier that morning.

"I'll drink your blood," Secrist said, jabbing the air with his knife. "I'll lick it from the rocks." He was squinting, as if he couldn't see Thealos anymore.

Thealos moved backwards, foot over foot, crossing the distance to the portal. He could see Secrist stagger now, his arm coming up to shield his face from the light. It was bright, as bright as the sun. Thealos felt the hair on the back of his neck rise as the magic whispered again.

—I am the Silverkin Crystal—

The words came with a shriek of light that nearly blinded Thealos. Spinning around, he squinted at the stone archway suspended by two pillars sculpted like gryphons. The searing light came from within the archway, brighter than the sun at noonday. He didn't know how he could see anything at all, but there it was. Still squinting, Thealos approached the pillars. The light drowned out details, blurring the pathway to follow. He heard Secrist screaming in pain, but he no longer smelled the Forbidden magic. The Silverkin soothed him with its voice, comforting. Thealos touched the stone portal. He ran his hand along the cool chiseled stone.

Without a look back, Thealos entered the archway.

XXXIV

A stone doorway, beveled and hewn by expert crafts-
men, opened at the end of the portal. The Otsquare
was behind Thealos now, its blue light nothing but a
mirror-like face. Wrapped in comforting folds of magic, he
entered the chamber. The stillness was perfect, soothing and
calm. The magic greeted him as its son. There were no torch
racks on the walls, only small inlets with blue stones that
gave off a tranquil glow. Not even a mote of dust swirled
in the air. The chamber felt...clean. Thealos was aware of
his boots and soiled clothes and every crumb of mud. The
sweat cooled on his forehead and back and he found himself
shivering.

It only took a moment to look over the chamber, for it was
small. It was octagonal in shape and one stone inlet of light
glowed from each facet of the wall. The domed ceiling was
too a little too tall to reach, and the entire chamber seemed
carved out of some fine-grained gray rock he did not recognize. Its texture and feel was similar to the granite temple
of Keasorn in Avisahn, except the stone was smoother, more
like marble. Behind him, the gryphon arches led back to the
tunnels. The wall opposite the arches also had an opening,
and he saw a thin stairwell leading down and away. That
surprised him – he hadn't been expecting another way out.

Thealos stared at the center of the chamber and folded his
arms. There were no shadows in the room. Not one. The room

was level all around, but it dipped bowl-like in the center, a very gentle grade. He noticed a pattern on the floor. From opposite walls, the pattern took shape. Thealos cocked his head to examine it. Two thin slats of stone met in the center of the chamber. He nodded, recognizing it. An octagon with a cross-mark inside. It was the symbol on Jaerod's amulet and sword-pommel.

—Claim me—

The voice whispered to him from the center of the rotunda. At the junction of the cross in the center of the room was a thinly carved symbol — two offset squares. It was larger than his hand and nearly indistinguishable. Thealos walked towards it. But as he stepped into the gently sloping bowl, a stream of light came from the ceiling, startling him. The pillar of white fire joined the center of the dome to the Otsquare etched in the floor.

"Son of Quicksilver, welcome."

It was a different voice, Silvan in tongue and style. A man's voice, gentle yet firm. He hesitated, listening to it.

"We created the Silverkin to challenge the danger of Firekin. We are the Mages of Safehome and thus have we always done."

Thealos swallowed, feeling gooseflesh prickle down his arms. The voice sounded...almost familiar. He hesitated, listening as it continued.

"The Crystal was forged and laid within a bed of Hothstone so that none could disturb it. Until now. You are here because you have never touched or tasted that which is Forbidden us. Before you can claim the magic, you must receive a Foretelling. Look into the light and see what was, what is, and what may be. Have courage, Son of Quicksilver. The future has yet to be tamed."

Thealos shivered. The words sent chills through his body. The Mages of Safehome. Who were they? He remembered Jaerod and Justin speaking about them. Both seemed to know what they were. But he knew nothing of their order or what they represented, except a constant struggle against the Sorian. Wishing he had asked more questions, Thealos stared at the chamber walls. One way in. Another way out.

The Silverkin Crystal in the crossroads. His heart calmed but his legs felt weak. He had come too far to quit now.

Walking down the thin slope of the bowl, he approached the shaft of light going ceiling to floor. Streamers of light rose and fell. He reached out and touched it, bathing his hand in the brilliance. It was like touching a cloud. The smell of the room was peaceful and inviting. He felt safe, for the first time since he had left Avisahn. He was among his people. Protected and sheltered.

Taking a deep breath, he stood before the pillar of light. Leaning forward, he looked into it.

* * *

The rush and shock of magic was so strong Thealos gasped. It was like dunking his head into an iced over pond. He couldn't move or twitch. His eyes burned, but he couldn't blink to water them. He stood frozen, helpless, and felt a surge of panic rise up in his throat. The glowing pillar held him fast, swirling with color and light. He could not see the rest of the chamber, only the blinding light. He felt eddies of Silvan magic swirl up in the rotunda around him, bulging and burgeoning until it filled the rock with fury. It was like a thousand Wolfsmen blades singing in his veins at once. He felt something inside him rip loose. Drowning in the magic, he struggled to keep sense of who he was and what he was.

Then he saw it.

A whisper of stillness cracked over the room, taming the surging tide of Silvan magic. He could see again, but he was no longer in the chamber. He was in a foamy-blue sky, soaring like a hawk. The magic buoyed him, easing him gently in its arms. He descended over a lush and beautiful valley, teeming with bishop pine and cedar. Groves of green maple with acres of orchards and grasslands in between stretched for miles and miles. His heart melted at the sight, at the vastness and immensity of it. Then he recognized what he was seeing. The Trident River! There were the granite cliffs of the Ravenstone! Looking to the side, he saw the sprawling city of Avisahn nestled against a bend in the river, parapets and towers lost in a dizzying sprawl of manors, parks, terraced walks, and fountains. It was not the Avisahn that he knew. The forest was too thick and vast, stretching from the Ravenstone to the Kingshadow. It was the land before the humans came. Before Sol-don-Orai was destroyed. The pang of longing filled him with such power that he started to weep. But the magic carried him away, following the twists and bends of the river until it flung him out over a huge bastion at the river's end, spilling roughly into the ocean. It was Sol, but glittering! Thealos saw a Silvan fleet, dozens of ships hugging the coast all the way to Jan Lee. There were hundreds of them!

He wanted to stop and take it all in, but the magic carried him on its wings, making him soar over the foam and waves, reaching across the broad expanse of it. There were ships heading south, braving the tides and crosswinds. Looking ahead, he saw the continent rushing towards him. A tangle of jungle and mountains with snow-capped peaks met him first. The distant coast of the Shoreland. Thealos had never been there, for the Shae did not control that far south. Over the windy peaks he traveled, slipping through gorges that shouldered higher than the Kingshadow mountains. When he reached the top, he swore with amazement.

Hunkered down beyond the mountains was a valley so vast it could have swallowed Dos-Aralon and Avisahn together. Emerald fields flanked by towering redwood and alder stretched out for miles filled with pastures feeding thousands of ox, horse, and sheep. Mines rich with veins of iron, gold, and silver exploded with wealth and promise. He could not see the end of the valley, so distant and vast. There had to be a million humans living there in the homelands and farmlands stretching along the nape of the mountains all the way to the sea. It was a vast and rich country. Cities dotted the land, hundreds of them. Towers yearning to touch the sky wrestled with domed assemblies, all glimmering with gold paving. The magic eased him down slowly, gently, through a pink rainsquall at sunset – closer to the earth, closer to the rich dark soil that drank in the rain from the skies. And there, feeding the land with its magic, Thealos saw the Everoot. Flecks of blue and violet danced in fields acres wide. The Earth magic sang with glory.

Darkness fell across his vision and when the sun rose, the smell of smoke and char stung his nose. The magic hoisted him again, zooming across the sky. He twisted around, seeing the veil of smoke and haze lingering over the dark valley. Homesteads were ruined and abandoned. Fires burned constantly from shattered palaces and desolate parks. He saw two armies marching in the valley, marching from destruction to destruction. Their minions spread death and havoc. Thealos saw the struggle, looping low so that he could see their faces. Faces full of hate and fury with drops of juice trickling down their chins. It was Everoot again. The two armies clashed fiercely, leaving fields of blood and the dead. But the dead rose and continued to fight, death begetting life over and over. Endlessly. The hot fires burned and ravaged the earth, but men would not die. They fought over the Everoot, to dig out the last remnants of it. To control it all.

Thealos watched with disgust as the scene changed, growing darker and darker. He did not understand the magic of the vision and how it worked, but he did understand the mood of the land and was not just seeing the inhabitants with his eyes. The Earth magic whispered its secrets to him. The dead were in piles now, in furrows that stretched like grain rows. He watched arrows hailing down from the skies, dropping men to agonizing ends as the Deathbane-coated tips robbed their lives. The armies were more cautious now, the warriors dwindling fewer and fewer in number. The entire land was desolate, save a few cloistered cities that barred either side from entering. Thealos watched in horror as the armies struck again, hammering at each other viciously, dwindling fewer and fewer.

Then the wind started to blow.

Thealos felt the eddies of magic shift with the jerking motion of the winds. It was blowing eastwards, towards the sea. He watched in moments as the fields turned brown, and the earth became pockmarked and cracked. The armies continued to fight for control of the Everoot, but then men were dying of thirst. There was no water, nothing to feed the plant, to keep it alive and whole. He listened to the screams of the dying and shuddered in his soul from the total destruction. It collapsed, crumbling like a castle made of blasted sand. The magic pulled him away, dragging him from the terrible scene. He wanted to weep again at the destruction of so many. Dust blew over the land, clouds of thick black dust and ash. It choked the life out of everything.

Thealos turned over and saw the sea, zipping across the eddies of water that separated them. He was ashore immediately. Groves of trees stretched all the way to the sea, but he saw the moors and a lone hill. In the moors, he saw a citadel, a watchpost that huddled in the midst of the trees. It was Silvan with the banners of House Silverborne flapping on the poles. It was a different crest, though similar to the one he remembered. The rising sun of Silverborne was garnished with green oak leaves and settled on a field of black – the color of war. Cradled in the arms of the magic, Thealos could see the details clearly, burning in his mind. He swooped low before he saw the Mages.

There were three, tall Silvan men with green cloaks and tassels. Each one was flanked by a Sleepwalker bearing a medallion on their chest and a long sword at their hip. Thealos watched intently. The Mages were speaking to a remnant of Shae around the watchpost. He watched the Mages raise their hands and one tilted his head back, singing. The earth opened beneath them, unfolding like a rose. There was a light in the sky, stabbing down like the sun and then a shadow smothered them. Looking up, Thealos saw a city emerge from the clouds, wider than the watchpost, nearly as wide as Avisahn itself. It descended from the heavens and hovered there, an obelisk in the sky. Thealos waited, watching in amazement. The city was enormous, more beautiful than anything he had ever seen. He had heard of the city of Safehome. He was certain Keasorn himself belonged there.

A rotunda gradually descended from the floating city, carved out of living rock. It went into the open earth where the Mages waited. The low rumble of thunder sounded and the huge city was gone. It was happening so quickly, Thealos longed to learn more. Who were the Mages? Why did only one of them sing? Where did the Sleepwalkers come from? Why were they speaking to the Shae near the watchpost and not in it? The magic pulled him again, drifting across the forest a short way. In the darkest, thickest portion of the forest, he watched another set of Mages at a pond planting clumps of Everoot at the base of a beautiful, secluded waterfall. Justin was there, his arms folded imperiously. One of the Mages touched the Warder Shae's forehead and there was a flash of light.

Darkness washed over Thealos. He was back in the rotunda, his legs wobbling. Then the magic swept him up again, easing him back into the sky. He looked down across and saw that the forest had receded to a tangle of crooked cedar and vine maple. He watched as scores and scores of Bandit soldiers scraped the last of the Everoot from the trees and boulders, tossing the clumps into barrows and baskets. They were destroying the peaceful glen, turning the pond and forest into a filthy network of sluices and gutters. This was not the past. It was happening at that moment. Thealos could hear their grunts, he could see the flexing muscles of their shoulders as they worked. The Sorian who had faced Jaerod stood nearby, her dark eyes smiling. She wanted the Everoot used, she wanted the Deathbane to murder. To cause havoc in the valley. To destroy what she could not control. Yes, she wanted to see Ballinaire destroyed too, waiting quietly to place another in his stead. Slowly, Thealos felt himself drawn away from the glen, away from the harvesting. He wanted to know more. He had to learn more!

The magic took him to the road that sliced through the forest where the Bandit army waited just beyond the screen of trees. In the morning, it would come into the city as the fog shielded it from the eyes of the bastion walkers. The doors would be opened to let them in, and the war with Dos-Aralon would begin. There would be no siege. It would fall in a day, just as Jaerod had said. Again the magic was pulling him back, drawing him across the moors to the fortress. He fought against it, tried to stop himself, but the magic tethered him.

There was so much to learn! The intents and thoughts of the
Bandits were made plain to him. He saw everything, if but
for a moment. He turned and saw Landmoor rising up from
the mist. He watched Allavin Devers and Ticastasy scramble
out of the mouth of the ruined shrine, followed by Bandits
and Kiran Thall. They were worried about him. Allavin was
praying Thealos would make it through, but the woodsman
felt his duty to protect Ticastasy. She was worrying even
more and grieving for Flent. Her heart was breaking. Tears
stung his eyes and he yearned to reach out to her, to let her
know he was safe and to comfort her because of Flent's death.
But the magic would not let him. It whisked Thealos down
the halls, past a screaming Secrist who thrashed against the
blue light, trying to shove himself through the Otsquare.
The man's thoughts were all madness, placed there by the
Sorian woman. With one intent – to kill Thealos. The blue
light snared Thealos, bringing him back inside with a violent
jerk.

Darkness.

The vision opened a third time and Thealos saw himself
kneeling in a pool of light in the middle of the rotunda. He
watched his actions, saw the look of determination on his
own face. Reaching into the Otsquare embedded in the floor,
he withdrew a silver amulet and chain with a blue sapphire.
The jewel was the size of an egg, garnished with Silvan runes.
In his mind, he watched as the blue lights in the rotunda
winked out, leaving only himself and the glowing Silverkin
Crystal. He was alone, but only for a moment. Secrist came
into the rotunda, his eyes mad and hateful. Thealos watched
himself scramble backwards before the magic surged to life
on its own, flaring brilliantly in the darkness. It ripped the
motes of Deathbane from the dagger and wrapped the Kiran
Thall in folds of blue fire. The fire spread throughout the
tunnels, stealing Forbidden magic from every nook and corner. The fire burned fast and quick, slamming into the aged
Sorian with its full intensity, dropping the man to his knees.
Ballinaire staggered and choked, appearing to age years in
moments. Every shard of darkness and filth was licked up by
the flames before rushing back. Thealos could see it all.

The fire rushed back, gathering like a storm and capturing the magic within the blue sapphire. No, there was something else too. Thealos watched the Forbidden magic course through his body and into the Crystal. Yes, the Firekin was swallowed by the Crystal's power, but it passed through him first! The evil went through his body like water, sickening him. And he watched as he collapsed in a heap on the floor, helpless as the Crystal winked out. He understood. He finally understood! The magic of the Silverkin required a terrible price. Thealos winced as the Kiran Thall lunged forward and kicked him in the ribs. He flinched as he watched Secrist pummel him again, ripping the Silvan magic from his hand. He understood it too clearly. The Crystal searched and trapped Forbidden magic. But whoever wielded it could feel the Firekin as it was captured. The artifact did not stop men of flesh and blood. It would not stop the Bandit Army. Secrist held the magic triumphantly in his hand, staring at its weight and power. The madness was gone. Looking down at the crumpled Shae, Secrist dropped low and slit his throat.

The vision started to fade, snapping him back to the present. In the distance, he heard the Sorian woman's voice welcome Secrist back and demand he give the Silverkin to her.

And Thealos knew that he would.

* * *

No! Thealos blinked awake. He lay on his back on the floor of the rotunda, soaked with sweat. The light in the center of the octagonal room was gone, but the blue stones from the eight walls shone, leaving no shadows on the floor. Thealos' hand was near the Otsquare etched at the bottom. Waiting for him.

—*Son of Quicksilver*—

The magic beckoned to him, insistent, like Shae barters whispering through the rock to wake him to his needs and offer their wares. It felt the presence of Forbidden magic near, it hungered to lash out at it with its power. Thealos recoiled, scrambling to get away from the center of the chamber.

—*Claim me*—

Thealos panted heavily. The images of the light were so vivid, he felt he had lived them. He saw himself dead on the floor, over and over again. It wasn't the fear of dying that filled his stomach with snakes. If he knew that both Sorian would be harmed by the Silverkin, that the war would not continue – he would gladly give his life. He had seen what happened in Sol-don-Orai. He couldn't let that happen to his people. His mind felt like it would burst like a melon. But he also knew that the Everoot still being harvested out in the moors would not be banished by the Silverkin. The Bandits would still be able to turn it into Deathbane. And there would be nothing left to stop them if the Silverkin belonged to the Sorian.

—*I have waited for you. You are the rightful heir. Claim me!*—

Over and over, Thealos saw it in his mind. The Sorian would get the Silverkin. The war would start across the land and no one in Avisahn would know what had happened. The futility of it all sickened him. It could not be happening like this. He clenched his fists and swore. No! He was too close to back away now. If he could take the Silverkin and run away, if he could...

But would that really change what would happen? The warding failed as soon as the Silverkin was taken. The Otsquare in the hall would no longer shelter him. And when Secrist attacked, the Silverkin would surge to life of its own will. Thealos doubted that he would be able to control it. It was all so clear to him. So brutally clear. He knew now why Jaerod had sought him out. The Sleepwalker had known that Thealos could get the Silverkin but would not be able to protect it. Thealos bowed his head in despair. There was no one left to protect him. Not Sturnin, not Flent. Not even Allavin Devers.

"Jaerod!"

Thealos clenched his hands, staring at the symbol on the floor. The Silverkin whispered to him and demanded he take it. His mind raced furiously. What if he waited? Surely

Secrist would not stay out there forever? Surely someone would come? But how would he know when that happened? He was still hungry and had no provisions or supplies at all. How long could he afford to wait before seizing it? Then he remembered. In the morning, the Bandit army would seize Landmoor.

It would be almost impossible to get out with it then.

He knew in his heart what he needed to do. If he could get out of Landmoor that night, the fog would hide his trail and give him a chance to slip away. Back to Avisahn. Back home. The Shae had no idea what they were up against. And if they hesitated in this war, if they stood apart as they had for so many years, it would be too late. Dry sobs threatened to shake loose inside him, but he felt that he had no tears left after all he had seen in the Foretelling. Someone had to warn the Shae. He had nothing to offer as proof to Laisha or the Sunedrion. No evidence at all. Not even a tiny stub of Everoot. He stared back down at the small Otsquare etched on the floor. His fingers twitched, but he clenched his hand into a fist. If he took the Silverkin he would probably die. If he died, the Sorian would claim it. But if he went back to Avisahn, they would try him as a traitor. What were his choices then really?

A thought struck him. What if he made the Shae come to the Shoreland to get him?

Looking up, Thealos stared at the other doorway and the thin stairwell leading out of the chamber. Had the Mages of Safehome known all those centuries ago that he would need another way out of there?

Think it through, he told himself. The Foretelling had given him the information he needed to survive. He knew the past. He knew the present. He knew what would happen if he tried to claim the Silverkin now. Despite the threat of Secrist, the presence of a Sorian within the tunnels was probably enough to provoke the Silverkin's magic. He had no idea how long the consequence of the magic would sicken him. All that Foridden magic, churning inside of him, before being captured within the stone. He could be sick and weak for days...for even longer. No – he had to abandon the tunnels. The Silverkin was still safe. The Bandits would not be able to take it if he left it there. He would need protectors. He would need an entire company of Crimson Wolfsmen. Chewing on his lip, he thought about the alternatives.

There was really only one choice to be made. If he had felt the prick of awareness on the back of his neck – the assurance that a Sleepwalker was nearby to defend him, he would never have hesitated claiming the magic. But that wasn't an option to him. There were no Sleepwalkers waiting for him. And without food, water, or weapons, it would be difficult enough making it back across the Shadows Wood. If he delayed much longer, by morning it would be impossible to get out.

Stifling the urgent whispers of the Silverkin, Thealos left the rotunda and descended the narrow stairs.

XXXV

The Shoreland fog cloaked the moors in thick gray folds. It would take the sun hours to work through it and restore some warmth to Thealos' body. He couldn't remember when he had been so cold or so hungry. Or so discouraged. The wild berries and mushrooms he'd eaten left an empty feeling inside and juice stains on his fingers. He worked his way east of Landmoor along the jagged edge of the Shadows Wood. Until he was certain he was past the bulk of Tsyrke's army, he didn't dare try crossing the forest. One thought burned in his mind. Meet up with Allavin and Ticastasy in Castun. It kept his boots shuffling one after the other. He'd abandoned stepwalking hours earlier to cover more ground. His eyes drooped as he walked. To Castun. *Just a little further,* he told himself.

The small trading post was a good hike from the south fringe of the forest. He hoped to be there in two days if he could manage it, but he needed sleep. Every jackdaw jumping on the branches or fluttering by made his head jerk. Wiping his mouth, he plodded ahead. He knew enough about the forest to keep himself alive. But his hunger wasn't getting any smaller. Without a hunting bow and dagger, he wouldn't be able to do any real cooking. Castun – just a little further. A fresh hot stew served in a trencher bowl teased his imagination. Some cool Silvan wine for his thirst.

The Shadows Wood stretched for miles ahead of him,

sparking visions of the vast forest he had seen in the
Foretelling. The memory was still sharp in his mind. Had
the magic really shown him the past? His heart ached at
the thought. So many had died in Sol-don-Orai. Suddenly,
he remembered the look on Sturnin's face as the dagger
plunged into him. The Deathbane had ripped the life from
him. He bit his lip, wincing. The knight had saved his life. If
he hadn't wrestled Secrist down, the Kiran Thall might have
killed him too.

Thealos folded his arms tightly to stop shuddering. He
had to stop thinking about it, for that way led to madness.
He made a silent vow – the knights of Owen Draw would
learn about Sturnin's courage. Thealos would see to that. His
legs throbbed and he stumbled over some exposed roots and
went down in a patch of witch-thorn. The witch-thorn cut up
his hands and stung. Rising up, he looked around, amazed to
find himself in the thick of the forest. He couldn't remember
how long he had been walking and didn't remember when he
had decided to enter the woods. Rubbing his eyes and sucking on the bleeding pricks to soothe his hands, he sat down
on the log of a felled tree and looked for the sun. His stomach
gave off a dull ache, reminding him again of his hunger.

"Think, Thealos," he muttered to himself. He rubbed his
forehead. The road leading to Castun would be to the west.
So would the Bandit army if he wasn't careful. He dropped
down from the twisted trunk and started off again, heading
north he thought. His mind swam with fatigue, blurring the
trees and juniper shrubs ahead of him. He was so tired! He
had dozed in the dungeon beneath Landmoor. But the truth
of it was that he hadn't slept well since Avisahn.

Clumsily, Thealos staggered on. He tried stepwalking
again, but that only slowed him down. His thoughts danced
like fireflies. To blot out the pain in his hands and legs he
composed a letter in his mind to send to Avisahn. What could
he write that would have the Shae army rushing in? *To the
Council Elder of Vannier—greetings. During my travels, I've
missed the turnish pastries from the baking guilds the most
and wondered if you could spare a plate of them. The Silvan
wine in Castun is decent, I'm pleased to report. Haven't tried*

the Spider Ale yet – sorry to disappoint you. I could use a bag of Aralonian pieces and wondered if you could ask my Correl for me. You are so very good at extortion, I'm sure he'll listen to you. And if you could tell the Princess of Avisahn that I'm forming a rebellion against her Sovereignty down here in the Shoreland, that would also be much appreciated. I've found a nice abandoned Shae watchpost to get things started –and the view of the moors is quite exceptional. With fondest regards, Thealos Quickfellow.

Thealos rubbed his bleary eyes and chuckled to himself. He would send a separate message to Laisha as well – phrased differently of course. He could pay a runner to get them to Dos-Aralon and maybe to one of the merchants Correl worked with. He didn't dare go back himself. If Nordain caught him first, he wouldn't be given the chance to defend himself. The trial could drag on for months, and the Shae didn't have months. They could no longer hide behind the Trident river. They could no longer afford to remain behind and watch. The Silverkin Crystal would not destroy the Bandit army in the Shoreland. He knew that much for certain. The Shae army would need to rise itself in war once again. It hadn't happened since the Purge Wars. But it was going to happen again. Oh, he couldn't wait to see the look on Nordain's face when he was forced to admit that Thealos had been right!

Thealos kept walking. He might rouse the Shae army, but he would still need to convince them on the right course of action. And how would he do that without proof? Allavin Devers would help him. He was a Shaefellow and a tracker for Dos-Aralon. Maybe his word would help sway them. There was Ticastasy too. Yes, she'd be safer in Avisahn than remaining down in Castun. He shook his head – what was he thinking? Two humans – he doubted the Sunedrion would even let them speak. But they had both seen the Everoot. That made three witnesses, which were necessary according to the law. Thealos muttered a curse. Two humans and a Kilshae – wonderful! If only he had been able to save a little bit of Everoot. To show them that it was real. And Justin – poor Justin! Thealos felt his heart throb with regret. The

Warder Shae was still back in Landmoor locked up in a cell. He didn't even want to *be* in Landmoor – he had insisted on going to Avisahn instead. Thealos wished that he had. He stopped, feeling the sense of failure rise up in him like a hungry wave. Biting his lip, he shook his head and kept walking. He could not quit. He would not quit! He would make the Shae listen. Somehow, he would convince them.

His foot snagged in another twisted root and this time he went down hard. Blackness washed over him along with a queasy feeling. His ankle throbbed. Thealos breathed out slowly, trying to steady himself with the pain. He'd rest for a moment, just until the pain subsided...

He slept.

Thealos awoke with a jolt. He had been dreaming of his Wolfsman blade. The one the Sorian had destroyed. In his mind, he saw the gemstone eyes wink with power, trembling with Silvan magic. The presence was so strong, he thought he could reach out and touch it. The forest was shaded, swallowed by the shadows of dusk. Sweet Vannier, how long had he slept? Coming fully awake, he sensed the presence of the Shae all around him.

As Thealos raised his head, he saw a leaf-bladed short sword pointed at his neck.

At first he didn't believe his eyes, that it was only the remnants of a dream, but two other Wolfsmen appeared from the thick brush clogging the path in the woods. He recognized the man standing over him, the leader. They had met in Sol.

The Crimson Wolfsman Lor studied him shrewdly. "*So, you're alive after all.*"

He sounded surprised. Thealos' ankle murmured in pain as he tried to bring himself to his knees. He was still dazed. Three Crimson Wolfsmen. His breath started to choke off in panic. *Not now,* he thought. *Sweet Vannier, not yet!* He wasn't ready to return to Avisahn. No, it was too soon. Without any evidence, they would mock his story and imprison him.

Thealos tried to speak, but his throat was thick and his mouth too dry. He shook his head and grunted, trying to work some spit into his mouth.

The Wolfsman crouched on one knee and handed him a flask. Thealos gulped the leather-flavored water down and noticed that the Lor hadn't lowered the short sword yet. He was still on guard, curiously watching the woods around Thealos.

"*You are weary, Kil-quickfellow,*" the Wolfsman said with more than a hint of disdain. "*When did you escape the human army?*"

Thealos stared into the man's blue eyes. "How did you find me?"

The Wolfsman gave him a thin smile. "*It was not that difficult,*" he said mockingly. "*I have another quaere with me. Where is the Sleepwalker you fled with from Sol?*"

Thealos shook his head. Seven Crimson Wolfsmen sent to bring him back to Avisahn? *Hate, I'm in more trouble than I thought!* "What...what was your name?" Thealos stammered.

"*I am Xenon Ironwolf, Watcher Lor of Sol.*" His eyes narrowed – probably because Thealos wasn't using Silvan. "*And you are under arrest by the Shae Council of Elders for high treason. You've led us on a chase over half the valley. Are you tired of running yet, boy?*"

Thealos shoved the flask into his hand. "*I will go with you willingly, Xenon. But I need to go to Castun first. It's a town not far from here and on the way back. If we can stop...*"

The Wolfsman smirked. "*I think not.*"

Thealos ground his teeth, losing his temper in a snap of emotions. "You do not understand what is happening down here, Xenon. You have no comprehension of the danger. It is your duty to protect our people. For the love of Keasorn, listen to me! The humans are using Forbidden magic. They will use it against us. I have evidence of this, but it is in Castun. Please...please take me there on the way. It won't delay us long, maybe a day."

Xenon shook his head. "*It is you who does not understand, Kil-quickfellow. You have been summoned by the Council of Elders. I arrested you in Sol, but you would not come willingly. I'll truss you in ropes if I must. But you will come with us.*"

"Please!" Thealos begged. "At least send one of your men to Castun for me!"

Xenon shook his head and stared at him coldly. *"To be killed by a Sleepwalker like the Kiran Thall were? I'd go myself if I believed you were honorable. You've shamed your family and your people. You are Kilshae now and have lost the use of your true family name. Remember that, Kil-quickfellow."* He rose and glared down at Thealos. *"Bind him."*

Thealos winced as the Wolfsmen tied his wrists behind his back. He stared at the Lor and nearly choked and he tried to speak. He used Silvan this time. *"I am Thealos Quickfellow, an heir of Quicksilver. And I have not received anathema yet. I am a Shae."*

"You can call yourself the 'king of linseed oil' for all that I care. Until we get back to Avisahn. Until you answer for your crimes before the Shae Council of Elders and the Sunedrion." Xenon made hand motions to start off into the woods.

* * *

Ticastasy walked with her arms folded. Allavin's cloak draped over her shoulders, but it wasn't enough to stop the chilling feeling in her heart. She was exhausted and more than once, the observant woodsman had to keep her from walking right into a tree. She had watched the evil dagger steal Sturnin Goff's life. If Flent had fallen in the same manner, she would never forgive Tsyrke. Not ever. Her mind had been made up on that point.

"Watch the roots," Allavin warned, alerting her just in time to slow and watch her step, crunching through the dried fragments of branches and debris. Allavin walked behind her, using the wide broom of a cedar branch to mask their trail as they passed. Twice during the journey they had hidden in swamp gullies as the Kiran Thall roamed the woods looking for them. But Allavin had kept them safe.

"How far do you think it is to Castun?" she mumbled. "We've been walking all day."

"We'll get there soon. I don't know about you, but I could use a soft pillow tonight."

"Mmmm," she replied, barely able to speak. She paused as he approached and shared some water from his flask with her. The water was warm but it soothed her throat. She felt a pang of guilt, knowing that Quickfellow didn't even have a dagger to use or a blanket to roll up in. She looked down at herself. The gown he had given her was mud-spattered and torn. She'd worn it to impress Tsyrke and to lie to him. To stab him in the heart as he had done to her. She wiped her eyes, her thoughts lost in a hazy cloud. What was she going to do? Where could she go? Quickfellow had said he would meet them in Castun. Was he a new path her future was going to take? A barter's son was definitely more realistic than a Silvan prince.

"Come on, lass. Let's keep going."

Ticastasy nodded and started trudging through the woods again. When they came to the edge of the forest, she nearly cried with relief. Castun would be close. As she started walking again, more confidently now, she felt Allavin catch her arm.

"What is it?"

"Smoke," he whispered, pointing.

She squinted and realized it herself. Castun was burning.

Sagging to her knees in the dry prairie grass, she started to cry in thick choking sobs. She felt Allavin's arm slide around her shoulders. She could barely hear him over own ragged tears.

"This happens in war," he said and squeezed. "And it's only going to get worse."

* * *

Ticastasy awoke later hearing voices whispering softly in the musical language of the Shae. She didn't know how long she'd been asleep, but it was night again and she was vaguely aware of falling asleep on Allavin's warm cloak. As she slowly sat up, she wondered with a surge of hope if Quickfellow had caught up with them.

It was Jaerod.

"She's awake," the Sleepwalker said as she hurried to rise. He reached over and pulled some food out of his pack and offered it to her. She took it hungrily.

"Jaerod just finished telling me what happened," Allavin said while she ate. He shook his head and sighed with disbelief.

"Hello, Ticastasy," Jaerod said, his face impassive.

She nodded in welcome and pulled the cloak around her shoulders. She was relieved to see him alive, but where was Quickfellow? "Where have you been?"

Allavin answered for him. "The Sorian tried to kill him, but he used some magic to bring him back to the city he comes from – somewhere in the East Kingdoms? He's been hurrying back to join us, but knew he came too late."

"I thought you were Quickfellow's protector?" she said, wiping the crumbs from her mouth. The bread was wonderful.

"He's safe, at least for now. He was found by the Crimson Wolfsmen earlier today," Jaerod answered. "They're bringing him back to Avisahn right now. I'm going to join him after I leave you both."

She nodded, feeling miserable. "Did he...get what he came here to get?"

Jaerod looked at her seriously and shook his head. There was something in his eyes as he looked at her. She couldn't decide what it was. Compassion? Pity? "The warding is still in place. One of the Sorian has left something there in case the warding fails. From what Allavin has told me, I'm not sure Thealos was able to get the magic safely. If he took it, the warding would have vanished."

Ticastasy sighed wearily. "Then we failed, didn't we?"

Jaerod smiled and put his hand on her shoulder. "We only fail if we stop trying. I don't think Thealos is going to quit...do you?"

She thought about it a moment, feeling a fluttering of hope in her heart. "He's pretty stubborn, isn't he?"

"He's very stubborn. When he comes back to the Shoreland, he'll bring a Silvan army with him. He'll need you both as he's needed you before. Be watching for him. Be waiting."

"We will," Allavin promised – and she knew he meant it for both of them.

* * *

Tsyrke reached down and picked the snapped necklace from the dirty straw. The sparrow pendant shimmered in the torchlight coming from the hall outside the cell. He closed the necklace into his fist, squeezing tightly.

"What happened?" he asked huskily, staring at the lump of char sprawled near the cell wall. If she was dead, he would never forgive himself.

Mage stepped near the stain sprawled against the far wall. "Have your men wrap this in wet blankets and bury it under stones."

"Who was it?" Tsyrke asked. "The knight?"

"I can only guess. There is no spark of Life magic left here to read. The victims of Deathbane are nameless. It could as easily have been the Shae."

Tsyrke squeezed the pendant, feeling the metal bite into his palm. She had cast the pendant away. It was his only link to her, allowing him to find her no matter where she was. It had surprised and worried him that she had stayed so long in the cell. When his soldiers pounded on the door, warning that the dungeons had been breached and that men were dying swiftly to some unknown plague, he had feared the worst. He still feared it. Fury boiled and raged inside him. There were too many players, too many risks. The walls of his life were tottering, ready to collapse. By the Druids, if he went down, he would bring as many as he could down in ashes with him.

He stood slowly, feeling his bones ache and his heart bleed. "Who knows about the Deathbane," he asked Mage with a thick voice, aware that they both already knew the answer to that question. Their eyes met in the stillness of the cell. "I've had enough of her meddling."

* * *

Dujahn of the Gray Legion walked down the tunnel corridor, keeping wary of the Bandits who saw him pass. He doubted any of them would recognize him or even be able to describe him if pressed. The city had fallen so quickly, it was almost a shame. Not even a skirmish. The garrison cells were teeming with prisoners, mostly soldiers who hadn't sworn allegiance to Ballinaire yet. But the palace dungeon held the most dangerous enemies, and they would probably spend the entire war in the cramped cells, hungry for even a whisper of sunlight. These were men not even Ballinaire dared trust.

Passing under a ring of light from a flickering torch, he paused to study the cells. Where was it? Each cell was shielded by a huge iron door with thick rivets and hinges. Miestri had told him what to look for. A rat hissed at him from the rafters as he passed by. Scowling at it, he kept walking.

The orb in his pocket suddenly glowed with warmth, burning against his leg. He reached in and retrieved it. It glowed like firelight, casting hazy shadows on the floor around him. He stopped and looked above the cell door. There was a marking there in the stone – he'd missed it completely walking by.

Reaching to his belt, he unfastened a key ring and searched for the right one. It fit into the lock with a loud click. Twisting it, the lock gave way. He grabbed the handle and pulled the door open.

The hazy light from the orb revealed a Shae huddled in the corner. His eyes glowed in the dark.

"Ah, there you are," Dujahn said, unnerved at the look the Shae gave him. "The Lady of Vale is ready for your report. She sent me to bring you to her pavilion." Dujahn hesitated. The Shae looked at him coldly and spat something in Silvan.

"That's right, you only speak the tongue of the Shae," Dujahn went on in stumbling Silvan. He really wasn't very good at it yet, but it was something to work on. *"Are you ready? The Lady of Vale wishes to speak to you."*

"And who is that?" the Shae asked softly, angrily.

"She said you would remember her when you remembered your name."

The Shae shifted and rose slowly, long thin arms folded imperiously. *"And how does she know my name?"*

Dujahn smirked. *"Because she was the one who took it from you. Don't you remember it, Ravin Silversheir?"*

The orb flashed a wicked glow and the Shae sank to his knees, clutching his head in agony. He screamed, full of pain and loathing. Dujahn watched him, mesmerized. But when the onslaught of pain had finally passed, the blue-robed Shae recovered and stared up at him, a submissive look on his face. His eyes were glowing the same color as the orb.

"I will serve my Lady," he whispered, his eyes filling with tears.

ABOUT THE AUTHOR

A writer since high school, Jeff Wheeler's interests include medieval history, playing music, Chinese martial arts, publishing *Deep Magic*, and spending time with family. He lives in Rocklin, California with his wife and two children.

He welcomes reader response at www.jeff-wheeler.com.

Made in the USA
Middletown, DE
02 January 2017